SOUTH OF LITTLE ROCK

A NOVEL

GEORGE ROLLIE ADAMS

BARN LOFT
PRESS

Publisher's Cataloging-In-Publication Data
(Prepared by The Donohue Group, Inc.)

Names: Adams, George Rollie, author.
Title: South of Little Rock : a novel / George Rollie Adams.
Description: Second edition. | [Pittsford, New York] : Barn Loft Press,
    [2019] | Previously published: [United States] : Outskirts Press,
    [2019]. | Includes bibliographical references.
Identifiers: ISBN 9781733366908 (paperback) | ISBN 9781733366915 (hardback) |
    ISBN 9781733366922 (ebook)
Subjects: LCSH: African Americans—Civil rights—Arkansas—Little Rock—History—
    20th century—Fiction. | Civil rights movements—Arkansas—Little Rock—
    History—20th century—Fiction. | School integration—Arkansas—Little Rock—
    History—20th century—Fiction. | Little Rock (Ark.)—Race relations—History—
    20th century—Fiction. | LCGFT: Historical fiction.
Classification: LCC PS3601.D3745 S68 2019 (print) | LCC PS3601.D3745
    (ebook) | DDC 813/.6—dc23

🏠 **BARN LOFT** PRESS
Paperback ISBN: 978-1-7333669-0-8
Hardback ISBN: 978-1-7333669-1-5
eBook ISBN: 978-1-7333669-2-2

Cover Photo © 2019 www.gettyimages.com. All rights reserved—used with permission.
Author photo courtesy Allison C. McGrath.

Barn Loft Press and the "BLP" logo are trademarks of Barn Loft Press.
PRINTED IN THE UNITED STATES OF AMERICA

FOR

Diana, Brady, Amy, and Amanda

CHAPTER 1

Sam Tate and his son Billy were the only whites among the ballplayers sweating in the July sun. Gran had warned Sam about coming here. "It ain't right," she said, "and people will talk." He thought no one would notice, let alone care. But someone did. As the sharp crack of bat against ball echoed across the weed-infested park, a lone figure watching from a pine thicket high up beyond right field shifted sideways to keep out of sight.

"Catch it, Mr. Billy! Run, Mr. Billy! You can do it, Mr. Billy!" the batter and other Black Tigers shouted. In Unionville, like everywhere in southern Arkansas in 1957, blacks said "Mister" to all white males, even twelve-year-olds.

"Go get it, son!" Sam yelled from near first base.

The baseball sailed high and deep toward the unpainted board fence, and the boy ran barefoot and shirtless, straining to make the grab.

"Faster, Mr. Billy, faster!" Leon Jackson, the Black Tigers' player-manager called from center. He had invited the Tates here. This was their third practice with the Black Tigers on the town's only regulation diamond. The Unionville School District had built it after World War II for the white high school. For a while, a white amateur team, the Lumbermen, played on it and Sam anchored their infield. When the club folded after a few years for lack of enough players, the district let the Black Tigers use the field twice a week in summer. But no school board member

1

ever thought whites might play with them.

Being here meant a lot to Sam. In the five years since his wife died giving birth to their daughter Mary Jane, he had filled his spare time with baseball. He read about it, listened to it, talked about it, and played it. At forty-six, he could still hit, run, and throw. Until recently, though, he had only been playing in his horse pasture with Billy.

When the ball, stained brown from heavy use, smacked into the boy's well-oiled glove, the players shouted, "Rabbit on the run, Mr. Billy, rabbit on the run! Throw it to second, Mr. Billy!"

Billy pivoted, skipped forward, and put his entire body behind a throw to cut down an imaginary base runner. The ball landed short but everyone hollered approval anyway. Sam wished Judith Ann could see how hard their son played and what fun he was having. Along with her sandy hair and blue eyes, Billy also had her spunk. She would be proud of him.

"That's some ballplayer you've got there, Mr. Sam," Leon said, as he trotted in from the outfield. "You want to take a few cuts? See what you can do with B. J.'s fastball today? I'm gon' catch him a spell." B. J. Long was the team's ace pitcher.

Sam had been waiting for the chance and he and Leon moved off toward the first-base dugout, a wooden bench under a shed covered with tarpaper. One end had been boarded up to hold grounds-keeping tools and the Black Tigers had leaned their bats against the cobbled door. Sam picked out a Mickey Mantle model and grabbed two others to swing with it off to the side.

While he limbered up, he watched Leon strap on shin guards. He was a few years younger than Sam, a tad taller at six three or so, and dark as midnight. Leon owned a dry-cleaning shop at the end of an alley behind Farmer's State Bank, directly across Main Street from Sam's Oklahoma Tire and Supply store.

He and Sam discovered a shared passion for baseball when Leon bought his team's first bats and balls at Sam's store. Soon they were exchanging Major League scores and statistics when they met on the street or in the bank.

When they bumped into each other the day after the All-Star Game, Leon got so excited talking about Minnie Minoso's spectacular game-ending catch that he asked Sam to come to the Black Tigers' Wednesday afternoon practice. In summer, Unionville stores closed at noon on Wednesdays so their owners and employees could do chores, go fishing, or loaf. With time to run some errands and still get to the workout, Sam accepted the invite and asked if he could bring Billy. They felt a little out of place that first time but now they just played ball.

As Leon settled behind the plate, Sam tossed the extra bats aside, reset his cap over wet black hair, and stepped into the right-handed batter's box. His sleeveless undershirt, tucked into khaki pants, was also sweat soaked, and his arm and shoulder muscles, toughened by years of hard work, glistened in the heat. He took a couple of practice swings then dug his cleats into the dirt and stared toward the mound, body relaxed, eyes on the ball in the pitcher's hand.

B. J., a brown beanpole propping up a pair of faded overalls, went into his exaggerated Satchel Paige windup, kicked his left leg high, and tossed an off-speed pitch straight down the middle. Sam swung easily and lofted a long fly to left, where Charlie Foster stood dead in his tracks and hauled it in. Two medium fastballs followed. Sam cut early and a little high on the first one and pulled it on the ground outside third base. He hit the second one on the nose, to left again. Charlie backpedaled and hauled it in just short of the fence.

"Rabbit on the run!" Leon yelled. "Rabbit on the run!"

Sam stepped back and Leon turned to his left, still in his catcher's crouch.

"No need to stir around when Charlie's throwing," he said. The ball left Charlie's hand just above his head and rose scarcely more than twenty feet before arcing down and popping into Leon's mitt waist high about two feet inside the base line.

"He's not throwing so good today," Leon said, looking up at Sam and smiling. "He made me reach for it."

Sam grinned and stepped back into the box. "Come on. Let's see some more heat," he called to B. J. "I'm feeling my Wheaties now."

The skinny pitcher spat a stream of Beech-Nut tobacco juice toward short and toed the rubber again. Without a word, he added twenty miles an hour to his next offering. Sam hit it smack on the fat part of the bat and sent it soaring over Charlie's head into a stand of oak trees beyond the fence. One of the other Black Tigers scrambled over the boards to retrieve it.

"Way to hit, Mr. Sam! Way to hit!" the players shouted.

Sam blasted the next one farther into the trees but more toward center. Beyond right field, the man on the hill retreated deeper into the shadows.

"Give me some breaking stuff now," Sam called to B. J. "I'm ready for it."

"You sure about that, Mr. Sam?" Leon asked. "He's looking awful good out there."

"You bet." Then louder to B. J., "Show me all you've got."

B. J. spat another stream of brown slime and turned the ball over in his bony fingers. "All right, Mr. Sam," he said after a moment, "if you really want her, here she comes." He wound up like a windmill again and unleashed a nasty pitch that curved sharply down and across the outside edge of the plate. Sam swung hard, grunted, and missed by half a foot. The other players held back grins.

"Let me see that again," Sam called.

B. J.'s eyes twinkled. "All right, sir." He let fly a second time with the same result.

"Again," Sam said, and inched closer to the plate. Even with the adjustment, he managed only to trickle the ball down the first base line.

"Goddamn it, B. J., what do you call that pitch?" Sam called out. He was a deacon in the First Baptist Church, but like his daddy before him, he could cuss a blue streak when the mood took him.

B. J. spat again. "I call her Miss Lilabell."

"Why's that?"

"Because she's sneakier than Delilah and wickeder than Jezebel."

"Well, I don't think I need to see Miss Lilabell again today. Go back to the straight stuff."

After a few more swings, Sam stepped away so others could hit, grabbed his glove from the dugout, and headed out to join Billy shagging flies. The Black Tigers had let the boy bat earlier and he remained content to run down balls for them.

As Sam jogged across the infield, he watched the players running, catching, and throwing and listened to them whistling and calling to each other. He admired their skill and easy manner and wondered what it would be like to play in a game with them. If the Lumbermen could have used black players, he thought, there might still be a team he could play on. Like most everything else, though, the Tri-County League was segregated. Meanwhile, the Black Tigers played pickup games with black squads from other towns, and until now no whites paid them any attention.

When Sam reached right field and turned to face the batter, the man on the hill slipped from his hiding spot, looped around to his truck on the far side, and drove off without anyone seeing him.

CHAPTER 2

Five hundred miles north of Unionville, Larkin and Velma Reeves were worried. Larkin, a thin man with slicked-back hair and a pencil moustache, pushed the afternoon newspaper aside, set a serving tray on the patio table, and handed glasses of iced lemonade to Velma and their daughter Becky. They sat on cedar chairs he had built, along with the table, in the basement of their suburban Kirkwood, Missouri, home. July had brought sweltering heat and the women were wearing sundresses and sandals. Larkin had on Bermuda shorts. They had been arguing off and on since last evening. Becky had an offer to teach seventh grade in Unionville, Arkansas, and Larkin, a high school principal for twenty-six years, did not want his only child taking a job in a school she had never seen in some small town in the middle of nowhere. More than that, even though she was thirty-five, he hated the thought of her moving so far away.

"You'd be better off laying out a year and waiting for something to open up around here," he said, nodding toward the St. Louis skyline.

"Dad, I love you," Becky said, flashing a dimpled smile and flipping strands of auburn hair away from sparkling brown eyes, "but you and Mom are overreacting and you know it." Gestures like these had melted her father's resolve before but not this time. He and Velma, who taught third grade, were proud that Becky had followed in their footsteps, but the Unionville position seemed risky.

It had come open when the woman holding it quit unexpectedly and, according to Becky's understanding, took a similar position elsewhere. With the start of school only weeks away, Unionville officials scoured Arkansas and every neighboring state in search of a replacement, posting as many ads as they could afford and conducting interviews by telephone. They learned little about Becky except that she had a teaching certificate and experience, was not married, and could relocate on short notice. She learned even less about them.

"You haven't met anyone down there," Larkin said, frowning. "You don't even know what kind of facilities they have or what textbooks they're using."

"Come on! They said I'd be teaching in a practically new building. And you know I've never been tied to textbooks. You and Mom taught me better than that."

"Honey," Becky's mother asked, trying a different approach, "are you sure you can drive that far?" A trim woman admired for her Latin good looks and sunny humor, Velma normally did not worry out loud like this. When Becky had come down with polio during her teens, Velma helped her work through months of hospitalization and painful therapy and later encouraged her to chase her dreams. Now, however, Velma seemed willing to do anything to keep her daughter from going south, even reminding her how hard she found long drives because the polio had left one leg shorter than the other.

"I have to do it, Mom," Becky said, putting her hand on Velma's arm. "I want to work and I still like being in a classroom." She had been seeking an assistant principal's job or similar position but had exhausted all possibilities for the coming school year. Since finishing her master's at the University of Missouri in the spring, she had gone on nine interviews and received zero offers. More than one recruiter, after seeing her limp, suggested that helping to manage an entire school would be too much for her.

Velma took a deep breath and let it out slowly, searching for the right words. "I understand how you feel," she said, "but this just seems too rushed."

Becky sighed and sat back. For a long time, all three sipped their lemonade in silence. A light breeze stirred the warm air and raised the scent of potted petunias.

"Look, Mom, Dad," Becky said finally, as she leaned forward and set her glass on the table, "I've handled a lot of different situations and I can handle this one. It'll be fine until I can get something else, so I'm taking it."

They had to admit she had always been resourceful. After beating polio, she had worked during most of World War II as a clerk in an aircraft factory then earned a degree from nearby Fontbonne University and taught at a private academy in Illinois before going to graduate school.

"Becky," Velma said, coming to what concerned her most, "there are a lot of mean-spirited people down South. The farther you go, the worse it gets. I looked up Unionville on the map. It's not far from that place in Mississippi where someone killed that poor Emmett Till boy just because he said, 'Bye, baby,' to a white girl. And you know what it was like for your Great-grandmother Charlene and your Grandmother Abigail living in New Orleans."

"But Mom, that was a long time ago. And they were madams for gosh sakes."

"Yes, they were, but they didn't have much choice about it. That's why Momma sent me up here to live with Cousin Lottie—to get me away from all that. Now I wish they'd given me Lottie's last name too."

"What difference does that make?"

"None probably," Velma said, "but Clémence isn't exactly common, and Momma and Grandma both owned a lot of property. What do you think will happen if somebody down there starts nosing around?"

"Oh, Mom," Becky said, getting up to clear the table, "no one up here has ever bothered about you, and no one down there is going to bother about me."

CHAPTER 3

"Gran's gon' be mad again, ain't she?" Billy asked, as he climbed into the Ford pickup with the Oklahoma Tire and Supply Company's OTASCO logo on the sides. He and Sam were leaving their fourth Black Tigers practice in as many weeks. They smelled bad and dripped sweat on the seats but Sam did not mind. He felt the kind of tired that satisfies both body and soul.

"Yeah, I reckon so, son," he said, starting the engine, "but you let me worry about that. And don't say 'ain't.' Your momma taught you better."

Dusk trailed close behind when they pulled into the gravel driveway on the northwestern edge of Unionville, but they still had time to pick the purple-hull peas they had not gotten to before heading off to play ball. The white frame house set well back from the street, and Sam parked in front of the matching garage that still held the Ford Victoria Sam had bought for Judith Ann and now drove only on Sundays and family outings. As he and Billy climbed out of the truck, Gran and Mary Jane came from behind the house.

"Daddy, Daddy!" called the freckled-faced little girl rushing toward him in t-shirt and shorts, pigtails flying. "You're home! I helped Gran feed the chickens. Ain't you proud of me?"

"Yes, I am, sweetheart," Sam said, grinning broadly. He reached down, swept her into his arms, smelled the sweetness of her sun-bleached hair, and overlooked her grammar. "I'm very proud of you." Like Billy, she had been a planned baby, long tried for, and Sam had promised Judith Ann before she died that he would pay attention to their education. With Gran's help in almost every way except Billy's homework—she had done all her book learning in a one-room school—he kept his word, most of the time.

"Where have y'all been?" Gran asked, as if she did not know. "Them peas are gon' dry up if y'all don't hurry up and pick them. Dadgum it anyway! I don't know why y'all want to go off over there with them coloreds."

"But Gran," Billy said, "they're good ballplayers. And Leon says I'm good too."

"That don't make me no never mind," she said. She wore a flour-sack apron over a faded house dress, and a bonnet covered her white hair, up in a bun as always. Wire-rimmed glasses perched on her nose. "It ain't about you. It's about appearances and what's proper, and y'all ain't got no business being over there."

Gran was knee-high to nothing and pushing eighty-one, but she ran the Tate household. She had been born Ida Belle Pruett, the youngest of six children, on a hardscrabble farm just ten miles away, the same year Rutherford B. Hayes entered the White House and ended Radical Reconstruction. Her daddy fought under the Confederate stars and bars at Gettysburg, Cold Harbor, and dozens of other places where men killed each other mostly because of slavery. She grew up listening to him rail about Northern carpetbaggers and Southern scalawags, and she was firmly committed to the notion that whites and blacks each had a place and ought to stay in it.

"Aw, Momma, let the boy alone," Sam said with a shrug. "It's just good clean fun. It doesn't mean anything."

"Yeah, it does. It ain't fitting and sooner or later you're gon' see that."

While Gran took Mary Jane inside to wash up and help set the table, Sam and Billy left their baseball gear on the back porch and headed through the yard toward the vegetable garden. The Tate homeplace covered seven acres and Sam loved every inch of it. Elm, oak, and messy chinaberry trees dotted the large front yard, and out back a tin barn with a new coat of red paint held hay and oats and gave cover to Old Ned, a chestnut gelding still good for plowing and gentle enough for the kids to ride. A small outbuilding housed laying hens and another held pullets for fattening until Gran wrung their necks for Sunday dinners.

The garden lay between the house and barn. A mesh-and-barbed-wire fence kept Old Ned and varmints out. Billy did not say anything more until he and Sam got through the gate, grabbed bushel baskets from a post, and starting picking. Then he asked, "Daddy, what did Gran mean back there? I don't understand what's wrong with playing ball with Leon or what it is you're gon' see."

"There's nothing wrong with it, Billy, and I'm not gon' see anything but B. J.'s curve ball coming off the fat part of my bat one of these days. Gran just doesn't understand baseball, that's all. Hurry up now and let's get these peas done."

Except for Mary Jane, no one said much during supper. Gran was still puffed up like an old sitting hen, and Sam and Billy concentrated on the warmed-over pork chops, butter beans, and sweet corn they washed down with milk from jelly glasses.

After supper, Gran said, "I'm gon' work on my new quilt. What peas y'all don't shell tonight, Ollie Mae can do in the morning." Ollie Mae Green was the part-time cook and maid Sam hired after Judith Ann died. She worked for the Tates on Tuesdays, Thursdays, and Saturdays.

Most times when Gran was piecing and quilting, she worked in her sitting room on her own side of the house, but when she was cutting out pattern pieces, she liked to spread her cloth, templates, and scissors on the pink-and-gray dinette table in the kitchen. While she arranged her things, Sam brought in a basket of peas from the back porch.

"I want my own bowl," Mary Jane said. Usually she worked from Sam's bowl or Gran's so they could help her cull any peas with brown spots.

"Okay," Sam said. "You're getting to be a big girl now."

He spread newspapers on the floor, took three large mixing bowls from a cupboard, put one on the table for himself, and handed one to each child. They dropped cross-legged to the linoleum floor and began helping themselves to pods from the field basket. Sam took a dinette chair. As they shelled, they tossed the hulls onto the newspapers.

Pleased with her new status as a pea sheller, Mary Jane said in the best grown-up voice she could muster, "So, Gran, what kind of quilt are you making this time?"

The little girl's manner and question warmed the room. Gran did not wear her false teeth except when she went to church or when special company came, and a toothless grin spread through her wrinkled face.

"I'm making you a memory quilt, hon. It's gon' be a sampler."

Gran had been quilting for as long as Sam could remember.

Every Tuesday morning at nine o'clock she got together with Emma Lou MacDonald and Almalee Jolly to quilt and gossip, and she was always showing him and the children something new she was working on.

"I got some of y'all's old clothes saved up," Gran said, "and I got more patterns than I'll ever have time to make up regular so I'm just gon' put a bunch of stuff in one quilt." From a lined oak basket woven years ago by her daddy, she lifted bits of cloth, laid them on the table, and shared the memories they held. "I done cut scraps out of the clothes," she said to Mary Jane. "Now I'm gon' cut my pattern pieces. This here blue scrap come from an apron I made for your momma when her and your daddy got married back in 'thirty-nine, and this red piece is from one of his old shirts when he worked at the gasoline plant out yonder at Newton Chapel."

"What's that black one?" Mary Jane asked. "It's not pretty like the others."

"That one's real special, hon. It come from the suit my daddy wore after he come home from the Civil War."

"Tell us some war stories, Gran," Billy said.

"Yeah," Mary Jane begged, "tell us about the soldiers."

Gran liked telling stories almost as much as she liked quilting. "Well," she said, taking scissors and cloth in hand, "your great-granddaddy joined up right off the bat with the Third Arkansas Regiment. Went all the way through the war and come out a captain. He said if General Stonewall Jackson hadn't got hisself killed at Chancellorsville, we'd have beat them Yankees."

As she talked, Billy hung on every word. Mary Jane did not understand much of it, but she liked listening and was waiting for the part about how the Confederates ran out of food and tried to make coffee from acorns.

Sam had heard it all dozens of times, and as Gran cut her shapes and talked, he slipped into memories of his own. How he came home from college short of money and went to work delivering groceries for Hadley's Food, Feed, and Seed. How he met and fell in love with Judith Ann. How he took out a loan and opened a general store across from the high school on Newton Chapel Road. And how he worked evenings at the gasoline plant during World War II to make his payments and put his little brother through college.

The storytelling and remembering continued until they shelled all the peas. Then Gran said, "I'm tired. I'm going to bed."

Sam glanced at the gingerbread clock sitting on a wall shelf. This was early for her. She usually sat up all hours listening to gospel singers and preachers on powerful radio stations in far-away Nashville, Tennessee, and Del Rio, Texas.

Sam said he would finish up in the kitchen, and while Gran put away her quilting stuff, he hugged the children and sent them off to get ready for bed. Afterward, as he washed and blanched the peas for freezing, he could not help worrying. He had been taking care of his mother ever since his daddy died. With his brother Herman out of college and off working in the Texas oil-fields, Sam and Judith Ann had moved in with Gran. That was when Sam sold the general store, borrowed more money, and bought the Otasco franchise and a sideline of building supplies.

"Can we sleep in the hall tonight, Daddy?" Mary Jane asked, padding into the kitchen carrying her well-worn Fuzzy Bear and dragging one of Gran's quilts. "I'm hot."

The Tates' Arctic Circle swamp cooler never lived up to its name, so Billy and Mary Jane liked to bed down on a pallet just inside the screened front door. There they could catch an oc-casional breeze and go to sleep listening to katydids, crickets, and the lonesome-sounding horns of freight trains traveling the Rock Island line.

"Sure," Sam said. "Just be sure to latch the door."

When he finished the peas, he switched off the kitchen light and went onto the back porch to have a Chesterfield. In the evening like this was about the only time he smoked and it had been his nightly habit for five years. Now, however, his thoughts turned less to Judith Ann than to Gran.

CHAPTER 4

On the first Saturday in August, Sam angled into his regular parking spot in front of the Otasco store. A two-story brick building with a white cast-iron front, it sat smack in the middle of a three-block stretch that most Unionville residents called "uptown." Although his watch said only a few minutes past seven, it seemed later. He liked to open early and catch folks on their way to work. Not a lot stopped in but he always felt better getting a head start on the day.

"Can I do the lock, Daddy?" Billy asked, jumping out of the truck.

"Here you go," Sam said, tossing the keys. "Let's get a move on." He brought Billy to the store nearly every Saturday and on most weekdays during the summer. The chores he did for a weekly allowance of a dollar and a fifty cents saved Sam time and helped Billy learn hard work.

Clad in a white t-shirt, jeans, and black, high-top tennis shoes, he swung open one of the two big glass doors and breathed in the smell of oiled floors, rubber tires, and car batteries. Sam, in a plaid shirt and khaki pants, walked up the center aisle between rows of Ben-Hur, Leonard, and TempMaster appliances. As he went, he pulled strings hanging from light fixtures near the high, pressed-tin ceiling, and fluorescent bulbs lit the store. Farther back, he switched on a huge electric fan mounted on a chrome stand and turned left under an open stairway into a partially enclosed office with a counter facing the sales floor. Here he unlocked the safe and started counting out change for the cash register, which sat on a long wrapping table out in the sales area. Billy fetched a broom from a closet under the stairs, swept the sidewalk, and began moving display goods outside, in front of tall plate glass windows flanking the entrance.

By the time Sam finished with the cash register, Billy had put out an assortment of Brunswick automobile tires, Lawn-Boy power mowers, and Flying-O bicycles. Then Sam helped him set up a tool rack loaded with rakes, hoes, and shovels. Neal O'Brien, who owned City Hardware across the street next to Farmers State Bank, also displayed merchandise this way. Would-be customers could stop and inspect the tread on a tire, get the feel of an ax, or check the bend of a fishing pole, and no one ever harmed anything.

As the Tates worked, steam began rising from Leon Jackson's dry-cleaning shop behind the bank. Fred Vestal parked his Chevy panel truck in front of his furniture store across the alley from the bank, got out, and waved. Sam and Billy waved back, and as they did, they saw skinny Jim Ed Davis pull his battered red-and-black International pickup into the back of the alley and go in the side door of the bank.

"I wonder what old Jim Ed is doing over there at this hour?" Sam said. "He couldn't be working."

Bank president Horace Bowman's black Lincoln was parked out front but he was always in early. In addition to being the majority stockholder in the bank, he owned Bowman Lumber Company and was by far the richest man in Unionville. He put in long hours watching over his holdings and Sam owed him more money than he liked to remember. Jim Ed, on the other hand, had not worked a lick since coming home from World

War II, having been a Navy cook. He lived in a rundown house
on a hundred acres west of town, and other than occasionally
selling some timber, he had no visible means of support. Some
folks said he lived off money his daddy left from years of selling
moonshine whiskey distilled in old car radiators.

"Maybe he's trying to borrow money without anybody
knowing it," Billy said.

"Yeah, maybe, but he's gon' be disappointed. Mr. Bowman
doesn't lend money to the likes of Jim Ed any time of day."

"Hey," Billy said, pointing, "here comes Scoggins."

"Mr. Scoggins, son," Sam said.

"Okay, Daddy."

Father and son watched Doyle Scoggins drive past in his
brand-new Chevy hardtop, tail fins glittering in the sun. The
Tates waved but Scoggins was fiddling with something on his
dashboard and did not see them. A slender, slump-shouldered
man who always wore long-sleeved khaki shirts and matching pants, he had worked the early shift at the Southwestern
Chemical plant up in El Dorado for so long that even on his
days off, he got up and went to Emmett's Café for coffee. The
only difference was that on those occasions he left his old GMC
work truck at home and drove what he called his "Sunday-go-
to-meeting car," despite no one ever having known him to go to
church, or much of anywhere else except uptown on Saturdays.
The Chevy was his only luxury and he kept it shined up like a
gold watch. A few weeks back, he had let Billy sit in the driver's
seat and breathe in the new-car smell.

Just as the Tates were setting out the last of their display
goods, two pulpwood trucks passed through town heading south
for some rural timber-cutting site. Billy turned just in time to
see them. They had "O. H. Trucking" painted on the doors.

"There goes Otis, Daddy," Billy said, pointing to Otis Henderson, shortstop for the Black Tigers.

"Yep," Sam said, as Otis waved.

Finished with opening the store, Sam and Billy exchanged grins of satisfaction and turned to other chores.

CHAPTER 5

A block and a half up the street from the Otasco store, Preston Upshaw, new owner and editor of the weekly *Unionville Times*, locked the front door of his board-and-batten newspaper office and headed off to sell more ads for his first issue. Traffic had picked up on Main Street, people bustled in and out of Emmett's Café next door, and men were unloading a transport truck in front of the Ford dealership across the highway. Upshaw had a hunch this would be a good day for business and he decided to start with Sam Tate.

"Hey, boy! Where's your daddy?" Upshaw called out moments later in a raspy voice that startled Billy, who had just scattered oiled sawdust on Sam's dark wood floors and was sweeping the aisles front to back.

The newspaper man, short and fiftyish with a marked paunch and thinning brown hair, scanned the store for its owner. Even though it was midsummer, he wore a faded corduroy sport coat over his white shirt and loosely knotted necktie.

"I'm back here," Sam said from his desk behind the office counter. Upshaw had been in town only a few weeks, but already his persistent sales pitches had become irritating.

"Have you decided about that ad yet, Mr. Tate?" Upshaw asked, trying to strike a smooth salesman's tone while forcing a smile across his fleshy face. "Like I explained last week, this is a really good deal—two ads, one-quarter page or larger, for the price of one if you commit to six months. But you have to let me know soon. This offer's only good till I get the first issue out."

"I already told you," Sam said, only now looking up from his work, "I'm not interested. I'll take an eighth page, and that's just to be neighborly, because I don't need it. Everybody who's gon' buy from me already knows this place. All I have to do is keep the doors open and put up these specials they send me from Tulsa." He motioned toward paper banners hanging from wires stretched between two balconies that ran along the sides of the store to a mezzanine above the office. He closed the file he was working on, got up, and came around the stairs. "Take it or leave it."

"You can't afford to pass this up," Upshaw said. "I'm gon' quadruple old man Trammell's circulation."

Until April, Wilbur Trammell had owned and published the *Unionville Times* for nearly forty years, writing the copy and setting the type by hand with a single assistant. He had died at age eighty-four and his only heir, a daughter who lived in Mississippi, had put the paper up for sale. The first time anyone recalled seeing Upshaw was when he turned up at Emmett's Café for breakfast one morning, having moved into a tiny apartment in a back corner of the newspaper office the night before.

"I can pass up any damn thing I want to," Sam said, his aggravation growing. "Besides, I don't believe you can get that many subscribers around here."

Upshaw stood speechless, jowls twitching. This was not the response he wanted, nor did he like the tone of it. Before buying the *Unionville Times*, he was an assistant editor at the *Daily Ledger* in Hattiesburg, Mississippi. Having long wanted to publish his own paper, he chose the *Unionville Times* because it fit his pocketbook and the town seemed to fit his vision.

He had driven up from Hattiesburg one Saturday in May, stopped for gas at the Sinclair station, strolled up and down Main Street, and rode around a few side streets. He discovered that Unionville was not one town, but rather two adjoining towns with the same name. They sat straddle of US 167, which was also Main Street, and along both sides of State Line Road—one town in Arkansas, 130 miles south of Little Rock, and the other in Louisiana, 130 miles north of Alexandria. The gas station attendant told him the only nearby town of any appreciable size was El Dorado, population twenty-five thousand, some 20 miles north and seat of Union County.

According to highway signs at the town limits, each Unionville had a few more than one thousand citizens. Upshaw found out later that two-thirds of the Louisiana residents lived in Tonti Parish on the east side of the highway and the other one-third lived in Claiborne Parish on the west side. The fellow pumping gas said each Unionville had its own mayor and town council, but in everyday life, just about everyone treated the two towns like they were one. Upshaw could see they even shared the only traffic light. It hung smack-dab between them, above State Line Road. He guessed it was put there mostly to slow down big trucks and Yankee tourists passing through on their way to Dallas and New Orleans.

Upshaw could also see that most of the town's businesses stood along the last two blocks of the highway before it left Arkansas and the first block after it entered Louisiana, and he came to learn that locals considered the last block on the Arkansas side the town's commercial center.

On that visit, Upshaw noted a barbershop and newsstand, a drug store, a dry goods store, the Otasco store, a grocery, a variety store and shoe repair shop, and Hadley's Food, Feed, and

Seed on the west side of the street. On the east side, he saw the post office, another dry goods store, City Hardware, the bank, Vestal's Furniture Store, a flower shop, another grocery, and Liberty Theater. All of them looked like potential advertisers, plus Upshaw liked how the theater had a separate entrance for blacks around on the side, off State Line Road.

He paid the service station guy and took a drive around. In addition to the newspaper building, he counted half a dozen more businesses elsewhere along Main Street, including the Ford dealership, another feedstore, a pool hall and domino parlor with a dentist's office in back, a small office building for the telephone and electric companies, and Emmett's Café, which doubled as a Trailways bus station. Mixed in with them were a meeting hall for each town and, on the Arkansas side, a firehouse. Scattered along other streets, he saw Methodist, Presbyterian, and Baptist churches, a doctor's office, a funeral parlor, and two little mom-and-pop grocery stores whose owners apparently lived in back. Among this last group, only the funeral parlor interested him. Undertakers advertised discreetly but dependably.

A little way east of the highway he found the Rock Island Railroad tracks, an ice plant, two lumber mills, and a pulpwood yard—good signs all. On the main roads, only passenger cars and pickups outnumbered wood and lumber trucks. In the lumber trucks, he saw prosperity. In the pickups, most of them carrying shotguns and rifles in their rear windows, he saw men whose emotions he believed he could stir.

Upshaw did not venture into the black sections of town and missed the two black churches, Sadie Rose Washington's juke joint, Black Tiger shortstop Charlie Foster's auto-repair shop, and pitcher B. J. Long's plumbing service. But he would not have cared about them anyway.

In less than an hour, Upshaw decided Unionville could support the type of weekly news operation he dreamed about. With plenty of potential advertisers, two town governments, and growing civil rights unrest across the South to work with, he was confident he could use pointed reporting and editorializing to build a healthy circulation. In addition, the Louisiana side offered the colorful shenanigans of Governor Earl Long, while the Arkansas side boasted the rising star of Governor Orval Faubus. Having long admired the way Faubus had used the *Madison County Record*, a little daily up in the Ozarks, to launch his political career, Upshaw hoped to do the same here.

Today, when he regained the starch drained by Sam's back talk, Upshaw said, "Old man Trammell didn't know how to run a paper. I'm gon' make the *Unionville Times* first-rate. Folks are gon' be holding their breath for every issue."

"Well," Sam said, "I wish you luck, because you're gon' need it. But I'm not taking out any quarter-page ads."

"I'll be back," Upshaw said, leaving. "You'll change your mind when you see my stories."

CHAPTER 6

Seeing Upshaw coming out of the Otasco Store set Ruthelle Ponder on edge. She was not overly friendly to anyone early in the morning and she especially disliked people she considered pushy. A tall, bony woman in her mid-fifties, she shoved her glasses up on her nose, waited for a car to pass, and crossed the street in the middle of the block. Known to everyone as Miss Ruthelle, she was Sam's bookkeeper and, when it was not too much trouble, his sales clerk.

She fussed over Sam's books like they were hers, which was mostly why he tolerated her. Sometimes when he was not there, she did not even bother to leave her office chair to help customers. "Y'all help yourselves," she would call out, peering over the counter and trusting that whatever folks picked up they would bring to the back so she could cash them out. Having never married, she had no children and did not much care for Billy. Sam let him wait on customers buying fish hooks, bicycle parts, and other small items, but Miss Ruthelle did not believe a kid his age should have his fingers in the cash drawer. Billy liked having her around, though, because she kept a jar of jelly beans in her desk and he had fun sneaking a few every chance he got.

"What did that man want?" she asked, as soon as she came through the double front doors, propped open to help circulate the warm air. "You know we don't have money to throw away with him."

27

"Don't worry, Miss Ruthelle," Sam said, both pleased and amused. "I sent him packing."

"Well, it's a good thing," she said, heading straight for her chair. "I saw Lester Grimes coming up the sidewalk. Don't let him come in here and waste our time either."

Lester and his younger brother Odell owned the barbershop and newsstand, and when Lester was not sounding off about one thing or another in his own place of business, he liked to drop in on other merchants and hold forth in theirs. The Otasco store was one of his favorite destinations and he showed up at least once a day. Miss Ruthelle usually liked folks stopping in to gab, especially when they hung around the office counter or cash register table so she could stay put. But Lester loved telling off-color jokes and Miss Ruthelle did not like that one bit. Sam did not care for Lester much either because he was a gossip and had an opinion about everything. But he was a fellow businessman, and despite a big gut and limited mobility due to his unbridled fondness for corn bread and gravy, he was chief of the whites-only volunteer fire department, a job no one else wanted.

"Hey, Billy, you missed a spot up front here," Lester said, as soon as he got inside. As he walked to the back, his starched white barber's jacket rustling with every step, he shouted, "Hey, Sam, did you hear the one about the traveling salesman and the farmer's daughter up in Tennessee? Oh, Miss Ruthelle, I didn't see you there. How're you this fine morning? I bet you've heard it, ain't you?" She shot him a go-to-blazes look as he turned, grinning, to the purpose of his visit.

"Sam, I'm reminding everybody to be at fire practice Monday night. We got the new helmets in and we're gon' be passing them out."

Sam said he would. As a member of the Arkansas-side town

council, he had been pushing for as much new fire equipment as their strapped budget could support.

His fire-chief business done, Lester switched subjects. "You buying any ads from Upshaw, Sam? He's been after me ever since he hit town, and I see he's out hustling again this morning."

"Only what I used to buy from old man Trammell. Are you?"

"I don't know what I'm gon' do yet," Lester said, turning to leave. Halfway to the door, he called over his shoulder, "Miss Ruthelle, now don't you go telling anybody about that traveling salesman, you hear?"

Miss Ruthelle bore down on her pencil so hard she snapped the lead.

As soon as Billy finished sweeping the floors and emptying the trash, he headed to the post office to get the mail and the *El Dorado Daily News*. The *Unionville Times* had never printed much more than town news, school doings, legal notices, obituaries, and birth and wedding announcements, so most people also subscribed to the countywide paper. Some also took the *Shreveport Times* from down in Louisiana or the *Arkansas Gazette* from up in Little Rock or read them for free at the barbershop and newsstand.

A lot of folks had the El Dorado paper delivered, but at least as many got it through same-day drop-off at the post office. Billy liked the Tates' getting it that way because when he was working at the store, he could see the Major League box scores early and talk about them with Sam between customers and chores. They were keeping close track of the St. Louis Cardinals trying to catch the Milwaukee Braves for the National League pennant.

When Billy left the post office and started back across the

highway, he was studying something else, however. Like a lot of boys in Unionville, Billy considered the wooden signs that hung under the sheds on most store fronts inviting targets for showing off. Extending nearly half the width of the sidewalks, the hand-lettered boards hung from wires and hinges, and if swatted hard enough, they would swing back and forth. A kid could measure his growth by which ones he could reach on a running jump. Maybe today he could finally hit the Unionville Variety and Shoe Repair sign. Tucking the newspaper and mail under his right arm like a football, Billy sprinted forward, but just as he started to leap he heard a shout from behind.

"Stop that right now!"

Claude Satterfield, the Arkansas-side marshal, had just turned the corner at Hadley's Food, Feed, and Seed, having walked from his home a few blocks west on First Street. Mr. Claude, as everyone called him, was barely five six, did not weigh much more than a sack of horse feed, and was somewhere on the far side of seventy, but no one messed with him. He always wore a black felt hat, black suit coat with his badge pinned to the front, and khaki pants with a leather-covered blackjack rammed in a back pocket so that the handle stuck out from under the back of his coat. He did not carry a gun, but his getup set him apart, and stories abounded about how in his younger days he had used his noggin knocker to crack skulls and crush collarbones. About the only crime other than an occasional fistfight or incident of public drunkenness that most folks could recall, though, was a bank hold-up back before World War II. The robbers had gotten clean away in a beat-up old Ford, while Mr. Claude, who did not have a car and did not know how to drive anyway, had stood in the middle of the street waving his blackjack and shouting, "Come back here, you low-down sons of bitches!" But no one ever brought that up in Mr. Claude's presence.

On hearing the old man's voice, Billy stopped cold. He knew what was coming. Mr. Claude took him by the arm and marched him down the street and into the Otasco store.

"Sam," the scrappy little lawman said loudly for full effect, "this is the third time I've caught this boy running on the sidewalk. If he does it again, I'm gon' have to put him in the pokey."

"I'll make sure he doesn't, Mr. Claude," Sam replied. He took the mail and paper from Billy and said, "Come to the back, son. I want to talk to you."

Miss Ruthelle, who had watched the brief scene, returned to her books, hiding a smirk.

Billy hated that his daddy took away a week's allowance and today's sports page, but at least Pete and Dwayne Jones, due at the store any time now, had not seen him in Mr. Claude's grasp. A powerful black man almost as tall as Leon but a whole lot bigger around the middle and in the behind, Pete worked at the store two Saturdays a month. Sometimes during the summer, he brought his son with him. Dwayne was a year or two older than Billy, and Sam paid the boy thirty-five cents to help pick up trash and cut weeds in the alley next to Lawson's Dry Goods and around the Otasco store warehouse out back.

Almost every time Dwayne came, he and Billy took breaks together and played games between warehouses and among piles of trash waiting to be hauled away. The boys never saw each other any other time, though. White kids went to school on the west side of town and black kids went to school on the east side. Billy never questioned that, just as he never questioned the "Whites Only" and "Colored" signs on the separate rest rooms at gas stations and the separate waiting rooms at the doctor's office and the train depot. He saw all of that as simply how things were. He did not know that all over the South, after the Civil War, men like his great-granddaddy had passed Jim Crow laws to enforce such ways of behaving. He also did not know that now other men were willing to do whatever was necessary to keep things that way.

CHAPTER 7

Becky Reeves's shoulders and leg ached as she pulled her green Plymouth off highway 167 and into a Mobil station on the north side of El Dorado. Night and a light drizzle had started to fall and she was anxious to get to Unionville, but first she needed gas, a rest room, and food. She had been driving all day, having left her parents' home in Missouri before dawn and stopped only twice.

"Fill it up and check the oil, please," she said, getting out. "Are the rest rooms locked?"

"Yes, ma'am," the pimple-faced attendant said. "The keys are hanging inside the door there." He pulled a dirty rag from grease-stained coveralls, wiped his forehead, and stood staring as Becky, in a sleeveless yellow dress, closed the car door and started toward the office.

"Are you going to put gas in it, or not?" she asked over her shoulder.

"Yes, ma'am," he said, removing the gas cap from the sedan and flipping the switch on the pump. He kept gawking as Becky walked across the pavement. She sensed his eyes on her but kept going. People often stared at her and she had learned to ignore it. She had a face and figure that would turn any man's head but most folks stared because of her limp.

"Are there any restaurants near here?" she asked a few minutes later, as she paid the bill.

"There's an A&W drive-in about a mile up the highway and the Flamingo Motel's a little ways past that. They have a café but I ain't never ate there."

A dirty rest room and limited options for food added to Becky's fatigue. Her parents had urged her not to drive straight through but she had insisted. She was eager to settle into the furnished apartment the Unionville School District had recommended and start getting ready for her students. It was Tuesday, August 20, and classes started in two weeks.

Expecting she would have to make tomorrow's breakfast from two huge bags of groceries her mother had thrust into the car when she said goodbye, Becky picked the Flamingo over the hamburger place. The menu was about as appealing as the three pink birds blinking on the motel's neon sign, but the food and coffee were hot, and she lingered longer than she had intended.

When she left the café, rain was falling in sheets and it slowed her drive through El Dorado and on down to Unionville. According to directions taken over the phone, her apartment was in Hazel Brantley's home, on the east side of the highway four blocks north of State Line Road. Because Unionville had no intown mail delivery, the houses did not have numbers on them. School superintendent Vernon Appleby's secretary had said to look for a white frame house with a double carport, full front porch, and two front doors. That had sounded easy enough, but few houses on either side of the street had any lights on inside or out, and in the rain they all looked pretty much alike. Becky missed the Brantley place on the first pass and had to go on to State Line Road, turn around, and count streets on the way back.

A late-model Chevy sat in the left side of the carport but the other side was empty. Becky turned into the short driveway and parked in the vacant spot. Lights came on in the house, and as she climbed wooden steps to the porch, her landlady flipped on a bright outdoor light. Dressed in a pink bathrobe, she remained inside peering through a slightly open door at the far end. Becky crossed to that side and could see just enough to determine that the woman was short, stout, and likely old enough to draw Social Security.

"Who are you and what do you want?" she demanded through the screen door. "I got a shotgun and I'll use it!"

"Mrs. Brantley?" Becky asked, wondering if she had the right house after all.

"Yeah, what is it?"

"I'm Rebecca Reeves. Becky. Your new tenant."

"How's that? Who'd you say?"

"I'm Becky Reeves. The school district arranged for me to rent your apartment. They said they would tell you I was arriving today."

"Well, why didn't you say so? Wait right there. I'll get your key." Hazel disappeared inside for a moment. When she came out, she leaned a .12-gauge pump against the door facing.

"Sorry if I scared you, hon," Hazel said. "It's awful late and a widow woman living alone in this town has to take precautions. We've got a marshal that don't drive and a night watchman that's plum loco. Folks have to protect their ownselves. Here's the key to your side of the house. Open it up and go on in."

"Do you have a lot of crime in Unionville?" Becky asked, taking the key and being careful not to brush against the shotgun.

"None except for somebody getting a snootful now and again, but if any robbing and stuff ever starts, I aim to be ready for it."

Becky walked to her end of the porch, pulled open the screen, and unlocked the door. The upper half had a single glass pane covered by lace curtains. She stepped inside and Hazel followed. The apartment smelled of Pine-Sol and Clorox.

"I had my colored woman clean it good for you yesterday," Hazel said, flipping on the lights. "This here's your living room. Your kitchen's through there. Bedroom's behind it. Bathroom's off the bedroom. What you do in here is your business but I don't like noise at night. I'm a light sleeper. I've always had teachers living here and most of them have been quiet."

Becky couldn't help grinning. "I assure you, Mrs. Brantley, I'm not a rowdy person. May I ask if this is where the teacher whose place I'm taking lived?"

"Sure is, hon. And she didn't get no new job like they said neither. She went and got herself pregnant and had to get married. Fellow that knocked her up is from someplace down in Louisiana. But I can't tell you about it. It's all hush-hush and I hate gossip. I'll say this, though. Folks around here don't like that kind of carrying on. They'll be all in a stew when word gets out, and you can bet it will when that baby comes. Of course, if she hadn't been running around with three or four men at once, it probably wouldn't have happened. She went gallivanting off with one or another of them near about every weekend. Sure didn't set no good example for kids, I'll tell you."

When Becky did not reply, Hazel said, "Well, hon, if you need anything in here, you let me know. How about your stuff? Want me to help you unload your car?"

The offer seemed more a desire to snoop than to help. "Thank you, but no," Becky said. "I don't have much and I can manage fine."

"Okay. Well, why don't you come over in the morning about eight and I'll give you some breakfast and tell you all about

Unionville. And you can tell me all about yourself."

"All right, Mrs. Brantley, I appreciate that. I'll see you tomorrow."

"Call me Hazel, hon," the landlady said, as she went out the door.

A friendly sort, Becky thought, but not somebody you would want to confide in. The apartment was better than she expected. The linoleum floors and wallpaper looked almost new. In addition to a sofa and other usual furnishings, the living room had a writing desk, TV, and window fan. Small hallways with closets connected the three rooms. The bedroom had a dresser, a chest-of-drawers, and an iron bedstead painted white. Her mother's blue-and-white Shoofly quilt would look good there, Becky decided.

She had not fibbed about unloading the Plymouth being quick work. She had brought only two suitcases of clothes, a couple of hats, some sheets and towels, and a few kitchen items. Her books, Remington typewriter, portable Singer sewing machine, three quilts, and the two bags of groceries rounded out her cargo.

Becky took greatest care with the quilts. She had brought two of her mother's and one she had made herself, plus material she had been saving for a Sun Bonnet Sue appliqué. She had learned to quilt while recovering from polio and she expected that once she got into a routine at school, she would have plenty of time for it in a place as small and quiet as Unionville.

CHAPTER 8

The Tates looked forward to Tuesdays. Gran got to quilt with her friends. Mary Jane liked how they made a fuss over her. Billy got to borrow another stack of baseball novels from the bookmobile. And Sam liked seeing all of them happy.

He was getting ready to leave for the Otasco store. "Daddy loves you, sweetheart," he told Mary Jane, as he loosed her from a hug and set her on the kitchen floor.

"I love you too, Daddy," she said, clutching Fuzzy Bear in one hand and tugging at her nightgown with the other.

"Billy, you be careful crossing State Line Road," Sam said, as he headed out the back door, "and get some books for Mary Jane. Y'all mind your grandmother, now."

By the time Ollie Mae Greene arrived to help with the rest of the day's chores, Gran had fetched her basket of quilt pieces, gotten out her special-recipe tea cakes, and started making fresh lemonade. Emma Lou MacDonald, Almalee Jolly, and Gran had been quilting together every week for more than twenty years. Nothing short of illness kept them from it. Besides sharing a passion for quilts, they had all grown up on farms, lived through two world wars, made it through the Depression, nurtured marriages, raised children on a shoestring, and lost loved ones. In their minds, they had the wisdom that comes with long life, and they liked sharing it with each other and anyone else who would listen. Because Gran did not drive and Emma Lou and Almalee did, they always met at the Tate home.

"Come on, Ollie Mae," Gran said. "Let's get going. They're gon' be here any minute." Dark, middle-aged, and nearly as round as she was tall, Ollie Mae had raised children in circumstances just as hard as Gran but with lots less money and working six days a week in someone else's house to boot. The experience had made her strong and patient.

"Yes, ma'am," Ollie Mae said, taking her white apron out of a paper bag and slipping it over a plain housedress. She had only three work dresses but whichever one she wore was always clean and freshly pressed. Gran expected that but never gave any thought to how Ollie Mae managed it. "I see Mr. Sam picked a mess of snap beans and tomatoes and left them on the back porch this morning," she said. "Y'all want them for dinner?"

"Yeah," Gran answered, pulling out a dinette chair and sitting down, "with mashed potatoes and steak. Take a package out of the freezer."

Sam bought entire sides of beef and got them cut and wrapped at a processing plant in El Dorado. Like gardening, it saved money. Every now and then, Gran would send a package home with Ollie Mae. Her husband, who drove a truck for South Arkansas Oak Flooring, would fuss when she brought it in, saying they did not need any white folks' handouts, and she would tell him she had more than earned it.

As soon as she put away her paper bag, Ollie Mae took a closer look at Gran. She often sat in the kitchen and talked with Ollie Mae about weather, recipes, and religion, but almost never on quilting days. On those, every minute went into getting ready for Emma Lou and Almalee.

"Y'all feeling all right this morning, Mrs. Tate?"

"I'm fine," Gran said after a moment. "I didn't sleep good last night, and I'm thinking about my memory quilt. I've got scraps and patterns for everybody. It's gon' be a keepsake."

"It sure sounds like it," Ollie Mae said. She quilted, too, though more from necessity than for pleasure. Instead of hand-stitching her tops, batting, and backing together in fancy designs like Gran and her friends, Ollie Mae usually just sewed around the edges and took heavy thread and tied the middles together in several places because it was faster. "That'll go in Miss Mary Jane's hope chest someday, I reckon, won't it?" Ollie Mae asked. The little girl, who was sitting under the table rocking Fuzzy Bear, looked up and smiled.

"Yeah, it will," Gran said. "She never knew her momma or her Granddaddy Tate. I want her to have something with the whole family in it, something she can wrap up in and feel all of us around her."

"That's real nice, Mrs. Tate," Ollie Mae said, as she washed the breakfast dishes. "My boys don't care about quilts, but I've made a bunch for my grandbabies and their mommas. It's a good feeling to give them something that has your ownself in it, something you made with your own hands."

"Yeah, it is, Ollie Mae. It sure is," Gran said.

When Gran heard the crunch of automobile tires on gravel, she pulled herself up, smoothed out her dress, and headed off to greet her friends. "Set out them tea cakes and lemonade at ten o'clock," she ordered Ollie Mae. "Mary Jane, get yourself dressed then you can come sit with us."

By the time Gran got to the front door, Emma Lou was

puffing up the porch steps. Close to Gran in age but a head taller, she had a sunny round face and an obvious weakness for her own cooking and was hauling a large quilted bag with an unfinished Double Irish Chain quilt spilling over the sides.

"Morning, Ida Belle," she said. "Sure is hot, ain't it?" She wore a blue print dress and her stockings were rolled down to her ankles like Gran's.

Almalee, tall, slender, and youngest of the three, slid from under the steering wheel of her year-old Ford Fairlane, slammed her door harder than usual, and went around to close the passenger door Emma Lou had left open.

"I'll be there in a minute," Almalee said, her sparrow-like face screwed up in a frown. "Lordy! Some people just don't pay no mind!" She wore a green print dress and would never roll her stockings down, no matter how hot it got.

"Y'all come on in," Gran said. "I done started a new quilt and I want to show you what I'm gon' do."

"I'm starting a new one too," Alamalee said. "It's gon' be a Triple Irish Chain with a zigzag border," she added in a boastful tone the others let pass.

Gran ushered them through the screen door and across a short hallway into her spotless sitting room. Each woman took her usual place, Emma Lou in a straight chair that suited her back, Almalee on the gray armless sofa, and Gran in her padded rocking chair. A pair of south-facing windows with curtains tied back and paper shades rolled halfway up let in the morning sun. A large photograph of her daddy in his black suit hung in an oval frame above a table-model Philco radio in the corner.

As the quilters began pulling out their sewing things, Mary Jane, now in a t-shirt and shorts, scurried into the room with a doll and a shoe box and settled under a quilting frame that held a nearly finished Grandmother's Flower Garden quilt. Gran worked on it evenings now and again, often while telling the children stories. The shoe box held a needle, thread, and scraps of cloth Gran had cut for doll clothes. Mary Jane was learning needlework the same way her grandmother had.

"Gosh almighty!" Emma Lou said, when she saw Gran's pile of quilt pieces. "You've been busy."

"I'm making another sampler," Gran said. Like most women who had been quilting for years, she had already made several. "This one's gon' be a memory quilt for Mary Jane." Gran held up the bits of cloth one by one, proudly identifying where each came from. Emma Lou and Almalee joined in the remembering.

"Why, I recollect that gray scrap," Emma Lou said, smiling. "That's from one of Judith Ann's Sunday-go-to-meeting dresses. She wore it plum out."

"Yep," Gran said.

"I remember that navy piece," Almalee recalled, as she reached into her bag for a spool of thread. "It's from one of your old smocks. I was with you when you got the material for it on sale up at Lawson's. That was the day I bought that brown linen suit that looked so good on me." She glanced up again as she threaded her needle. "And that pink seersucker piece there, that's from one of Mary Jane's baby dresses."

"Yep," Gran said again. "Judith Ann made it when she was expecting. She just knew she was gon' have a girl."

Emma Lou peered over her glasses at Mary Jane, who seemed caught up in her own stitching.

"Ida Belle, do you think Sam's ever gon' get married again?" Emma Lou asked quietly.

"I know who'd be just right for him," Almalee said, not looking up. "I told Opal the other day she ought to stop in the store every now and then and buy something. Sam's so shy, he ain't never gon' ask her out if he don't think she's interested." Opal was Almalee's only child and her chief project aside from quilting. Thinner than her mother and nearing forty, Opal worked as a bookkeeper in an El Dorado bank and rode back and forth with another woman and two men. The carpooling provided all the contact she wanted with people of the male persuasion.

"I'm sure Opal isn't interested in Sam," Emma Lou said. "Why don't you just let that girl alone, Almalee? She'll find herself a husband if she ever decides she wants one."

Mary Jane still seemed busy, so Emma Lou returned to her question. "You and Sam are doing a fine job with these kids, Ida Belle," she said, "but they really ought to have a momma, and Sam's still a good-looking man. I know he could..."

"Let me show y'all what blocks I'm making," Gran cut in, as Mary Jane looked up. "I'm gon' have a Log Cabin block and a Wild Geese Flying block for my daddy and a Dove in the Window block and a Pear Basket block for my momma."

"Lucille Taylor made a Pear Basket quilt a while back," Almalee said, eyes still glued to her work. "She had it up at the county fair. Won a blue ribbon too. Oh, it was pretty. Had lots of browns and yellows and tiny little stitches. Not as fine as mine, though." Lucille and her sister, Mae Vinnie, were seamstresses and owned a dry-cleaning shop favored by most white women.

Gran ignored Almalee and kept talking about the sampler, calling out the squares she was making for each family member, including a Dutch Girl for Mary Jane.

"I made a Dutch Girl quilt for Opal when she was little," Almalee said. "She's still got it. I'll bring it over and show it to y'all. No! I'll get Opal to bring it over and show it to Mary Jane. I bet Sam would like to see it too."

Gran and Emma Lou continued to ignore Almalee.

"What blocks you got in mind for yourself?" Emma Lou asked.

"I ain't decided yet, but I'm thinking about a Sunflower and a Rolling Star. Then I'm gon' need two more to finish it all out so I have four squares across and five down."

"That's gon' be real pretty," Emma Lou said, tilting her head and picturing the finished work of art. "What color lattice and border are you gon' put on it?"

"I'm thinking about making both of them some sort of cream color so all the blocks will stand out nice."

"That's it," Almalee said. "I'll get Opal to wear her cream-colored dress when she brings her quilt over to show Sam. It always looks so nice on her."

While his grandmother quilted and his sister played, Billy headed for the bookmobile, the closest thing Unionville had to a public library. It came from Homer, over in Claiborne Parish, but because Unionville had a consolidated school district that included both sides of town, everyone could check out books— everyone, that is, except blacks. No law kept them from it but custom did. During the school year, the bookmobile came to the white elementary school on the Arkansas side, and during the summer it parked next to Unionville Feeds way down on the Louisiana side.

As long as Billy stayed off the highway and out of the quarters, he was allowed to ride his bike just about anywhere in town. This morning he peddled three blocks to the white elementary and high schools on Newton Chapel Road, then ten blocks south, across State Line Road to Lafayette Street, and east two blocks to the feedstore on US 167.

As usual, he arrived in the parking lot before any other library users. He leaned his bike against the shaded side of the tin-clad store building and waited. By the time the huge brown bookmobile rolled in, several other people had joined him. As soon as the driver opened the rear door and put down the wooden steps, Billy smelled the books. The odor always reminded him of the piles of *Saturday Evening Post* magazines his mother saved and the endless evenings she spent reading stories to him. She taught him to love books long before he started school, and if there had not been a line of folks behind him, he could have spent the whole morning in the big truck. In only a few minutes, however, he found two baseball novels he had not read and four Little Golden Books for Mary Jane. He realized she was getting too old for them but he knew she still loved them.

As Billy stood at the checkout desk behind the driver's seat, he saw Crazy Dan Malone on the other side of the highway pushing his beat-up wooden wheelbarrow along Lafayette west toward the bookmobile. As far as anyone knew, he was a hobo when he wandered into Unionville a few years back. For a while, he rambled around knocking on doors and begging for handouts and work. Then Alan Poindexter, chief bookkeeper at Bowman Lumber Company and current mayor of the Arkansas side, offered him use of an abandoned tool shed behind the lumber mill, off State Line Road over in Tonti Parish. He still lived there, and Alan gave him occasional odd jobs around the property. Most other folks did not pay him much mind.

Well past middle age and slight in build, Crazy Dan had a stringy gray beard and a cheap glass eye that did not match his good one. He wore heavily patched bib overalls and a shapeless brown hat, and everywhere he went, he pushed his once-green cart, its wobbly iron wheel grating on paved surfaces.

"Mrs. Thompson," Billy asked the bookmobile attendant, "would it be all right if I just sit over there and read a spell?" He nodded toward the vacant driver's seat.

"I'm sorry, Billy, but that's against the rules. Are you feeling all right, hon?"

"Yes, ma'am. I'm okay," he said. He ducked his head, slipped through the exit, and headed straight for his bike.

"Hey, Billy!" Crazy Dan yelled, as soon as he crossed to the feedstore side of the highway, his high-pitched voice jarring everyone in line. "How's my daddy this morning?"

One of Crazy Dan's greatest joys in life, or so it seemed to Billy, was picking at him by claiming to be Sam's son. It had started several years ago for no apparent reason except Sam gave Crazy Dan the wheelbarrow for some work in the Otasco warehouse. At first, the old man's antics had been only a little bothersome. Now, however, several older boys got a kick out of teasing Billy about being Crazy Dan's brother, and the whole mess was nearly impossible to stomach.

Because Billy could not ride on the highway and Crazy Dan now stood between the feedstore and Lafayette Street, he had the boy cornered in plain view of all the bookmobile patrons.

"Hey, Billy!" the old man shouted again. "You know Sam's my daddy, don't you? He told me hisself. He gimme this here wheelbarrow. He said he wants me to come live with y'all. What do you think of that? Huh? Huh?" His laughter, sharp and loud, like a chicken squawking, echoed through the parking lot.

Billy's mother had told him the best way to deal with teasers was to tell them to stop, and if they would not, try to ignore them. The first tactic had only encouraged Crazy Dan and Billy had long since given up on it. He put his books in his handlebar basket, pushed his bicycle past the old man and the onlookers, and got on and rode away as fast as he could. The bystanders went back to talking and Crazy Dan turned and went up the highway. Even when Billy was blocks away, though, the old man's screeching still rang in his ears.

⁓

When Billy got home, Emma Lou and Almalee were still there and Mary Jane was sitting on the front porch swing waiting for him. She was hugging a worn Log Cabin quilt that she and Billy used for daytime naps and lying around. He took the familiar coverlet and spread it in the shade of a huge elm tree in the front yard. If he read to his sister for a while, she would be satisfied and soon go off to do something else. Then he could read one of his baseball novels till noon when Sam came home for dinner and brought the newspaper with yesterday's box scores.

Billy opened *Howdy Doody and the Princess*, but before he could begin, Mary Jane asked, "Are we gon' get a new momma?"

"Where in tarnation did you get an idea like that?"

"Mrs. MacDonald and Mrs. Jolly were talking to Gran about it. Mrs. MacDonald said we ought to have a momma."

"We don't need a momma. We've got Gran. She takes good care of us."

"Yeah, I know, but you and Daddy are always talking about Momma, and I can't even remember her. It's not fair." Mary Jane's lips quivered and tears welled in her eyes.

CHAPTER 9

Preston Upshaw crushed another cigarette in the ashtray on his cluttered desk, folded his arms above his belly, and stared through a cloud of smoke at the mocked-up headline for his first issue of the *Unionville Times*. Advertising sales were running ahead of any old man Trammell ever generated but not hitting levels Upshaw expected.

"Those merchants will come around when they see this," he said to Pearl Goodbar, his assistant. She had worked for Wilbur Trammel until he died and Upshaw had kept her on. She was having trouble learning to operate the new Linotype machine, but when she was not grumbling about the pile of loose boards and other mess the installers left after they tore out a wall to get the thing into the building, she was proving good at editing copy and writing local stories. Upshaw read the headline aloud, "'Hell on the Way.' Yeah, that'll do it," he said. "We'll run 'Crisis in Little Rock' as a subhead."

This was exactly the sort of moment Upshaw had been waiting for. He assumed a lot of folks in southern Arkansas and northern Louisiana believed as he did that a growing number of northern do-gooders, liberal judges, and rabble-rousing black ministers were rallying around *Brown v. Board of Education*, the Supreme Court's 1954 ruling to integrate public schools. He also figured his readers knew about the bus boycott started by some black woman named Rosa Parks over in Montgomery,

Alabama, a year and a half ago and how this past spring Martin Luther King, Jr., led tens of thousands of followers on a march in Washington, DC. Surely, too, Upshaw guessed, all of this riled his readers as much it did him and, like him, they resented how the NAACP and the Southern Christian Leadership Conference kept pushing harder and harder for all sorts of civil rights for black people.

On his sales rounds, Upshaw had heard enough talk to know that most people in Unionville assumed that the long-antic-ipated integration of Little Rock schools would take place in September. He also knew, however, that opposition was building in the capital, and he both welcomed it personally and saw it as something he could stoke in Unionville for profit.

"I tell you, Mrs. Goodbar," he said, "folks around here are apathetic and I'm gon' fix that. Integration can be stopped if people will just wake up. If they don't, what's happening in Little Rock is gon' happen down here."

"What does 'Hell on the Way' mean?" Pearl asked, coming over to his desk. She brushed a strand of brown hair away from her gold-rimmed glasses and picked up the headline sheet. Now in her early forties, she had taught high school English before leaving to raise two daughters. When the youngest entered sixth grade, she answered an ad from Wilbur Trammel because she liked to write. She had learned a lot from him but she was not accustomed to turning out headlines like these.

"I mean," Upshaw said, "that if the Little Rock school board tries to go ahead with the Blossom Plan to integrate—Virgil Blossom is the superintendent of schools up there—some folks are gon' fight to stop it."

"Who said so?"

"Martin Smitherman. He's a big-wheel lawyer in the Capital

Citizens' Council. Ran for Congress a couple of years ago. Knows what he's talking about. He's not the only one either. Brother Walter Paxson, that radio preacher over in Texas, said it too. The Citizens' Council brought him to Little Rock earlier this summer. It's all right here in my story," Upshaw said, digging for a page of copy. He read aloud, "'There are people left yet in the South who love God and their nation enough to shed blood if necessary to stop this work of Satan.'"

"He said that back in the summer sometime?"

"Yeah, June I think."

Pearl sat down on a cane-bottomed chair, one of half a dozen scattered around the huge office and printing room. "Isn't that old news?" she asked. "I remember Jim Johnson talking about it during the last gubernatorial election. You know about him, I suppose. He's from Crossett, just over in Ashley County. It's a lumber town, a lot like Unionville, only bigger."

"Sure, I know about Johnson," Upshaw said. "He might have won if he hadn't gon' around busting up Faubus's rallies with bullhorns and calling him a communist. Anyway, this isn't old news to anyone who's forgotten about it or didn't hear it in the first place. And I'll tell you something else. I grew up watching my momma work beside coloreds in Mississippi cotton fields and I don't intend to watch a whole generation of white kids going to school with them. People in Unionville are gon' start thinking differently now. I'm gon' see to it."

"Isn't this headline a little strong?"

"It's nothing you need to worry about," Upshaw snapped. "You just stick to editing. I'll worry about the content."

Pearl got up and went back to her desk. Whatever she thought about her new boss, she could not afford to talk back to him. She needed her job. Her husband worked for a wholesale grocery house in El Dorado, and sending their daughters to college was going to take every dollar their family could scrape together.

Upshaw lit another cigarette, took a long draw, and picked up the headline sheet again.

"Yes, sir," he said, "this will stir things up."

CHAPTER 10

Becky woke up early, eager to see Unionville and her new school. She finished squaring away her things, put on a white blouse and dark skirt, and went next door for breakfast. Her landlady, in her pink bathrobe again, welcomed her to a spic-and-span apartment smelling of fresh coffee. The kitchen table held cereal, bananas, poached eggs, whole-wheat toast, and orange juice—not at all what Becky had expected.

"Doctor told me to watch what I eat," Hazel said. "I hope this is okay."

"It's lovely and I'm starving."

"Well, you just sit right down and help yourself, hon. Did you sleep all right?"

"I tossed and turned a bit," Becky said, taking a chair between corner windows overlooking a small yard with beds of colorful flowers. "Guess I'll have to get used to the cars on the highway at night. Was I dreaming, or is there some kind of mill close by? I thought I heard a steam whistle early this morning."

"Yeah, you did," Hazel said, pouring the coffee. "Unionville's got two lumber mills. Both of them used to blow whistles to wake up the help in the morning. Blew them every time they had a shift change and at dinnertime too. They've all but quit now, though. The one you heard was down by the depot. They blow it mostly for old time's sake. Goes off at six o'clock every morning, rain or shine. When the wind's blowing this way, it's really loud."

"Then I won't have to set my alarm clock."

"Nope, hon, probably not. Nobody sleeps late in this town." Hazel sat down and picked up a plate of toast to pass. "Is everything all right in the apartment?"

"Everything except a dripping faucet in the kitchen," Becky said, taking the plate. "It needs a new washer. But you needn't trouble yourself about it. I can fix it."

"Oh, hon, you don't have to bother with that. We have a plumber in Unionville, a colored boy. I can get him to come take care of it."

"No, please. There's nothing to it. I need to go out and buy an iron and an ironing board, and I can pick up a washer and fix it in a jiffy. I keep a tool kit in my car."

Hazel beamed. This would save her three dollars, at least. "Well, ain't you something, hon? I just know we're gon' get along good. That girl before you, she was always bothering me to get this, that, or the other thing done for her. I tell you what, my late departed husband—God rest his soul—he wouldn't have put up with it. He was a good man, though. Worked down at Bowman Lumber Company."

Becky helped herself to eggs.

"That's the mill that's got the whistle," Hazel said. "Old Horace Bowman, he's the big shot around town. Folks say he's got more money than God. I believe it too. Lives in a house big enough for half the Baptist congregation. That's the church you want to go to, by the way. Brother Byrd, he's a real hellfire-and-brimstone preacher. Makes the hair crawl on the back of your neck. Oh, listen to me, hon, running on so. Let me tell you where to buy things. We got some good stores in Unionville."

Hazel recommended the Feed and Seed and Perry's for groceries, the Otasco store for the iron and the rubber washer, the variety store for the ironing board, and the Taylor sisters for dry cleaning. She offered to let Becky use her washing machine and dryer if Becky did her laundry in the daytime. Then came the inevitable.

"So, tell me hon, if you don't mind my asking, what happened to your leg, and why ain't a pretty gal like you married? Is your leg the reason? If it is, that's too bad."

Becky had heard the questions too many times to count. She took a sip of coffee and gave her standard answers.

"I had polio when I was a teenager and I've yet to meet the man I want to marry."

She had shared an initial attraction with more than one man but had not admired any deeply, and none had seemed comfortable with her. At one point, she wondered if any man ever would be, but now she was not sure she cared. She was a lot more concerned about getting an opportunity to run a school someday.

After breakfast, Becky removed the worn washer from her kitchen faucet. Outside, trees and grass still wet from last night's rain glittered in the early morning sun and the air was sticky. She decided to check in at school first and do her shopping later. The campus was close by and easy to find. She drove three blocks north on the highway then one block west on Newton Chapel Road.

The school was larger than she expected. A corrugated-tin bus repair shop and three elementary buildings of varying styles stood along the north side of the road. From phone conversations, she knew she would be teaching in the one-story concrete-block structure that sat between the repair shop and a two-story brick building that looked like it might have housed the entire school at some earlier time. A white frame structure with slides, swings, and seesaws out front lay west of it. Behind the buildings, playgrounds and sports fields extended north to woods and east to the highway.

The high school and district offices occupied three brick buildings on the south side of the road. Becky parked the Plymouth in front of the largest, climbed half a dozen steps to the main entrance, and entered through a pair of glass doors propped open with wooden blocks. The building smelled of aging books and cleaning solvents.

She crossed the oiled wood floor to an open door with "Office" painted yellow on a glass pane. Inside, a middle-aged woman looked up from her typewriter. "Morning," she said, peering over eyeglasses. "What can I do for you?"

"I'm Rebecca Reeves, your new seventh-grade teacher. Folks call me Becky."

"I'm Hilda Starr, Superintendent Appleby's secretary. We talked on the phone. We've been expecting you. Have a seat and I'll tell him you're here."

Becky thanked her and chose the nearest chair. Several minutes passed before Hilda returned. "Mr. Appleby will see you now," she said. "You stopped in at just the right time. I'll take you back."

"Hello, Miss Reeves," Appleby said, rising as Becky walked into a large room with a long row of windows overlooking the street. The other three walls were bare except for pictures of several US presidents. An American flag stood in one corner. A slender woman with white hair and piercing eyes sat at the far end of a conference table filled with papers. "This is Gladys Woodhead, the elementary school principal," Appleby said, "We're delighted to see you."

"I hope you had a good trip down," Woodhead said. She remained seated.

"How do you do?" Becky replied. "The drive was fine and I'm happy to be here." She walked across the room and shook hands with her new bosses, and Hilda returned to her desk.

"Well," Appleby said, then paused, searching for words. His globe-like face and thick, black-rimmed glasses reminded Becky of an owl. Strands of brown hair were plastered over his mostly bare scalp. Suspenders and a wide tie stretched over his stomach.

"You didn't tell us you had a handicap," he blurted finally. "I hope you're gon' be able to hold up."

"The forms you sent didn't provide a space for it and I didn't consider it pertinent," Becky replied. "I assure you, I'll manage nicely."

"I hope so," Woodhead said, motioning Becky to sit down. "This is my last year before retirement and I don't want any more surprises or any trouble."

She told Becky her classroom was not ready but Hilda had her student list and textbooks. "Our seventh graders don't change classes the way they do in some of the bigger schools," Woodhead explained, "so you'll teach all subjects. You can come back Friday and I'll give you a tour if you want one. We have a faculty meeting next Wednesday morning at nine. Don't be late."

"I won't," Becky said, smiling despite Woodhead's sharp manner. "I'm looking forward to getting started."

"How'd it go?" Hilda asked, when Becky returned to the reception area.

"They said I have to fill out more forms and you have my class list and books."

Hilda handed over a file. "The forms are in here. They're self-explanatory and you can bring them back next week. Your class list is in there too. You have thirty students and the other seventh-grade teacher has twenty-nine. Lily Poindexter is her name. You'll like her. Her husband is the mayor on the Arkansas side. And don't mind Mr. Appleby and Mrs. Woodhead. They're always a little anxious before school starts. We get funds from two states and students from one county and two parishes, and we have to keep separate records on all of them. It gets complicated. Your textbooks are on top of the cabinet over there. You need a hand?"

"No. I can manage. I came prepared." Becky took a drawstring bag from her purse and began filling it.

"What did you think of Mrs. Brantley?" Hilda asked. "She's a character, isn't she?"

"She certainly seems well versed on the community."

"Yeah, Hazel loves to talk, but when you get down to it, she's really pretty nice. Well, if you need anything, give me a call. My home number is in the file. Don't hesitate to use it."

Becky returned to her car, drove slowly past her building, then headed for Unionville's tiny business district.

"Baseball's not gon' be the same anymore," Sam said. He, Billy, Lester Grimes, and Neal O'Brien were gathered around the Otasco store cash register.

"I never liked any of them New York teams, not even when the Yankees had Ruth and Gehrig," Lester said, shifting some of his bulk from one leg to the other. "But the Giants go back a long ways. They ain't San Francisco Giants. Ain't now and won't never be."

Three days earlier, the Giants had announced they were moving to California beginning next season, and baseball fans were unhappy just about everywhere except on the West Coast.

"I read the Dodgers might move out there too," Neal said. A slim, studious-looking man with thick brown hair and glasses, he always wore sport shirts and dress slacks in keeping with his position as president of the Arkansas-side town council. The job did not require much, but he liked it and moved among his fellow merchants as if they were family and the whole town his backyard. "The story said they started thinking about it right after the Braves moved to Milwaukee and the Browns went to Baltimore." The Braves had moved from Boston and the Browns from St. Louis.

"Better be careful what you say about the Braves," Lester said, winking. "Billy's a big fan of theirs. Ain't you, boy?"

"No, sir," he said. "I like the Cardinals."

"Well, Billy," Neal said, "I hope you're not counting on them catching the Braves this year. Looks like Milwaukee's pretty much got it locked up."

"Yes, sir," Billy said, "I know how it looks but I'm hoping."

As the merchants and Billy talked, Becky parked in front of the store, got out, and came inside. Everyone looked around at her. Knowing that Miss Ruthelle was unlikely to offer to assist her, Sam headed up front.

"Hi, I'm Sam Tate," he said, introducing himself as he would to any new customer. "May I help you?"

He was not looking at her the way he would look at some other new customer, though. Like everyone else who saw her for the first time, he noticed her limp, but he was also looking at how her shoulder-length hair framed her eyes and her dimples, how her breasts filled her blouse, and how tan she was, as if she spent a lot of time outdoors. She seemed bright, warm, and desirable all at the same time. He had not looked at a woman this way since Judith Ann.

"Yes, hi, I'm Becky Reeves, the new seventh-grade teacher over at the school, and I need an electric iron and a half-inch faucet washer."

Becky's answer surprised Sam. He was not used to women asking for faucet washers.

The mention of seventh grade caught Billy's attention and he edged toward the center aisle. He might be in her class when school started. Neal and Lester inched forward too.

"All right, let's start with the iron," Sam said, and motioned Becky toward an aisle on his right. "We have several kinds." As she moved past him, he drew in the smell of her perfume, sweet but light and cool.

She knew the type of iron she wanted and grabbed it.

"Now, about that washer," he said, showing her to the other side of the store. "Do you need someone to install it for you?"

"No," she said, smiling, her dimples deepening. "I can do it myself."

"Well," he stammered, color rising to his cheeks, "I can recommend a good plumber and I'll be happy to get ahold of him for you."

"No, really, I can do it," she said in a confident tone Sam liked. "How much do I owe you?"

"Let's ring it up," he said, and led her back to the cash register. The onlookers scattered, each suddenly interested in car parts, fishing tackle, and assorted other merchandise.

"I suppose you're renting Hazel Brantley's apartment," Sam said, trying to extend the conversation as he totaled the sale. He regretted the comment as soon as he made it. He was afraid it seemed nosy.

"Yes," Becky said in a cheerful tone. "I'm in the teachers' suite."

"I bet you're finding out all about Unionville, too, at no extra cost." He wondered where she came from but did not ask. "My son's gon' be in the seventh grade this year. Maybe he'll be in your class. Billy, come on over here and meet Miss Reeves." Sam had noted right off that she was not wearing a wedding band.

"Hi, Billy," Becky said, extending her hand. "I'm glad to meet you. Are you looking forward to school?"

He shook hands with her. "Well, yes, ma'am, I guess so."

"He's all wrapped up in baseball right now," Sam said. "But he enjoys school once it gets going."

"Oh?" Becky said, smiling again. "Who's your favorite team, Billy?"

"The Cardinals. Me and Daddy like Stan Musial." Sam grimaced at Billy's bad grammar but Becky gave no sign of noticing.

"Well, now. How about that? The Cards are my favorite team too. I'm from St. Louis, or at least from near there."

"Have you ever seen them play?" Billy asked, wide-eyed that someone standing right here in his daddy's store might have seen his heroes in person.

"Yes, I have. Not often, but a few times."

"Wow!" Billy said. He wanted to ask more questions but felt Sam's hand on his shoulder and kept quiet.

Becky picked up the paper bag containing her purchases. "Sometime after school starts," she said, "whether you're in my class or not, I'll tell you all about Busch Stadium. That's where the Cards play, but I expect you know that already."

"Yes, ma'am, that'd be great! Thank you!"

"Okay, then, I'll see you at school," she said.

"Well, welcome to Unionville, Miss Reeves," Sam blurted, trying to keep her longer but unable to think of anything else to say. "I hope you enjoy it here."

"Call me Becky, please, and I'm sure I will," she said, and headed for the door.

The onlookers moved back to their places around the cash register.

"That's sure a fine-looking woman," Neal said, when she was out of earshot. "Wonder what happened to her leg?"

"Sure is a pity, ain't it?" Lester said. "But did you get a load of them headlights? Man, oh man, has she got a pair!"

Miss Ruthelle, who had been watching from the office, almost choked on the soda she was sipping. She coughed and Lester burst out laughing.

"Knock it off, Lester." Sam said. "That might be Billy's teacher you're talking about. Besides, she seems really nice." He walked to the display of irons and pretended to rearrange them but kept his eyes on Becky as she got in her car and drove away.

CHAPTER 11

"Daddy, this looks like a good day for baseball," Billy said on the third Wednesday afternoon in August. He was looking through the truck windshield at a sunny sky with fluffy white clouds. "Do you think we'll finish in time to go practice with the Black Tigers?" Father and son were headed to Bowman Lumber Company to get some one-by-fours to replace rotting boards in the back porch.

"I hope so," Sam said. I'd like to get another shot at B. J.'s curve ball."

"Do you think he's as good as Warren Spahn, Daddy?"

"No. B. J.'s good but he's not that good. Are you thinking about Spahn because he's killing the Cardinals?"

"Yes, sir, I guess so. He's sure pitching up a storm." The Braves left-hander was headed toward his eighth twenty-win season and Milwaukee had opened a big lead on St. Louis.

"You mean 'surely,' not 'sure,'" Sam said.

"Daddy, why do I always have to say 'surely'? You don't."

"I try to, son. I just forget sometimes, like you do. You know your momma wanted you to use good grammar. It'll help you get ahead someday. Do you understand that?"

"Yes, sir, I guess so," Billy said, as they slowed to turn onto the short mill access road. When they went through the gate to the huge lumber yard, he said, "Look, there's Mr. Davis. I guess he's got some work to do too."

"Yep, wonders never cease," Sam said. He glanced at Jim Ed Davis's pickup coming past them. A shotgun and a .22-caliber rifle hung on the rack behind the seat and a dozen rough two-by-fours stuck out the back.

Bowman Lumber Company sprawled over twenty-plus acres south of State Line Road across from the Unionville depot. The Rock Island Railroad tracks ran along the east side. A white frame office stood to the left of the entrance road and Horace Bowman's Lincoln sat in the gravel parking lot, close to the steps. On the right, the former company store, a large, aging frame building with a railed porch, faced the office. Back when it was legal, Bowman paid his workers in script good only for groceries, dry goods, and housewares in the commissary. He had long since sold it for a big profit, and even though the mill now paid in real money, most of the mill hands remained deeply in debt to the current owner.

Many of the workers still lived in unpainted company houses on the other side of the railroad tracks. The tiny shotgun structures lined both sides of State Line Road and several side streets and made up the southern end of the quarters. The remainder extended north along the tracks past South Arkansas Oak Flooring. Houses up there were better. Leon Jackson, B. J. Long, Otis Henderson, Charlie Foster, and Ollie Mae Greene all lived there, and the black school—a rambling three-story wood structure—was there too.

Sam drove past the mill office and commissary into the work yard. Coming here always made him think of Judith Ann. For weeks after they met, he had made repeated trips to the mill to buy lumber he did not need just so he could see her again. This time, he surprised himself by also thinking of Becky Reeves. Meeting her made him realize how much he missed the touch of a woman.

Behind the office, a tin-roofed storage building extended south along a rail spur for nearly the length of a football field. Loading docks covered by sheds ran along both sides of the massive structure. The dock on the east side was for railroad cars and the one on the west side was for trucks. Beyond the storage building, steam rose from a drying kiln, and beyond it, tin-covered log-sawing and lumber-planing buildings towered above everything. A mountain of sawdust lay at the end of the yard. On the west side of the property, large stacks of low-grade lumber sat graying in the sun and piles of logs awaited sawing. West of these, a chainlink fence separated the mill grounds from the backyards of houses in the adjoining white neighborhood.

Sam parked near the center of the long storage building, and even before he and Billy got out of the truck, they could smell the resin-laden odor of fresh-cut lumber and hear the deafening whine of giant circular saws. They walked through the nearest of several breezeways looking for the dock foreman. Jack Metcalf, an athletic-looking man wearing jeans and a sweat-stained baseball cap greeted them, clipboard in hand.

"Hey, Sam, Billy," Metcalf said over the roar. "What can I do for you?"

"I need a couple dozen one-by-fours, eight-footers," Sam replied, "and I'd like to pick them out myself."

"Sure thing. They're down at the far end. You and Billy just grab a push-truck and help yourselves. Give me a holler when you're done."

"Okay, son," Sam asked, as he and Billly reached the bins of one-by-fours, "what do you remember about picking out good boards?"

"Make sure they're straight and don't have knotholes in them."

"Attaboy."

They made their selection, got a sales slip from Metcalf, loaded the truck, and drove around to the office. Inside, a varnished wood counter separated a waiting area from desks piled high with papers and file folders. A clerk sat at each one, and beyond them Billy could see a workroom and two private offices, all paneled.

"Hello, Sam," said the attractive blond at the middle desk, as she got up and came to the counter. The polished top reflected her bright red dress. "I haven't seen you in a while. Hey, Billy, how're you doing? Fixing to build something?"

Gloria Tucker was in her early forties but looked younger. She had worked with Judith Ann and was married to one of Sam's long-time friends. Arlan Tucker owned Tucker Funeral Home and liked to hang out at the Otasco store.

"No, ma'am," Billy started, "me and Daddy are just working on the back porch. We..."

Before Billy could finish, Horace Bowman burst out of the office on the right.

"Sam!" he bellowed. "How's business?"

A short, stout man with thinning gray hair, Bowman always spoke this way to people who owed him money, and most considered the question dead serious. He was straining the seams of a blue seersucker suit and gripping a battered leather briefcase in one hand and a well-chewed cigar in the other.

As he pushed through a swinging gate at the end of the counter and scurried toward the front door, he looked even more sour-faced than usual. Sam could never understand how a person said to have as much money as Bowman never seemed happy. No one seemed to know exactly how he got his start, but most folks believed he made his first big wad by grabbing land for unpaid taxes then selling the timber and mineral rights. Some joked that he still had the first dollar he ever earned, but in addition to buying a new car every couple of years, he owned a huge brick house, where he lived alone, having never married.

"Business is pretty good, Mr. Bowman," Sam said. "How're you today?"

"Doing all right," Bowman said, as he went out the front door.

"Is something bothering him?" Sam asked Gloria. "He's in a mighty big hurry."

"I don't know. Jim Ed Davis was back there a little while ago and he tore out of here too. They might have been dickering over timber but you never can tell what either one of them is up to."

"This is the last one, Billy," Sam said, nailing the board in place. "We'll paint it all later. You pick up these scraps and take them to the trash heap. I'll put up the tools, then we'll go play some ball." He started wiping off his hammer and square.

"Can I go too, Daddy?" Mary Jane asked, bored now with playing on the tire swing hanging from the big elm tree out front.

"I reckon so, sweetheart. I tell you what. If you'll sit in the stands and stay put while I try to hit Miss Lilabell, I'll play catch with you while Billy shags flies. But you better let me tell your grandmother. She's not gon' like it."

"You're not gon' hit somebody, are you Daddy? You said it was bad to hit people."

"No, Mary Jane. Miss Lilabell isn't a person. That's what B. J. Long calls his curve ball. It's like a nickname."

When Gran heard their plans, she reacted about as Sam had expected. "That's no place for a little girl!" she said. "And you ain't got no business over there neither. I done told you!"

Sam said he would be home in time to pick beans and corn before dark, then he grabbed his and Billy's baseball gear and whisked the kids into the truck.

"Why doesn't Gran like black people?" Mary Jane asked, as they drove away. "I like Ollie Mae. She cooks good and she tells me about games she used to play when she was little."

"Gran likes them all right," Sam said. "She just doesn't believe white people and black people ought to mix—you know, live together and such."

"We're not gon' bring the ballplayers home, are we, Daddy?"

"No sweetheart," Sam said, smiling, "We're just gon' play some ball with them."

The Black Tigers were well into their practice when the Tates walked into the ballpark. They took seats on the bleachers behind the wire backstop and waited for Leon Jackson to see them. He was behind the plate and B. J. Long was on the mound—one a bundle of muscle, the other skin and bones.

When Leon turned to run down a foul ball, he spotted Sam and called out, "Hey, Mr. Sam. Want to get yourself a bat and come hit a few? B. J.'s got Miss Lilabell working good today."

"You got it, Leon. Be right there," Sam said. He changed into his cleats, found the Mickey Mantle bat, swung it a few times with a big-handled Jackie Robinson model, and stepped to the plate.

"How're you today, Mr. Sam?" B. J. greeted him. "You want to try Miss Lilabell again? She's feeling mighty fine this afternoon."

Aware that he had arrived near the end of the team's practice, Sam called, "Just gimme a couple of straight ones so I can get my timing then bring her on. I'll be ready."

B. J. went through his usual windup, limbs flying every which way, and put an off-speed fastball down the middle. Sam hit it on a line over short.

"Yea, Daddy!" yelled Mary Jane. "Yea, Daddy!"

Sam lifted the second pitch, another medium fastball, to deep center, and Mary Jane cheered again. After a few more knocks, he stepped out of the box, adjusted his cap, grabbed a handful of dirt, and rubbed it in his palms. Batter, pitcher, and catcher all knew it was time for Miss Lilabell. When Sam stepped back in, B. J. was smiling.

"Uh oh, watch out now," Leon said through his catcher's mask. "When ole B. J. grins like that, it's not a good sign for the batter."

Yeah, Sam thought, he knows he's got my number. Then to B. J., "Come on, let's see her."

B. J. spat a brown blob toward third base then wound up and let fly. Sam knew at once this was not the real Miss Lilabell. He started his hands in motion, kept his head down and eyes on the ball, and put his entire body into his swing. The Louisville Slugger caught the ball just as it broke across the outside corner and sent it soaring over the right field fence. The solid hit felt good all the way through his wrists and up his arms. He knew, however, that B. J. had taken something off the pitch and so did everyone else in the ball park—everyone except Billy and Mary Jane. B. J. had thrown that one for them.

Sam wanted to try another one but he knew that refusing B. J.'s gift and calling for the real Miss Lilabell now would be insulting. Besides, he also understood, like every player on the field, that B. J. could throw it a dozen times full tilt, and he would never put a good hit on it. Still, they all shouted, "Good hit, Mr. Sam, good hit!"

In the stands, Billy whistled and clapped his hands. Mary

Jane yelled, "Yea, Daddy! Yea, Daddy!"

When Sam turned from watching the ball clear the fence and looked at B. J., the lanky pitcher, still grinning, tipped his cap. Sam tipped his in return and neither spoke. Behind the plate, Leon looked up and said quietly, "He's a good man, Mr. Sam, he's a good man."

On the hill beyond right field the man in the edge of the woods did not understand what had just passed between Sam and the black ballplayers. But he knew there was something about it he did not like.

CHAPTER 12

"Georgia Speakers Blast Integration Order," read the head-line in the *El Dorado Daily News* on Friday, August 23. Becky knew plans were afoot to integrate Little Rock schools, but she was surprised to see banner stories about it in southern Arkansas.

The night before, the Capital Citizens' Council had brought two of the country's best-known segregationists—Marvin Griffin, Governor of Georgia, and Roy V. Harris, president of the anti-integrationist White Citizens' Councils of America—to Little Rock to speak to three hundred people over dinner. They said the *Brown v. Board of Education* decision would destroy the American form of government and white people should not stand for it.

After the speeches, rowdies threw a rock through the living-room window of state NAACP head Daisy Bates. She and her husband had been publishing the *Arkansas State Press,* a weekly civil rights voice, for more than fifteen years, and she had recently become primary advisor to seventeen black students handpicked by Superintendent Blossom to attend Little Rock Central High School. A note attached to the rock was short and to the point: "Stone this time. Dynamite next."

Hazel Brantley, still playing welcome-wagon hostess, had brought the newspaper to Becky and now sat waiting for her to finish the lead story.

"Don't that beat all?" Hazel said, when Becky handed back the paper. "I swear! I don't know why them coloreds want to go to white schools. They ought to stay in their own place."

"What place is that?" Becky asked, although she knew full well what Hazel meant.

"You know," Hazel said. "If the good Lord had meant for whites and coloreds to mix, he'd have made them the same color. But he didn't."

"I don't know what God meant when he made people different colors," Becky said, "but I doubt he intended for folks to behave as contentiously as we do. I expect he envisioned a more harmonious society."

While Hazel struggled to come up with a reply, Becky remembered her mother's warning about moving down South then pushed the thought aside.

Others in Unionville were also reading and talking about the Little Rock dinner. A copy of the *Arkansas Gazette*, which carried a headline announcing, "Citizens' Council Crowd Applauds Speech against Race Integration," lay face up on a chair in the barbershop and newsstand.

"It's too bad Griffin ain't governor of Arkansas," Lester Grimes said, clicking his scissors to shake off snips of Sam's hair. "He'd send all them wooly-headed N-double-A-C-P troublemakers packing. Faubus ought to be taking notes. He's been way too liberal with coloreds."

"The problem is ole Faubus is a goddamn nigger lover!" Jim Ed Davis said from the other barber chair.

"You got that right," Odell Grimes said. "He never should've let things get this far."

Although he was two years younger than his brother Lester, heavier, and a lot thicker between the ears, Odell bore a striking family resemblance.

"The problem is that old Daisy Bates," Jim Ed said, wagging his finger. "Somebody ought to tar and feather her and every one of them no-account commies helping her."

"Put your blooming hand down before I cut your finger off!" Odell yelled. "You don't get a haircut but once in a coon's age and then you can't sit still. You ain't got no place to go."

"I got business to take care of," Jim Ed said. "Hurry up, before I get out of this chair and tie your tail in a knot."

Jim Ed was the only man in town smaller than Mr. Claude, but unlike the marshal, he did not scare anybody.

"You ain't gon' do nothing," Odell said, "but run your mouth."

"Yeah, Jim Ed, you're all talk," Lester chimed in. "You're always popping off about doing some big thing or other but you never do it."

"Aw, leave him alone," Sam said. He did not care about Jim Ed, but especially now that he had met Becky Reeves, he wanted to make sure Lester paid attention to what he was doing and gave him a good haircut.

"Say, Jim Ed," Sam asked, trying to change the subject, "didn't I see you buying two-by-fours down at the mill the other day? You building something?"

"It ain't none of your damn business what I'm doing, Sam. That's what's wrong with this town. Everybody's too damned nosy."

"All right," Sam said. "No need to get all riled up. I was just being neighborly."

"No, you wasn't. You was nosing into my business. You want to talk about something, why don't you tell Lester and Odell about how you been playing baseball with them coloreds."

"What's this?" Lester asked, his voice rising at the thought of something new he could tell around.

"Not that it's any of your concern, or anyone else's," Sam said, "but Billy and I have been practicing with the Black Tigers. They're good ballplayers."

"Yeah? Well, you know what I think, Sam?" Jim Ed asked, as Odell removed the cover cloth and started shaking it. "I think you might be a nigger lover, too, just like ole Faubus. Odell, what do you think?" Jim Ed stepped out of the chair and nodded toward Sam. "You think ole Sam here is a nigger lover?"

Odell did not say anything. He knew to keep his mouth shut.

"Lester, stop cutting a minute," Sam said, leaning forward, his patience at an end. "Jim Ed, people are tired of hearing you blow off all the time and if you don't learn to control your tongue, one of these days somebody's gon' yank it out of your head and shove it up your ass."

The comment surprised everyone, including Sam. He was not sure what exactly made him so mad. But he did feel he had been defending the ballplayers as well as himself.

Across the street, Reverend Hosea Moseley, pastor of the Mt. Zion Baptist Church, stopped in to see Leon Jackson. Sawed-off broom handles propped up wooden window shutters on his tin building behind the bank, and the sliding door was pushed all the way open in a losing effort against the heat. The odor of cleaning fluid spilled into the alley, and inside, a trio of dim light bulbs dangled from the ceiling.

"Have you seen the El Dorado paper this morning?" Moseley asked. A thin man in his sixties, he had close-cut gray hair and wore a white shirt and dress pants shiny from long use.

"Yes, sir, I have," Leon said. He reached for a hanger, put a newly pressed suit coat on it, and looked at the preacher. "Is that worrying you?"

"Yeah, it is," Moseley said. He moved aside so Leon could hang up the coat. "This kind of thing can get folks all stirred up. We ain't had any serious trouble with whites around here and I sure don't want to see none now."

Leon stopped working and looked at his visitor. Moseley had been a respected leader in Unionville's black community for as long as anyone could remember. Like many other blacks his age in the South, he had been limited to an eighth-grade education, and like most small-town black pastors, he had learned the Bible and preaching by sitting through long hours of Baptist Youth Training Union lessons and listening to dozens of older ministers tongue-lash their congregations one minute and inspire them the next.

"I'm with you, Reverend. But maybe Mrs. Bates can make some headway up there. If she does, it'll help us all down the road. Anyway, we just have to be ready to deal with whatever comes."

Leon spoke from disposition and experience. He had learned strength and patience from his daddy and seen violence in World War II. Whites knew he was a veteran, but they assumed he drove trucks, built barracks, or worked in mess halls. They were unaware that he fought with the famed all-black 92nd Infantry Division in Italy and earned a Purple Heart. They also did not understand the tunes they heard him singing or humming quietly in his shop or around town. His daddy had been a crew leader for Rock Island Railroad Gandy dancers and led the call-and-response songs that helped his crew work in tandem.

Pick and shovel...huh,
Am so heavy...huh,
Heavy as lead...huh,
Picking, shov'ling...huh,
Till I'm dead...huh,
Till I'm dead...huh.

Some songs were for dragging cross ties, some for wrestling rails, and some for driving spikes and tamping gravel. Leon knew them all.

Like Moseley, he had been quietly following civil rights activities across the country. His wife Wanda worked in the office at the black school and their daughter was attending Southern University in Baton Rouge on a partial scholarship. Few whites knew she was in college, and if they had known, they would have wondered how the Jacksons paid for it. Many already puzzled over how Leon afforded the spiffy two-year-old Ford Fairlane he drove. Blacks knew, though. In addition to operating the dry-cleaning shop, he loaned out money at considerable interest and won piles more shooting craps at Sadie Rose Washington's place deep in the quarters on Friday and Saturday nights.

Leon and Moseley got most of their civil rights news from the *Pittsburgh Courier,* one of the nation's biggest black newspapers. Circulating unnoticed by Unionville whites, the paper came weekly by mail to Moseley, to his fellow pastor at the A.M.E. church, and to a handful of lay leaders then passed, dog-eared, from reader to reader. Eventually copies ended up in the barber's corner at Sadie Rose's, where men read and discussed the contents between tall tales about sports and women.

"You're right about staying ready," Moseley said, as he watched Leon press another coat. "So far, I haven't heard anything unusual from any of the sisters, so that's good." In addition to the *Courier*, Unionville blacks had a local grapevine, also unknown to whites. Cooks and maids overhead conversations in white homes every day and shared them throughout the black community. This told which whites were fair, or the least prejudiced, and which should be avoided. "We still need to keep our eyes and ears open, though," Moseley said.

"Don't you fret none, Reverend," Leon said. "We're watching."

Later in the day and farther up the street, on the other side, Upshaw sat at his desk with the El Dorado and Little Rock papers spread out in front of him. His coat hung over the back of his chair and a cigarette smoldered on the edge of his butt-filled ashtray. He had finished printing his first edition of the *Unionville Times* an hour ago, but because most people got it by mail, they would not see it until Saturday morning at the earliest. Both the *El Dorado Daily News* and the *Arkansas Gazette* had beaten him to the punch on coverage about the Capital Citizens' Council meeting and the harassment of Daisy Bates. This was not the sort of beginning he wanted.

"Well, I guess it could be a blessing in disguise," he said to Pearl, who was rolling copies of the *Unionville Times* and applying address labels. "People will know I wrote my stories first. These others just prove I'm right about a hell of a fight coming."

"Do you think whoever threatened Daisy Bates with that note would really try to blow up her house?" Pearl asked.

"I wouldn't bet against it," he said, smiling.

CHAPTER 13

Sam and Billy had barely finished putting out display merchandise on Saturday morning when Boomer Jenkins came stomping through the wide-open front doors.

"Hey, Sam, you got any fishing line worth a damn?" he called, his deep voice filling the store and startling Miss Ruthelle. Billy heard it way in back where he was emptying sawdust from sweeping. He picked up his broom and hurried up front.

A powerful, craggy-faced man, Boomer's real name was Jeremiah, but folks called him Boomer because it was easier to say and suited his personality and the noise he made walking and talking. He had lost his left leg below the knee in World War II. No one knew exactly how because he never told the story the same way twice. All anyone knew for sure was that he had been a medical corpsman. The army gave him an artificial leg, but when he got home, he threw it away and carved one out of cypress wood. Black leather straps around his stump and waist held the contraption in place, and a metal rod welded to the clutch pedal of his Dodge pickup enabled him to drive. He always wore a floppy black hat and carried a big hunting knife in a black scabbard that stood out against his khaki clothes. Because of his getup, size, and gruffness, most people gave him a wide berth and he loved it.

"You bet," Sam said, parking a hand truck loaded with cartons of auto parts. "I'll be with you in a second."

"Well, I sure hope you've got something better than the crap you sold me last time," Boomer said. "It wouldn't hold squat. I can't make a living if my trotlines keep breaking." Boomer lived way back in Corney Bayou over in Claiborne Parish and stretched his disabled veteran's pension by supplying catfish and frog legs to restaurants in nearby towns. Jim Ed Davis was about the only friend he had, and they had little in common other than military service and a strong dislike for blacks.

"Morning, Miss Ruthelle, how're you doing?"

"You watch your language Boomer Jenkins!" she called from the office. "There're women and children here!" Not much intimidated Miss Ruthelle.

"Excuse me, Miss Ruthelle. I sure as hell didn't mean no offense," Boomer said, laughing.

"Boomer, look on the second shelf there," Sam said, walking over. He had barely gotten the words out of his mouth when Elmer Spurlock came into the store.

"Good morning sinners!" he called out.

"Damn it," Boomer muttered under his breath. "If I'd known that Bible-thumping son of a bitch was gon' show up, I'd have went to the hardware store."

"Good morning, Brother Spurlock," Sam said, using the title whites preferred for their preachers. "I'll be with you as soon as I finish here."

"That's all right, Sam," Spurlock said. "I just need a little paint for one of the Sunday school rooms. I expect Miss Ruthelle can help me."

"What color do you want?" she growled, making no attempt to hide feeling put out by having to get up from her chair.

Spurlock played shepherd to a flock of independent Baptists six miles west of town on Newton Chapel Road. The congregation rejected all mainstream Baptist organizations and took every word of the Bible literally. Their part-time preacher was pushing sixty, had a barrel chest and a face like a bulldog, and had not needed a comb in years. In addition to being a self-taught preacher, he also drove a school bus and painted houses when he could get the work. His once-white coveralls, which he wore everywhere except to church, had almost as many stains as the bed of the eight-year-old Chevy pickup he used to haul his ladders and scaffolding.

While Sam helped Boomer and Miss Ruthelle waited on Spurlock, Lester Grimes came rolling in from the sidewalk, belly jiggling and mouth running. "Hey, Sam, did you see the new *Unionville Times*? Upshaw's got more information about that mess in Little Rock."

"What's it say, Lester?" Spurlock asked. He had hated blacks ever since he was a boy growing up dirt poor next to the quarters in Magnolia, over in Columbia County. The only thing that gave his family an edge over their neighbors was skin color, and he was paying close attention to what was happening in Little Rock.

"It says here there's gon' be bloodshed," Lester reported.

"Let me see that," Spurlock demanded.

Lester handed over the paper. "This Brother Paxson is a good man," Spurlock said after a moment. "I hear him on the radio sometimes. He knows the scriptures. And he's right. All these integrationists are doing the devil's work and they're gon' be punished in eternal damnation."

"I don't care nothing about no preachers, no scriptures, and no eternal damnation," Boomer said," but I've heard about Daisy Bates, and I for one ain't gon' put up with none of her crap. If somebody don't settle that fuss up there pretty quick, first thing you know, all the coloreds down here are gon' be acting up."

"I sure hope not," Spurlock said. "We don't need integration in Unionville. Our schools are fine the way they are."

"Amen," Miss Ruthelle chimed in.

Sam did not say anything. His customers' opinions were no surprise, but the depth of their anger was. He had to admit that Upshaw's first issue had hit home with at least some folks.

Later, after everyone had left and Miss Ruthelle had gone back to her invoices and sales receipts, Billy asked, "Daddy, is there gon' be some kind of fight? I don't understand what that was all about just now."

"No, son, I don't think so," Sam said, as he opened a carton of fuel pumps. "There're just some folks up in Little Rock that want colored kids to go to school with white kids."

"Why, Daddy?"

"Well, son," Sam said, placing two pumps on a shelf, "I guess they think colored kids will learn more that way. Reach in that box there and hand me some more of these."

"Can't they learn stuff in their own schools?" Billy asked, grabbing two boxes.

"Yeah, seems like they can. Give me some more."

"Why's everything separate anyway, Daddy?"

"Colored people have different ways than we do."

"I still don't get it," Billy said, digging out two more pumps. "Like Mary Jane was saying about Ollie Mae the other day, she does things just like we do. And Leon and B. J. play ball just like we do."

Sam did not know what to say to that. All his life he had heard Gran and other white people fuss and cuss about black folks and never thought much about it. He had known them only as people he sold things to or hired to do unskilled work. Since his last practice with the Black Tigers, however, he had been thinking a lot about the ballplayers. He saw them differently someway but he was not sure how exactly, or why.

"Speaking of baseball," he said, changing the subject, "I think maybe the Cardinals are on the TV *Game of the Week* today. Why don't you go get the newspaper and see? Maybe we can watch a few innings after dinner."

CHAPTER 14

Billy's questions were still bothering Sam Sunday morning, but he pushed them aside when he started up the Ford Victoria and backed it out of the garage. Weather permitting, the Tates went to church every week. Usually only heavy rain kept them away and even that never stopped Sam. He had been elected a deacon two years ago and he took the responsibility seriously. Truth be told, he did not understand why the congregation chose him. He certainly did not toe all the biblical marks Brother Walter Byrd harped on every week. Maybe it was his business experience they liked. In any case, seeing that Billy and Mary Jane got to church regularly was part of his promise to Judith Ann, so he remained as faithful as he could.

The First Baptist Church was a white-painted brick building two blocks west of the business district. It had a two-story education wing in back and a tall steeple above a front entrance set off by white columns. Its size and design showed that Southern Baptists were the largest denomination in Unionville. They had even made sure to build their steeple higher than the Presbyterians and put in more stained glass than the Methodists.

Most who attended regular services arrived in time for Sunday school at a quarter to ten, but some came only for preaching at eleven o'clock. These usually got their choice of seats before Bible study ended. Folks coming from Sunday school would enter the worship hall from doors on either side of the pulpit and fill in the remaining spots. Sam always sat on the left near the back with Billy and Mary Jane, and Gran always took a place down front on the right with her friends, Emma Lou and Almalee. They liked being close to the choir and the pianist.

Today, when Sam came from his men's class, he saw Billy and Mary Jane sitting in a pew behind Hazel Brantley, who had brought Becky Reeves. She was reading her bulletin and did not see him but Hazel did and grinned. As he walked up the aisle, he reached to straighten the horses-heads tie Billy had given him last Father's Day to go with his navy-blue suit.

Becky, in a blue linen suit and matching pillbox hat looked even more beautiful than she had in the store a few days earlier. Aware that he was staring, he forced his eyes away until just before he came even with her. When he glanced at her again, she looked up, smiled, and mouthed, "Good morning." He smiled back, nodded, and took his seat.

Once there, he could not keep his eyes off Becky's hair and shoulders. He noticed every time she shifted in her seat, tried to picture her at a Cardinals game, and wondered what she would think of Brother Byrd.

A wiry man in his late forties, Byrd had curly brown hair, boundless energy, and possibly the most unusual preparation of any Southern Baptist minister below the Mason-Dixon Line. He had grown up in Detroit, clashed with the law in his youth, and become a drifter and an alcoholic by his twenty-first birthday. Sometime before World War II, a Baptist minister in New Orleans found him drunk in a French Quarter alley and helped him turn his life around and get through college and the seminary. Almost every time he faulted his listeners for some sin or other, he cited a firsthand encounter with it and they loved listening to him.

After an interlude of organ and piano music, Byrd rose from a chair behind the carved oak pulpit and started the service with spirited singing of "Sunshine in My Soul" and "Send the Light." Even though the songs were unfamiliar to Becky, she found them easy to follow in the hymnal and sang in a warm soprano voice everyone noticed.

The traditional welcome and announcements followed. All eyes turned toward Becky when she raised her hand as a visitor and took a guest card from an usher. Next came the passing of collection plates and a choir special. The plain-clothed singers delivered "His Eye Is on the Sparrow" in moving fashion with Opal Jolly, a gifted contralto, singing two verses solo. Her mother Almalee sat with her hands clasped over her heart and beamed like a peacock at her daughter.

Once the choir finished, everyone was ready for hellfire and brimstone and Byrd did not disappoint them. His theme was almost always the same—repent, trust in the Lord, and live right—but he never delivered it the same way twice. He did, however, always quote scriptures, wave his Bible, tell stories, pace up and down, yell, whisper, and fume. Today was no exception and when he finished, he led the choir in singing, "Softly and Tenderly," about Jesus calling for sinners to come home to God.

When Byrd offered his closing prayer, though, he broke with tradition. Normally he did not believe in mixing politics with religion, but this time he called for "divine guidance for all those responsible for making critical decisions in our capital city" and for "patience and Christian behavior on the part of all the citizens of our state and community." Some in the congregation already had their minds on dinner and other after-church plans and failed to notice these lines in the prayer. Others found them a bit puzzling but thought little more about them. A few wondered, however, whether they signaled a potentially disturbing attitude about integration. For Sam, they brought Billy's questions back in mind.

There was nothing vague about anything Brother Elmer Spurlock said that same hour at Mercy Baptist Mission out on Newton Chapel Road. He had no qualms about taking on political subjects, and when his congregation gathered in the simply furnished little white frame building, he had a direct message in mind. He started the service with the congregation singing "Stand Up for Jesus," "Rise Up, O Men of God," and "Onward Christian Soldiers," all of them calls to action.

> Onward Christian soldiers,
> Marching as to war,
> With the cross of Jesus
> Going on before!

The mission had no organ and no choir, but the piano player could really tickle the ivories, and the worshipers sang with full voice and conviction.

When it came to pulpit theatrics, Spurlock took a backseat to none, and before saying a word, he shucked his brown suit coat and rolled up his sleeves. Even with the windows open and ceiling fans going full tilt, he had worked up a sweat, and his shirt stuck to his bulky body like wet wallpaper. He preached from Genesis 9:18-25, a biblical passage that many whites had misinterpreted for generations. It told how, after the great flood, Noah's son Ham saw his father naked and drunk on wine. IInstead of showing respect and giving him clothes, Ham called his brothers, Shem and Japeth, to come see the spectacle. Unlike Ham, they covered their father without looking at him. When the old man woke up and learned what had happened, he put a curse on Ham's son, Canaan, making him a servant forever.

"Negroes," Spurlock wailed, "are descended from Canaan, and these passages prove that God meant them to be inferior and separate!" Bending phrases from the opening songs, he called on his flock to, "Rise up, end the night of wrong, and make the Satan-helpers who're hollering for integration flee."

When he finished, rather than a traditional closing hymn, he chose "We're Marching to Zion" and sent his listeners away confident that his way would carry them "to the beautiful city of God."

Another Unionville minister also took note of the events in the state capital. At the Mt. Zion Baptist Church, a concrete-block building two blocks east of US 167, in the shadow of South Arkansas Oak Flooring, Reverend Hosea Moseley stood in front of a choir wearing homemade red robes and behind a pulpit built by church members. He prayed for guidance and started his service with devotional singing. Standing between the pulpit and the congregation, deacons B. J. Long of the Black Tigers and Pete Jones, who worked part-time at the Otasco store, took turns calling out the lines of "Sweet Hour of Prayer" one by one, and the worshipers, accompanied by piano, repeated each in turn.

> Sweet hour of prayer, sweet hour of prayer
> That calls me from a world of care
> And bids me at my Father's throne
> Make all my wants and wishes known!

Lining out the words was hardly necessary because everyone knew them, but the traditional practice of call and response always gave comfort and created unity.

Next came songs that spoke of better days ahead. Call and response continued, but the choir, which included the Tates' cook Ollie Mae Greene and Black Tiger Charlie Foster, led the way in stirring renditions of "The Unclouded Day," "When the Roll Is Called up Yonder," and "Peace in the Valley." An electric guitar and drums were soon brought into accompaniment, and the music carried for blocks beyond the church's open windows. Finally, from "On Jordan's Stormy Banks," Leon and Wanda Jackson and the others sang about heading for the Promised Land, where Jesus reigns and worries disappear.

Now the church folks felt uplifted and ready for the sermon. Clutching his King James Bible, the only version any Unionville Baptists, black or white, used, Moseley quoted from Mark 12:30-31, "Thou shalt love the Lord thy God with all thy heart," and "Thou shalt love thy neighbor as thyself. There is no other commandment greater than these." Then he came immediately to his point. "I know there's some troubling stuff going on up yonder in Little Rock. Some troubling stuff! But brothers and sisters, I also know God is with us. I know it in my heart. But there's three things we're gon' have to do. Listen to me, now! Three things! Say it back to me, 'Three things.'"

"Three things," the congregation said in unison.

"You tell it, Reverend," several called out. "You tell it."

"We've got to remember that God calls on us to love our neighbors, all of them, black and white. We mustn't hate white people no matter what. It's not God's way. We're all His children."

"Amen!" several worshipers called out.

"Praise Jesus!" others shouted.

"And I believe," Moseley went on, "God's gon' open up their eyes someday. I really do. He's gon' open up their eyes!"

"Amen! Praise Jesus!" the calls came. The preacher and his

listeners were falling into a rhythm now. Words and feelings flowed like a rushing stream.

"Second, we've got to pray. Y'all hear me now! We've got to pray for those brave children up yonder in Little Rock, and we've got to pray for our own children right here in Unionville. Pray for their safety. Pray for their futures."

"Preach Reverend! Preach Reverend!"

"The world is changing and someday our children are gon' have opportunities we've never had. Lord, keep our children safe for a greater day!"

"Amen! Praise Jesus!"

"Lord, keep our children safe on their long journey."

"Amen! Praise Jesus!"

"And last, we've got to keep our eyes open and be vigilant. The Bible says, 'Be vigilant!' Most white folks here abouts are God-fearing people, and they're not gon' do something crazy, like what's been threatened on Mrs. Bates up there in Little Rock. But there's some others I'm not so sure about, especially since we don't know what kind of things that new newspaper-man is liable to write. So y'all be on your best behavior. Don't y'all go out of your way to provoke nobody. And y'all keep a close watch on our children. You hear me? Keep a close watch on them!"

"Preach Reverend!"

Before Moseley finished, he worked in plenty about sin and repentance and the service ended with everyone singing "Amazing Grace."

> I once was lost but now am found,
> Was blind but now I see.
> 'Twas grace that taught my heart to fear,
> And grace my fears relieved.

After the benediction at the First Baptist Church, most eyes turned to Becky as folks stood to leave.

"Who's that?" Almalee asked, leaning over to Gran and Emma Lou. "She don't look like anybody from around here."

"She must be that new schoolteacher Billy's been talking about," Gran said in a disapproving tone. "She's from up North somewhere—a Yankee."

"She sure is a pretty thing, isn't she," Emma Lou said, smiling.

Gran and Almalee both grunted in response.

"Morning, Becky, welcome to First Baptist Church," Sam said, as she exited her row. "Morning, Hazel."

Becky smiled, dimples flashing. "Hello, Sam. Hi, Billy. Is this pretty girl your sister?"

"Yes, ma'am," Billy said. He looked spiffy in a white sport coat and navy slacks. "This is Mary Jane. She's five." She had on a blue dress with a bow in the back.

"Hello, Mary Jane," Becky said. "How are you?" She wondered where the children's mother was but did not ask.

"Mary Jane's our pride and joy," Sam said, and before he could say anything else, other folks crowded around. Hazel busied herself making introductions and sharing the limelight. Some people came over to be friendly but some only wanted a closer look. It was not often that Unionville got a new teacher, and a good looking one who limped and appeared on the scene so close to the start of classes fueled all sorts of speculation.

CHAPTER 15

By the time the quilters gathered in Gran's sitting room on Tuesday morning, Billy had gone to the bookmobile and Mary Jane had gone outside to play on the tire swing. With no one except Ollie Mae to hear, the conversation turned quickly to Becky.

"Lucille Taylor said she saw her in Perry's buying groceries," Almalee said from her customary place on the sofa. "She bought Animal Crackers. Can you imagine that—a grown woman, a schoolteacher with no kids, eating Animal Crackers? Don't that beat all?"

"Gosh almighty, Almalee," Emma Lou said. "I don't know who's a worse busybody—Lucille or you. I have to admit, though, I wish I could've seen Betty Sue Perry when she first laid eyes on Miss Reeves. I bet the last thing she wanted to see in Unionville was another unattached woman as pretty as she is." Betty Sue was shapely, blond, twice divorced with two children, and in high pursuit of husband number three.

"You really think Becky Reeves is pretty?" Almalee asked. She was laying out her Triple Irish Chain pieces. "I wouldn't think men would find her appealing, what with that crippled leg and all. I wonder what happened to her? Reckon she was born with it?"

"I don't know what happened to her, hon," Emma Lou said, "but she sure was born with everything else she needs and then some. Didn't you see Fred Vestal hanging around her outside after church? He looked like a puppy panting after a bowl of milk. What do you think, Ida Belle?"

"All I know is she's a Yankee," Gran said, frowning. She reached into her basket for another piece of cloth. "We don't need no Yankee down here teaching our kids. No telling what kind of crazy notions she'll give them."

"You really think she's a Yankee?" Almalee asked. "Hazel Brantley says she don't talk much like one."

"She's from Missouri," Gran said. "It sure ain't no Confederate state."

"Sounds like you Tates have been talking a lot about Miss Reeves," Emma Lou said. She stopped sewing and looked up at Gran. "Do you think Sam is interested in her? Wouldn't that be something?"

"Sam don't have truck for no Yankee woman," Gran declared.

"Of course he don't," Almalee agreed. She didn't want to hear Sam linked with anyone but her Opal. "Speaking of crazy notions," she said, pulling a stitch tight, "what do y'all think is gon' happen up there at Little Rock? It sure is a mess."

"It's all that low-down Daisy Bates's doing," Gran said. "I don't know who she thinks she is, sitting up there like Miss High and Mighty stirring up trouble. She was raised right over yonder at Huttig and it's littler than Unionville. Why, she don't have any more sense than these coloreds around here."

"Shhh! Ida Belle," Emma Lou whispered. "Ollie Mae will hear you."

"Won't make me no never mind if she does," Gran said. "She knows it's the truth. Whoever threw that rock through that window would have saved everybody a lot of time if he'd have skipped the note and just gon' straight for the dynamite."

"That's awfully un-Christian, Ida Belle," Emma Lou said. "I'm surprised at you!"

"Aw, nobody wants to hurt her," Gran said. "They just want to scare her. That's what the night riders done when my daddy was alive. When coloreds got to acting uppity, the Ku Kluxers just put on their robes and rode around making a lot of racket to scare them. It worked every time."

"Billy, hon, you need to choose something and make room for other folks," the librarian said in the bookmobile. The line of waiting library users snaked out the rear door and across the parking lot.

"I can't find anything," he said, shoulders slumped. "You only have one baseball story I haven't read."

"Well, then, what about something different? We have some very interesting young people's biographies of presidents."

"No thank you, ma'am. I want to read some more about baseball before school starts."

"What's that one you're holding?"

"It's *The Battery for Madison High*. It's about twins on a high school team."

"Yes, I know that one," the librarian said. "It's by Al Hirshberg. We have another baseball book he wrote but it's probably a little too grown-up for you."

"What is it?" Billy asked, his interest spiked by her caution.

"It's called *Fear Strikes Out*. It's a biography of Jimmy Piersall. He's the..."

"I know him," Billy interrupted. "He's the centerfielder for the Boston Red Sox."

"That's right. He and Mr. Hirshberg wrote the book together."

"Can I check it out?"

"I don't know if that's a good idea, hon. It wasn't written for children. It's about Jimmy Piersall's nervous breakdown."

"Please," Billy pleaded. "I know about him being sick. There's a picture show about it. I bet my daddy would let me read it. I bet he'd even read it with me."

"Okay, but you be sure and tell your daddy that I let you have it on condition that he does."

For Mary Jane, Billy had found two Little Golden Books, and while the librarian processed his selections, he looked out the windshield for Crazy Dan. The old man was nowhere in sight and Billy hurried outside, put the books in his bicycle basket, and headed west on Lafayette Street. Moments later, as he turned north onto Elm, he saw the figure and heard the voice he dreaded.

"Hey Billy!" Crazy Dan cackled. "How's my daddy this morning?"

The old man was dead ahead in the middle of the street, approaching in a near trot, his wheelbarrow squeaking and grinding on the pea gravel. This time Billy had no intention of pretending not to hear. He stopped, got off his bike, reached into his jeans pocket, and brought out a handful of rocks he had picked up earlier in a drainage ditch.

"Crazy Dan, you stop talking about my daddy!" Billy warned.

"He ain't your daddy! He's mine!" the old man shouted, still coming.

Billy gripped one of the rocks, stepped forward like a pitcher, and hurled a bullet that struck the front of Crazy Dan's wheelbarrow and bounced away.

"Hey, boy! Don't be chunking no rocks at me!" he hollered in a commanding tone Billy had not heard him use before. The old man stopped, put the wheelbarrow down, and glared at the boy.

Scared now more than angry, Billy fired three more rocks one after another. Crazy Dan ducked and the first sailed over his head. The second glanced off one of the wheelbarrow handles. As Crazy Dan leaned to avoid the ricochet, the third one caught him on his ear and knocked his hat off. If he had not moved, it would have hit him square on the nose. For a moment, man and boy stood equally shocked, staring at each other. Crazy Dan touched his fingers to his ear and felt blood. He fished into an overalls pocket, came out with a dirty rag, and held it to his head.

"I'm gon' tell Sam what you did, boy," the wounded teaser said, "and he ain't gon' like it." He looked at the rag and stuffed it back in his pocket. Then he picked up his hat, grabbed his wheelbarrow handles, and turned back the way he had come.

Billy looked around to see if the shouting had drawn any attention. As far as he could tell, it had not. He retreated to his bicycle and put up the kickstand but did not get on right away. Throwing the rocks felt good when he let fly with them, but he only meant to scare the old man, not hurt him. He knew his mother would not have liked it, and he knew if Crazy Dan told his daddy, he would almost certainly dish out some sort of punishment.

After thinking about that for a moment, Billy jumped on the bike and pedaled as fast as he could to the Otasco store. He cut through the row of warehouses in back, rode up the ramp to the store's loading dock, dropped the kickstand, and went in the back door. Sam was at the cash register talking with Arlan Tucker, the undertaker, a stocky man who always had a ready smile.

"Hey, Billy, what've you been up to?" Tucker asked.

"Hi, Mr. Tucker," Billy said. Then, ignoring Tucker's question, he asked, "Daddy, can I talk to you?"

"It's all right, Sam," Tucker said, "I've got to get going."

"What is it, son?" Sam asked, as Tucker left.

"Not here, Daddy." Billy nodded toward Miss Ruthelle, hunkered down in her usual spot in the office. They walked back to the loading dock.

"What is it, Billy?" Sam asked again, when they were outside. "Did you spend your allowance already?"

"No, sir," Billy said, twisting one of his bicycle handlebars. "I did something I don't think you're gon' like."

"Why don't you tell me about it?" Sam asked. He leaned against a wooden work bench.

"Well, you know how Crazy Dan's always teasing me about you being his daddy?" Billy asked.

Sam hated how Crazy Dan bothered Billy. "Yeah, I do and you just have to ignore him. I've told him a bunch of times to leave you alone, and he always says he will, but either he's lying, or he doesn't understand, or he forgets. Is it getting worse?"

"Yes, sir, but that's not exactly what I wanted to tell you."

"Well, what is it then?"

Billy poured out the entire story, starting with his other recent encounter and ending with the rock throwing and Crazy Dan's threat.

A silence broken only by the sounds of traffic on nearby streets fell over father and son. Sam pushed back an impulse to find Crazy Dan and beat the hell out of him. Obviously trying to reason with him did no good.

"Billy," Sam said, after reining in his temper, "there are two things I want you to remember. The first one is that trying to scare somebody isn't the way to settle anything. I admit I've done it myself, more than once. Matter of fact, I did it to Jim Ed Davis just the other day. Sometimes it gets you what you want for a little while. But in the long run, it doesn't really accomplish much. It just hurts people. The second thing I want you to remember is that I'm proud of you for telling me what happened. Now, what are you going to do the next time he teases you?"

"I'm gon' do what Momma always said. I'm gon' keep on going and not pay him any mind."

"Right," Sam said, squeezing Billy's shoulder. "You go on home now and enjoy your books."

"I got one for both of us, Daddy. Look," Billy said, reaching into his bicycle basket. "It's about Jimmy Piersall. The librarian said I could take it if you'd read it with me."

"All right, it's a deal. Piersall's trying to learn not to fight with teasers too."

While Gran and her friends were quilting and Billy was dealing with Crazy Dan, Governor Faubus was maneuvering to stay in line with public opinion against integrating public schools in Little Rock. When the Central High Mothers' League—a newly formed auxiliary of the Capital Citizens' Council—filed suit in Pulaski County to keep the Blossom Plan for integration from going into effect, Faubus went to court with them and lied. He said he had reports that people were buying knives and pistols in record numbers and bands of armed men were traveling to Little Rock in caravans of cars and trucks. The judge believed him and issued an injunction postponing integration. That night, Blossom Plan opponents celebrated by driving up and down the street outside Daisy Bates's ranch-style home honking their horns and shouting racial slurs.

The next morning dark clouds gathered early over southern

Arkansas, and by noon a light but steady rain had set in, the sort that could last all day. At the newspaper office, however, Upshaw could not have felt sunnier as he banged out a story about the governor's testimony and the court decision.

When he finished, Upshaw leaned back from his typewriter, pouched out his stomach, and locked his hands behind his head. "Man," he said to Pearl Goodbar, "this proves Martin Smitherman and that Dallas preacher were right. There's gon' be bloodshed if Daisy Bates and the rest of that bunch don't come to their senses."

"I'm beginning to think you'd like to see that," Pearl said from her desk halfway across the huge room.

"Mrs. Goodbar," Upshaw said, grinning, "if I wasn't so happy about the prospects of this paper, I'd take offense at that remark. Violence sells papers." He unlocked his hands, leaned forward, and reached for more typing paper. "Set up for a headline that says, 'Armed Men Oppose Integration,' and another one that says, 'Blossom Plan Shot Down in Court.'"

The plan was not dead long. On Friday morning, a federal judge in Little Rock, responding to a petition by civil rights attorney Thurgood Marshall, dismissed the county court injunction and ruled that the integration of Central High should proceed. By that time, the *Unionville Times* had already come off the press with Upshaw's stories outdated.

"I don't care what the damn judged said," Upshaw told Pearl. "I'm sure there's gon' be violence, and my guns-and-knives story is gon' help it along."

Most Unionville merchants stayed open until eight o'clock
or after on Saturday nights. A lot of people worked six days a
week and this was the only time they had to shop. Some folks
liked catching a double feature or the late show at the Liberty
Theater. And some liked just hanging around and watching others come and go. The Otasco store was one of the places where
white men gathered to gab, lie, and ruminate, along with the
barbershop and newsstand and the pool hall and domino parlor.
Teenagers always took over Emmett's Café.

Miss Ruthelle had Saturday nights off and did not miss being
there when the Otasco regulars talked sports and politics and
told tall tales. Not one of them recalled when he started hanging
out there but it was now their habit. On the last Saturday night
in August, they drifted in after supper as always, made themselves at home, and got right to one of their favorite topics.

"Too bad it wasn't the *Game of the Week*," Houston Holloway
said from his seat on the mezzanine steps. Tall and trim, he was a
pump operator at the Ark-La-Tex Oil refinery and always wore
cowboy boots when not at work. "The radio announcer said the
fight started when one of the Braves slid into the Reds' second
baseman."

"Yeah, I heard that too," Doyle Scoggins said from his perch
on an empty nail keg turned upside down. "They said both
benches cleared." He dropped his cigarette butt on the heavily
oiled floor, mashed it with his shoe, and reached into his shirt
pocket for his Zippo lighter and a new pack of Lucky Strikes. No
one said anything about the way he put out his cigarette, but they
all knew he would never treat his new Chevy that way.

"Who won the game?" Sam asked from his usual spot near
the cash register.

"The Braves, 14 to 4," Scoggins said. He blew smoke through

thin lips and a crooked nose smashed years earlier in a wreck with a lumber truck driven by one of Horace Bowman's mill hands. "They hit five home runs."

"I reckon the Reds' fighting didn't prove much, did it?" Sam said, looking at Billy, who sat nearby on the wrapping counter.

"Say, Sam," Scoggins cut in before Billy could reply, "What's up with you and Billy playing ball with ole Leon Jackson and them?"

"I suppose you heard about that from Lester, huh?" Sam asked.

"A lot of folks know about it," Scoggins said. "You sure you ought to be doing that?"

"Sam, you didn't think you could play ball with coloreds and folks not talk about it, did you?" asked Doc Perkins, the town's only physician. He had helped himself to Sam's office chair, as usual, and moved it out next to the stairs. Doc had a dignified but grandfatherly face, was still close to his playing weight as a former Tulane University fullback, and always wore a black suit and tie.

"Are those boys any good?" Holloway asked. He had held down right field for the Unionville Lumbermen in the old Tri-County League and still itched to play sometimes.

"Yeah, as a matter of fact, they're darned good," Sam said. "They're all slick fielders. Leon Jackson can hit the ball a mile. B. J. Long's got the best curve ball I ever saw. And Charlie Foster's got a rifle for an arm."

"Yeah, but ain't you afraid that y'all's being over there will cause some kind of trouble?" Scoggins asked. He was holding the Zippo between his thumb and middle finger and turning it round and round against his knee.

"I don't see any harm in it. Do you?" He looked at Scoggins

and then at the others, one by one.

"It don't bother me none," Tucker said. "It's about the same as going hunting with them. I do it all the time."

"It don't bother me neither," Holloway said, banging a fist into his other hand as if it were a baseball glove. "Shoot, I wouldn't mind going with you some time."

"Well," Scoggins said, "you sure as hell won't ever see me out there with them."

"I don't care one way or the other," Doc said, "but I expect some folks will get their knickers in a knot over it."

"To hell with them," Sam said. "It's none of their business. Anyway, I won't be going any more. They got rained out Wednesday and Labor Day is their last game." To change the subject, he asked, "What do y'all think about what's happening in Little Rock? Doc, you think there's gon' be violence up there?"

"Probably not," Doc said. He leaned back in his chair and slid his hands into his pants pockets as if gathering his thoughts. "Faubus has too many weapons, what with the state police and all. Besides, I think he just made up those armed caravans he was talking about. I'd be more worried about something happening down here when the integrationists set their sights on us."

"You really believe they will, Doc?" Tucker asked.

"Yeah, I believe eventually they're gon' go after schools all over the place. It's the law, after all."

"Well, I hope my kids are out and gone by then," Tucker said. He and Gloria had a daughter in high school and twin boys a couple of years behind her. "I don't want them to have to deal with it."

Scoggins crushed another butt and reached for his Lucky Strikes again. "There has to be some way to stop it," he said.

"Nope," Doc said. "It's coming."

CHAPTER 16

Becky Reeves spent Saturday afternoon and night working on her Sun Bonnet Sue quilt. During the week, she had gone to the teachers' meeting, put pictures up in her classroom, and completed lesson plans for three weeks. Fred Vestal called from the furniture store and, with apologies for waiting until the last minute, invited her to supper and a picture show in El Dorado, but she turned him down, blaming a tiring week. He struck her as nice but uninteresting and she planned to spend the whole holiday weekend sewing. Then Hazel Brantley popped over from next door and invited her to go to church again.

All over the country, people woke up on Sunday before Labor Day looking forward to one last chance to catch the monster fish that kept getting away, go water skiing, or grill steaks in the backyard.

Sam got up thinking about church and wondering if Becky would be there. Earlier in the week, he had learned that Billy was going to be in her class. He was excited about having a teacher who had a firsthand acquaintance with the Cardinals, and Sam expected he would try to sit near her again today.

Sure enough, when Sunday school ended and Sam walked in for worship, he saw Becky sitting in the same place as last week, with Billy and Mary Jane right behind her. Becky had on a pale green blouse and a white hat with little feathers, and Sam thought she belonged on a movie poster. Both she and Hazel, who was sitting beside her again, were reading their bulletins. Becky glanced up, saw Sam walking up the aisle, and smiled. He smiled back, and when he pulled even with her row, she mouthed, "Good morning." He did the same, took his seat, and tried to focus on his bulletin.

The service followed a predictable track. Opal Jolly sang a moving solo of "Just a Closer Walk with Thee" and Brother Byrd preached another one of his spellbinding sermons. When he finished, he prayed for "peaceful resolution of the differences within our state." This time a few more members than last week noticed his vague reference to the events in Little Rock, but again, most in the congregation were already planning dinner and the rest of the day.

When the worshipers began filing out, Becky turned toward Sam and the children. "Hello, Tate family. Billy, are you ready for school on Tuesday? I suppose you know we'll be learning things together."

"Yes, ma'am," Billy said, smiling from ear to ear and buttoning his sports jacket like a grownup. "I'm anxious to hear all about Busch Stadium."

"That's great," Becky said, as they all moved into the aisle. "We'll have some other interesting things to talk about too. It'll be a fun year."

"I've never seen him so ready for school to start," Sam said, walking slowly alongside Becky. He noticed she was wearing the same perfume she had on the day she came into the Otasco store. "How about you?" he asked, breathing in the pleasing scent. "Is Hazel taking good care of you?" He spoke loudly enough for the landlady, now ahead of him, to hear.

"Yes, Hazel has told me everything I need to know about Unionville, and I'm anxious to get going on Tuesday." Becky did not say that Hazel had also passed along just about everything she knew about Sam and his family.

"Well, if there's anything we Tates can do for you, don't hesitate to let us know," Sam said, unable to come up with anything better.

"Thank you. I appreciate that. Hey, Mary Jane. How are you today? That surely is a pretty dress you're wearing."

"My grandmother made it," Mary Jane said, walking on the other side of her daddy.

"Well, she certainly is a good seamstress."

"Gran makes quilts too," Mary Jane added.

"Oh, does she?" Becky said. "So do I."

Across the sanctuary, Emma Lou nudged Gran. "Looks like Sam and that new teacher are getting along good. They sure make a handsome couple."

"Emma Lou, you know I don't want to hear that kind of talk," Gran said. "I done told you. Sam ain't got truck for no Yankee woman. He's just being polite."

"Ida Belle's right," Almalee leaned over and whispered to her shorter companions. "I'm sure when Sam's ready to think about marrying again, he's gon' want a nice southern girl like Opal."

"Did I say anything about marriage?" Emma Lou asked. "Gosh almighty, y'all!"

Later, when the Tates were driving home, Gran asked Sam, "What were you and that Yankee schoolteacher talking about?"

"We were just exchanging the time of day, Momma."

"She makes quilts, Gran," Mary Jane said, "just like you."

"That'll be the day."

As always after Sunday dinner, Sam and Billy helped Gran

clean up the kitchen, then Sam played games with Mary Jane and read to her. In mid-afternoon, he and Billy gathered balls, bats, and gloves and headed to the horse pasture. Old Ned, long experienced with flying baseballs, took to the barn as soon as he saw them coming.

They followed a routine. First, they used shovels and a wheelbarrow to pick up fresh horse apples. Then came a game of catch to warm up and, after that, batting for Billy. Unionville did not have a Little League and Billy had never played in a real game. The closest he ever came were occasional sandlot games with friends in the summer and during recess at school.

To compensate, Sam had built a low mound and a small chicken-wire backstop at home, and he made their Sunday afternoons special by calling out imaginary hitting situations. Billy had a good eye for the ball and took in batting tips like Old Ned's saddle blanket soaked up sweat. Sam rarely had to remind him anymore to keep his back elbow up. "This next one's gon' have a bend in it," Sam said, after Billy murdered a batch of straight pitches. Sam threw a slow curve, and Billy smashed it toward what would have been right field on a real ball diamond.

"Good hit!" Sam called. He loved watching Billy swing.

After a while they switched to fielding, first with grounders then fly balls, Billy's favorites. When they finished, they went to the back porch, sat in the shade, and drank lemonade with Mary Jane and Gran. Although Gran didn't like baseball, she liked seeing Sam and Billy play together and she always made them something cold to drink afterward.

"Billy," Sam asked, as they cooled off, "how would you like to go see the Black Tigers play a real game tomorrow afternoon? Provided we get all our chores done in time." After Labor Day, stores no longer closed on Wednesday afternoons, and Sam always used the holiday to get work done around home.

"Yes, sir!" Billy said. "That'd be great!"

"Sam!" Gran said, puffing up. "I done told you! Y'all ain't got no business over there with them coloreds, especially with all that mess going on up at Little Rock. People are gon' talk and they're gon' stop buying from you."

"No, they won't, not as long as I have what they want and the price is right. Besides, if someone doesn't like it, that's their problem. I'd a whole lot rather be sitting over at the ball park watching a good ball game with coloreds than sitting in the barbershop getting a haircut with the likes of Jim Ed Davis."

"Well, I don't like it," Gran said.

On Monday morning, Sam got up early, hitched up Old Ned, and tilled the garden for a fall crop of turnip greens. He had them planted before anyone else woke up. After breakfast, Billy helped harvest several long rows of peanuts, which he and Sam stacked under a fenced-in shed behind the barn. In a week or two, Billy and Mary Jane would help pull them off the vines for drying. During the winter, Sam kept a pan full roasting on the big flat-top gas heater at the store. They attracted customers and fueled the Saturday night bull sessions.

Sam and Billy worked past noon, and when they finished, Gran told them, "Me and Mary Jane ate already and what's left is cold. I didn't aim to keep food warm just so y'all could run off over there and mix with them coloreds."

As he and Billy headed for the ball park after a dinner of warmed-up leftovers, Sam began to feel a little unsure about going. Whites never attended Black Tiger games and despite how he and Billy had been practicing with the team, he was not sure they would be welcome. If they went, no one would ask them to leave, but he did not want to embarrass Leon Jackson. So, instead of going through the ticket gate, Sam parked on the school grounds and he and Billy walked between the woods and the outfield fence and sat down in the grass well outside the unenclosed right field foul line.

A hundred or more people were scattered around the small grandstand and along the foul lines near the dugouts but none paid the uninvited guests any attention. Sam and Billy had never seen the Black Tigers in uniform, and although their cream-colored suits were old and worn, they looked sharp. Each shirt had a homemade orange "U" stitched to the front and a homemade black number sewed on the back. Their caps were plain black and their stockings orange.

"Looks like they got those uniforms used somewhere, but I bet they still had to save up a long time for them," Sam said.

"I bet Leon cleans them in his shop," Billy said. "Look, there he is, coming out of the dugout. He's got on shin guards and stuff. There comes B. J. too. I bet he's pitching."

Being the home team, the Black Tigers took the field first. Their opponents, the Strong Cyclones from over near Crossett, batted first. Their uniforms were old, too, and some were not complete, but still they looked good. The pants and shirts were gray and the stockings, homemade numbers, and caps red.

"Come on, B. J.! You're the man, B. J! Show him your smoke, B. J.! He can't hit!" some of the Black Tigers yelled when the first Strong hitter stepped into the batter's box. Others whistled encouragement.

B. J. Long peered in at Leon to get the sign for the first pitch then went into his windmill windup and let fly. Ball striking mitt sounded like a rifle shot. The hitter never moved his bat.

"Strriikee!" the umpire bellowed.

"Wow!" Billy said.

The next pitch made the same sound, only this time the batter swung and missed.

"Strriikee two!" the ump bellowed again.

"Watch for Miss Lilabell this time," Sam said.

B. J. got Leon's sign, wound up, and delivered.

"Ungh!" The batter's strained exhale could be heard all over the park as he missed B. J.'s favorite pitch by a foot.

"Strriikee three! You're out!" the umpire yelled.

Leon shot the ball to the third baseman and the players whipped it around the infield and yelled, "Atta boy, B. J.! Way to pitch!" The crowd cheered loudly.

"Daddy, this is exciting," Billy said.

"Yeah, it is," Sam agreed. He was glad they came.

The next two batters went down in order, one on another strikeout and one on a weak grounder to Otis Henderson at short. When the Cyclones took the field, a giant of a man strode to the mound. He was bigger than Leon and blazed his warm-up pitches to the plate. Otis led off for the Black Tigers and went down swinging on three straight fastballs. Charlie Foster came up next and fouled off two fastballs before bouncing a ball weakly to short. Leon strode from the on-deck circle to bat third.

"If that pitcher keeps on throwing fastballs, Leon's gon' park one," Sam told Billy. "Just you watch."

The first pitch popped loudly into the catcher's mitt. Leon took it for a strike.

"That's okay," Sam said. "He's just getting the timing down."

The second pitch was another fastball in the strike zone, and again Leon watched it go by without moving the bat held high behind his head. The pitcher, sure now that he had the upper

107

hand, wound up and delivered again. This time, Leon stepped forward, put his weight into a perfectly timed swing, and used his wrists to snap the bat into the ball. It exploded off the barrel, rose on a steady line over second base, and looked as if it were still climbing when it cleared the center field fence.

"What did I tell you?" Sam said, clapping.

The Cyclones' pitcher learned from Leon's blast and started mixing his deliveries, but he was no match for B. J. By the eighth inning, Unionville led 9 to 0. Leon slugged another home run in the fourth, this one a towering fly to left, and no Strong batter hit the ball out of the infield. With a win well in hand, Leon took B. J. out of the game to give another Black Tiger a chance to pitch. When Leon walked to the mound to go over signs at the start of the inning, he looked out toward Sam and Billy and tipped his cap. Billy waved back and Sam gave a thumbs up.

"Looks like the Black Tigers about have it wrapped up." Sam said. "Let's go so I can read some to Mary Jane before supper."

"Just one more batter, please?" Billy begged.

"All right," Sam said, sitting back down on the grass.

The Strong hitter lined the new hurler's first pitch toward the gap in left center field.

"That might be a double," Sam said, as Charlie Foster raced to his left.

"Rabbit on the run!" Billy shouted, as the batter rounded first base. The Black Tigers were yelling too. "Rabbit on the run! Rabbit on the run!"

Charlie scooped the skidding ball off the grass, pivoted, and hurled it on a line to second. It arrived before the runner could even start his slide.

"Out by a mile, Daddy!"

"Son," Sam said, "that fellow was out as soon as he decided

to go to second. He just didn't know it. Come on. We have to go home now."

"Okay, Daddy. Mary Jane's probably waiting for you."

When Sam and Billy rose to leave, so did the man looking on from the woods on the hill behind them.

While Sam and Billy watched the Black Tigers, the Braves swept a doubleheader from the Cubs in Chicago and the Cardinals lost a pair to the Reds in Cincinnati. This put the Cardinals eight and one-half games back in the National League pennant race.

In Little Rock, School Superintendent Virgil Blossom, NAACP leader Daisy Bates, and parents of the seventeen students scheduled to enter Central High School on Tuesday morning suffered a much more important setback. Frightened by all the talk of violence, eight of the students and their families went to Blossom's office and withdrew their applications to attend Central. While that was going on, the superintendent's secretary received a telephone call from a man who refused to give his name but claimed some two hundred armed men were on their way to Little Rock to "get" Blossom. After reporting the call to the police, Blossom telephoned Faubus and asked for more protection. He responded by scheduling a statewide television address for late that evening.

The Tates stayed too busy to watch a lot of television but each had favorite shows. Mary Jane loved *Howdy Doody*, Billy never missed *Dragnet*, and he and the adults watched *Gunsmoke* every week. They all liked *I Love Lucy*, and Gran and the children often watched *Father Knows Best*. Sam stopped watching it after Mary

Jane said, "Daddy, I wish I had a momma like Mrs. Anderson." If Tucker had not called Sam to tell him about the governor's speech, he would have missed it.

A little before ten o'clock, with Billy and Mary Jane long in bed, Sam and Gran sat silently in the living room waiting for the broadcast. He thought about how his mother seemed to tire so easily of late, how much things had changed during her lifetime, and how they would surely change more, even drastically from her point of view. He wondered how much longer he, Billy, and Mary Jane would have her.

Like Sam and Gran, people all over Arkansas sat in front of their TVs or near their radios. When Faubus appeared on the screen in stark black and white with his hair slicked back from his jowly face, he looked worried. He talked about the need for deliberate rather than quick change and explained how he had asked the courts for more time to work out the details of integration and how federal judges had rejected his pleas.

Now, he said, a telephone campaign was underway to assemble a large crowd of protesters at Little Rock Central High School at six o'clock the next morning. Repeating rumors like ones he had described in court earlier, he said he had reports that caravans would converge on Little Rock from all over the state. "If that happens and Negro students attempt to enter the school," he speculated, "blood will run in the streets." Accordingly, he said he had called out the National Guard to keep order and protect lives and property. The troops were already in place as he spoke, having arrived an hour earlier in jeeps, trucks, and half-tracks, and were armed with rifles, bayonets, tear gas, and riot clubs.

Faubus went on to say he had come to the inevitable conclusion that, for the time being, schools in Pulaski County must remain segregated. In violation of a federal court order, he directed that the integration of Little Rock Central High School be put on hold.

The broadcast sent shock waves across the state. Regardless of position, responsibility, or opinion, everyone saw that the dispute had become a crisis.

"It's about time somebody showed some gumption," Gran said, when Faubus finished speaking.

Sam got up and turned off the set. "I'm not so sure it was gumption, Momma. Looks like he's just postponing something that's gon' happen no matter what he does."

Elsewhere in Unionville, Brother Spurlock reached for a pack of cigarettes and a notepad. Preston Upshaw went to his typewriter. Reverend Moseley got down on his knees. Principal Woodhead went to bed fearing her last school year might not go as smoothly as she had hoped. And Becky Reeves began making new lesson plans.

CHAPTER 17

On Tuesday morning, Becky stood on the courtyard sidewalk outside her classroom welcoming students to the first day of school. The weather was mild and sunny and the air was filled with anticipation and promise.

"Good morning. Welcome to seventh grade. I'm Miss Reeves," she said to the children as they drifted in alone or in small groups. "How are you? What's your name?" She would not remember all of them from this, but she had posted a temporary seating chart, and as she greeted them, she told them to find their designated seats.

"Good morning, Miss Reeves," Billy said, when he walked up.

"Good morning, Billy," she said to the only student she knew. He grinned with pride.

Becky also counted the children as they arrived. Most of the sixteen girls wore dresses but some sported widely flared poodle skirts. Most of the fourteen boys wore checkered sports shirts and brand-new jeans that threw off a heavy smell of dyed cotton.

Few students noticed Becky's leg until she walked to her desk and stood in front of it. Earlier, she had written her name on the blackboard behind it. She waited while the last students took their seats and all grew quiet. Another, longer blackboard ran along the wall to her right, parallel to the courtyard outside. Bulletin boards covered the back wall. Hand-cranked windows lined the one on her left, offering a view of the bus repair shop. Billy sat near the middle of the first row, next to the long blackboard.

Becky looked around the classroom, savoring the moment, as her students waited for direction. She expected to spend seven hours a day, five days a week with them over the next nine months, and she wanted to give each the best chance to enjoy school and make the next grade.

"My name is Miss Reeves," she said. "Welcome to seventh grade." She walked a little way toward the door, paused, and then crossed the room to the windows. The children stared. A few exchanged looks but none said anything.

"As I'm sure you all know," she resumed, "this is my first year in Unionville. You probably noticed that I limp when I walk and you may be curious to know why. I had polio when I was about your age, before we had vaccines to prevent it. My leg doesn't hurt and it doesn't keep me from doing most things I want to do. If you ever want to ask me anything about it, you may do so. I won't mind."

Before going to sleep last night and again this morning, she had considered saying something about the National Guard having been called out in Little Rock. She doubted many of her students had seen or heard the governor's speech, though she suspected it might have been talked about over breakfast in some homes. Because the issue was unlikely to be resolved any time soon and the first day of class was always tense, she decided not to bring it up unless one of the children asked about it. She planned to get to it soon enough, however.

"Now," she said, "I'd like to learn more about you."

While students from New York to California had mostly ordinary opening days, those entering Central High School passed
under the watchful eyes of the entire nation and 270 Arkansas
National Guardsmen. All 1,878 students who entered were
white. After Faubus's speech, the school board had asked parents
of the nine remaining black children selected under the Blossom
Plan for integrating the school to keep them home pending further legal action.

The spectacle created immediate reactions. Segregationists
drew encouragement from it and integrationists felt disillu-
sioned and outraged. News media everywhere pointed out that
Faubus was the first southern governor to try to exert state authority to stop federally ordered integration.

Sam chose not to mention Little Rock at breakfast and Gran
kept silent about it too. He also delayed going to work so he
could see Billy off for his first day of class. Miss Ruthelle opened
the Otasco store for him, and by the time Sam got there, Lester
Grimes had already stopped in to talk.

When Sam walked in, the portly barber was saying, "I still
can't believe Faubus did it." He turned to Sam and asked, "Did
you see him on TV last night?"

"Yeah, I saw him," Sam said. He kept walking, turned under
the stairs to the closet, and emerged with a broom and a bucket
of oiled sawdust.

"Well, what do you think?" Lester asked. "You reckon ole
Orval is finally seeing the light?"

"No, I think he's just beating a dead horse. Washington's not
gon' let him get away with it."

"You know, Sam, you're starting to worry me. First, you're
playing baseball with coloreds and now you're talking against
states' rights."

"Damn it, Lester," Sam snapped. "Why don't you go bother somebody else and let me work?"

⌒

Across the street, Leon Jackson held down the lid of his pressing machine and gave a pair of pants a shot of steam. Heat smothered the tin building like a blanket, and he wiped his forehead with the back of his hand before looking up at Reverend Moseley. The preacher had stopped in moments earlier, worried now more than ever that the trouble in Little Rock might cause problems in Unionville.

"I agree it's bothersome, Reverend," Leon said. "All that talk about knives and guns up there might give folks down here ideas, but I don't know what more we can do." He did not tell the preacher about having twice seen the shadow of someone creeping among the warehouses out back while he was opening the shop in predawn hours to get a head start on his work. "You were smart to tell parents to make sure their kids don't stay out after dark. And having the deacons take turns staying in the church and watching it at night is good too."

Moseley was standing just inside the doorway and before he replied, he looked around to make sure no one was coming. "I guess I worry most about our womenfolk walking back and forth to work over to the white side of town. You know what happened to Mrs. Bates's momma over in Huttig when Daisy was a baby."

"Yeah, I know. Three white men raped and killed her. But I expect the most our womenfolk are gon' have to put up with is some name calling. It makes me mad as hell—excuse me, Reverend—to think about it, but bad as that is, at least it's nothing new. Tell you what. After prayer meeting tomorrow night,

115

why don't you get all the men folk together? Just say you have some kind of special church business or something. When we get them separated from the women, we'll ask the ones that have cars or trucks to keep an extra lookout."

"That's a good idea, Leon, but are you gon' be at prayer meeting tomorrow? Seems like you been worshiping baseball more than the Lord on Wednesdays."

"Baseball season's over for the Black Tigers, Reverend. You know that. You just want to remind me that I've been backsliding. I'll be there."

A few hours later a federal judge ordered the integration of Central High School to proceed the following day despite the National Guard. "It's my constitutional duty," he said. Superintendent Blossom advised parents of the nine black children to send them to school but not go with them. He feared that if black adults showed up, white protesters would riot. All nine families passed a restless afternoon and evening. Daisy Bates spent hours talking with police officials and black ministers to see if some of them would accompany the children, but the police said the National Guard had made the school off limits to them, and the preachers agreed with Blossom. Finally, well past midnight, Bates phoned eight homes and arranged for the students to meet her at a central location the next morning. She and her husband planned to escort them the rest of the way in a group so they would not have to face a potential mob alone. But Elizabeth Eckford's family did not have a phone and Bates, exhausted, forgot to arrange another way to get the message to her.

The next day, Wednesday, September 4, subscribers of the *Arkansas Gazette* woke up to a front-page editorial titled "The

Crisis Mr. Faubus Made." It said the governor was posing possibly the most serious constitutional question since the Civil War. "The issue is no longer segregation versus integration," editor Harry Ashmore wrote, "but rather a question of the supremacy of the government of the United States in all matters of the law." The national administration, he speculated, would not allow such a basic question to remain unresolved.

At the Eckford home, Elizabeth, the daughter of a Missouri Pacific maintenance worker, put on a brand-new black-and-white dress her mother had sewn especially for her first day of school. The family prayed for her safety and Elizabeth, unaware that the other students were traveling together by private car, took a public bus to a stop near Central High.

When she got off and approached the school on foot, she saw the National Guardsmen and a crowd of four hundred whites. Her heart raced but she was determined not to disappoint her family and continued walking just as she had been instructed. The brownish brick building itself was enough to scare any new student, even in ordinary times. It had a seven-story central tower and two five-story wings that spread over most of two city blocks. As Elizabeth made her way toward the main entrance, the protesters closed in behind her and started calling her names.

"Two, four, six, eight," they chanted, "we ain't gon' integrate!"

When Elizabeth reached the line of guardsmen, she saw white students passing between them, but the soldiers barred her way with bayonets. She tried several times to get through. Someone in the crowd yelled, "Lynch her!" Someone else shouted, "Go home, you nigger bitch! You ain't going to our school!"

Elizabeth walked back to the bus stop and sat on a bench. There was no other place to go. A white reporter from the *New*

York Times sat down next to her to hold off the mob, and eventually a white woman whose husband was a professor at all-black Philander Smith College helped her onto a bus and accompanied her home.

The other black students also failed to get past the guardsmen and returned to their families shaken and anxious.

CHAPTER 18

At the *Unionville Times*, Upshaw could not believe he had so much material for his next issue. The paper did not generate enough revenue for a wire service but he did not need one. He had been up since Monday night watching newscasts, listening to the radio, pouring over daily papers, and making phone calls, and he had churned out more copy than he could print. He was tired, rumpled, and smelled of stale cigarette smoke, but he could not have been happier.

"This is great stuff," he told Pearl, during a break to grab more coffee from the pot on a hot plate near his desk. "Faubus showed Daisy Bates he's not gon' be pushed around, and now other southern governors won't be afraid to stand up too."

"Have you finished what you're going to lead with this week?" Pearl asked from her desk. She had written all the birth, death, and wedding announcements and was nearly ready to start copy-editing Upshaw's pieces. "Today's Wednesday, you know."

"Yes and no," he said, sitting down again. "I've got a bunch of stuff ready to go, but I'm gon' wait a while longer and see if anything else breaks. I don't care if it takes all night."

On Thursday, newspapers around the world carried stories and pictures of the armed guardsmen blocking the black students in front of Central High School and the protesters jeering at them. In Little Rock, Mayor Woodrow W. Mann questioned Faubus's claims about growing weapons sales, and in Washington, the Justice Department considered legal action against him.

In Unionville, Upshaw decided to start the day with some fieldwork. Normally, he made his own meals in his tiny apartment in back of the workroom. This saved time and money and spared him the company of people he regarded as his intellectual inferiors. However, this morning he wanted to hear what folks were saying. He cleaned up and headed next door for breakfast at the café.

Emmett's place always smelled of tobacco smoke and cooking grease but its customers varied according to day and hour. At noon on weekdays, the café served a regular crowd of store owners, clerks, delivery men, and truck drivers. Friday nights drew a different bunch of regulars for fish suppers. On Sundays, church folks dropped in for open-faced roast beef sandwiches and mashed potatoes. On Saturday mornings, loafers took up most of the seats drinking coffee and talking sports. And after supper on Fridays and Saturdays, teenagers gathered to sip cherry cokes, play pinball, and listen to Elvis Presley and Jerry Lee Lewis on the jukebox. The rest of the time, breakfast and supper belonged mostly to single adults and married ones disgruntled with life at home.

Emmett Ledbetter gladly served them all but felt most comfortable with the weekday and Saturday morning regulars. Pale and baggy-eyed, he had lived on cheeseburgers for most of his fifty-plus years and looked it. Except that he had grown up somewhere in Claiborne Parish, never married, and bought the café shortly after World War II, no one knew much about him. Like Jim Ed Davis, he drove an International truck that had seen better days, but he did not venture out much other than to the bank and the barbershop, and even then, he always dressed the same way, in wrinkled slacks, a white long-sleeve shirt with cuffs rolled up to his elbows, and a grease-stained apron. His favorite pastime was drinking bootleg whiskey but he was smart enough not to let his customers smell it on him. A favored few, however, had a secret password they could use to get a cup of coffee that was against the law in dry Anderson Township.

Upshaw took a stool at one end of the counter so he could see everyone seated along it as well as folks in booths along the wall and at tables in the middle of the floor. He did not recognize any of the customers but suspected many shared his views. The only questions he had were how deep their convictions ran and how worked up they were over Little Rock.

"By god, if I'd been there, I'd have laid one of them monkeys out cold," Jim Ed Davis was saying near the middle of the counter. "I think they got off easy. Of all the nerve! They tried to walk in there just like they owned the place."

"Hell, I'd have just shot the first one that showed up," Crow Hicks, the Arkansas-side night watchman, said through a mouthful of fried sausage. "That would've scattered the rest of them." A tall, bony man about Emmett's age, Crow held his job only because Mayor Alan Poindexter could not get anyone else to take it and the town council thought he was better than no watchman at all. All he had to do was walk around after dark and make sure all the stores were locked up tight and no kids were out on the streets too late.

It was probably a good thing for the mayor's minor political career that most people did not see Crow very often, else some of them would have kicked up a fuss. In the daytime he either slept, played dominos, or shot pool. He always wore bib overalls stained with tobacco, and unlike Mr. Claude, he carried a gun, on duty and off. It was a long-barreled .38 Smith & Wesson, and he packed it in a leather holster strapped around his waist with a long belt pulled tight so the end hung way down. A lot of people were afraid of him simply because of how he looked.

"I ain't never seen a nigger that was worth a damn," Crow added. "It wouldn't bother me none to shoot one of them anytime."

Upshaw wondered if the mayor or any of the council members had ever heard their night officer talk this way.

"I tell y'all, before old Faubus called up them guard boys, I was about ready to go up there myself," Odell Grimes put in. On a break from the barbershop, he was taking up two stools next to Crow and working on his second order of pancakes.

"Aw, crap, Odell, who do you expect to believe that?" Boomer Jenkins challenged from the other end of the counter. "You ain't got the balls for something like that. You'd piss your pants and turn around and come home before you even got there."

"Would you go?" Odell asked, taking no offense at Boomer's remark.

"Hell no. I ain't got no time for it. But I'll tell you one thing, if these coloreds down here ever start up with that crap, I'm gon' be in the thick of it. I don't see no need to put up with it."

Because Boomer did not come to town much, Upshaw had not seen him before. He noted the big outdoorsman's steely eyes, knife, and hunter's bearing and knew instantly he was more dangerous than the skinny man with the gun.

"What'll you have this morning, Mr. Upshaw?" Emmett asked, walking down to the end of the counter.

"Black coffee and a stack of pancakes. And bring me a side order of bacon."

Upshaw had not been especially hungry when he came in,

but having heard the kind of talk he hoped for, he suddenly had a huge appetite. He did not know whether Little Rock really had segregationists armed with knives and guns but Unionville certainly did. And he had not been the only one to hear them spouting off about what they would do. He wondered how many more there were like these. Plenty, he expected.

"You won't make it home for supper tonight," Upshaw told Pearl when he returned to the newspaper office. "I've decided how I want to play this and I have to do some rewriting."

Becky had decided how to play it, too, but not without some anxious moments the night before. When Faubus had called out the National Guard on Monday, she had seen only the historical and legal implications. However, on Wednesday, after the soldiers turned back Elizabeth Eckford with bayonets and the mob yelled, "Lynch her," Becky began to give her mother's warning about moving to Unionville serious thought.

That night, after watching the news on TV, she went to her hall closet, took down a shirt box of photographs, and carried it into the living room. She had not intended to bring them with her, but her mother had hidden the box in one of the grocery bags she slipped into Becky's car back in Kirkwood. It was Velma's not so subtle way of reminding her daughter that she had made a potentially dangerous decision and should be careful.

Becky put the box on the coffee table next to a half-drunk cup of tea and sat on the sofa. She had not opened the box after discovering it in the grocery bag, but she knew what was in it. Now, she slowly removed the lid and sifted through the contents. When she came to the pictures of her Great-grandmother Charlene and Grandmother Abigail, she took them out, stared at them for a long time, and recalled the stories her mother told her before college.

Velma did not want to upset Becky or change anything about their lives, but she wanted her to know the truth about her family. As Becky examined the pictures, she could almost hear Velma explaining that she was what white people in New Orleans called an octoroon and how they bought sexual favors from her mother and grandmother but scorned them because of their race. Until now, that kind of hatred never seemed this real or this close. Becky had always lived and passed as white without thinking about it. She was sympathetic toward blacks but never thought of herself as one. Not even the growing civil rights movement had made her question her sense of who she was. Now, for the first time, she considered the potential consequences of someone learning that legally she was black. The prospect of discovery was so new and seemed so unlikely, however, that she stubbornly dismissed it. No one had discovered her mother and no one would discover her, she decided. She put the photographs back in the box and put the box back in the closet.

CHAPTER 19

On Thursday morning, as soon as Becky's students saw her finish the mandatory attendance and school lunch paperwork and drop it in the collections box outside the door, they started asking questions about Little Rock. She knew the subject was potentially explosive, but it offered too good a teaching opportunity to pass up, and she had come prepared. She intended to approach it candidly and in the context of what her students were already expected to learn about the Constitution and the federal system of government.

Glen Ray Plunkett, a chunky boy sitting midway back next to the windows got in the first one. "Miss Reeves, are we gon' have niggers trying to get in our school?"

There it is, Becky thought. Children get right to the point. And they repeat what they hear at home.

"My daddy says there's gon' be another Civil War," Tommy Ingram, a skinny boy with freckles, offered from the back of the room as soon as she turned around. "He says somebody's gon' get killed. Is that right, Miss Reeves? Is there gon' be another Civil War? Are people gon' get killed?"

Becky took her time moving to the front of her desk, leaning against the edge, and looking around the classroom at her students. The children waited for her reply.

"Class," she said, "you are asking good questions about very important events—the type of events that are written about in history books—and we're going to explore the answers togeth-er. Let's start by listing all the questions you have, then we'll talk about which ones you want to explore first."

A neatly dressed girl in the front row raised her hand.

"Yes, Barbara?" Becky asked.

"Miss Reeves, do you mean we're gon' do history first? Isn't this supposed to be math time?" Math was Barbara Ames's favor-ite subject.

"Yes, Barbara, we are—this morning at least. But first, there is one rule we all must follow in our discussion. We will, none of us, use the terms 'nigger' or 'colored.' The proper word is 'Negro.'" Becky went around her desk to the blackboard. "Now then," she said, "let's write down all our questions. Then we'll decide where to begin."

That evening in more than one Unionville home, parents and seventh-grade students discussed the day's American history lesson.

"She said we can't say 'nigger' or 'colored,'" Glen Ray told his parents.

"Well, son, you don't have to pay no mind to some old-maid Yankee schoolteacher," Bobby Jack Plunkett said. "I know lots of people and I got some pull around that school. If she gives you any trouble, I'll fix it." Bobby Jack, a deliveryman for the Coca-Cola bottling plant in El Dorado, had been a star athlete at Unionville High School. "You do what she tells you in class and what I tell you otherwise. You hear?"

"Yeah, Pops, I hear," Glen Ray said.

Barbara Ames told her parents that Becky had messed up the class schedule and had not spent enough time on math, something the entire Ames family regarded as far more important than history or current events. Barbara's father, Howard, was an accountant for Ark-La-Tex Oil in El Dorado, and he and her mother both expected their only daughter to follow in his footsteps.

"Don't you worry, honey," Howard said. "If she keeps it up, I'll talk to Mrs. Woodhead. Principals have to make teachers stick to the curriculum."

During supper at the Tate house Billy said, "Miss Reeves is real interesting, Daddy."

"'Really,' Billy, not 'real,'" Sam corrected. "I bet that's because she told you all about the Cardinals, huh?"

"No, sir, she hasn't mentioned the Cardinals yet." He gulped down half a glass of milk. "We talked about Little Rock, Governor Faubus, and integration," Billy said, his face glowing with enthusiasm.

"For crying out loud!" Gran said. She leaned back in her chair. "I knew that woman was gon' fill your head with trash. What's she telling y'all?"

"Well," Billy said, "we talked about how there are state governments and the federal government and how the Constitution tells what kinds of things each one can do and what they can't do."

"That's very good, Billy," Sam said proudly. "What else did she tell you?"

"We talked about how segregationists want to keep black and white schools separate and how integrationists want blacks and whites to go to school together. Of course, I knew that before."

"And I guess she told you she's one of them integrationists, didn't she?" Gran fumed.

"Actually, she didn't say what she is," Billy said. He took another long drink of milk. "She said the segregationists and the integrationists are lined up against each other like two football teams and they both have to play by the rules. The rules are in the Constitution and the courts are like the referees. They're gon' make everybody follow the rules. And, oh yeah, she said we should say 'Negro,' not 'nigger' or 'colored.'"

"Well, I never!" Gran snorted.

"You really like Miss Reeves, don't you?" Sam asked.

"Yes, sir, I sure do."

"'Surely,'" Billy, "'surely,'" Sam said almost absent-mindedly. His thoughts had turned to how pretty Becky looked in church last Sunday and whether she would be there again this week.

CHAPTER 20

Hundreds of folks in Unionville and countless other people across Arkansas and the rest of the country woke up on Friday morning unable to get Little Rock off their minds. The growing crisis was becoming one of the most dramatic news events since World War II. Even the *New York Times* gave the story front-page coverage. The major TV networks readied film of Little Rock for their evening news shows, the editors of *Time* and *Life* magazines worked on feature stories for upcoming issues, and in countries behind the Iron Curtain, state-run media outlets cited the goings-on as proof that American democracy had failed.

When Pearl Goodbar walked into the messy *Unionville Times* workroom at six o'clock, she had gotten only four hours of sleep. She found Upshaw in the same shape she had left him the night before—down to his shirt-sleeves, grease-smeared, and switching back and forth between wiping the Linotype machine with a kerosene-soaked rag and banging on it with a wrench.

"How's it coming?" she asked coolly.

"You're just in time. I'm almost done, but I swear, if I could get my hands on the idiot that used vegetable oil to grease this thing, I'd make him eat it."

Upshaw had tried to follow the dog-eared maintenance manual he had gotten with the used machine, but he never dreamed the previous owner had failed to lubricate it properly. He had let the moving parts get all gummed up, and they froze while Pearl was setting type for this week's press run. To meet the mailing deadline, they would have to work flat-out all day and hope nothing else went wrong.

"There's fresh coffee," Upshaw said. "Help yourself."

Pearl put her purse and lunch bag in her desk and reached for her mug without saying anything. Upshaw's unexpected gesture surprised her but she chalked it up to excitement about his second issue. He had rewritten his main stories with blinding speed on Thursday morning.

"This stuff is so good, it practically writes itself," he had said.

She had to admit it was dramatic. Under the huge front-page banner, "Faubus Stands Tall, Bars Negroes," Upshaw praised the governor for facing up to "misguided Yankee integrationists who so love the black man that they are willing to defy the rights of states to run their own affairs." Making no effort at straightforward reporting, the editor declared, "Arkansas's leader is deservedly destined to become a nationwide symbol for right-thinking Americans who abhor the abuse of federal power."

In a separate story under the headline, "Concerned Citizens Fight Back," Upshaw described the threats against Daisy Bates and the unconfirmed rumors that caravans of armed citizens were descending on Little Rock to help make certain Central High School remained segregated. "Responsible Arkansans are making their feelings known and their voices heard," he wrote.

In addition, copying a tactic from the *Arkansas Gazette,* he had penned a front-page editorial, though with a completely different tone than Harry Ashmore's piece a few days earlier. Leading with the title, "It Can Happen Here," Upshaw stated, "If Negroes enter the top public high school in the capital, others of their race will be emboldened to enroll in white schools across the state, and the result will be chaos. It will happen quickly and un-controllably and Unionville will not be spared. People of good moral character must step forward and oppose it."

He stopped banging, came from behind the Linotype machine, and grabbed a rag to wipe his hands.

"Okay, that does it," he said. "Get over here, Mrs. Goodbar, and finish setting the copy so we can crank up the press."

By Friday night, most white people in Unionville were thinking more about high school football than about anything in Little Rock. Bobcat games were the biggest social events of the year. Even when the team played on the road, parents and fans turned out to cheer. The season opener—at Lewisville, seventy-five miles west, over near Texarkana—shoved other concerns aside for at least a little while.

Coaches and players loaded up the district's best school bus and left Unionville in midafternoon so they could stop in Stamps for an early supper. The band left later in the second-best bus, aiming to arrive just before game time. Two dozen cars carrying parents and fans followed close behind. Unfortunately, they returned home disappointed, as the team played hard but suffered a disappointing 14 to 13 loss.

The next morning, as on every Saturday during football season, conversation at Emmett's Café and at the barbershop and newsstand revolved around the game.

"I just don't understand why we punted with three minutes left to play," mill foreman Jack Metcalf said. He was waiting his turn for a haircut. His son, Ronnie, was a junior halfback for the Bobcats. "We should've gone for the first down."

"Yeah," Rufus Keller, owner of the former mill commissary,

said through a cloud of powder, as Odell Grimes dusted loose hair off the back of his neck. "I couldn't believe it. What was coach thinking?"

"He wasn't thinking, if you ask me," Bobby Jack Plunkett, the Coca-Cola deliveryman, said from Lester Grimes's chair. "Fourth and five on their forty-one-yard line? He should've went for it. I'd have run a reverse around the right end. Hell, I bet my Glen Ray could've made it and he ain't but in the seventh grade."

"Well, cheer up," Odell said. "Maybe the Bobcats will have some of them big colored boys blocking for Ronnie next year. Ain't that a hell of a thought?"

"It ain't gon' happen," Lester said. "Folks are gon' fight back, just like Upshaw's saying. Did y'all see the papers this morning? Look at the *Arkansas Gazette* over there," he said, pointing to a wall rack near Metcalf. "Somebody burned a cross in the mayor's yard up there last night," Lester said, referring to Little Rock. "That ought to send a signal that good people ain't gon' tolerate integration."

Lester's comments were exactly the kind of talk Upshaw expected to hear when he went to Emmett's Café for breakfast again. He wanted to see how folks responded to this week's *Unionville Times*, and he especially looked forward to hearing from the men he had seen at the café on Thursday. When he walked in, however, none of them were there.

He sat midway along the counter and ordered coffee and two eggs over easy with toast and juice. Although he was disappointed at not seeing the gun-toting night watchman and the knife-carrying man with the wooden leg, he still hoped to hear something he could use.

"How many yards did Ronnie Metcalf gain?" Doyle Scoggins asked no one in particular. He was sitting near the end of the counter where he could keep an eye on his new Chevy parked outside.

"Near about a hundred and fifty," a mechanic from the Ford dealership across the highway said. "That boy can flat out run. Nobody came within ten feet of him on that sweep in the second quarter. Man, that was pretty!"

"Coach should've called that again the last time we had the ball instead of kicking," another diner said.

"Naw, the Lewisville coaches were watching for it after that first one," a third man chimed in. "Ronnie didn't gain nothing on sweeps in the second half."

This was not what Upshaw had anticipated. Had these folks not read his paper? There should have been enough time to pick it up at the post office or grab it from the rack outside the café. What would it take to get people off their duffs? He decided to wait until afternoon then make the rounds of the merchants again, see what else he could hear, and try selling more ads.

Billy did not find all he was looking for, either, when he paid twenty cents to see the Saturday matinee at the Liberty. He figured *Gun Fight at the O.K. Corral* would be full of gunplay right from the start, and he did not expect all the fuss Burt Lancaster and Kirk Douglas made over Rhonda Fleming before the big shoot-out at the end. When he walked out of the dark movie house into the bright sun, he was in much the same frame of mind as Upshaw had been upon leaving the café earlier. At least Randy Lawson had taken time off from shining shoes at the barbershop and newsstand to go along with him.

As the boys crossed the street so Randy could catch the late afternoon crowd of folks wanting haircuts and shines for Sunday, they saw Upshaw coming out of Lawson's Dry Goods.

"I bet that newspaper man's been trying to sell ads to my daddy again," Randy said.

"Yeah, he's been pestering my daddy too. He's sure a strange bird. Don't bother speaking to him. He don't care for kids."

"I know. He's been in the barbershop a couple of times. I asked him if he wanted a shoeshine and he acted like he didn't even hear me."

"I bet he could use one," Billy said, as they slipped between two parked cars onto the sidewalk. "He's always walking. I've never seen him in a car."

"He's got one of those stake-bodied trucks. You know—the kind with side planks, like the ones they use at the Feed and Seed. I saw him buying gas at the Sinclair station."

As Randy peeled off and Billy continued toward the Otasco store, Upshaw ducked in its front door. He was just starting his spiel when Billy arrived moments later.

"Mr. Tate, I know you said you didn't want a larger ad, but in view of my growing circulation, I thought you might have changed your mind."

"No. I haven't," Sam said, hitching up his pants impatiently.

"I'll tell you what," Upshaw persisted. "I'll still let you have a whole series at my original introductory price."

"Nope, I don't want it."

"Man, I don't understand you," Upshaw said, his frustration showing. "Didn't you read my stories today? Don't you see I'm trying to help this town?"

Sam glanced at Billy and tried to come up with a measured response. "Look, I don't know what you wrote, because I've been too busy to read your blooming paper. And right now, I don't care what's in it. I've told you more than once I'm not gon' take out a bigger ad and I'm not gon' change my mind. Don't ask me about it again. If you do, I'm gon' stop buying ads altogether. Period. End of discussion."

"All right, but read today's issue," Upshaw said, heading for the door. "It's important."

"Daddy, your face is red," Billy said, when the editor was out of earshot.

"Yeah, son, I know. How was the picture show?"

"What do you think is gon' happen?" Hazel asked, as Becky took a load of laundry out of her landlady's clothes dryer late Saturday afternoon. The *Unionville Times* lay on the kitchen table. "Do you think coloreds are gon' try to go to our school?"

"I'm sure they will eventually," Becky said, carefully folding a blouse.

"But Mr. Upshaw seems to think it can be stopped," Hazel said. She put a lid on a boiler of potatoes, wiped her hands on her apron, and turned to face Becky. "He says all we have to do is take a stand."

Becky reached for another blouse. "Hazel, forget for a minute about whether you believe integration is right or wrong and think about how you, or anyone, would go about stopping it. There's no way to do it. The Supreme Court has ruled. School desegregation is the law of the land, and violence and intimidation won't prevent it. Negro leaders won't back down and the federal government is going to protect them. The only thing people like Governor Faubus and Mr. Upshaw can do is delay the inevitable and get a lot of people hurt in the meantime."

Hazel put both hands on her hips, squinched her eyes, and said after a moment, "You're for it, ain't you?"

Becky did not respond.

"Oh, my god!" Hazel exclaimed, "I got an integrationist living in my house! A sweet young thing like you. Why, I never dreamed."

"I never gave you any reason to believe otherwise," Becky said coolly. "But if you want me to find another place to live, I will."

"Oh, lands no!" Hazel said quickly. "At least you ain't running around carrying on about it. Why, if you left, hon, I'd have a devil of a time finding another tenant as nice as you. I like having you here, even if I don't understand you half the time. You're good company and you don't seem to mind my always running on. You don't have to move just because I don't agree with you about this colored business."

"You see, Hazel? People can be different, and even disagree, and still get along. Can't they?"

"Well, hon, I reckon so. Leastways, you and me can. You want to go to church with me again tomorrow?"

"I don't know. I'm making some changes in my lesson plans, and I may have to work on them all day tomorrow. Okay if I let you know in the morning?"

"Sure, hon, that's fine, but if you don't go, I think somebody's gon' be disappointed at not seeing you."

"Oh really, and who would that be?"

"Why, Sam Tate, of course. I told you I ain't never seen him smile at any woman like he smiles at you, except for his late wife."

Becky kept silent.

"You don't have to say nothing. I got eyes."

CHAPTER 21

On Sunday morning, Upshaw, still unhappy with the reception he had gotten around town on Saturday, poured over other papers and compared their stories to his. In an Associated Press piece in the *El Dorado Daily News*, a reporter asked who would give in first. "Will it be the president, committed to uphold the laws of the nation and the Supreme Court's anti-segregation ruling, or the governor, who defiantly used the Arkansas National Guard to prevent racial integration?" The *Arkansas Gazette* hoped Faubus would obey the federal edict. "If he refuses," the paper stated, "having used force himself, he would thus invite the federal government to reply in kind with consequences that defy the imagination."

Upshaw tossed his copy away in disgust. What a bunch of shortsighted pantywaists, he thought.

While politicians schemed and editors railed, most Unionville residents went about their usual Sunday routines. Folks attending church heard little that was new.

At First Baptist, Brother Byrd prayed more directly for "peaceful resolution of the crisis in Little Rock and good will among all people," and having read their morning papers, a larger number of the congregation took notice. Much to Sam's disappointment, Becky was not there.

At Mount Zion Baptist, Reverend Moseley repeated cautions he had been issuing for two weeks now.

At Mercy Baptist Mission, Brother Spurlock reported that someone from southern Arkansas—he did not know who—had sent Faubus a petition with more than three hundred signatures complimenting him for his stand against integration.

"I'm ashamed," Spurlock said, "that our congregation didn't take part in that effort and that we ain't doing more to support our governor, and I aim to take steps. I'll be calling on you faithful people to help out and I know I can count on you."

He did not say what he had in mind. He did not have to. Most in his congregation would follow wherever he led.

About eleven o'clock, three Unionville residents who had not followed their normal Sunday morning routines were beginning to wish they had. Jim Ed Davis pulled his battered pickup to the side of the highway about two miles north of Sheridan and thirty miles south of Little Rock. He opened his door, climbed out, and stood, hands on hips, while traffic swerved to avoid him. His passengers piled out of the other door and stormed around to his side.

"Dadblame it, Jim Ed! How could you run out of gas?" Odell Grimes whined in disbelief. Although it was September, it had been hot in the crowded cab and sweat dripped off the barber's round face onto his massive stomach. "How stupid are you?"

"I thought you filled it up when we stopped back yonder in Fordyce," Jim Ed said. He spun around and threw his faded International Harvester baseball cap to the ground. "You moron!" he shouted, turning back to Odell, "You said you'd pay for the gas if I'd do the driving. I told you when I went to take a crap we was gon' need gas. Why the hell do you think I parked by the goddamn gas pump?"

"Well, you didn't say we needed it right then," Odell came back. "Why didn't you say so! Besides, I had to go too. I was near about to pee my britches."

"I didn't see you going to the rest room!"

"I didn't. I went over behind that big dump truck."

"Goddamn it!" Jim Ed yelled, throwing his hands up. "Don't you know something like that could get us arrested before we do what we came for? Fordyce is a county seat. It ain't no hick town like Unionville. You're lucky nobody saw you."

"Nobody seen me but some snot-nosed kid."

"Did he say anything?"

"I don't know. I couldn't really tell," Odell said, putting his hands in his pockets.

"What'd he say?" Jim Ed demanded. "I know damn well he said something. I can tell by the dumb-ass look on your face."

"I ain't gon' tell you."

"Damn it, Odell! Did he say anything about calling the cops? He could have got my license number. You better tell me."

"I can't."

"If you don't tell me," Jim Ed threatened, "I'm gon' make you walk back to Sheridan to get the gas."

"He said 'mine's bigger than yours.'"

Jim Ed and Unionville night watchman Crow Hicks, the other passenger, doubled over with laughter. Odell stood motionless for a moment then took a swing at Jim Ed, missed, and fell against the side of the truck, ripping his trousers and skinning his leg.

"Dadblame it! Now look what you made me do!" he hollered. "I ruined my best pants."

"I told you this wasn't no dress-up trip," Jim Ed said. "Why didn't you wear hunting clothes like me?"

"Come on!" Crow said, using the back of his hand to wipe tobacco juice off his chin. "Cut the crap! What're we gon' do about gas? I want to get going and shoot me some coons." He was wearing his night watchman's badge and packing his Smith & Wesson revolver.

Inspired by Upshaw's editorial, the three men had left Unionville a little more than two hours earlier intent on joining one of the caravans of armed men they had been hearing about. They did not know exactly where they would find such a group, or what they would do when they got to Little Rock, but they figured that would become clear when they arrived. It was enough just to be armed and on the way. Two .12-gauge shotguns—an automatic and a double-barrel—hung in the rack behind the seat. Odell did not own a gun, but Jim Ed had left his twenty-two at home and brought a shotgun for his barber.

"All right, all right!" Jim Ed said. "I'll go get the gas. Y'all stay in the truck."

"It's hot in there," Odell complained.

"All right. Sit over there in the shade and don't go wandering off. Some idiot might come along and steal something."

"I'm hungry," Crow said. "Bring back something to eat."

"No! I ain't gon' do it. We'll eat when we get to Little Rock."

"You can at least get some goobers and moon pies."

"No!"

"Damn it!" Crow snapped. "Next time we're gon' come in my truck. It don't run good, but at least I know how to keep gas in it!" He drove a dilapidated gray Chevy with a Confederate flag painted on the tailgate.

"Bull shit! You ain't got no more sense than Odell," Jim Ed

said. He picked up his cap and started walking.

A little more than an hour later, a Texaco attendant brought Jim Ed back. Odell and Crow were asleep on the ditch bank, the passenger door of the truck was standing open, and an empty Bell jar was sitting on the running board. They had drunk a whole quart of moonshine. After the Texaco guy emptied a two-gallon can into the gas tank, Jim Ed poured a few drops into the top of the carburetor and cranked the engine. When the man left, Jim Ed walked over to his traveling companions and roused them enough to get them into the truck. Both were snoring when he reached Little Rock and pulled into a Gulf station.

After the attendant filled the tank and Jim Ed paid up and got directions to the capitol, he shook Odell and Crow. "Wake up! We're here."

"I'm hungry," Crow said, stretching.

"We ain't got time to eat. We're going to the capitol."

"What's there?"

"Faubus, you moron, and maybe them armed caravans he's been talking about," Jim Ed said, starting the engine.

"I got to pee," Odell said.

"You always got to pee," Jim Ed said, driving away from the gas pump. "We ain't got time. We're going to the capitol."

"Jim Ed, if you don't stop, I'm gon' pee my pants."

"Stop the damn truck!" Crow growled. "I got to go too."

"Aw, shit!" Jim Ed said, slamming on the brakes just before pulling onto the highway. "Y'all ain't nothing but trouble."

They were barely on the road again before Crow started begging Jim Ed to stop for food. He had to admit he was hungry, too, and he pulled into the parking lot of Mac's Diner, one of those shiny stainless-steel places popular with truck drivers and cops.

"This reminds me of Emmett's," Crow said, after they got inside. Jim Ed led the way to a booth and Odell followed and slid in opposite him. Crow plopped down next to Odell, with one leg in the aisle and his Smith & Wesson in plain view. He cut his eyes around the room then leaned toward his buddies. "Why's everybody looking at us?" he asked.

In a few moments, a middle-aged waitress came over with menus. She wore a hair net and a pink uniform with a name tag.

"We don't need menus, Mary," Jim Ed said, sitting up straighter and acting in charge. "Bring us all coffee and a stack of pancakes. We're in a hurry."

"I don't want no pancakes, Jim Ed. I want a hamburger," Odell said.

"Me too," Crow added.

"All right, coffee and three hamburgers, everything on them. Bring us some fries too."

They were about halfway through their meal when a Pulaski County sheriff's cruiser carrying two deputies pulled into the parking lot and stopped next to Jim Ed's truck. He watched them through the window as they got out, walked around the pickup, and looked in the windows and the back. They were wearing sunglasses, cowboy boots, western-style hats, and uniforms with sharp creases on the pants and shirts. When they finished their inspection, they came into the diner and stood just inside the doorway looking all around, glasses still on and thumbs hooked into belts holding nightsticks and pistols. After a few moments, they walked over to the booth where Jim Ed, Odell, and Crow were sitting.

"You boys belong to that old International out there?" the first deputy asked. He was tall, dark, and built like a Green Bay Packer. His face was blank under his dark glasses.

"Yeah," Jim Ed said. "It's mine. Is there a problem?"

"Don't know yet," the officer answered. "That truck's got a southern Arkansas plate. Where're y'all from?"

"Unionville," Crow said. "I'm the night watchman down there and I sure like meeting other lawmen. My name's Waylon Hicks but y'all can call me Crow. Everybody does."

"You got a license to carry that pistol, Mr. Hicks?" the officer asked.

Crow fished in his bib overalls, brought out his wallet, and produced the document. The officer took it, handed it to his partner, and asked, "What're you boys doing up here in Little Rock? You visiting somebody or something?"

"No, sir," Crow said. "We come up here to join one of them armed caravans and keep the coloreds out of y'all's schools."

"That's right," Odell piped up, feeling important. "We're gon' help the governor."

The second deputy, shorter, but also dark, muscular, and just as somber looking as his partner, shifted his weight, drew in a long breath, and let it out loud enough for everyone in the place to hear. "Governor Faubus is doing his best to keep armed ya-hoos like you out of Little Rock," he said.

Jim Ed slouched down in his seat. This wasn't going the way he planned.

The deputy handed back Crow's gun permit. "I tell you what, boys. I want you to put five dollars on the table then get up, go outside, and get in your truck. Then I want you to start it up, head south, and don't stop till y'all get back to Unionville. We're gon' be behind you until you get out of Pulaski County. If y'all so much as look back, we're gon' show all three of you the inside of the county jail."

"I sure would like to see y'all's pokey," Crow said. "I got a cousin what works at the Louisiana state pen down in Angola. Ouch! Quit punching me, Jim Ed!"

"Let's go! Get a move on!" the second deputy growled.

The trio scrambled to their feet but not fast enough to suit the first officer. He shoved Odell through the door then stood on the front steps with his partner and watched while Jim Ed and his buddies hustled into the pickup.

When the one-vehicle armed caravan was a couple of miles down the highway, Crow asked, "What are we gon' do now?"

"I don't know," Odell said, "but I think I peed my pants."

"Goddamn you, goddamn Upshaw, and goddamn that rag of his," Jim Ed said. "Just you wait till get my hands on that lying son of a bitch."

CHAPTER 22

On Sunday night, Faubus went on television again, this time to defend his use of the National Guard. He maintained that armed men still planned to come to Little Rock and cause trouble and said he intended to keep the guardsmen in place. Within hours, groups bigger and more menacing than Jim Ed Davis's motley crew seemed to prove the governor right. Before dawn on Monday, carloads of angry segregationists with guns drove from West Memphis, Blytheville, and other eastern Arkansas towns to Little Rock. When they saw the guardsmen, though, they turned around and went home. Despite their quick departure from the capital city, its mayor said, "The governor's defiant words and his actions come straight out of that period in our history when irresponsible men plunged this nation into a tragic Civil War."

On Monday morning, Becky rolled out her new lesson plans. She did not believe the growing crisis merited quite the dramatic comparison that the Little Rock mayor did, but she saw clear similarities and connections to earlier controversies about race and states' rights. She knew, however, that her students viewed the events in more personal terms.

Earlier they had asked: "Why do Negroes want to go to white schools? Will we have to let them? Who will make us?

Won't going to school with them hold us back? Will Negro kids eat in the lunch room with us? Will they ride our buses? What will happen if we just stay home? Is there going to be a war?"

Becky knew if she answered these questions the way she would like to, she would aggravate more than a few parents and probably school officials. But she was committed to good teaching and was more than a little pigheaded, so she decided to ditch the entire textbook approach to seventh-grade American history. She planned to teach things the students wanted to know and, in her opinion, they could use now.

The textbook started with the early explorers and moved through colonization, the American Revolution, westward expansion, the Civil War, industrialization, and the world wars. Knowing her students had already studied some of this in lower grades and would have another US history course in high school, Becky decided to start with the federal system of government and the Constitution, jump quickly to the Civil War and Reconstruction, and tie it all together with current events. She briefly considered whether she should tell Principal Woodhead and Lily Poindexter, the other seventh grade teacher, and decided not to. Neither Mrs. Woodhead nor anyone else had provided any instructions or guidance about proceeding through the textbooks page by page, but Becky still figured it was best to keep quiet about not doing it.

As soon as she finished her administrative reports, she asked her students to arrange their desks in six circles with five desks in each, then she handed a typewritten sheet to one student in each circle.

"Starting today," she said, "we're going to have social studies first thing in the morning and look at some of the questions you've asked about what's happening in Little Rock and why it's happening and how it might affect you." She told them they would work in groups until time for math then put their desks back in rows. Before she could explain further, Barbara Ames raised her hand.

"Yes, Barbara, what is it?"

"Miss Reeves, we're supposed to do math first."

"Barbara, I've decided to do social studies first so that from now on you can circle your desks while I'm filling out my reports. That way we'll have more time for math when we get to it later."

"Yes, Linda?" Becky said to a slender, blond-haired girl waving her hand from the middle of the room.

"What are we going to do in groups, Miss Reeves?"

"You're going to decide that partly for yourselves," Becky said, responding to Linda Perkins, granddaughter of Doc Perkins. "In each group, you will work on questions I give you for each unit, then you will share your answers with the rest of the class. You can do that however you want so long as you give some kind of verbal summary, like a talk or a skit, and make some kind of visual summary, like a drawing or a poster. After all the group presentations for each unit, each of you will write an essay about what you think is the most important thing you've learned." When she paused, Glen Ray Plunkett raised his hand.

"Yes, Glen Ray?" she asked.

"What're you gon' do while we're working? Ain't you gon' do no teaching?"

Becky smiled. "I'll give you an introduction to each unit and help each group as you go along." She looked around for any other hands then said, "Each group will have a different leader for every unit so everyone will have a turn. For starters, the group leaders will be those of you to whom I've given the assignment sheets—Linda Perkins, Barbara Ames, Carol Mason, Kenneth Greer, Glen Ray Plunkeet, and Billy Tate. I want each leader to get things started by reading your group's assignment aloud to the other members. Do it quietly so as not to disturb the other groups. Tomorrow I will provide mimeographed copies for everyone."

That night, again, Becky was the chief topic of conversation in several Unionville homes.

In the Ames household, the Ark-La-Tex Oil accountant was beside himself all through supper. "That woman is ruining things for Barbara," Howard said to his wife after their daughter had gone to bed. "I've got to get over there and let Mrs. Woodhead know we expect her to put a stop to this nonsense."

At the Plunkett house, Bobby Jack was also steaming, but for a different reason.

"First, you can't say 'nigger,' and now, you have to help her teach the class. That ain't right! I'm going over to that school first chance I get."

"Pops, I kind of liked being the leader of my group," Glen Ray said.

"Hell, boy, reading to a bunch of kids ain't leading. That ain't gon' teach you nothing. Being a general in the army is leading. Calling plays on a football field is leading. Giving orders to your dolly man is leading." Bobby Jack was so proud of his delivery-man's job that he had painted his pickup truck Coca-Cola red. "You ain't gon' learn nothing from play acting and poster making. That stuff's for sissies."

At the Tate home, school did not come up until everyone except Mary Jane was helping clean up after supper.

"So, what are the three branches of government, son?" Sam asked, when Billy mentioned having studied about them.

"Well," Billy said, taking a soapy plate from Sam and dipping it in hot rinse water, "there are three of them. First, there's the legislative branch—that's the Congress. It makes the laws. Then there's the executive branch—that's the president. It carries out the laws. And then there's the judicial branch—that's the courts. It explains the laws and settles arguments when people don't agree about them. I think Miss Reeves said that part's called 'interpreting.' Anyway, it's real interesting, Daddy, and it's all right there in the Constitution. Miss Reeves has a book with the whole thing in it."

"'Really,' Billy, not 'real,'" Sam said. "But, hey, I'm impressed. You learned a lot today. What do you think, Momma? I bet we've got us a lawyer in the making here."

Gran stopped wiping the table and looked over at Sam. "Well, Billy's sure enough smart," she said. "I just hope that woman don't get him all mixed up. She don't know how we do things down here, and there ain't no telling what she's teaching them kids. You better keep an eye on her."

"You know, Momma," Sam said, "that's exactly what I intend to do."

CHAPTER 23

When the fire siren went off a few minutes after two o'clock on Tuesday morning, its shrill whine jolted just about everyone in Unionville out of bed. People rushed to their windows or onto their porches to look for flames or an orange glow that would tell them where the fire was, and seeing none, they waited for the sound of the fire truck. It did not have a muffler, and the teeth-jarring racket it made when it got on the road was another way to tell where the fire might be. Meanwhile, volunteer fire fighters from both sides of town jumped into their clothes, ran to their cars and trucks, and headed for the firehouse.

"Can I go, Daddy? Please?" Billy begged, as Sam pulled on his shoes.

Mary Jane was also up, and echoing her brother. "Can I go too, Daddy? I'm big enough. I want to go too."

The children always asked to go when the siren went off at night, and a couple of times when Sam did not see a big blaze, he had let Billy tag along under strict orders to stay in the pickup.

"No. This is a school night," Sam said, avoiding the issue of who was and was not old enough. "Besides, I didn't see anything when I looked out. It's probably just a false alarm. Y'all go on back to sleep. I'll be home in a little while."

When Sam got to the highway and turned south toward town, he saw the fire truck heading toward him, siren blaring

and cab light hurling red streaks onto the houses along Main
Street. When it came alongside, he saw a truck driver from
Bowman Lumber Company behind the wheel and fire chief
Lester Grimes riding shotgun. Odell Grimes, Crow Hicks, and
Norm Patterson, an electrician at Ark-La-Tex Oil, were stand-
ing on the rear platform hanging onto handrails. Other fire fight-
ers trailed behind in their own vehicles. Sam edged to the curb,
reached under his seat for his new fire helmet, and got ready to
make a U-turn. Seconds later, Neal O'Brien signaled from his
City Hardware truck for Sam to cut in ahead of him.

Sam still did not see any sign of a blaze when the fire truck
turned right after just two blocks and headed east toward South
Arkansas Oak Flooring. Seconds later it slowed in front of Mt.
Zion Baptist Church. People were standing around out front,
and Sam figured there must have been a minor electrical fire and
they had already put it out.

Then, in light from the fire truck's high beams, he saw
it—a smoldering wooden cross leaning tall against the church's
charred lawn sign. There was no mistaking what had happened.
He had never seen a cross burning but he had heard plenty about
them.

He pulled to the side of the road, got out, and smelled the
stink of engine exhaust, smoldering wood, and burned grass.
Other men stopped their vehicles behind him and ran to catch
up, but there was little for them to do. Neal came up beside
him and they walked forward together bareheaded. There was
no need for helmets. Odell and Crow were standing in front
of the fire truck, hands on hips, staring. Lester and some of the
other first arrivals were hooking up a hose to spray the dying
embers and make sure the lawn did not catch up again. About a
dozen black men stood quietly a little way beyond the fire truck,

between the cross and the church. They had used a garden hose to douse the fire before the truck arrived. Sam could make out Reverend Moseley, Leon Jackson, B. J. Long, Otis Henderson, and other Black Tigers among them.

"What the hell?" Neal said, as Preston Upshaw ran past with his camera, bumping into people. "Damned fool." Neal rubbed his elbow. "I never thought I'd see anything like this around here. We haven't been having any trouble with the coloreds."

"Maybe someone got all worked up about what's happening in Little Rock," Sam said.

"Yeah. Could be. You see Mr. Claude anywhere? I don't think there's any law against burning crosses, but burning that church sign is vandalism."

"Maybe he wasn't able to catch a ride. I don't see Jesse either."

Jesse Culpepper, a Union County sheriff's deputy, lived up the highway a few miles and was assigned to patrol Unionville. He did not do much, though, except drive around town now and again, stop at Emmett's Café for coffee, and jawbone with whittlers under the big sycamore tree across the street. The rest of the time he just cruised up and down the highway and main county roads, occasionally stopping a speeder or responding to an accident.

"I'll ask Lester if he's seen them," Neal said. "I'm gon' get ahold of Sheriff Eubanks, too, and see if we can get a couple of extra patrol cars down here for the next night or two—just so people don't get nervous and start shooting at each other or something."

No whites had approached the group of black men, and Sam walked toward them, past the charred cross and the knot of fire fighters around it. Gran had told him how his granddaddy and his night rider friends burned crosses during Reconstruction, but those were only stories to him. This was real. The thing stood wet, foul-smelling, and threatening, never mind that who-ever put it there had run away in the dark. It was made of two-by-fours wrapped in burlap and was burned so badly Sam could not tell whether the boards were new or old. That would not have been much of a clue anyway. Nearly everyone had loose boards lying around somewhere. Sam guessed whoever put it there made it beforehand, brought it in a truck, leaned it against the sign, then poured kerosene or something on it to make it burn easily.

"Sure is a pretty sight, ain't it?" Odell Grimes asked, as Sam passed. "This'll make the coloreds around here think twice be-fore they try to pull any of that integration crap."

"Damn straight!" Crow said.

Sam stopped. "Did you boys do this?" he asked.

"No," Crow said. "I wish I had, though."

"Sam!" Lester Grimes said, jumping to his brother's defense. "You ain't got no right accusing anybody. Why don't you just mind your own business?"

"This is my business," Sam said. "It's town business and I'm on the council. Why don't you just do what you're supposed to do and spray that mess down again? And don't move it until Mr. Claude sees it."

"Who do you think you're ordering around? I know what to do. I'm the fire chief. Remember?"

"Then act like it," Sam snapped.

Meanwhile, the crowd continued to swell, and Upshaw stopped taking pictures and started looking for people to inter-view. He began with the fire chief and the night watchman.

When Sam reached Reverend Moseley and the folks stand-ing with him, they glanced at each other, and all except Leon inched back.

"Evening, everybody. I'm sorry about y'all's sign. Anybody see who did it?"

"No, sir, Mr. Sam," Moseley said. "Otis was getting coffee, and when he heard tires spinning and looked out, the thing was already burning and there wasn't anybody around."

"Otis, you were in the church at this hour?" Sam asked.

"Mr. Sam," Leon said, before Otis could answer, "ever since Mrs. Bates was threatened up at Little Rock, some of us have been worrying something like this might happen. We've been taking turns watching the church."

"We had to keep an eye on it," Moseley said, "but we'd sure appreciate it if you didn't tell anybody. It might make things worse."

"I don't see any reason to mention it," Sam said, "especially since no one saw anything. Anyway, we're gon' try to get the sheriff to do some more patrolling to make sure it doesn't happen again. Y'all probably want to clean up that mess as soon as you can, but you ought to leave it till Deputy Culpepper and Mr. Claude see it."

"Mr. Sam," Moseley said, "we got to get that thing down tonight. We don't want our children to see it. It'd scare them."

"Yeah, I guess it would. I'll see if I can hurry things up."

When Sam walked out of earshot, Leon said, "Y'all see, I told you. He's all right."

As Sam expected, all the Tates came to breakfast Tuesday morning wanting to hear about the fire. He had spent the rest of the night thinking about what to tell them. Seeing the men he played ball with act skittish with him and scared for their families bothered him. He knew his mother would not see things the way he did, and he did not believe Mary Jane needed to hear about it at all. However, he wanted Billy to understand what had happened, because other kids probably would be talking about it at school.

After everyone loaded their plates with pancakes, sausage patties, and syrup, Sam said, "All right. Here's what happened last night." He thought if he began in a way Mary Jane could follow, there would be less chance that anything Gran said or Billy asked would upset her. "Some bad men decided to scare some other people by burning a cross in their yard. It wasn't a nice thing to do, but no one was hurt, and the bad men won't do it again."

"How do you know the bad men won't do it again?" Mary Jane asked.

"Well, sweetheart," Sam said, "your daddy and Mr. Claude— you know who he is, he makes sure everyone obeys the laws— believe the bad men were just trying to get attention. But they know now that playing with fire and scaring people is bad."

"Where'd they burn it, Daddy?" Billy asked. "Was it Ku Kluxers like Gran's told us about? Were they wearing robes?"

Sam told where then said he did not believe there were any Klan members around Unionville.

"I figured this was gon' happen sooner or later," Gran said. "I been telling Emma Lou and Almalee that if we had a few night riders like when my daddy was alive, it would put a stop to all this integration mess."

"Momma, did you ever see a cross burning?" Sam asked.

"Nope. Always wished I had, though."

"Well," Sam said, reaching for another sausage patty, "it's not a very pretty sight. When you stand there looking at it and thinking about how somebody sneaked up with it, set it on fire, then ran away, it seems mean and cowardly. The people who go to that church didn't do anything to deserve something like that. I keep thinking about how scared Mary Jane would be if somebody did that to us, and it doesn't make me feel very good."

"Aw, Sam, nobody's gon' do that to us. And I'm telling you again, the only way to make coloreds stay in their place is to show them who's boss."

"Momma, like I said before, I don't know how much longer we're gon' be able to keep whites and coloreds separate. Doc Perkins is about the smartest man I know, and he believes integration is coming, like it or not."

Gran pushed her plate back and glared at her son. "Sam, you ought to be ashamed saying something like that in front of these kids. You ain't getting to be for it, are you? Good lord in heaven! Your daddy would turn over in his grave!"

"Daddy, are you an integrationist?" Billy asked.

"Son," Sam said. "Remember when you threw those rocks at Crazy Dan because you wanted to scare him and all it did was hurt him and make you feel bad?"

"Yes, sir."

"Well, all I'm saying is that whoever burned that cross last night was trying to scare someone and hurt them and their families, and I don't feel good about it. Do you understand that?"

"Yes, sir, but are you an integrationist?"

"Billy, I'm just a man who's trying to figure out what's right," Sam said.

"You mean you don't know, Daddy?"

"Son, I'm not sure just how I feel about it right now, but don't you worry about it. It's all right not to know something and take time to think it through."

Gran did not say anything but Sam could see she was seething.

"Daddy, can't you answer Billy's question?" Mary Jane asked.

She was looking for a way to get back into a conversation that was over her head.

"No, sweetheart, I can't, but I'm studying about it. Do you understand that?"

"No, sir."

"Well, it's like you learning your letters and numbers. If I keep trying, I'll figure it out."

When Ollie Mae Greene arrived after breakfast, neither she nor Gran mentioned what happened the night before. They had not talked about the ruckus in Little Rock since it began, and neither of them wanted to bring up the cross burning. Each knew that doing so would hurt how they got along every day and threaten a work situation she needed to hold onto.

Emma Lou MacDonald and Almalee Jolly would be arriving soon and wanting to talk about it, though, so Gran, thankful that her arm and shoulder were not hurting the way they did yesterday, went to the front porch to wait for them. Mary Jane followed her out and headed for the tire swing.

The quilting partners drove up in Almalee's Ford promptly at nine o'clock. Emma Lou scrambled out of the passenger side as quickly as her stout frame would allow, grasping her quilting bag in one hand and straightening her dress with the other.

"Ida Belle," she called from the driveway, "did you hear the news? Somebody must've heard you talking about those night riders."

"Wait!" Almalee said. "You left the door open again."

"Oh, shoot! Who cares about your blamed old door," Emma Lou said, turning back to close it. "I want to hear what Sam said about last night."

Almalee hurried to climb the porch steps first.

"I heard up at the post office that the whole Mt. Zion congregation was crying and carrying on like babies," she said. "Is that what Sam said too? I heard he was talking to some of them. Did Ollie Mae come to work today? She's goes to that church, don't she?"

"Yeah, she's here," Gran said. "Mary Jane!" she called. "You play out here a little longer, hon, then tell Ollie Mae I said to give you some lemonade." Gran did not want to scare the little girl any more than Sam did.

Emma Lou and Almalee filed into Gran's sitting room and took their usual seats. "Okay, Ida Belle," Almalee said, not bothering with her bag of cloth and thread. "Tell us what Sam said. We know he was there. You said somebody ought to do something like this and they did."

"There ain't nothing to tell," Gran said. She reached into her sewing basket. "It was done out when he got there."

"Did he say anything about who did it?" Emma Lou asked, as she began to sew.

"Nope. I don't guess anybody knows."

"Well, if I was betting, and I'm not," Emma Lou said, "I'd bet on Boomer Jenkins. I heard him tell a colored woman up at the Feed and Seed one day, 'If you don't get out of my way, I'm gon' take my knife and skin you right here.' Shoot! That even scared me."

"It wouldn't surprise me none if it was that old Crazy Dan Malone," Almalee said. "He gives me the creeps pushing that wheelbarrow around all the time and rooting through people's trash."

"Aw, Almalee, he's not smart enough to burn a cross," Emma Lou said, "and anyway, he couldn't have managed all the makings.

Besides, why would he want to? He practically lives with col-oreds down there at Bowman's mill."

"Let's talk about something else," Gran said. She was still struggling with how her son no longer seemed to agree with her about black people.

"All right, Ida Belle," Emma Lou said. "How're you coming with your memory quilt?"

CHAPTER 24

Neal O'Brien was setting out merchandise in front of City Hardware when Sam got to the Otasco store. He had taken longer than usual for breakfast. Neal watched him park, waited while a tractor-trailer rig rolled by, then hustled across the street. Sam saw him coming, opened one of the big front doors, and waited.

"Morning, Sam," Neal said, and did not wait for a reply. "The mayor said he'd call the sheriff this morning and see about getting some more patrols down here. I've been thinking about it, though, and I don't believe it'll happen again. Whoever did it probably just got all worked up, and now that he's got it out of his system, that'll be the end of it."

Sam said he hoped so, and Neal asked if he had been the one who had started the hat passing around. By custom, when a fire destroyed a house, barn, or other property, someone took up a collection to help the victim, white or black. Sam said he had. Then he asked if Neal had seen Jim Ed Davis at the fire.

"Come to think of it, I didn't," Neal said. He reached for a bicycle to set out. "You think he did it?"

"Well, it's the sort of thing he might think of and it's strange he didn't show up. He doesn't usually miss a fire. Of course, that's no proof. Heck, Crow Hicks is another one who could've done it."

"But he was on the fire truck," Neal said, taking a tire stand from Sam.

"He could've put the cross out, lit it up, and driven straight to the firehouse and been there when the call set off the siren," Sam said. "He knows we don't have any way of checking on his whereabouts."

"You think we ought to ask him about it?"

Sam rolled out the tool rack. "I don't know. I sort of did last night. He denied it, of course." He paused then said, "I suppose we ought to just wait and see if anything else happens or anyone starts talking."

As Neal was leaving, Miss Ruthelle arrived. She had heard the news from neighbors who had driven to the scene, but she still had questions for Sam. It was the same all over town. Everyone was talking about it. As soon as the Grimes brothers opened the barbershop and newsstand, Lester headed straight for the Otasco store. His desire to shoot the breeze with somebody other than Odell had overcome his anger with Sam from the night before.

"Hey, Miss Ruthelle," the butterball fire chief called in high spirits. "Did you hear the one about the Irish priest and the French madam?"

"Lester Grimes!" Miss Ruthelle said, swiveling in her chair and glaring over the office counter. "Don't you start with me this morning!"

He laughed and continued through the store until he found Sam out back stacking old car batteries on the loading dock for salvage.

"Hey, Sam. That was some doing last night, wasn't it? I bet them coloreds was scared, wasn't they? You talked to them. What'd they say?"

"The ones I talked to were mostly worried about their kids."

"Well, I hope they was scared. That's the whole point of

burning a cross. Scare them good so they'll stay in their place."

"Lester, you seem mighty pleased about all this," Sam said, lifting another battery. "Do you know who did it?"

"You're damn right I'm pleased. But no, I don't know who did it. Whoever it was, though, I'd like to shake his hand."

"Have you seen Boomer Jenkins lately?"

"Nope. You accusing him now?"

"No, I just haven't seen him in a while."

"Well, too bad he wasn't there. He'd have got a kick out of it."

Unlike Lester, Preston Upshaw did not care to talk to anyone but Pearl the morning after. He had gotten what he wanted the night before.

"Listen to this," he said, while she was getting coffee. He had been transcribing his notes and motioned her to a chair across from his desk. His coat was flung over one corner and he had not shaved or eaten. "It's from the volunteer fire chief. He said, 'It's about time somebody did more than talk about them coloreds getting uppity.' And here's another good one. It's from some guy named Bobby Jack Plunkett. He said, 'This'll make the coloreds think twice before they try to go to our schools.' And this one's from that Crow fellow, the Arkansas-side night watchman. He said, 'They ought to give whoever done this a medal.' This is good stuff. People are starting to wake up."

"That's surely a bunch of fine upstanding citizens you've got there," Pearl said. She got up and moved to her own desk. "You don't intend to print that stuff, do you?"

"Sure I do. It'll help folks stiffen their backbones, get them off their duffs. And it's gon' help sell subscriptions and advertising too. You'll see."

162

"Did you ask any of the church members what they thought?"

"Nope. No one cares what they think."

Before Pearl could reply, Elmer Spurlock came barging into the office wearing his size triple-X painter's coveralls and smelling of turpentine and cigarette smoke. Upshaw had never met the man, and he did not look like someone who would buy ads. "What do you want?" the editor growled.

"Morning, Mr. Upshaw," he said. "I'm Brother Spurlock, pastor of the Mercy Baptist Mission, out on Newton Chapel Road, and I'm a fan of yours."

"Is that so?" Upshaw said, rising from his desk with quickly gained interest. Nothing about the man suggested he was a preacher, but he had certainly started off the conversation fine. "What can I do for you?"

"Well, sir, I believe you and me see eye to eye about coloreds, and I think maybe we can help each other."

"Yeah? Then have a seat over here and tell me what's on your mind. Mrs. Goodbar, we got any more mugs anywhere?"

"Look in the cabinet under the hot plate," she said, keeping her eyes on her work and trying not to look too interested in what Spurlock had in mind.

"Mr. Upshaw," the preacher began, "I want the same thing you do. I want to see to it we don't end up like Little Rock. I don't believe God intended for whites and coloreds to mix, and I plan to do all I can to keep it from happening down here."

"We're in agreement so far," Upshaw said. He handed his guest a mug of coffee.

"I want to organize a chapter of the White Citizens' Council in Unionville, and I came to ask for your help. I think we need to get upstanding, right-minded people together and send a message to the governor that we're behind him and, at the same time, let the coloreds around here know we ain't never gon' tolerate integration. I've got some organizing literature and a place to meet, but I need help getting the word out. I'm hoping you'll run an announcement in the paper and maybe print up some flyers."

Upshaw felt almost like jumping out of his chair and shouting but he caught himself in time to keep the upper hand. "Brother Spurlock, I don't know you, and I'm not in the business of running free ads or printing flyers, but I tell you what. I agree that Unionville needs a Citizens' Council, so I'm gon' help you out. But don't tell anybody I gave you anything for free. First thing you know, all kinds of folks would be in here looking for handouts. When are you gon' have your first meeting and where's it gon' be?"

"It's gon' be out at my church on a Thursday night so it won't interfere with Wednesday prayer meeting. Friday would be better, but folks won't come when there's a football game. Let's say the twenty-sixth."

As Upshaw got up to signal the end of the meeting, he said, "I didn't see you over at that colored church last night. Were you there?"

"No. I live too far out to hear the siren. A couple of church members told me about it this morning. They said they tried to call me last night, but I was so tired from painting that I was plumb dead to the world and didn't hear the phone. And my wife's over to Magnolia. Her momma's sick."

"Well, Brother Spurlock, it's too bad you weren't there. It was a beautiful expression of free speech in action."

Becky had heard the siren and the fire truck but she did not learn about the cross burning until she was almost ready for school. One of Hazel Brantley's friends called her about it, and she came knocking on Becky's door right after hanging up the phone.

"They say nobody saw anything and they don't know who did it," Hazel said, "and they say the Negroes were bawling and taking on something awful."

Becky had not been prepared for anything like this. Being in a state where the governor used the National Guard to defy federal authority was one thing. Being in a town where someone burned a cross was something else. Her mother's warning flashed through her mind again and a shiver shot up her back.

"Thanks for letting me know," she said. "I expect a lot of the children will know, too, and they'll want to talk about it. I need to think about how to handle it."

Before going to her classroom, she stopped in the elementary school office to mimeograph a math quiz. The other teachers there were all talking about the cross burning.

"I think it's a good way to keep coloreds from trying to get into our school," one said.

"Yeah. I agree," another said.

No one asked Becky's opinion and she did not offer it. She got to her classroom just before the bell, and as soon as she walked in, the children began asking: "Who did it? What's it mean? What's gon' happen now?"

"All right class," she said, "go ahead and arrange your seats in groups like we discussed yesterday, and as soon as I finish the reports, we'll talk about it."

After Becky slipped the administrative forms into the holder outside the door, she went to the blackboard and wrote six terms in two columns:

Fear	Historical Symbol
Hate	Free Speech
Intimidation	Protest

Then she came around to the front of her desk, looked all around the room, and saw what every good teacher craved—students interested and eager to learn. Every one of them had turned in their seats to face her, waiting for what would happen next.

"Now then," she said, "yesterday, we started looking at how the federal government is organized, but today, we're going to put that on hold for a while and look at what happened here in Unionville early this morning. You will see in time that the two things are related. Because the cross burning happened only a few hours ago, none of us has all the facts, and I haven't had time to write out a lesson about it, but that doesn't matter. We know that sometime after midnight someone placed a wooden cross on the lawn of the Mt. Zion Baptist Church, set it on fire, and left without anyone seeing who did it. The fire fighters came but the blaze destroyed a church sign. Since that time, people have been talking about it all around town. Does anyone know anything more about it, other than that a parent or family friend was there?"

"My daddy said all them coloreds . . . , I mean Negroes, were hollering and crying," Glen Ray Plunkett said.

"Did he see them?" Becky asked.

"No, he said they quit before he got there. He said Crow Hicks told him about it."

"Anyone else?"

"My daddy says it'll cost at least fifty dollars to fix the sign," Barbara Ames added. "He's always right about numbers."

"Does anyone have any additional information to share?" All

were silent. "Okay," Becky said, walking over to the windows so that everyone could see the blackboard, "here's what we're going to do. On the board, I've written six possible reasons why someone might have burned the cross. Each of your groups is going to research why one of those might be the cause. Then you're going to explain it to the rest of the class, using the methods of presentation we talked about yesterday. You're going to need some help, so I will work with each group.

"To begin, I want you to find definitions for each term. Then I want you to search the First Amendment to the Constitution, the chapter on Reconstruction in your American history textbook, and the article on the Ku Klux Klan in the *World Book* and see if you can find examples of actions that are related to the definitions. You can also use two books I brought in this morning. They are on my desk. The first is volume two of *The Growth of the American Republic* by Samuel Eliot Morison and Henry Steele Commager. The second is *Black Reconstruction in America* by W. E. B. DuBois. Both are advanced reading but I'm confident you can use parts of them. You'll have to take turns, though.

"Write your examples down and I'll be around to talk with each group about how you're doing. When we're done with that, we're going to look at how the examples you picked might be similar to what happened here in Unionville. Group one on this side of the room will take the first term in the right-hand column, group two the second, and group three the third. Groups on the other side will do the same for the terms in the left-hand column. Does anyone have any questions?"

—⁓—

On Tuesday night, Becky's name came up yet again in family conversations around town.

"Hon, you mean to say she wasted the whole social studies lesson talking about the cross burning?" Barbara Ames's mother asked as they were setting the supper table.

"Not exactly, Momma. We're trying to find things from a long time ago that help explain it."

"That's the dumbest thing I ever heard of," Howard cut in from the kitchen, where he was making a salad. "It doesn't need any explaining. No one around here wants you kids going to school with coloreds, and someone decided to make it clear to them. It's simple logic."

"Well, Daddy," Barbara said. "It might not be. My group is looking at hate, and the person that burned the cross may have done it just because he hates Negroes. Another group is looking at fear. Some kids think the person who burned the cross wants to scare Negroes, but other ones think maybe the person who burned it is the one that's afraid."

"That's a bunch of baloney," Howard said. "No white people are afraid of coloreds. We just don't want to mix with them." To change the subject, he asked how math had gone. Then before Barbara could answer, he added, "I still intend to speak to Mrs. Woodhead about that woman."

Over at the Plunkett house, Bobby Jack was mad enough to chew nails. Glen Ray was in the group studying fear.

"That crooked-legged bitch is full of dog crap!" Bobby Jack yelled. He pushed back from the kitchen table and paced back and forth. "The man that burned that cross ain't scared of nobody. He may be the only person in town with guts enough to stand up against all these commie bozos that want you to go to school with a bunch of wooly-headed morons. They're the ones that was scared."

"But, Pops, if the man that burned the cross wasn't scared, too, why'd he run off the way he did?"

"Because that's the way cross burning's done, son. It scares the coloreds more if they don't know who did it. They don't know who to watch out for next."

"It sounds like you know a lot about cross burning, Pops. You ever burned any?"

"Well, if I had, boy, I wouldn't tell nobody about it, would I?"

"No, sir, I guess not."

"You're damn right. You just don't go around asking folks that kind of question. Things like that are supposed to be secret. I can tell you one thing, though. I ain't scared of no coloreds. Goddamn that woman!"

At the Tate home, the more Billy talked about his day in class, the farther the distance between Sam and his mother grew.

"I'm in the group that's looking at historical symbols," Billy said, helping himself to more black-eyed peas. "That's easy for me because of Gran's stories. Cross burnings are a way of telling Negroes they're supposed to stay separate. Only, Miss Reeves says they won't have no separate schools once the federal government enforces the law."

"It's 'any,' Billy, 'any separate schools,'" Sam corrected.

"Yes, sir. Anyway, the fear group has the most interesting part. Like you were saying this morning, whoever burned the cross is a coward, else he wouldn't have run off before anyone saw him. Miss Reeves says he's not scared of getting caught. He's scared he's gon' have to mix with coloreds, and that's why he's trying to intimidate them. That's a new word we learned, 'intimidate.'"

"You see, Sam!" Gran cried, red in the face. "That woman's filling his head plum full of nonsense. Didn't I tell you? She don't know what she's talking about. Ain't no cross burner scared of no coloreds! Billy, you don't be paying no attention to her."

"Momma, don't tell the boy that," Sam pleaded. "Of course, he's gon' pay attention to her. She's his teacher. And she's pretty darned smart too. Look how interested he is. When I studied history, all we did was memorize dates. I didn't get much of anything out of it."

"Well, if you ask me," Gran said, "he ain't getting nothing out of it either but a bunch of lies. I'll butt out because he's your son. But you're gon' be sorry you didn't listen to me."

They started arriving at Reverend Moseley's house a block north of Mt. Zion Baptist Church just after nine in the evening. They came in twos and threes, some on foot and some by truck or car. By ten o'clock there were a dozen of them. They waited quietly in the dark, some sitting in homemade cane-bottomed chairs on the narrow front porch and some on the steps. Each cradled a rifle or shotgun.

"What do you men intend to do?" Moseley asked, when the first ones showed up.

"We're gon' protect you and our property," Leon Jackson said. He was carrying a .12-gauge automatic shotgun. "We already saw that just keeping a lookout doesn't help, and the good Lord only knows what other fool ideas some of those jokers have. We don't aim to let them hurt you or the church. A bunch of brothers are over at Mt. Zion with guns right now."

"Y'all best go on home," Moseley said. "Nobody's gon' do

anything else this soon. Whoever did that last night is gon' sit back and enjoy it for a while. Besides, if anybody came around and any of y'all shot at them, you'd be the ones that'd get thrown in jail. Nobody'd take our side."

"You're probably right, Reverend," B. J. Long said, "but what happens to us don't matter as much. Besides, if any of that white trash sees a bunch of black men with guns, they'll probably run like hell. Excuse me, but it's the truth."

"That's right, it is," Ollie Mae Greene's husband said. "My wife heard they all think we was so scared last night that we was crying and carrying on. They won't be expecting us to stand up to them."

"Okay, I'm not gon' argue with you," Moseley said. "I admit my womenfolk are worried. I expect this might help them ease up some."

At half past ten, Mrs. Moseley and their daughter appeared on the porch with iced tea, coffee, pecan pie, and apple fritters. When everyone was served, the women retired, leaving the men to themselves. As time passed, their mood turned lighter.

"B. J., what do y'all expect to do with that twenty-two?" Pete Jones, the Otasco deliveryman, asked. He pointed at B. J.'s bolt-action rifle, now lying on the porch. "Hell, that ain't nothing but a popgun. Sorry, Reverend."

"Why, man," B. J. said, "I can knock the eye out of a squirrel at thirty yards while he's jumping from one tree to another one."

"Yeah, un huh," several men said, laughing.

"Aw, get on away from here," Pete said. "You can't do no such thing. Ain't nobody can shoot that good."

"Leon, you tell him," B. J. said.

"Why, he sure can," Leon said. "I've seen him shoot gnats off

171

a bullfrog without even making him jump."

"Yeah, and I got me a chicken that gives milk," Pete said.

There was a chorus of guffaws.

"I don't care nothing about no twenty-two neither," Otis Henderson said. "I want me something that'll make a lot of noise and a big hole. You throw this old .12-gauge on somebody and work the pump, why he'll mess his pants right where he stands."

"Yeah, you talking now, brother," another of the Mt. Zion faithful said. "Either that or he'll pucker so tight he'll be taking Ex-lax for a month."

There were more guffaws and Moseley and Leon exchanged a look. They knew that although their friends were not afraid for themselves, their wisecracking covered up deep concern for their families.

CHAPTER 25

For the next several days, a lot of folks in Unionville felt like they had as much race trouble as Little Rock. People spent hours speculating about who burned the cross and whether whoever it was would do it again, and they debated whether the two patrol cars Union County Sheriff Floyd Eubanks put to driving around town most every day after midnight were enough to stop it. All the while, Becky's students continued to study ways to account for it.

In Little Rock, the nine black students assigned to Central High School continued to stay home, while federal authorities took new legal actions. The Justice Department requested an injunction to make Governor Faubus stop interfering with court-ordered integration, and a judge granted it and set a hearing for September 20.

Because the cross was burned in the early morning, the *El Dorado Daily News* could not report it until the following day and did not give it much space. Upshaw planned to give it plenty. "Okay, Mrs. Goodbar," he said, handing her several pages as soon as she came in on Thursday morning, "here's our lead story and headline. Let's get cracking."

She took the papers, put her things away, and sat down to read. Under the headline "Burning Cross Says No to Integration,"

Upshaw had written, "In the early hours of Tuesday morning an unknown Unionville patriot made a bold point on behalf of all the white citizens of this proud community. He said no to integration in a courageous act whose meaning cannot be mistaken. Our town's white citizens would do well to thank him and vow to uphold the determined and heroic stand he has made. Our black citizens would do well to take his warning."

As Pearl read on, copyediting as she went, she saw that the piece reported every possible detail, including the quotes Upshaw had read to her from his interviews. Then came the last paragraph: "Our patriot has given us a fine example of free speech in action. Let us follow it and make sure that those who wish to step on the rights of states to manage their own affairs and those who wish to change our way of life in the South understand that all the rest of us clearly and unequivocally say, 'NO!'"

"Don't just sit there, woman," Upshaw demanded. "Get going on the Linotype. We've got a newspaper to get out."

"Mr. Upshaw, aren't you afraid this story will cause more trouble?"

"Well, Mrs. Goodbar, if you mean more good people showing they're not gon' tolerate integration, then no. In fact, I'm expecting it. Now get a move on."

"Did you see the lead story in the *El Dorado Daily News* this morning?" she asked, heading over to the Linotype machine. "Governor Faubus is meeting with President Eisenhower this weekend. Aren't we gon' report that?"

"Yeah, I saw it," Upshaw said. "I'm fixing to do a little piece on it now. It won't take long. They won't settle nothing by talking on some damn golf course."

By Friday there had not been any more trouble in Unionville, and the town's white citizens turned their attention to the first home football game, against the archrival Strong Bulldogs.

Game time was seven o'clock, but teachers and students started getting ready right after lunch. Following a pep rally in the gym, the football coaches mowed and marked the field. High school boys not on the team or in the band pitched in. Band and pep squad members took to the wooden bleachers to practice songs and yells. Becky and other elementary teachers assigned to work the concession stand sent their students to other teachers' classrooms and joined high school faculty members in opening, cleaning, and stocking the little frame building behind the home bleachers. When they finished shortly before five o'clock, they had less than an hour to dash home, clean up, and get back to work the game.

Families of Unionville students involved in the game began showing up a little before six and Strong folks not long after. The smell of hot dogs, hamburgers, and onions on the grill drew them to the concession stand as soon as they stepped out of their banner-draped buses and cars. By six-thirty, the gravel parking lot was full, cars and pickups were parked on side streets for blocks around, and several hundred people had arrived. None wore Sunday-go-to-meeting clothes but almost all were freshly scrubbed for the occasion. Mr. Claude and Crow Hicks were on hand to handle traffic and discourage rowdiness, along with county deputies who were not patrolling highways or pulling duty at games in other towns.

All the Bobcat football regulars followed routines of long habit. Tucker came early with his wife Gloria and brought his backup hearse, which doubled as the town ambulance, just in case a player got injured or some fan got too excited and fell off the bleachers or had a heart attack. He and Gloria, whose kids were in the band, then grabbed seats on the back row along the fifty-yard line. Doc Perkins and Neal O'Brien from City Hardware settled on the next row down with their families, and mill foreman Jack Metcalf and others with boys on the team found spots in surrounding seats. Volunteers lined up to carry the downs marker and yardage chains, and deliveryman Bobby Jack Plunkett and other former players gathered along the sidelines. Sam and Billy walked the four blocks from home and took seats Gloria saved for them. Mary Jane stayed home with Gran.

"Y'all ready for some head knocking?" Tucker asked the Tates when they arrived.

"Yes, sir," Billy said. "I bet we're gon' win tonight."

"This ought to be a good one," Sam said, being careful not to snag his dress pants on a splinter as he sat down. "They should be fired up after last week."

Things did not start well for Unionville. No one worried much when Strong won the coin toss and elected to receive. The Bobcats, wearing black and gold, lined up thinking more about what they would do when they got the ball than about stopping their white-clad opponents. A skinny Bulldog, whose shoulder pads were almost as wide as he was tall, took the kickoff on his own thirty-yard line, and before the dust settled he was standing in the Bobcat end zone.

"Man!" Neal said. "Where'd that kid come from?"

"Two bits, four bits, six bits, a dollar! All for the Bobcats stand up and holler!" the cheerleaders yelled, trying to boost the home side's dampened spirits. That helped the fans, but it was skill on the field that changed Unionville's fortunes. By half-time, Ronnie Metcalf had gained nearly a hundred yards and scored two touchdowns and the Bobcats were leading 20 to 7.

Fans always flocked to the concession stand between halves. Billy usually went right away with his friend Randy Lawson. Sam and Tucker usually waited until the band finished playing then argued all the way about who was buying.

They did not get far this night before Doyle Scoggins caught up to them and started telling about his sister's boy who played for some big school over in Shreveport. He said he was looking forward to putting some miles on his new Chevy going to watch the kid, but tonight's game was way down below Baton Rouge somewhere. Besides, he snorted, "The team down there has a bunch of coon-ass Cajuns on it and they are just about as good-for-nothing as niggers." By that point, Sam had stopped listening. The concession-stand window had come into view and he was looking for Becky. After a moment, he saw her turning toward the counter with a bottle of soda in each hand. She was wearing a black-and-yellow Bobcat vest over a white blouse, a strand of hair had fallen over one eye, and she looked as lovely here as she had in church.

"Sam!" Tucker said. "Didn't you hear me?"

"What? What'd you say?"

"I said, 'I'll buy this time.'"

"Oh, okay." Sam said, as Scoggins peeled off to talk to somebody else.

"Hello, Billy's dad," Becky said, when he and Tucker stepped up to the counter. "What can I get for you?"

"Hi, Becky. Three cokes, please, and say hello to Arlan Tucker. He talks a lot, but aside from being our undertaker, he's harmless. Tucker, Miss Reeves is the new seventh-grade teacher."

"Hi, Becky," Tucker said. "We met at church."

"Yes, that's right," she said. She put three bottles of Coca-Cola

177

on the counter and took the three dimes Sam held out to her. "Are you fellows enjoying the game?"

"Yes," Sam said. "Are you gon' get to see any of it?"

"I wish but I don't think so." She seemed about to say something else, but a woman wearing a Strong booster hat interrupted for popcorn, and Becky managed to say only, "Excuse me," and give a little wave.

As Sam and Tucker walked back to their seats, the stocky undertaker said, "Billy's new teacher sure is a good-looking woman, Sam. Boy, if I wasn't married, I'd be camping on her doorstep."

"You would, huh?"

"Like a bear after honey."

The two friends rejoined Gloria just as Unionville was receiving the second half kickoff. Ronnie returned it to the Strong thirty-five-yard line, scored on a sweep two plays later, and the Bulldogs never got back in the game.

With the outcome no longer in doubt, Sam's thoughts turned again to Becky. He had not asked a woman out in more than fifteen years and the thought of doing so now put butterflies in his stomach. About halfway through the fourth quarter, he asked the Tuckers and Billy if they wanted anything else to drink.

"You can bring me a coke," Tucker said.

"I'll go," Billy offered. "I want one."

"No, that's okay," Sam said. "I need to stretch my legs."

"Hey, Billy," Tucker said, turning and winking at Gloria. "I've been meaning to ask you how the Cardinals are doing."

While Tucker and Billy talked baseball, Sam made his way to the bottom of the bleachers and around to the concession stand. The parking lot was jammed with fans leaving by the carload, so this time he would have a better chance to talk to Becky and less chance of an audience. When he spotted her, she was giving change to the last customer in sight. Some of the other teachers had left already and the rest were getting things ready to close.

"Hi, Sam," she said, smiling, when he walked up. "Need another coke?"

"Hi, Becky. Yeah, three more." He put thirty cents on the counter, watched her fish the bottles out of a tub of ice water, and felt his heart beating faster. When she set the drinks in front of him, he leaned closer.

"What I really want," he said, lowering his voice, smiling, and trying to look playful, "is to know if you like catfish."

"What?" she said, surprised by the question.

"Catfish, do you like catfish?"

"Well, yes. I haven't had it in a long time, but I like it."

"Good," he said, glancing at the other teachers, all still busy. "I thought maybe, well, there's a great catfish place down near Monroe, and I'd love to buy you supper some evening and thank you for getting Billy so interested in history. How about it?"

Surprised again, she answered instinctively, teacher to parent, "Oh, Sam. That's very sweet, and I'd really like to accept, but I'm not sure it's a good idea. With Billy in my class, it could cause problems. But I do thank you."

Sam felt his face sag but he kept trying to smile.

"Well, that's a good point," he said, reaching for the drinks. "But if you change your mind, let me know. It's a standing offer. You have a rain check."

He turned and walked away without looking back. Becky watched until he was out of sight.

On Saturday morning, Preston Upshaw headed next door to Emmett's Café again, confident that this time people would be talking about the latest issue of the *Unionville Times*. As before, he took the last stool near the end of the counter so he could watch the entire room, and once again the only talk he heard was about the Bobcats and the Metcalf boy. Emmett came over to take the editor's order.

"Mr. Ledbetter," Upshaw said, "you're a regular advertiser in the *Unionville Times*. I wonder what you thought about today's issue."

"I ain't seen it. You want coffee?"

"Yeah, I reckon," Upshaw said, "You mean you weren't just a little curious to see what your local paper said about the cross burning?"

"I've done heard everything there is to know about it." Emmett pointed along the counter and toward the booths. "Folks in here ain't talked about nothing else all week."

"I don't hear anything but football this morning."

"That's because that's all there ever is on Saturdays during the season. You eating or not?"

"No, thanks. I think I'll go get a haircut."

His appetite ruined, Upshaw tossed a dime on the counter and headed for the door. Doyle Scoggins looked up from his ham and eggs, started to say something to the editor, but instead only noted his scowl and watched him leave.

As he made his way down the street, Upshaw decided to stop in the Otasco store and ask Sam Tate if he had seen the paper. When Upshaw got there, Sam was setting up a window display of fall sporting goods—everything from rifles and shotguns to footballs and basketballs. Deer-hunting season was weeks away, but squirrel season had opened. And even though the town was currently football crazy, a few boys and lots of girls were already practicing hoops.

"Morning, Mr. Tate," Upshaw said, trying his best to sound friendly.

"Morning," Sam replied without looking up. He put several cartons of ammunition in front of a stand holding seven shotguns and rifles, including a .22-caliber bolt-action with a telescopic sight.

"That's quite an arsenal you've got there," Upshaw observed. "Is that safe?"

"Yeah, the stand's locked. No one's gon' mess with them." Sam grabbed two hunting vests and a pair of skinning knives from a counter behind him.

"What would keep someone like that Crazy Dan fellow from just breaking the window and taking a weapon."

"It'd make too much noise. Someone would get here before he could get the locks off this stand or get it out of the window."

Upshaw glanced at the locks. "Yeah, I guess so. Anyway, I wonder if you saw my story on the cross burning this morning and what you thought about it."

"It so happens I did see it and I didn't care for it."

"Why not? I thought it was a good piece of journalism, if I do say so myself."

"You really want to know what I think, Upshaw?" Sam asked, turning to face his visitor.

"Yeah, that's why I stopped in. I thought maybe by now you could see that I'm turning the *Unionville Times* into a first-rate newspaper."

"Okay, here is it. I think you're more interested in Preston Upshaw than you are in Unionville. I don't much like some of the stuff you're writing. And when that series of ads I bought runs out, I don't think I'm gon' buy any more."

Upshaw glared at Sam for a moment then left without another word.

At the barbershop and newsstand, things started looking up. There, taped inside the glass door facing out, was the front page of the paper with Upshaw's photograph of the Grimes brothers and others spraying water on the charred cross. Lester and Odell both had customers in their chairs but they stopped cutting long enough to praise the story.

"I guess y'all like being celebrities," Upshaw said.

"Yeah," Odell replied, "we have us a couple more cross burnings, and we won't have to worry about Ronnie here having to line up behind no dumb coloreds next year." He patted his customer on the shoulder. "Ronnie, say hello to Mr. Upshaw."

That was more like it, Upshaw thought when he left the barbershop a little later. He saw Horace Bowman's Lincoln in front of the bank as usual and headed across the street. Bowman had bought ads for both the bank and the lumber mill and maybe now he could be persuaded to take bigger ones.

A light was on in the banker's office at the back of the lobby, but there was no receptionist at the desk outside his door, and curtains were drawn over the office windows. Through a crack, Upshaw could see a figure moving inside. With no choice other than to wait, he sat down on a vinyl-covered sofa.

In a few minutes, the office door opened and out came Jim Ed Davis, jaw set and lips tight. Upshaw recognized him from the time in Emmett's with the night watchman and the man with the wooden leg. Jim Ed recognized the newspaperman, too, and broke into a grin.

"Hey, Mr. Upshaw," he said, stopping. "I sure liked what you said in the paper this morning. You're right about the guy that burned the cross. Somebody ought to give him a reward or something."

Upshaw stood up. "I'm afraid you have me at a disadvantage," he said. "I've seen you around but I don't believe we've met."

"I'm Jim Ed Davis and I agree we've got to keep them coloreds in their place."

"Yes, sir, Mr. Davis, and by any means necessary. Say, I see you've been meeting with Mr. Bowman. Is everything alright? You looked worried when you came out." Upshaw was thinking maybe he ought to come back another time.

"No. Everything's fine. Old Bowman's all bark and no bite. You just got to make him the right proposition."

CHAPTER 26

When Sam walked into the First Baptist Church sanctuary on Sunday morning, he could not help looking around for Becky. He had thought about what she said at the football game and he knew she was right. People would talk, kids would hear, and they would tease Billy. Gran would have a fit, too, and while that mattered less, it was hard to dismiss. Still, he could not get Becky out of his mind.

He continued to look for her as he headed for his customary seat, and as he moved up the aisle he could hear that most folks who were not talking about the Strong game were talking about the cross burning. Becky was not there and Sam, disappointed, slid in beside Billy and Mary Jane.

As soon as Brother Byrd took his seat on the podium in front of the choir, folks could tell he was more wound up than usual. His tan suit was rumpled, his brown tie was crooked, sweat was beading on his forehead, and he looked grim, like he had just preached a funeral. His manner did not change when he went to the pulpit after the opening organ music. Instead of the usual fast-paced, bright-shining-light songs, he led the congregation in slow, God-the-Father hymns about Christian love. By the time he got to the second one, people were exchanging glances about the change in routine. Even children noticed the difference.

"Isn't the choir gon' sing?" Billy whispered to Sam.

When Byrd finally put down his hymnal, he picked up his

Bible and in a soft voice read his texts for the day. "Listen to First John, chapter four, verses twenty and twenty-one, 'If a man say, I love God, and hateth his brother, he is a liar; for he that loveth not his brother whom he hath seen, how can he love God whom he hath not seen?' And listen to Luke, chapter three, verse fourteen, 'Do violence to no man.'"

Some in the congregation started squirming in their seats, afraid of where their pastor might be headed. A few started getting hot under the collar.

For a moment after he finished reading, Byrd stood dead still, looking down at his open Bible. Then slowly he raised his head, looked out over the worshipers, and seemed to stare every one of them straight in the eyes.

"I am not an integrationist," he said, still speaking in a quiet, even tone, "but something vile happened in this community this week. And I'm here to tell you," he said, louder now, eyes glaring, "that it does not please the Lord!" Then "No!" he shouted, and banged his fist on the pulpit. "It does not please Him!"

"Amen!" Hollis Cook roared from over in the corner on the second row. The church's oldest deacon had dozed off during the scripture reading and his startled cry added to the congregation's growing unease.

"It doesn't matter what you believe about segregation or integration, about *Brown v. Board of Education,* about Little Rock Central High School, or about Orval Faubus," Byrd said. He moved to the other side of the pulpit and pointed at his audience. "Desecrating a place of worship is a despicable act. It's an act of hatred. It's an act of violence. And it's a sin in the eyes of God!"

Now, even more church members were looking around. Byrd could tell they did not like what he was saying but he kept going.

"I don't know who burned that cross on those church grounds over in the quarters," he said, walking around the pulpit again, "and who it was doesn't really matter. What matters," he shouted, "is that it was done out of hate!" Then, lowering his voice to a loud whisper, he said, "It was done to hurt and intimidate. What matters is how you respond to it. What matters is what you feel in your hearts. What matters is what happens next in our community because of it."

The preacher stepped off the podium, walked up to the front row of pews, and said in full voice, "People, we need to heed the words of the apostles. We need to love our brothers and do violence to no man." He paused, seemed to look everyone in the eyes again, remounted the podium, and shouted, "We need to obey the word of the Lord!"

By the time he finished, nearly everyone in the congregation was fidgeting, rolling up their bulletins, playing with their hands, or staring at him in disbelief. To many, his benediction, delivered as usual after he walked to the rear of the church, was as shocking as his sermon. He asked God's "blessings and protection for our fellow Christians in the Mt. Zion Baptist Church." Afterward, as he stood at the front door to greet people as they left, many worshipers stuck out their hands without speaking or looking up. Some tried to slip through unnoticed. Others avoided him altogether by leaving through the education wing in the back.

At Mt. Zion, everyone expected their minister to preach about the cross burning. Like always, Reverend Moseley started his service with prayer and devotional singing. Today, he chose hymns to remind his congregation of the importance of the cross of Jesus. B. J. Long and Pete Jones lined out the words of "The

Old Rugged Cross," always a favorite, and the worshipers sang about someday exchanging their cares for a crown in heaven. Next came "Burdens Are Lifted at Calvary," "When I Survey the Wondrous Cross," and "At the Cross," about having faith in God to lift life's burdens.

When the mood was right for preaching, Moseley, in black suit and tie, walked to his homemade pulpit and read from Psalm 147, "The Lord lifteth up the meek; He casteth the wicked down to the ground." Then he turned to the book of Matthew, chapter five, and read from Jesus's well-loved Sermon on the Mount, "Blessed are the meek; for they shall inherit the earth," and "Love your enemies, bless them that curse you, do good to them that hate you, and pray for them which despitefully use you, and persecute you."

Cries of "Amen!" and "Praise Jesus!" rang out all through the reading and continued as the pastor told his listeners they should not be afraid, because God would look out for them. "What y'all got to do," he said, "is keep your eyes on the cross of Jesus. That's the cross y'all want to be looking at. Don't' y'all be looking back at no burned cross. Y'all look at the cross of Jesus. Don't y'all be hating nobody neither. Don't y'all be trying to strike back at nobody. Y'all keep your eyes on the Lord's cross. The Lord's cross!"

"Preach Reverend!" the worshippers cried. "Amen! Praise Jesus!"

While Brother Byrd and Reverend Moseley condemned violence and preached good will, out at the Mercy Baptist Mission, Brother Spurlock was so pleased about the recent turn of events that he had gone out and bought a brand new white suit and red tie, and when he rose to the pulpit, he had the congregation

sing "God Bless America" as a prelude for talking about patrio-
tism. Next, unaware that a black man, Thomas A. Dorsey, had
arranged it, the burly preacher led the singing of "I'm on the
Battlefield for My Lord."

Spurlock's biblical text was short—Ecclesiastes 3:1-8,
words commonly attributed to Solomon, son of David. "To everything there is a season, and a time to every purpose under the
heaven" and "a time to love, and a time to hate; a time of war,
and a time of peace."

With sweat now beading on his bald head and staining the
armpits of his new suit, Spurlock put down his Bible, took off his
jacket, tossed it onto his chair, and turned back to the congregation. "My friends," he said, picking up his Bible again and holding
it high in the air, "this is the word of the Lord, and I'm here to
tell y'all that we're in a war, and this is not a time to love. Did
you hear what I said?" he yelled.

"Amen, brother!" several listeners called.

"This is a time of war!" Spurlock shouted again. "Our southern way of life is being threatened! Not in Alabama. Not in
Tennessee. Not in Little Rock. But right here in Unionville!"

He moved out in front of the pulpit and pointed his Bible at
his listeners.

"'Oh,' you say, 'there ain't no coloreds trying to go to our
schools. All that stuff's happening up in Little Rock.' I tell you it
may be in Little Rock now, but before you know it, it's gon' be
right here in Unionville. I thank the Lord there are at least two
men among us who know the truth. There are at least two brave
patriots in Unionville who ain't afraid to stand up for what they
believe. One of them is the man who burned that cross over
there at that colored church. The other one is Mr. Upshaw, the
new owner of our local paper."

The sweating preacher moved back behind the pulpit, laid his Bible on it, and gripped both sides.

"These men know what's at stake. I want y'all to heed their example and stand up and be counted. Don't let integrationists take away our freedom to live the way we want to! We got a right in Arkansas to live separate from the black race and we're not gon' give it up without a fight!"

Unionville residents who did not hear enough about integration during church and expected to learn more from their newspapers when they got home did not find much. But on Sunday night, ABC television correspondent Mike Wallace bombarded Faubus with questions during a live broadcast from the governor's mansion. Faubus said his calling out the National Guard had nothing to do with whether integration was legal. He repeated that he had done it only to prevent violence, and he hinted he might withdraw the soldiers sometime during the week.

Later in the evening, when reporters asked Daisy Bates if she intended to send the nine black students back to Central High the next morning, she said she planned to wait until the guardsmen were gone.

In Unionville on Monday evening, the Arkansas-side town council held its regular monthly meeting in the little municipal building across from Emmett's Café. The six men, all of them white, met every third Monday and usually did not have much to do except go over the town's limited finances, hear reports about the water system and volunteer fire department, and try to figure out how to stop big trucks from speeding through town on the highway.

Tonight, however, they had something new. As usual they were alone except for the mayor, even though their meetings were always open to the public. Summer was hanging on, and they had the windows and front door open and the overhead fan going against the heat, but about all that did was suck in the smell of cooking grease from the café across the street. An American flag stood in one back corner and an Arkansas flag in the other. A door in the center of the back wall led to a rear area with two empty jail cells—one for whites and one for blacks.

"Personally, I didn't mind the cross burning," Art Nelson said, leaning back in his wooden folding chair, "but I'd sure hate for it to lead to some other kind of trouble. That'd be bad for business." A small man with a thick mop of gray hair, Art had owned Unionville Feeds before selling too much on credit and going broke a couple of years back. He made a living now by doing tax returns and other bookkeeping chores around town.

"Well, it doesn't bother me like it does Brother Byrd," Fred Vestal said, "but I sure don't want to see any protesting and boycotting. I've got a warehouse full of furniture to sell."

Dave Westbrook, a heavy-set fellow with a deep tan, said, "Fred, I hear that preacher of yours is one of them integrationists. Folks were talking about him at the plant today. Is that right? Is he?" Westbrook, a Methodist, had just come off his shift at Southwestern Chemical in El Dorado. His silver hard hat sat in the middle of the table.

"Yeah, I heard that, too," said council president Neal O'Brien, who went to the Presbyterian church. He was chairing the meeting. "What about it, Sam? Is that true?"

"Aw," Sam said, "I think he was just preaching against violence."

"Well, I don't know," Fred said. "Some folks think that if

somebody burned down the Mt. Zion church, he'd be over there in half a second inviting them to come to ours."

For a moment, no one said anything. They were thinking about how folks would react to that.

"All right," Neal said, breaking the silence, "Does anyone think we need to do anything more except ask Sheriff Eubanks to keep up the extra patrols?"

"Yeah, I do," Westbrook said. "I don't see Mr. Claude as much as y'all do, but I'm wondering if maybe it's time to invest in a patrol car and find us a younger marshal, one that can drive."

"The town can't afford a patrol car," Neal said. "Besides, if we fired Mr. Claude, people would complain. They like him."

"Why don't we get the Ford place to donate a car," Westbrook suggested, ignoring the question of who would drive it.

"Not a chance," said Art, who did their accounting. "They're not doing well enough to afford it."

"Well, supposing we get Horace Bowman to donate it," Westbrook said. "He's got all the money in the world, and he's got more stuff that needs protecting than anybody else in town." Westbrook looked at the mayor. "Alan, you work for him. Do you think he'd do it?"

"Y'all are putting me on the spot," Alan said, slumping back in his seat and folding his arms, "but I doubt it. Anyway, I can't ask him. He'd bust a gut."

"Bowman won't help us," Art said. "When it comes to doing something for somebody other than himself, he's tighter than a tick's ass."

"Well," Sam said, after a deep breath, "I'm not afraid to ask him if we ever decide we need to, but whoever burned the cross has probably had his say and there won't be any more." He was not sure if he really believed that or just hoped it.

CHAPTER 27

"**I** swear, if it wasn't for them children, I never would set foot in church again while that man's there," Gran said. She, Emma Lou MacDonald, and Almalee Jolly had been quilting and talking about Brother Byrd's sermon for most of Tuesday morning. "As it is, I don't know how I'm gon' bear up to it. I just never heard that kind of talk from a white man. He ought to be ashamed."

She snipped a thread on the back of a Dutch Girl square, put it in her oak basket, and took out the Wild Geese Flying pieces cut from her daddy's suit. "I tell you," she said, her face red as the burgundy dress she was wearing, "that man ain't nothing but a low-down Yankee. I don't care how long he's been living down here."

"Now, Ida Belle," Emma Lou said, "I think we've been talking about Brother Byrd long enough. You're gon' have a stroke if you don't calm down."

"Well, I'll be surprised if the deacons don't give him a good talking to," Almalee said, failing to take the hint. "Did Sam say anything about them maybe doing that, Ida Belle?"

"No," Gran said. She did not add that after she had given Brother Byrd the devil in the car on the way home from church last Sunday, Sam had asked her not to criticize the preacher in front of the children. That had made her almost as mad as the sermon did.

As the third week of September wore on, things in Little Rock seemed at a standstill, and Preston Upshaw was struggling to come up with anything sensational enough for his September 21 issue. Finally, after grumbling and snapping at Pearl about every little detail of community news, he decided to make Faubus the main story.

"Sometimes," he told Pearl, "the obvious stares you in the face and you just don't see it."

While Upshaw schemed, others in Unionville were busy turning out copy for outlines, posters, and reports. Having finished studying possible reasons for the cross burning, Becky's seventh graders were writing about how in 1787 the lack of a strong central government led America's founding fathers to dump the Articles of Confederation in favor of the Constitution, how the federal system of government assigned some powers to the national government and others to the states, and how Supreme Court rulings interpret the Constitution and become the law of the land.

The students continued to talk about their studies at home.

"Did you know," Barbara asked her parents during supper at the Ames house on Thursday night, "when they were writing the Constitution, they had a big argument over counting slaves and had to settle it with a ratio?"

"Is that teacher of yours still fouling up the math lessons?" her father asked, as he helped himself to another roll.

"Well, yes and no, Daddy. We still aren't doing regular math first thing like Mrs. Poindexter's class, but today we learned about ratios during social studies, and it was interesting."

"Oh yeah? How's that?"

"Well, we started out talking about the Three-Fifths Compromise. You know, that's where people from the North and people from the South didn't agree about how to count slaves for taxes and representation in Congress, so they decided to count three-fifths of them. Then we did some ratio problems."

"I still don't like what that woman's doing," Howard said. "I'm gon' have to make some time to get over there and talk to Mrs. Woodhead."

At the Plunkett house, Bobby Jack was the one who brought up Becky Reeves. As he often did, he sat in the kitchen after supper finishing another beer while Glen Ray helped his mother.

"Boy," Bobby Jack asked, "did you tell that teacher of yours I don't want you doing no sissy stuff with posters and junk?"

"Pops, I can't tell her that. Besides, I'm learning things I didn't know."

"Well, by god, I can sure as hell tell old man Appleby," Bobby Jack said. "I bet you can't tell me one thing you learned from that woman that's worth a damn. Go on. Tell me something."

"You won't like it, Pops."

"I already know that but tell me anyway."

"We learned that the Supreme Court could have said a long time ago that Negroes can go to white schools. Right after the Civil War the Fourteenth Amendment said states had treat to Negroes the same as us."

"Do you hear the trash coming out of this boy's mouth?" Bobby Jack yelled to his wife. "Damn that woman!"

"Well, Miss Reeves says that sooner or later white kids and

Negro kids are gon' go to school together and ain't nobody can stop it."

"Oh, yeah," Bobby Jack said. "We'll see about that!"

⁓

At the Tate home, talk about school had upset Gran so much that Sam had started asking Billy about it during evening chores instead of during supper.

"You see, Daddy," Billy said, as they picked their way along a row of lima beans, "the colonies had been so scared of the king that when the founding fathers wrote the Constitution, they made a list of all the things the federal government could do, and then they said the states could do everything else. I forgot which amendment Miss Reeves said that was in. Anyway it's what people like Governor Faubus mean when they're talking about states' rights. Miss Reeves says he's not the first one to do it. She says we're gon' study about some of the others, too, but we haven't gotten that far yet."

Sam dropped a handful of beans into his basket, pictured Billy in Becky's classroom, and smiled.

"Billy, I remember you said Miss Reeves told you the Supreme Court acts kind of like a referee when there's an argument over the Constitution. What was the new word you learned for that?"

"I think it was 'interpreting.'"

"That's right," Sam said, resuming his picking. "It's finding out what something means and explaining it, like when Brother Byrd reads a verse from the Bible and says what he thinks it means."

"Daddy, is that why Gran got so mad at him last Sunday?"

"Well, kind of, Billy. Sometimes the way someone interprets something depends on what kind of experience they've had with it themselves, or what they've always heard about it. Gran sees Negroes and things like cross burning and night riders the way her daddy did. Brother Byrd sees them the way he thinks God does."

"You see them more like Brother Byrd, don't you, Daddy?"

"Yes, Billy, the more I think about it, the more I do."

CHAPTER 28

As soon as Lester Grimes saw the newspapers on Saturday morning, he headed straight for the Otasco store. He was so worked up he did not even speak to Miss Ruthelle.

"Well, Sam, I guess you were right," Lester said. He held out a copy of the *El Dorado Daily News*. Sam, who was still finishing his morning routine, took it and glanced at the headline.

"Federal Judge Grants Writ against Faubus," it proclaimed.

Sam had heard about the decision the night before. For the third time, a federal judge had ruled for integration in Little Rock, and Faubus had gone on TV again. He said he was withdrawing the National Guard and asked the NAACP to allow a cooling off period before continuing to push for integration. He said it would not succeed until the majority of white people accepted it, and it would hurt both races in any community where the feds forced it.

"Yeah, I know about it," Sam said, handing back the paper. "He said he's gon' appeal the decision but I don't imagine he'll get far with it."

"Well, he might. He's got a lot of support. Look here what Upshaw wrote," Lester said. He held out a copy of the *Unionville Times*. "Faubus Touted for President," the lead headline declared.

"I saw that too," Sam said. "Haven't you figured out that Upshaw's nothing but a blowhard?"

Lester gritted his teeth and turned red in the face. "You must

197

not have read the whole article. It says Faubus is getting tele-grams from folks wanting him to run. Some of them are from other governors."

"Come on, Lester. You know he doesn't have a snowball's chance in hell of getting elected president."

⌒‿⌒

"You mean he didn't even cuss?" Doc Perkins asked, when Sam told the Saturday night loafers what he had said to Lester.

"Nope," Sam said, "he tried to, but he just turned redder than one of those new fire fighters' hats and kept saying, 'But, but, but…,' and never got anything out. I laughed so hard even Miss Ruthelle got mad at me."

"I wish I'd seen it," Tucker said.

The usual folks were sitting around the Otasco store wait-ing to listen to University of Arkansas football. The Razorbacks were the heart and soul of sports and entertainment in the state, and although their main campus was way up in Fayetteville, they often played home games in Little Rock. The Razorback Radio Network carried announcer George Mooney's familiar play-by-play to every nook and cranny between Missouri and Louisiana, and even Doc, the Tulane alum, liked listening to it. Tonight, in the first game of the year, the Hogs were hosting the Oklahoma State University Cowboys in the capital. Little Rock hotels were full, restaurants were ready for postgame crowds, and despite a pouring rain, nearly twenty-five thousand fans were at War Memorial Stadium. Football had even muscled its way onto the front page of the *Arkansas Gazette*, right alongside politics and in-tegration. "Razorbacks Are Coming, Town Will Start Jumping," the morning headline declared.

The loafers had already argued about whether they had a

chance to win the Southwest Conference and go to the Cotton Bowl, who was the best Razorback quarterback, and whether Unionville's Ronnie Metcalf would play for the Hogs one day. He had gained more than one hundred fifty yards the night before in a 21 to 7 Bobcat win over Arcadia High School down in Louisiana, and Doc said he hoped the boy would go to Tulane.

With the countdown to kickoff seeming to take forever, Doyle Scoggins turned the talk to politics.

"What do y'all think is gon' happen Monday up at Central?" he asked. He sat on an upturned nail keg like always.

"Not too much, I'd bet," Doc said. He had Sam's office chair again. "There'll probably be some hotheads out there protesting, but I expect the cops will keep them in line. Those colored kids will get in and that'll be the end of it."

"Y'all think Faubus wants to be president?" Houston Holloway asked from his usual place on the railed stairway.

"Won't make any difference if he does," Doc said. "Folks up North wouldn't ever vote for him, and he's ticked off way too many folks down here."

Scoggins grimaced, as if disappointed about such an outcome. "Any of y'all going to that Citizens' Council meeting that Brother Spurlock's getting up Thursday night?" he asked.

"No," Tucker said, leaning against a display counter, "I don't have time for it."

"Not me," Sam said. He hefted himself onto the wrapping table. "I don't want to listen to a bunch of loud mouths blowing off. I get enough of it around here—present company excepted, of course."

"I don't know," Doc said, "it might be interesting just to see what ole Spurlock's got up his sleeve."

"Yeah, I think it will too," Scoggins said.

Just then George Mooney's voice came over the radio and everyone got quiet again. The game did not start well for the Razorbacks. They scored a touchdown on the first snap, but someone jumped off sides and the play was called back. After that, no one scored on the muddy field for two quarters. In the second half, though, Arkansas kept the Cowboys backed up on their own end of the field and managed to grind out two touchdowns. The win left the whole state in a good mood.

For many Arkansans, the good feeling from the football game carried over into Sunday. The *Arkansas Gazette* put the Razorbacks on page one again, right alongside stories suggesting a lot of people believed the Little Rock crisis was over now that the National Guardsmen had left.

Mayor Woodrow Mann said Little Rock police would be on hand at Central High on Monday morning to keep the peace. "The eyes of the nation and the world will be on us," he said, and the city would be cast in a better light.

Many other Arkansans were not happy, however, including an entire Baptist congregation in Unionville.

"Them federal judges are instruments of the devil," Brother Spurlock railed to a full house at Mercy Baptist Mission. He was decked out in his new white suit again and waving his Bible every which way. "It hurts to see our governor knuckling under to them," he said. "I want y'all to come on out to the Citizens' Council meeting Thursday night. We're gon' get organized and make sure we don't have race mixing down here."

"Don't you worry, Brother Spurlock, "we'll be there," the men in his flock told him as they shook his hand after the service.

At the First Baptist Church, Brother Byrd preached to a lot of empty seats and more than a few members who would rather have been someplace else. Light rain had been falling since sunup, and Gran and a lot of other folks seized that as an excuse to stay home. Sam left Billy and Mary Jane with her and came alone. People had been whispering all week about Byrd's last sermon and some still had questions about where he stood. Head deacon Fred Vestal had called a special meeting of church leaders for after preaching.

During the service, Sam found himself thinking less about the sermon than about family matters. Most of what went through his mind was not new. He liked the way his kids were growing up. Billy was responsible and doing well in school and Mary Jane was sweet and bright as could be. He imagined them at home with Gran and thought about how much they loved her. Once his mind started wandering, he could not rein it in. He thought about Judith Ann, as he frequently did, and he thought about Becky, something he found himself doing more and more despite how pointless it seemed. He wished she were here today. He was glad Billy was in her class but it was hard to avoid wondering how things might be different if he were not.

Brother Byrd delivered one of his traditional sermons, and after the benediction, when everyone but the deacons had left, they gathered in the front pews with the pastor. Among Southern Baptists, deacons managed all church business through regular monthly gatherings, so if they met any other time, it was a serious matter. Fred, looking worried, stood up and called the group to order.

"We're here," he said, "because after Brother Byrd's sermon

last week some of y'all and some of our other members had a few questions about what steps we should take in view of certain future possibilities."

"Yeah," one deacon spoke up, anxious to get on with the matter at hand. "Brother Byrd, you said you ain't an integrationist, but after that sermon you preached, I guess some of us ain't so sure. We want to know what you have to say about that and what you'd do if coloreds tried to come to our church."

"Yeah, that's right," Norm Patterson, the Ark-La-Tex Oil electrician seconded.

"Yeah," echoed Hollis Cook, wide awake for a change. "We don't want no coloreds in here."

"Amen," said several others. Sam and Doc exchanged glances but kept quiet.

"All right, fellows, take it easy," Fred said. "Brother Byrd, I'm sorry, but you see what the issue is and how strong folks feel about it. We need you to speak to it."

Fred sat down and Byrd got to his feet and turned to face the deacons.

"Men," he said, "I'm gon' ignore the fact that we started this meeting without our customary prayer for God to give us wisdom. I'm gon' ignore the fact that some of y'all have been talking behind my back all week instead of coming directly to me like you should have. And I'm gon' ignore the fact that some of y'all didn't listen very well to what I said last week. Let me see if I can make it simple for you."

Feet shuffled on the floor and butts shifted in the pews.

"I'm gon' say this just once. I am not an integrationist. I'm afraid it would lead eventually to mixing the white and black races through marriage, and I don't want that.

"But, now, as a practical matter, I don't believe y'all are as much worried about what I think, or what I would do if Negroes were to show up here some morning, as you are concerned about what you'd do. Y'all don't want them here, but you're deacons, and you're embarrassed about the likelihood that you wouldn't behave like Christians."

There was more squirming but no one said anything.

"Y'all are already thinking that you'd either tell them they can't come into the house of the Lord, or you'd leave it your-selves because you don't want to worship with them. Y'all know both those things are wrong in God's eyes, and you don't want to have to do either of them and feel ashamed. But knowing that you'd probably do one or the other, y'all want me to say that I wouldn't let them in. That way you'll be off the hook.

"I can tell y'all right now I'm not gon' make those personal decisions for you. You're gon' have to do it. I believe all people, regardless of color, are God's children, and we ought not hate somebody or mistreat them just because of the color of their skin. Hating is a sin, pure and simple, just like desecrating a church is a sin. If Negroes show up here some Sunday morning and want to worship with us, I'm gon' invite them in and go on with the service, and that's what I hope y'all will do too. I won't especially like doing it but I believe that's what the Lord would want. When Paul was instructing the Ephesians about Christ's church, he said, 'One Lord, one faith, one baptism. One God and Father of all, who is above all, and through all, and in you all.' That's in chapter four, if y'all want to look it up."

Hollis started to speak but Byrd held up a hand to si-lence him.

"Now, I hate to give y'all any consolation, because you don't deserve it. But I have one more thing to say. I don't believe the Negroes in Unionville want to come to our church any more than you want to go to theirs. They take just as much pride in their church as you do in this one and they have their own way of doing things. I'm pretty sure they don't want to give that up. One or two of them might want to come over here a time or two just to see if they can, but after they do, that'll be the end of it.

"That's all I have to say on the subject, and while I feel like God still wants me to be your pastor, if you think different, you can let me know." With that, he headed for his office.

For what seemed a long time, no one said anything. Sam looked at Doc, he winked, and Sam grinned back at him. Fred got back to his feet.

"Well, I guess that was clear enough," he said. "Are y'all ready to adjourn?"

"No. I ain't," Norm Patterson said. "I got a suggestion. I think we ought to go talk to the folks over at Mt. Zion and ask them if they mean to try to come over here, and if they say they do, then tell them they ain't welcome."

"Norm," Fred asked, "did you hear what Brother Byrd just said?"

"Yeah, I heard him. Maybe we can just ask them what their intentions are. See what they're thinking."

"Just who do you recommend for that job, Norm?" one of the other deacons asked. "You volunteering?"

"I was thinking Sam could do it. He seems to be pretty tight with them. I hear he's been playing baseball with some of them, and I saw him talking to them that night the cross was burned."

"No, uh-uh." Sam said, shaking his head. "I couldn't do that. Besides, I agree with the preacher. The best thing is to just leave it alone."

"I move we appoint Sam to go talk to them," Norm said.

"I second," Hollis said. "You got to take a vote on it, Fred."

"Okay. Motion made and seconded. All in favor raise your hand."

"Look, now, y'all. I don't want to do this," Sam protested.

Everyone looked around while Fred counted. "Seven ayes and five nays. The motion's passed," he said. "I'm sorry, Sam, the majority want you to do it."

CHAPTER 29

By eight o-clock Monday morning, Elizabeth Eckford and her eight fellow students were assembled in Daisy Bates's Little Rock living room. News reports said hundreds of segregationists had gathered at Central High School to block their entrance. Despite the danger, Bates and another NAACP official loaded the students into two cars, drove them along a little-used route to the school, and hustled them through a side entrance before the crowd could stop them.

Outside, too late, the mob yelled, "Keep the niggers out!" Inside, white students did more than hurl insults. They spit, hit, and kicked at the nine black kids. Some teachers tried to stop the abuse but others only watched. By noon, it was clear that things were getting out of hand both in the building and on the streets. Police officials ordered Elizabeth and the other students taken out through a basement exit and driven home.

This did not stop the uproar, however. Many in the mob were unaware that the black students had left. Segregationists, who had come from Citizens' Councils all over the state and beyond, beat two reporters and eventually gained brief entry to the school. Exaggerated radio reporting created panic and street fights broke out at several places in the city and carried into the evening. White people and black threw bottles, hurled bricks, and broke car windows. Shortly before midnight, fifteen police patrol units were needed to turn back carloads of angry whites trying to get into Daisy Bates's neighborhood with guns and dynamite.

⌒

Meanwhile, in midafternoon, as disturbances continued in the capital, Superintendent Appleby and Principal Woodhead prepared to deal with what they regarded as disorder in Unionville's seventh grade. They dispatched Hilda Starr, Appleby's secretary, to take over Becky's class and send her across the street to meet with her bosses in the high school conference room. When Becky walked in, Appleby and Woodhead were sitting reared back in their chairs with their palms pressing on the table.

"Miss Reeves," Woodhead said, skipping hello and an invitation to sit, "I told you the first time I saw you that I didn't want any surprises this year. Who gave you permission not to follow the social studies textbook approved by this school district?"

Becky looked from the principal to the superintendent and back again.

"I'm not sure I understand what you mean," she said. "I'm using the textbook."

"Maybe you are," Woodhead said, "but you're not following it in chronological order like you're supposed to."

"I didn't know that was a requirement."

"Well, it is," Woodhead snapped.

"I don't recall being told that specifically, and I'm pretty sure it's not in any of the written materials I received," Becky said firmly, surprising the officials.

"Now see here, young woman," Appleby said. "Don't you get snippy with us. You know very well what we're talking about. We know you've got those students of yours doing all kinds of projects and stuff while you're just sitting round doing nothing.

We also know you've got your schedule so messed up your kids don't know when to study what. And we know you're teaching integration."

So that's what this is about, Becky thought, integration. It fit with all she had been hearing and seeing in Unionville. She had figured she might get complaints about her methods but she had not expected such a direct charge. Still, she did not intend to back down from what she considered good teaching.

"Mr. Appleby, I don't know where you got those impressions, but you and Mrs. Woodhead are welcome to come over and observe my class any time. The children and I will be glad to have you."

The superintendent looked nervously at Woodhead, who seemed ready to explode, and then back at Becky, who merely smiled.

"I don't have time to be traipsing around to everybody's classroom watching them teach," he said. "We've got parents complaining. These are people we've known a long time, and I'm sure they wouldn't be calling us if you were doing what you're supposed to."

Appleby paused but Becky did not say anything more.

"Well?" Woodhead asked impatiently.

"Well, what?" Becky asked, as if she did not understand the implied question.

"What do you intend to do about this?"

"I plan to continue teaching my class like always, and I'd really like you both to come and observe. If you do, I think you'll find that whatever complaints you've received are unfounded. My students are engaged and they're doing good work."

"I'm afraid it's too late for that," Appleby said. "This is a small town and too many parents are upset. If you're not willing to cooperate, we're gon' have a special meeting of the school board Wednesday night to review your performance and your contract."

"And you're confident you can review my performance without observing me in my classroom?" Becky asked, not giving an inch.

"That's right. Now, I'll ask you one more time. Are you gon' cooperate?"

"I'm not going to change the way I teach, if that's what you mean."

"All right, then. We'll see you here at seven-thirty Wednesday night."

CHAPTER 30

When Governor Faubus, who had gone out of town, got word of the new violence in Little Rock on Monday morning, he called on people in Arkansas not to take the law into their own hands and hinted he might call out the National Guard again.

Meanwhile, President Eisenhower called the disturbances disgraceful and said he would use the full power of the United States to carry out the order of the federal courts. The next day, headlines in the *Arkansas Gazette* and other papers announced, "Ike Clears Way to Send Troops."

In Unionville, Lester Grimes had heard about the president's decision on TV the night before, and he was out bright and early looking for somebody to complain to. This time he bypassed the Otasco store and struck out for Emmett's. Finding the café crowd already stirred up, he took a counter stool and signaled for coffee. For once, however, he did more listening than talking.

"By god, I'm glad I ain't in the army now," Boomer Jenkins was saying midway down the counter. He sat sideways, his wooden leg sticking out into the aisle. "It's a damn sorry thing for the president to use soldiers to make white kids go to school with a bunch of burr heads. I swear if I had kids, wouldn't nobody make me send them to school with the black bastards. I'd keep them home."

"I think ole Ike's turning into a commie just like them damned federal judges," Jim Ed Davis said from a booth where he was sitting with Crow Hicks. "I'd love to cut every damn one of them's nuts off."

"I'll help you do it," Crow Hicks said. "I ain't fixing to mix with no niggers."

"Well, I tell you right now," Boomer said. "If Eisenhower sends troops up there, there's only two ways we're gon' stop integration down here. The first one is to keep the coloreds scared and the second one is to shoot some of them if they try something."

When Pearl got to the newspaper office, she found Preston Upshaw in deep conversation with Elmer Spurlock. The editor was sitting at his desk, the preacher had pulled a chair up to one side of it, and papers were scattered between two drained coffee mugs on top. As Pearl approached, Spurlock crushed a cigarette in Upshaw's ashtray, raked in the papers, and stood up.

"Well, I best be getting on to my painting job," the preacher said. "I'll see you out at the church Thursday night." Turning to Pearl, he said, "Good morning, Mrs. Goodbar. You're welcome to come too. The meeting's open to everybody, men and women."

"I expect Mr. Upshaw will fill me in on it," Pearl said.

"If you don't come," Spurlock said from the doorway, "you're gon' be missing something mighty important."

"What's the something important he's talking about?" Pearl asked, after he left.

"He's just talking about getting the Citizens' Council started. We have to get people organized. Brother Spurlock's gon' see to it."

"Seems to me you're taking more than a journalistic interest in what he's up to," Pearl said.

"I reckon that's a matter of perspective, Mrs. Goodbar. I feel a responsibility to help people see the trouble they're facing, and I'm gon' speak at the meeting. It'll help us get more subscribers."

"It's true," Almalee Jolly said from Gran's sofa. "I heard it on the news last night. They said Eisenhower's gon' send troops today."

"He's a dadgum Yankee Republican," Gran said, frowning. She was sitting in her rocker and had her feet planted on her padded shotgun shell crate like she meant to push it through the floor. "He's just like them good-for-nothings my daddy had to deal with when he come home from Virginia. I swan! He must be rolling over in his grave. This is gon' be like Reconstruction all over again."

"Gran, can people really roll over in their graves?" Mary Jane asked. She was sitting under her grandmother's quilting frame again, rocking one of her favorite dolls to sleep.

"No, hon, that's just a saying. It means if that person was alive now, they wouldn't like something they was seeing or hearing."

"Are you about to tell us some stories?"

"No, hon, not this time," Gran said. Then to her friends she said, "Every time she hears me mention my daddy she thinks I'm gon' tell stories." She glanced around at his picture over the radio. "The ones that come to mind now, though, I sure can't tell to children. Some of the stuff them Yankees did to people would make the hair stand up on the back of your neck. It makes me sick to think about it."

"What did they do, Gran? What makes you sick?" Mary Jane asked.

"I'm not really gon' be sick, hon. That's just a saying too. You go on with your playing and don't be paying so much attention to grown-up talk."

"You don't really think our soldiers would do any of that stuff now, do you?" Emma Lou asked. "This is not the same thing."

"Well," Gran said, "it sure feels like it to me. We got Yankee politicians stirring up the coloreds, carpetbaggers like that Reeves woman down here meddling in our schools, and the army butting in. My daddy used to say if it smells like a skunk, it probably is, and this mess sure stinks."

At six-forty on Tuesday afternoon, five hundred members of the US Army's elite 101st Airborne Division from Fort Campbell, Kentucky, moved into position around Central High School. A subdued crowd of about a hundred citizens, mostly women and children, watched as the soldiers set up a tent camp behind the school.

A little more than two hours later, millions of Americans gathered around their radios and TVs to find out what Eisenhower had to say about the troops' mission. All the Tates except Mary Jane waited in Sam's living room. He wanted Billy to see history being made but that was not all. Sam also wanted to see how well Becky's teaching had prepared his son to understand what was happening.

Earlier in the day, Tucker had dropped by the Otasco store with news about the unannounced school board meeting set for Wednesday night.

"I know you, Sam," Tucker said, as the two men stood out back on the loading dock. "I can tell you're more than a little partial to Becky Reeves, and seeing as how Billy is in her class, I thought you ought to know."

"How'd you hear about it?"

"The superintendent called to see if my sister might be willing to start back teaching and commute from up at Smackover if they fire Becky. I told him she wouldn't be any more interested now than she was when they asked her last summer. Anyway, Appleby said a bunch of parents are complaining and they're gon' be at the meeting."

Sam had thought about Tucker's news the rest of the day.

At nine o'clock, the president came on TV from the White House. He said he had been vacationing in Rhode Island but had flown back to Washington because, "I felt that, in speaking from the house of Lincoln, Jackson, and Wilson, my words would better convey both the sadness I feel and the firmness with which I intend to pursue this course until the orders of the federal court at Little Rock can be executed without interference."

Eisenhower reviewed the history of the crisis then declared, "The very basis of our individual rights and freedoms rests upon the certainty that the president and the executive branch of government will support and ensure the carrying out of the decisions of the federal courts." He said he was confident that most Arkansans were people of good will who would obey the law even if they disagreed with it. What he did not say was that he had called all ten thousand Arkansas National Guardsmen into federal service and ordered them to stand by at their respective armories. This would keep Faubus from trying to use them to complicate matters further.

"Well, Billy," Sam asked, when Eisenhower finished, "did you understand the president?"

"Yes, sir, I think so. He said pretty much the same thing we've been studying at school. The courts have said what the law means and the president has to make everybody go by it. It don't really matter if we like it or not."

Sam let his son's grammar pass. "Do you have any questions?"

"No, sir. I don't think so."

"Okay. Why don't you go on to bed? We'll see you in the morning."

Gran said good night to Billy but otherwise kept quiet until he left the room. Then she said, frowning, "Sam, that Yankee teacher has plum ruined that boy. He don't see nothing at all wrong with them soldiers coming down here and making our children go to school with coloreds. I can't believe you're letting her fill his head with this stuff."

"Momma," Sam said, "I know you're not gon' like hearing this, but times are changing. There's not a thing anyone can do to stop integration of the schools. Someday Billy and Mary Jane both are gon' have to deal with it, and I'd a whole lot rather they understand it than to go around beating their heads up against something they can't do anything about. This way they can just concentrate on getting a good education."

"You think that's what I'm doing? Beating my head up against a wall? Good god in heaven! I don't know what's come over you. Has that Reeves woman got you all hot to trot? You better stay away from her. She ain't fit for you."

Sam kept silent for a moment then sat forward in his chair.

"Momma, I know all this is hard for you and I'm sorry about that. I've already said just about all I can about Billy's schooling, but there is one more thing about Becky, and you may as well know about it. There are some parents that don't like her any more than you do and they're trying to get her fired. There's a special school board meeting about it tomorrow night, and I'm going, and if I get a chance, I'm gon' stick up for her because I think she's doing a good job. Billy's learning things he needs to know and he's enjoying it. I want him to keep on."

"Well, I don't like it one bit."

"I know you don't and I'm sorry about that because I love you. But you and I are just gon' have to agree to disagree about this."

Gran looked at her son for a long moment then pulled herself up out of her chair. "I'm tired," she said. "I'm going to bed."

"500 US Troops Fly into Little Rock on Ike's Orders." "Southern Governors Prepare for Showdown on Rights." The headlines seemed to explode across the top of the *El Dorado Daily News* on Wednesday morning. Having now signed up for home delivery, Becky read the paper over breakfast and decided immediately to use it in the day's social studies lesson. The first two pages read almost like a textbook on federal versus states' rights. One story described the arrival of the troops. Another quoted the president. Another quoted various southern governors. Most of them either condemned the president's action or questioned the necessity of it, but by the time the troop planes stopped flying into Little Rock, there were more than one thousand soldiers in the city, with the federalized Arkansas National Guard available if needed.

By eight o'clock, Elizabeth Eckford and the other eight black Central High School students had gathered at Daisy Bates's home just as they had two days earlier. This time, however, two jeeploads of heavily armed paratroopers escorted their station wagon to the front entrance of the school while military helicopters fluttered overhead. Angry segregationists lined the surrounding streets and shouted racial slurs but troops held them back with bayonets. A squad of twenty soldiers shepherded the nine students up Central's front steps. Inside, paratroopers walked them to their various classes and stood guard outside the classroom doors. White students taunted the nine just like on Monday, but this time they made it through the entire school day. In the afternoon, members of the 101st Airborne took them safely back to Daisy Bates's house.

Tomorrow they would try to do it all over again.

CHAPTER 31

Becky walked into the crowded Unionville High School conference room a few minutes before seven-thirty in the evening wearing her blue linen suit and carrying her homemade book bag. Hilda Starr, there to take notes for Superintendent Appleby and the school board, smiled and motioned her to a chair at one end of the long meeting table. A large man with coarse white hair, heavy frown lines, and a deep tan sat at the other end. He wore a wrinkled white shirt with sleeves rolled up to his elbows and looked eager to get things started. Becky had not seen him before but she assumed he was Herbert Kramer, president of the school board. He had a large dairy farm west of town, dabbled in timber, and was a deacon at Mercy Baptist Mission.

Appleby, fiddling with a pencil, sat to the right of Kramer, and Gladys Woodhead, arms folded across her chest, sat to his left. Four other men Becky had never seen before occupied the remaining seats at the table. All had papers in front of them and Becky guessed they were school board members. Kramer shuffled through a file folder while the others talked quietly about the weather. A dozen or so people sat in chairs around the sides of the room, watching as Becky took her seat. She figured most of them were parents and relatives but she recognized only Doc Perkins and Sam. When her gaze met Sam's, he winked, attempting to signal his support, and she nodded just enough to acknowledge it.

After a few minutes, Kramer rapped his knuckles on the table and started the proceedings. "This is a special meeting of the Board of the Unionville School District," he said, "and we're gon' dispense with the normal order of business. Let the record show that all members are present."

Then he turned to Becky. "Miss Reeves," he said, "I'm Herbert Kramer, president of the board. Superintendent Appleby and Principal Woodhead have gotten a lot of complaints about you, and we're here tonight to decide whether we ought to keep you or fire you. We're gon' hear from the administration first. Then we're gon' hear from some of the good people who've got kids in your class. After that, you'll get a chance to talk." He turned to the superintendent. "Vernon, you want to start?"

"Yes, sir," Appleby said, hunching forward in his chair. "Miss Reeves is one of two seventh-grade teachers. She was hired just before school started. Mrs. Woodhead and I have received a number of complaints that she isn't teaching like the rest of our faculty. We talked to her about it, and she not only admitted it, she said she wouldn't stop doing it. She's not following the regular seventh-grade schedule or the regular social studies curriculum. And she's teaching integration."

"Mr. Kramer," Becky said, raising her hand and trying to interrupt.

"Not now, young lady. You'll get your turn," the board president said. "Go on, Vernon."

"That's about it," Appleby said. "She's not doing what she's supposed to, and she was insubordinate when we asked her to follow normal procedures. A lot of parents are here tonight and they can verify what I'm reporting about her work."

"All right," Kramer said. He looked around the room. "Any of y'all got anything you want to say?"

"Yes, I do," Howard Ames said, rising from his seat. Other than Appleby and Doc, he was the only person in the room wearing a suit and tie.

"All right, Howard, go ahead on," Kramer said.

"Miss Reeves has her educational priorities out of focus," Ames said, reading from notes on a clipboard. "Mathematics is the foundation of order, discipline, and a structured mind and life. It is the most important subject in school, and until Miss Reeves arrived, it was always taught first thing in the morning. That way it not only received the attention it merited, it also paved the way for learning other subjects. Miss Reeves is teaching social studies first. That interferes with good fundamental education practices and I can prove it. My daughter's planning to major in accounting in college, and up to this year, she's always made straight A-pluses in math. In Miss Reeves's class, she already has two A-minuses on tests. I charge that Miss Reeves is endangering my daughter's future."

Despite the serious purpose of the meeting, several folks could not suppress giggles. Woodhead glared at each of the guilty.

"Who else?" Kramer asked.

"Me," Bobby Jack Plunkett said, jumping up from a seat along the wall behind Woodhead. Even though the temperature was in the seventies, he had squeezed into one of his old Bobcat letter jackets. "That woman's got them kids doing all the work while she sits around on her fanny doing nothing. And she's got boys like my Glen Ray doing sissy stuff like cutting things out of newspapers and magazines and making posters and crap. That ain't teaching them nothing useful. And she won't even let them talk natural neither. They can't even say 'nigger.' They have to say 'Negro,'" he said, drawing out the last word for emphasis. "And she's told them they're gon' have to go to school with coloreds, and there ain't nothing nobody can do about it. She ain't no fit teacher."

"Okay, anybody else?"

"Yeah," DeWitt Ingram said, rising from a chair across the room. He put on his Bowman truck driver's cap then remembered where he was and snatched it off. "That ain't all. She's teaching communism too."

"DeWitt, that's a new allegation," Kramer said. "How do you know she's teaching communism? What's she been saying about it?"

"Well, I don't know exactly. My son, Tommy, he brought home one of her books, and my brother-in-law was visiting from down at Homer, and he saw it and said a communist wrote it. Sonny—that's my brother-in-law—he's in the Citizens' Council down there and they know about them things. It was wrote by one of them coloreds that got up the N-double-A-C-P. His name's Elbert Bose or something like that. Sonny said he's wrote a whole bunch of books. Anyway, Sonny said a few years back the government tried him for being a Russian spy and he got off scot free."

All around the room people exchanged looks of surprise and, in some cases, anger. Kramer tossed the pencil he was holding onto the table and sat back in his chair.

"Miss Reeves," he said, glaring at her. "What have you got to say for yourself?"

Sam, sitting next to Howard Ames, leaned forward in his seat.

"Mr. Kramer and other members of the board," she said calmly, "I know my teaching methods are different but I believe I can answer all of your concerns. Some of the statements you have heard this evening are correct, and some are the result of misconceptions and are not accurate. It's true that I've changed the teaching schedule, but I'm using the social studies textbook, and my students are studying the main aspects of the curriculum.

"I have invited Mr. Appleby and Mrs. Woodhead to observe my class, but so far they haven't been able to do so. My invitation still stands and I'm happy to extend the same to any of you gentlemen and to any parents who may be interested. I would be glad to have you visit. But since you haven't had that opportunity, I'd like to tell you what we're doing in my class and why. May I do that?"

Kramer folded his arms. "Yeah, go ahead on," he said, in a tone that made clear he wished she had not asked.

Appleby and Woodhead looked on with clinched teeth.

"I would be willing to bet," Becky continued, "that most of you here tonight hated history when you went to school, or at least you found it boring. I would also wager that you felt that way because about all you learned were facts and dates for tests then you forgot most of them. I expect that little, if any, of what you studied seemed relevant to anything going on around you."

As Becky glanced around the room, only Doc and Sam were smiling, but a few folks looked thoughtful, and she could tell she had struck a familiar chord with at least some of them.

"I believe studying history ought to be meaningful," she said. "It ought to help us understand things that are happening today. And when it does, it's also interesting. No matter what your personal views are about the events in Little Rock, you have to admit that they are steeped in history. Everything that's going on there is a consequence of things that happened in the past. There are connections to the founding of our country, the formation of the federal government, various crises we have endured, the decisions we as a nation made on those occasions, and how people felt about them then and still feel about them now. Your children came to me interested in what they were hearing and seeing in the news, and I'm helping them explore things they want to know about. We may be skipping a few pages in the social studies textbook here and there, but my students are doing good work, and they're going to remember what they're learning because it's not superficial. It's real to them, so it's going to stay with them."

"Yeah, that's just what we're afraid of," Bobby Jack said loudly from the side. "You're teaching them to be nigger lovers."

"Yeah!" Ingram said.

Some of the other parents nodded in agreement. Others shifted in their chairs and whispered to their neighbors. School board members looked to see how their colleagues were reacting.

Sam had kept quiet for as long as he could. "May I say something?" he asked, standing and hitching up his dress slacks.

"Is your boy in her room?" Kramer asked.

"Yeah, he is."

"Okay, go ahead on."

"I haven't been to Miss Reeves's class," Sam said, "but I agree with everything she's saying about history and about our children wanting to understand what's happening now. I've never seen my son so interested in school. He tells me almost every day what he's learning, and I'm amazed by how much he knows and how well he understands how government works."

Bobby Jack jumped to his feet. "Oh, yeah?" he said. "My boy knows all that stuff, too, but what good is it? She ain't doing nothing but teaching integration."

"I'm not sure what you mean by 'teaching integration,'" Sam said, as Bobby Jack sat back down, "but if you mean teaching them to like it, or be for it, that's not the understanding I have.

I think Miss Reeves is smart enough to know that what our kids think about integration is a matter for us parents. My boy says she told them that the Supreme Court has declared that school integration is the law of the land. That's true and it's not teaching integration."

"What about that, Miss Reeves?" Kramer asked. "Is that right, what Sam said?"

"Yes, sir," Becky replied. "It is."

"Did you also tell them that they'd have to go to school with coloreds someday?" the board president asked.

"I told them that eventually schools will be integrated all over the country, even in Unionville."

"There, you see!" Bobby Jack shouted. "She's teaching integration."

Kramer rapped the table again. Appleby and Woodhead leaned back in their chairs and exchanged pleased looks behind Kramer. The board members were hearing firsthand what parents had complained about.

Sam, still standing, ignored Kramer's attempt to regain control of the meeting. "No, Bobby Jack," Sam said, "she's only telling them what the law is. And unless the law changes, you can bet your life that one of these days every public school will be integrated. It doesn't matter whether we like it or not." Then he turned to Kramer. "I'm no attorney, Herbert, but I don't see how you can fire a teacher for teaching facts. If that's not illegal, it ought to be."

Several people started talking at the same time. Sam sat down and Kramer knocked his knuckles against the table again.

Travis Swilley, a board member and part-time farmer who worked as a machinist at Southwestern Chemical, leaned toward Becky. "Miss Reeves, what about what DeWitt said a while ago there? Are you teaching communism and making your students read stuff some communist wrote?"

"No, sir," Becky said, opening her drawstring bag. "The only time the word 'communist' has come up so far in my class was when a student asked if President Eisenhower is a communist. He said he had heard it at home. Look, here is the book Mr. Ingram was referring to," she said, reaching into her bag and placing the seven-hundred-fifty-page volume on the table. "Tommy told me his father and uncle had been talking about it, so I brought it this evening. It's by W. E. B. DuBois and it's a history of Reconstruction. When the children asked questions about the cross burning here in Unionville, I let them read about cross burnings that happened after the Civil War. I'd be happy to lend this to anyone who'd like to read it, but I assure you that the word 'communism' doesn't appear in it."

Both Swilley and Kramer stared at the massive volume for a moment but neither had any desire to read it. No one else moved to pick it up either.

"Is there anybody else that wants to speak?" the board president asked.

"What about the teaching schedule?" Howard Ames asked. "She didn't deny she's fouling up math instruction. Make her admit it."

"Yeah, Miss Reeves, what do you have to say about that?" Kramer asked.

"I changed the schedule because the children were coming in every morning with so many questions about current events that most of them weren't ready to settle down and do math. I thought if we did social studies first I could capture that interest and also make it easier for them to concentrate on math later. Mr. Ames, this may not have worked as well for your daughter because she is so personally motivated to like math, but it has proven very effective for the rest of the class, and I've tried to meet your daughter's needs by working math problems into social studies whenever possible. She may have told you, for example, about studying the Three-Fifths Compromise." Becky turned to the board president. "Mr. Kramer, would it be all right to ask the other parents here if their children have been performing as well in math this year as in previous years? I'm confident they will tell you that's the case."

Kramer glanced around the room and he could tell by the sheepish expressions on people's faces that Becky was right.

"Nope," Kramer said. "We're not gon' do that. Does anybody have anything else?" he asked.

Becky raised her hand.

"What is it now, Miss Reeves?"

"Well, sir," she said, "I've told you what I've been doing and why, but because this is a meeting about my contract, I want to point out for the record that there is nothing in that document that defines the school curriculum or calls upon me to teach according to any particular schedule or methodology. I'm not an attorney either, nor have I retained one so far, but I feel confident that I have not violated my contract or any written policies of the Unionville School District." She had not planned to imply that she might take some kind of legal action, but after Sam's comment about whether the board had grounds for firing her, she thought she might as well plant the idea of such a thing in the members' minds.

Doc rose from his chair and cleared his throat.

"You got something to say, Doc?" Kramer asked.

"Yes. I do. I've sat in a lot of classrooms in my day and I've been attending school board meetings for a lot of years. In all that time, I don't believe I've ever listened to a teacher that sounded more competent and more sensible than Miss Reeves. I've got a granddaughter in her class, and I'm reasonably familiar with what's been going on there. I delivered most of the kids she's teaching and I think it'd be a crying shame to take her away from them."

"All right," Kramer said, "do board members have any more questions?"

No one said anything.

"Well, then," he asked, "does any member want to make a motion?"

"I do," Swilley spoke up. "I move we revoke Miss Reeves's contract on the grounds that she broke it when she violated standard procedures."

"Is there a second?"

Again no one said anything.

"All right, I'll second it myself," Kramer said in an irritated tone.

"You can't do that," board member Russell Hadley from the Feed and Seed said, peering over his gold-rimmed glasses. "You can't second your own motion. It's against *Robert's Rules of Order*."

"Anybody got a copy of *Robert's Rules*?" Kramer asked. He knew no one did. Procedural questions had come up before and the board had more than once instructed Appleby to get a copy. However, Kramer had always told him afterward to forget it, and the superintendent never crossed the man who signed his pay check. "No? Then I'm calling the question. We have a motion and a second to terminate Miss Reeves's contract. All in favor raise your hands."

The room was so quiet folks could hear insects and tree frogs calling outside the open windows. Kramer and Swilley hoisted their arms and waited for others but none showed.

"Come on. Y'all ain't done voting, are you?" Kramer asked.

None of the members moved.

"All right," the board president said, his frustration growing. "Is there anybody against the motion?"

Hadley put his hand up and everyone looked immediately at the other two members, Gene Ragsdale, owner of Gene's Dry Goods, and Ray Tillman, another dairy farmer. After glancing first at Hadley and then at Sam, Ragsdale raised his hand. A few onlookers gasped but most were not surprised. A former Unionville basketball star, he had a long history of giving money to both the white and the black high school teams. The black school had won several state championships in the Negro athletic association, and Ragsdale had displayed their trophies in his store windows.

When Tillman saw there were two votes to dismiss Becky and two to retain her, he lowered his gaze to the table top and mumbled, "I abstain."

"Oh, for goodness sakes!" Woodhead cried.

"He can't do that, can he?" Bobby Jack asked loudly.

Others in the room sat searching each other's faces for reactions and wondering if they had heard correctly.

"Order!" Kramer said, raising his voice and rapping the table. "Ray, why ain't you voting one way or the other? I know you ain't got no conflict of interest."

"I ain't exactly sure," Tillman said. "I know Mr. Appleby and Mrs. Woodhead don't like her teaching and I believe in supporting the administration. I sure don't want no integration neither, but I kind of like what she said about helping kids learn something more than just a bunch of facts to pass tests. Seems to me we could use more teachers like that. So I figure since the vote's tied, I'll just leave it that way."

Groans went up from most of the parents. Kramer, Appleby, and Woodhead stared at Tillman in disbelief. Becky looked over at Doc and mouthed, "Thank you." Then she looked at Sam and smiled. He smiled back and winked again.

"God help us all," Kramer said. "Motion's denied. Meeting's adjourned."

CHAPTER 32

On Thursday morning, the *El Dorado Daily News* carried a huge headline announcing, "Negro Students Enter Central behind Steel of Federal Army." In Unionville, however, most folks were talking about the school board meeting. News of it raced across town, fueled mostly by the parents who had tried to get Becky reprimanded or fired.

About ten o'clock, Lester found Sam in the back of the Otasco store rearranging a rack of tangled automobile exhaust pipes. "I hear you and Doc saved that new teacher's job last night," the gossipy barber said, eager to get a firsthand account.

Sam wrestled one of the crooked pipes from the bottom of the stand and put it up top. "We spoke up for her," he said, "if that's what you mean."

"My brother Odell saw Bobby Jack Plunkett at the café this morning and he was sure ticked off," Lester said. "He told everyone he figured old Doc was just trying to make sure that grandkid of his got good grades but you was probably looking for a way to get into Becky Reeves's britches."

"Goddamn that sorry son of a bitch! He's got shit for brains!" Sam shouted. He kicked at the bottom tier of pipes and the whole rack went crashing to the floor. The clanging was followed in quick succession by a scream and the sound of glass breaking.

Miss Ruthelle burst into the aisle. "What's going on back here? You scared me so bad I dropped my jelly bean jar!"

Sam stood with his hands on his hips looking at the mess he had made, while Lester, choking with laughter, tried to find an escape route through the jumbled pipes.

"It's nothing, Miss Ruthelle," Sam said. "I just lost my temper for a minute."

"I think I hit a nerve," Lester said, moving back a safe distance.

"What do you mean?" Miss Ruthelle asked.

"Your boss here went to bat for that new teacher at the school board meeting last night and he's pretty touchy about it this morning. That's all."

"I hear some folks think she's an integrationist," Miss Ruthelle said. "You sure you ought to be taking up for her? It might not be good for business."

"I tell you what, Miss Ruthelle. I don't mean any disrespect, but when it comes to making decisions about my kids and their schooling, I don't care much about how it affects business. Anyway, this isn't gon' hurt the store."

"Sam," Lester put in, "I ain't saying Miss Ruthelle's right, but I hear the school board vote is gon' come up at the Citizens' Council meeting tonight. I expect they're gon' have a big crowd too. Brother Spurlock's got them flyers plastered on near about every telephone pole in town. Are you going?"

"Maybe I will, just so I know what they're up to." Truth was he had already decided to go. When he opened the store this morning, he found a tightly folded note wedged into the door-jamb. Scrawled on a scrap torn off a brown paper bag, it read, "You better watch yourself nigger lover!"

Remembering having threatened Jim Ed Davis in the barbershop, Sam figured this was just the sort of thing he would do for revenge. It was also something Bobby Jack Plunkett, who had been plenty worked up at the board meeting, would stoop to. Whoever it was, Sam did not think leaving an anonymous threat amounted to much, but to be safe, he took a snub-nose .38 Smith & Wesson off the display shelf, loaded it, and stuck it in a tool box under his truck seat. He already kept one hidden under the cash register table and another at home.

That evening, when Sam, Doc, and Tucker drove up to the Mercy Baptist Mission a little before seven-thirty, they saw a surprising number of cars and trucks parked among the tall pine trees on the church grounds.

"I didn't think they'd get this good a turnout," Tucker said.

Recalling that Doc had said he might go to the meeting, Sam had phoned him and asked to tag along. Then he had gotten ahold of Tucker and persuaded him to come too.

Doc found a spot where his DeSoto would not get blocked in, and he and his passengers got out and joined others walking toward the entrance. Patriotic music from a portable loudspeaker spilled through open church windows, and a man standing in the shadows hid the glow of his cigarette and strained to hear what the new arrivals were saying.

Inside, a large Confederate flag hung in front of the baptistery. Taped to the pulpit was a round white cardboard sign with the words "Citizens' Council" printed in black around the top edge and "Unionville, Arkansas" hand-lettered around the bottom. The middle had a picture of crossed US and Confederate flags.

Sam and his friends slid into the back row of pews. He estimated the crowd at about seventy-five people. Boomer Jenkins was sitting down front on one side with Crow Hicks. Bobby Jack Plunkett, DeWitt Ingram, and the Grimes brothers sat across from them. School board members Herbert Kramer and Travis Swilley sat a few rows back. As other folks continued to arrive, Doyle Scoggins strolled down the aisle and slipped in behind the board members. Moments later Jim Ed Davis came rushing in, slapped Boomer on the shoulder, and nudged him to move over and make room.

"I bet this is the only time some of these ole boys have ever been in a church for anything but a funeral," Tucker whispered.

When the music stopped, the audience grew quiet. Elmer Spurlock came out a side door, followed by Preston Upshaw and a man Sam recognized as a state senator from over in Claiborne Parish. All three mounted the platform and stood behind the pulpit. Spurlock, jacketless with shirt sleeves rolled partway up his meaty forearms, asked everyone to stand for the playing of "The Star Spangled Banner" and "Dixie."

After everyone had sat down, he said, "Ladies and Gentlemen, we're gathered here tonight because our southern way of life is under attack and we don't intend to stand for it any longer. There's a black menace bearing down on us and it's coming from two directions. It's coming from coloreds who can't wait to get in our classrooms so then they can get in our bedrooms, and it's coming from heathen federal judges who're determined to help the cursed sons and daughters of Canaan run over the white race. We're gon' stop it dead in its tracks."

He explained quickly how he had gotten approval from the Association of Citizens' Councils of Arkansas to start a chapter in Unionville and how he wanted everyone to sign up at the end of the meeting. Then he said, "Right now, though, it's my privilege to present a man who don't need no introduction to folks that believe in states' rights and segregation. He's the Honorable Leland P. Farley, president of the Association of Citizens' Councils of Louisiana. He drove up here from Summerfield to lend us a hand, and I want y'all to give him a real Arkansas welcome."

The senator was a powerful man well known for his racist views and his ambition to follow Earl Long into the Louisiana statehouse. Except for Sam, Doc, Tucker, and a handful of others, everyone in the audience yelled and whistled. When the crowd fell quiet, Farley buttoned his suit coat and approached the lectern. He wore a white shirt and a blue tie decorated with Confederate flags.

"My friends," he said, "I don't have the pleasure of living in the great state of Arkansas, but I know there's good citizens here tonight from both your 'Land of Opportunity' and my 'Sportsman's Paradise,' and I'm pleased to be with y'all. And just like y'all, I'm saddened that the president of the United States has seen fit to send federal soldiers to occupy y'all's capital and force y'all's children to go to school with Negroes. But y'all are doing the right thing by getting organized and showing that we southerners are tired of being pushed around by ignorant bureaucrats and judges up in Washington, DC. We've got more than a hundred thousand people enrolled in Citizens' Councils in Louisiana, and I know y'all have got a strong association here in Arkansas. You good people can make it even stronger. We're all gon' stand up for states' rights together, and before the sun sets on this sorry chapter in the history of our glorious country, we're gon' win."

Jim Ed and Boomer led almost everyone in standing to applaud and whistle, and Spurlock waved a fist in the air. Sam, Doc, and Tucker sat silently. When the racket died down, Farley carried on for half an hour about what he considered the perils of integration. When he finished, Spurlock returned to the pulpit.

"Now we have another treat in store for us," he said. "We're lucky to have right here in Unionville a man of great God-given talent to understand and write about government and the rights of states to take care of their own affairs. He ain't been with us very long, but he's already showed us he cares about our community and he's willing to speak out for what he believes. I'm pleased now to introduce Mr. Preston Upshaw, owner, publisher, and editor of the *Unionville Times*."

Upshaw, wearing his trusty corduroy jacket and a tie, stepped forward amid light handclapping, laid some notes on the pulpit, and looked out at the audience.

"He looks a little green around the gills," Tucker whispered.

"Don't start counting your money yet, undertaker, he's not gon' die from it," Doc whispered back. "Just give him a minute. He'll come up with some hot air and snake oil."

"Good people of Unionville," Upshaw said, "I'm honored to be here in the company of folks who know what's best for this great country of ours and who have the guts to stand up and be counted when misguided federal officials try to tear down all the rights and traditions we prize here in the South."

The crew down front burst out cheering again and other folks joined in.

Doc leaned over to Sam and Tucker again. "I bet that bunch had more than a few nips of hooch before they came in here."

"I'm not gon' take a lot of y'all's time tonight," Upshaw continued, "I just want to say I'm glad to see that the very thing I've been urging in my paper for several weeks now is starting to take hold. People are beginning to pay attention to the fact that if this racial menace threatening us isn't stopped, we're gon' have coloreds sitting in class with our kids, riding on school buses with them, and eating in the school lunchroom with them. And the good Lord only knows what'll come next. I'm not gon' go into detail tonight about all the steps we can take to prevent all that because y'all can read all about them in my paper Saturday morning. Anyone who doesn't have a subscription to the *Times* can sign up for one before you leave this evening."

Doc leaned over again. "There's the commercial."

"There're two other things y'all need to do tonight too," Upshaw went on. "The first one is to join our Citizens' Council. The second one is to sign this letter we have up here at the front to thank Governor Faubus for the courageous stand he's been taking against tyranny. I appreciate y'all listening to me and I thank y'all for standing up for the right we have under the Constitution of the United States to live the way we want to in the State of Arkansas without interference from Washington."

Amid more cheering and applause, Upshaw stepped off the platform. He sat down next to Farley, and Spurlock returned to the pulpit.

"Before we end," he said, "does anyone have any questions or anything y'all want to say?"

Bobby Jack leaped to his feet. He was wearing one of his too-tight letter jackets again. "Yeah," he said. "I want to know if there's anything we can do to get rid of a schoolteacher that's teaching integration. We got one of them and the school board ain't gon' do nothing about it."

"I've heard about that woman," Spurlock said, "and I know about last night's meeting too. Matter of fact, we've got two members of the school board here with us tonight. It's too bad they were the only ones that had backbone enough to do what was right. The way I understand it, unless the board takes it up again and somebody changes their vote, there ain't much nobody can do except try to make sure she don't get no contract to teach here again next year. Is that about right, Mr. Kramer?"

The school board president pulled his bulk to a standing position and rested his hands on the back of the pew in front of him. "Yeah, Brother Spurlock, it may be," Kramer growled. "We probably don't have legal grounds to fire her right now. She'd have to violate her contract somehow before we could get rid of her, and it doesn't look like she's done that yet. I ain't give up on the idea, though. I'm gon' keep looking into it. In the meantime, folks can write letters to Mr. Upshaw's paper and see if that'll persuade her to quit."

Sam nudged Doc and whispered, "Let's get out of here. I've heard enough."

CHAPTER 33

The next day, people were talking about the Citizens' Council meeting all over town. Men hanging out at the barbershop, in the pool hall, and under the whittlers' tree speculated about what might happen next. Customers at Emmett's, women buying groceries and getting their hair done, and people passing each other on the streets swapped rumors about it. And folks at home tied up party lines repeating hearsay.

Come Friday evening, though, attention shifted to the Bobcats' football game with the Pineview Panthers. They hailed from way over in Webster Parish and had a big line and lots of rough players. As usual, parents, students, and fans started arriving early for the game. Mr. Claude, Crow Hicks, and some sheriff's deputies were on hand again to direct traffic and keep order. Becky Reeves had drawn concession stand duty again. As Sam and Billy took their usual seats with the Tuckers, the sweet smell of Half and Half pipe tobacco drifted over the stands, and most folks talked football or baseball.

"Hey Billy," Neal O'Brien called. "Too bad about the Cardinals. Who you rooting for in the World Series?" Milwaukee had clinched the National League pennant earlier in the week and was set to square off against the New York Yankees on Wednesday.

"I reckon I'll pull for the Braves," Billy said. "The Yankees have won plenty already."

"It's gon' be a good one," Neal said.

"What do y'all think our chances are tonight?" Sam asked no one in particular. "Those Pineview boys look pretty good out there." They were yelling and racing around like thoroughbreds in red and white.

"Yeah, I hear they're a tough bunch," Tucker said.

When the Bobcats, wearing their familiar black and yellow, lost the coin toss and lined up to kick off, the Panthers huddled briefly in front of their bench across the field, then let out a roar and sprinted out to receive the ball. Once they had it, they plodded downfield three and four yards at a time to take a 7 to 0 lead. The Bobcats did not get untracked until a minute before halftime, when Ronnie Metcalf got loose around the left end for sixty yards and a touchdown. The Bobcats converted the extra point to tie the game.

As soon as the whistle blew, Billy took off with Randy Lawson, and after a band show with twirling fire batons, Sam and Tucker headed to the concession stand. On the way, they saw school board members Russell Hadley and Gene Ragsdale standing off to one side, smoking cigarettes and talking quietly.

"Excuse me a minute, Tucker," Sam said, and walked over.

"I'm sorry to interrupt, fellows, but I wanted to thank you for the way you voted the other night. Like I said then, I think Miss Reeves is doing a fine job."

"We've heard that from some of the other parents, too, Sam," Hadley said. "But I have to tell you, most of them are against her."

"You reckon they might still find a way to fire her?" Sam asked.

"Probably not," Hadley said. "If nothing else, it'd be darned near impossible to find a replacement this time of year. I doubt Kramer gives a damn about that, but we do, and I expect Ray Tillman understands it too."

"Well, y'all did the right thing," Sam said, turning to go.

Tucker had wandered off somewhere and with halftime winding down, Sam continued on to get their drinks. When he saw Becky behind the counter, his breathing went shallow, and he was glad he had worn a starched shirt and his good slacks again. The lines were long as usual and when he got to the front, he had three dimes ready.

"Hi, Becky," he said, putting the coins on the counter. "Three cokes, please."

"Coming right up, sir," she said, smiling and reaching into an iced tub. She was wearing her black-and-yellow Bobcat vest again and Sam admired the way it fit her and her personality.

She set the drinks on the counter and reached for the dimes. "Will we see you again in the fourth quarter?"

"You can count on it."

"Great," she said, smiling before moving to the next customer.

For a while in the third quarter, the teams battled back and forth between the thirty-yard lines. Then Ronnie broke several long gainers and by early in the fourth quarter Unionville led 21 to 7.

"Anyone want anything from the concession stand?" Sam asked the Tuckers and Billy.

"No. I'm all set," Gloria said.

"Me too," Tucker said. He glanced at Gloria and winked.

"I want a coke, Daddy. Want me to come with you?" Billy asked.

"No, that's okay, son, you stay here and watch the game. I'll bring you one."

"Say, Billy," Tucker said, "I've been sitting here trying to make out a pitching rotation for the Braves in the series. I can't decide if I'd start Spahn or Burdette. Who'd you lead off with?"

With Billy occupied, Sam made his way around back of the bleachers, but his heart sank when he saw the concession stand. The line was long and included a gaggle of folks from church. Eventually, however, most customers broke away, their arms loaded with refreshments. Other teachers were helping the few that remained and Becky began wiping down the counter. She smiled when Sam approached. He grinned back and each spoke at the same time.

"Hi, Sam."

"I'm back for a couple of more cokes."

They laughed and he held up a dollar bill.

"You have a minute?" she asked.

"Yeah, sure."

Becky motioned him to her left, opened the side door of the stand, and stepped gingerly off the raised floor to the ground. Sam moved around to meet her and she pushed the door closed.

"Here," she said, extending her right hand as if she were holding something between her thumb and index finger. Nothing was there.

"What's this?" Sam asked, pretending to take the imaginary object.

"It's the rain check you gave me. I've been thinking about those catfish."

"I'd be pleased to redeem it, if you really want to."

"I do. Hazel tells me that everyone's already talking about me and how you and Doc defended me Wednesday night, so I can't see where our going out to dinner would add much more fuel to the fire."

"Great," Sam said, reaching for her hand and squeezing it gently. She squeezed back. Her skin was soft and smooth. "How about this Sunday? It's about an hour's drive. I could pick you up at five and we could be back by nine or ten."

"That'd be wonderful," Becky said, touching his arm with her free hand. "I'd better get back inside now."

"Casual dress," Sam said, as he released her hand.

When Becky got back behind the counter, Sam was heading for the bleachers. Then he remembered the drinks and came back. He and Becky only smiled as she took his dollar and handed him two drinks and his change.

When Sam got back to his seat, Unionville was kicking a field goal to make the score 24 to 7 and ensure themselves a three-one record. As everyone stood up to leave, Sam leaned over and spoke quietly to Gloria and Tucker. "I'm going out of town for a while Sunday evening. Would it be okay for Billy to call y'all if he and Momma need anything while I'm gone?"

Gloria smiled and Tucker put his hand on Sam's shoulder. "We'll be glad to help, buddy."

CHAPTER 34

Because Unionville school officials always kept the football lights on until everyone found their cars in the parking lot and on the side streets, no one noticed anything unusual after the game until they got some distance from the field.

Sam and Billy were among the first to discover that something was amiss. On their way home, everything seemed darker than usual. Both streetlights near the Tate house were out and broken glass lay on the ground around the poles.

"What happened, Daddy?" Billy asked.

"I don't know, son," Sam said. "I'll call somebody about fixing them."

Walking home along Elm Street, Mr. Claude discovered three streetlights out near his house, and when he opened his front door, his phone was ringing and the mayor was on the other end. Alan Poindexter had counted six streetlights out in the business district and put a call into Arkansas Power & Light in El Dorado. He asked Mr. Claude to walk uptown, find Crow Hicks, check storefronts and windows, then wait for the emergency crew in front of the utility office.

While Mr. Claude and Crow kept an eye on Main Street, the power crew arrived and took a quick drive around town to check lights, lines, and switches.

When they got back, they reported sixteen lights out—eleven on the Arkansas side and five on the Louisiana side.

"What do y'all think?" Mr. Claude asked.

"We'll have them on again pretty quick, but y'all need to know somebody shot them out," one of the repairmen said. "Whoever it was probably used a high-powered BB gun or pellet rifle, or maybe a twenty-two with rat shot. Other than uptown here, all the damage is clustered around your house and over by Sam Tate's place. Have y'all pissed somebody off?"

On Saturday morning, Upshaw was strutting around his office like a bantam rooster. He had sold more than a dozen new subscriptions at the Citizens' Council meeting, people all over Unionville were talking about the streetlights, and he thought today's issue of the *Unionville Times* was his best yet.

Under the headline "Citizens' Council Formed," he described the organizing meeting as the start of a new chapter in Unionville history and called Leland Farley and Elmer Spurlock men of foresight and courage, willing to stand up and be counted.

In a front-page editorial titled "Beat Back the Black Menace," he called on his readers to take four steps to stop integration. "Start by joining the Citizens' Council," he urged. "Attend its monthly meetings, sign its petitions, and go to rallies it will sponsor. Second, write your representatives in Washington and ask them to vote against all civil rights legislation. Third, vote only for political candidates that actively oppose integration. And last, refuse to patronize any businesses owned or operated by persons who favor or aid integration in any manner whatsoever."

When Miss Ruthelle read Upshaw's editorial, she brought it straight to Sam.

"I told you so," she said. "This last part is you. He's talking about you playing ball with them coloreds and taking that Reeves woman's side at the school board meeting."

"Maybe so," Sam said, "but it doesn't matter because no one's gon' listen to him."

"Don't' you think maybe that's why somebody shot out the streetlights around your house?" Miss Ruthelle asked. "Upshaw's probably not the only one that has it in for you."

Sam did not tell her about the note in the front door.

Even before Miss Ruthelle's complaining and speculating, Sam's morning did not go well. He got out of bed looking forward to seeing Becky in just thirty-six hours, but he still had not figured out what to tell his family. Then Neal O' Brien stopped by and said he had called a council meeting for nine-thirty to get a report on the streetlights from Mr. Claude and deputy Culpepper. Sam was expecting a load of building supplies to arrive from Shreveport soon, but he said he would be there if he could.

The delivery held Sam up, and when he got to the town hall, three police cruisers, all with different markings, were parked out front, and Mr. Claude and Jesse Culpepper were coming out the door with a deputy from Claiborne Parish and two from Tonti Parish.

"You boys find out who did it?" Sam asked.

"Not yet," Mr. Claude said. The deputies did not say anything. Jesse, a lanky redhead with a boardinghouse reach, spread a map out on the hood of his patrol car and the officers huddled around it.

All the council members except Dave Westbrook, who was

working a shift at the chemical plant, were inside with Alan Poindexter and Eddie Dunn, mayor of the Louisiana side. The folks over there did not have a marshal, so Dunn, a long-legged pipeline walker for Ark-La-Tex Oil, had called in the deputies from Homer and Farmerville. Everyone was standing except Alan, who sat on the edge of his desk.

"I can't believe there weren't any witnesses," he said, shrugging his fleshy shoulders. "Not everyone was at the football game."

"Have they already talked to all the neighbors around where the lights were shot out?" Sam asked.

"Almost," Neal said, "and so far, they don't have anything. I just keep thinking that if whoever did it thought we had a police car on patrol, they probably wouldn't have had the nerve to do it in the first place. Maybe we do need one."

"I was for it the first time it came up," Lawrence Perkins said. "It's a big expense, but it'd be like buying insurance." After tying to follow in his father Doc Perkins's footsteps, he had dropped out of medical school and become a successful insurance agent.

"It wouldn't have mattered last night whether we had a police car or not," said Art Nelson, the former feedstore owner. "All the law would have been at the game anyway."

"I know there weren't any county boys patrolling last night, but are they still cruising around town every now and then otherwise?" Fred Vestal asked.

"Yeah, one cruiser at least twice and sometimes three times a night," Alan replied.

"Well," Neal said, looking to wrap up the meeting, "the deputies all seem to think it was just a prank. I don't guess there's much we can do now but wait and see if something turns up."

"I don't know if it was a prank or not," Sam said, "but Lester

Grimes stopped in the store this morning after you were there, Neal, and he said there was a lot of talk over at the café that Negroes did it to get back for the cross burning. I don't think they did, because they're smart enough to know they'd just be inviting more trouble. Right now, though, it doesn't matter much whether they did it or not, because if a few hotheads believe they did, things could turn bad."

On Saturday afternoon, the Razorbacks beat the University of Tulsa Golden Hurricane 41 to 14, and twenty thousand fans in Fayetteville and tens of thousands more throughout the state once again put racial tensions aside for a few hours.

Sam was not able to, though. He had the game on at the store and caught some of it between customers, but he kept thinking about the council meeting and the talk that Negroes might have shot out the streetlights. He wondered if they knew some folks blamed them. He doubted whether any of them had seen anything, but he figured that if any of them knew something, it would be Leon. Most folks had probably already picked up their cleaning for the weekend, and now would be as good a time as any to pop across the street and talk to him.

Leon had his sleeves rolled up and was adjusting a piece of equipment when Sam walked in and asked if he had a minute.

"Yes, sir. What can I do for you?" Leon asked. He tossed his screwdriver into a toolbox, picked up a rag, and began wiping his hands. His white shirt was spotless and Sam wondered how he managed to work on machinery and stay that clean.

"I guess you heard about all those streetlights getting shot out," Sam said.

"Yes, sir. It sure is worrisome."

"I suppose you know some white folks are gon' say some of y'all did it to get back for the cross burning."

Leon rubbed his hands harder and laid the rag on the tool-box. "Yes, sir. Reverend Moseley was talking just this morning about folks maybe blaming us. But Mr. Sam, we'd be plumb crazy to do something like that. We don't want any more trouble."

"Yeah, I know. It wouldn't make any sense." Sam looked down at the floor and did not say anything for a moment. Then he decided that if he were ever going to do what his fellow deacons had asked him to, this was as good a time as any.

"Speaking of Reverend Moseley," he said, "did you know some folks have the idea that some of y'all's members might want to come over to First Baptist?"

Leon tilted his head and squinted at his guest. "Mr. Sam, are you joshing me?"

"No, I'm not kidding. Some folks are concerned about it."

Leon grinned. "I don't mean any disrespect, Mr. Sam, but those people sure don't know much about us folks and our churches. None of us want to go to any white church. Why, some of our brothers and sisters, they just about live for Sunday meeting. It's what keeps them going. Wouldn't nothing make them give it up. If you don't mind me saying so, y'all's services are awful short and y'all don't sing near as much as we do. Y'all do it different too. Y'all don't do any lining and calling or any shouting and clapping. Church just wouldn't be the same to us without that. Why we have some sisters that can just about raise the roof when they cut loose. No, sir. There's no way we'd give that up."

"How do you know so much about our services?" Sam asked, surprised.

"Well, sir, Wanda's brother is the janitor at the First Baptist up at Camden. I went up there and helped out one Sunday when he was sick, and I could hear the preaching and the singing while we were picking up the Sunday school rooms. Like I said, I don't mean any disrespect, but the Holy Ghost, he just gets hold of us different."

"Yeah, I reckon so," Sam said. "I can hear y'all singing sometimes at night when I'm outside at home and the wind's blowing right." He paused, then said, "Well, for whatever it's worth, the parish and county deputies think it was probably just some pranksters that shot out the streetlights, but if you hear anything, they need to know about it. If you want to, you can just tell me. I'll get word to them."

"I'll do that, Mr. Sam, but don't be expecting something. We just plain don't know nothing about it."

CHAPTER 35

By Saturday night, all the streetlights were back on, and on Sunday morning, most folks went about their normal routines. Brother Byrd preached a regular hellfire-and-brimstone sermon about sin and repentance. Reverend Moseley led a service of cautious thanksgiving for the safety of the black students in Little Rock. And Brother Spurlock, coming off what he regarded as a hugely successful first meeting of the Citizens' Council, dished out another serving of rants based on what he believed the Bible said about the races.

Becky stayed home again and Sam found himself thinking more about supper with her than about Byrd's sermon, and he chided himself for feeling like a schoolboy. He thought about Judith Ann, too, and wondered what she would think. Probably she would be pleased. She had loved him too much not to be. He tried to convince himself that going out to eat was just that, simply sharing a meal and conversation, but he knew there was more to it.

While Sam was at church, Becky was getting ready for next week's classes. At least she was trying to. She kept thinking about all the things that had happened over the past month and a half. The cross burning worried her some but she loved teaching more than anything, and all the controversy around Little Rock

provided as challenging and potentially rewarding an opportunity as any teacher could hope for. She disliked the opposition to
her methods, but she felt confident about them and convinced
herself that the school board vote had at least put the matter to
rest officially. She just needed to make sure her efforts helped
her students and did not distract them.

As she thought about that, she began once more to question
the wisdom of seeing Sam. Most likely one of them would not
take to the other. But suppose they hit it off, and she had to admit that part of her hoped they would—he seemed nice and she
liked his looks—then what? That could be complicated in lots of
ways. Eventually, she told herself it was only supper and there
was no need for concern.

"Maybe it was a coincidence," Sam told Becky, "or maybe
the bad-debt companies figured there'd be more demand for
their services at the end of the year. Anyway, we're always busy
in December because we carry the best selection of toys anywhere around, and I'd hired Art to help out. It'd only been a few
months since he'd gone out of business at his feedstore, and it
seemed like every time we got really busy, another bill collector
would come looking for him. So, one day Billy and I had a bunch
of bicycle assemblies backed up, Art and Miss Ruthelle had customers three deep, and this man came in—big tall fellow with a
fancy hat and briefcase. Walked in just like he owned the place,
came up to the cash register table, looked around, and said so
everyone could hear him, 'Where's Art Nelson? I'm looking for
him.'"

Becky smiled as Sam unfolded his story.

"Well," Sam said, "something about the way the fellow was

acting and the way he said it just hit me wrong. It was sort of like he was from the big city and didn't need to be polite to a bunch of hicks. I went over to him, said who I was, and asked if I could help. He said, 'I was told I could find Art Nelson here. I'm a bill collector, and I'm here to help him collect some of those bad debts that made him go bankrupt.' Everyone in the store heard him. I looked over at Art and I could tell he was embarrassed, and something just came over me on the spot. 'He's over there.' I said. 'The guy with the gray hair. But he's hard of hearing. You have to talk loud to him.'"

Becky's smile grew wider.

"Art heard me," Sam went on, "and the fellow walked over to him and said really loud, 'I'm from Wilcox-Barker Associates up in Little Rock and I'm here to collect your bad debts.' Art put his hand up to his ear and said, 'You'll have to speak up. I'm a little hard of hearing.' By this time everyone had stopped to look and the fellow got even louder. 'I'm from Wilcox-Barker Associates up in Little Rock and I'm here to collect your bad debts!' Art just gave him a puzzled look and shook his head. This time the fellow got up on his tiptoes and yelled down so loud he turned red in the face. 'I'm from Wilcox-Barker Associates up in Little Rock, and I'm here to collect your bad debts! If you'll hire us, we'll find the low-down scoundrels that stiffed you or we'll find the cemetery they're in!' About that time, Miss Ruthelle, who was probably the only person in the store who didn't know what was going on, came over to Art and asked him in her normal voice if Mrs. Goodbar had ever called back about the red transistor radio, because someone else wanted it. 'Nope,' Art said, 'she hasn't called.'"

Becky burst into laughter.

"That broke up everybody," Sam said. "The fellow's mouth

dropped open, and he just stood there looking around at all of us with this peculiar expression on his face, like maybe he'd just discovered his fly was open or something, and that only made them laugh louder. He was so mad he couldn't talk. Just turned around and walked out. I guess that was mean of us, me especially, but I couldn't help it. I don't like people who act like they're better than everybody else or try to take advantage of other folks when they're down."

Sam and Becky were sitting at a corner table in Aunt June's Seafood House a little way north of Monroe, Louisiana, sipping sweetened iced tea out of Ball jars and waiting for their orders of hot-water bread, scalloped potatoes, and catfish fillets cooked in buttermilk batter. Fishing tackle and boat paddles decorated the paneled walls. A red-and-white-checkered cloth covered the table and complemented Becky's white sweater and Sam's brand-new gray shirt. In the center of the table, a Mason jar held a bouquet of late-blooming tiger lilies.

Sam had felt a little awkward when he picked Becky up in what he still regarded as Judith Ann's car, but the feeling had passed quickly. He told her about the restaurant and they talked about food. That led to gardening and she asked him how he became a merchant instead of a farmer. Then he asked her how she came to be a teacher, and as they drove through north Louisiana's rolling red clay hills, their initial attraction grew.

"That's the funniest story I've heard in a long time," Becky said, when she finally stopped laughing. "You really taught that bill collector a good lesson about manners."

She took a sip of tea and Sam could not help staring. Her auburn hair caught the late-afternoon sun coming through the window, and the more he looked at her, the more beautiful she seemed.

"To tell you the truth," Sam said, "I'm not sure why I told you that."

"Well, I'm glad you did. It tells me you enjoy what you do and you're passionate about what you believe in. But I already knew that. I saw it at the board meeting the other night. Like I said before, I'm really grateful to you and Doc." She reached over and placed her hand on Sam's. "You two stuck your necks out for me."

"No, I'm grateful to you for what you're doing for Billy."

"Sam," she said, sitting back in her chair, "if you don't mind my asking, what did you tell him about this evening?"

"I didn't tell him anything about it," he said, fingering his silverware. "I fibbed to the whole family. I said I had a meeting about church business."

"Oh?"

"Well, that way I didn't have to explain why I took the car instead of the truck. Besides, I didn't know if I'd ever need to tell them anything else."

Becky didn't reply but he could tell that she was mulling over his answer.

"You see," he continued, "I figured that if you didn't want to see me again after tonight, Billy didn't need to know we went out. And if you did, then I'd have more time to figure out what to tell him."

"That's logical and it would work the other way around too."

"What do you mean?"

Becky learned forward again. "I mean that if you didn't want to see me again, you wouldn't have to explain that to him either."

"There wasn't any chance of that happening."

"Well, then, mister," Becky said, placing her hand back on Sam's, "I think you'd better get to work on how to explain that you were with me."

Driving back to Unionville after supper, they talked about Billy and Mary Jane and told each other about their own childhoods and what they did during the war. They did not discuss what was going on in Unionville. When they pulled into the driveway at Hazel Brantley's a little after ten o'clock, she had the porch light on.

"I see your landlady's waiting up for you," Sam said, as he opened the passenger door and held out his hand. "I bet she's watching out the window and she'll be on the phone all day tomorrow."

"I don't think she will," Becky said, almost whispering as they walked up the steps, still holding hands. "I haven't figured out why exactly, but she really seems to like me. She treats me more like a daughter than a tenant. And she's fond of you, too, in case you didn't know it. I know she's a gossip but we might prove the exception. You better come inside to say goodnight, though, because the other neighbors are probably watching too."

Sam closed the door behind them and Becky eased close to him. He drank in her perfume and his hands felt the soft warmth of her back through her sweater. She put her hands on his shoulders, stood on tiptoes, and kissed him on the lips. He slid his hands higher, pulled her closer, and returned her kiss.

"Becky, this has been a terrific evening," he said. "Are you game to do it again?"

"I'd love to," she said, stepping back and moving her hands gently along his upper arms.

"Great! The Bobcats are playing at Norphlet Friday night and you won't have to work. How about then? There's a nice steakhouse down at Ruston and I could pick you up about a quarter to seven."

"That's perfect."

CHAPTER 36

Sam did not sleep well Sunday night. He could not stop think-ing about Becky's smile and touch and trying to decide what to say to his family. Gran worried him most. He did not know which he dreaded more, telling her or listening to her fuss. At daybreak, he got dressed and went to the garden. The sky glowed orange and red, dew glistened on the plants, and the morning air was cool and refreshing. He did some planting, fed Old Ned, then picked a mess of green beans and headed for the house to talk to his mother before the children got up.

The smell of fresh coffee greeted him at the back porch. He left the beans and his work boots there, brushed the dirt off his overalls, and found Gran inside making breakfast.

"Morning, Momma. It's nice out today. I put in some more greens and some spinach and left a basket of beans on the porch. We can snap them tonight."

"Don't track up my kitchen," she said, not bothering to look up.

"I want to talk to you," he said. He moved a dinette chair next to the counter where she was working.

Gran kept stirring her pancake batter. She was freshly scrubbed, had her hair up in her customary bun, and wore a flour-sack apron over her dress even though she did not need it. Despite being so short she had trouble reaching the cupboard, she never spilled anything or made a mess when she cooked.

"Momma, I wish you'd use that electric mixer I brought home for you. It'd save time and be easier on you."

"You know I don't like them fancy machines."

Sam shifted in his chair.

"You might as well come on out with it," Gran said. "I can tell something's on your mind and I know it ain't Billy's schooling. I already told you what I think and you already told me you ain't gon' listen to me."

"Well, I'm sorry we can't see eye to eye about that, but there's something else I need to tell you before you hear it from Almalee Jolly or somebody."

Gran stopped stirring for a second then started up again without looking at him.

"You're probably not gon' like this either, but you have to know about it, and you're gon' have to understand it's something I want to do. I know you don't like Becky Reeves, but she's really nice, and I like her a lot. I took her to supper last night and I'm gon' do it again Friday." He felt like he ought to say more, but he couldn't think of anything, so he stopped to let what he had already said sink in.

Gran set the bowl on the counter and turned to her son. She looked like she had just lost something she prized and could never get back.

"What do you think Judith Ann would say about you spending time with a woman like that, a Yankee carpetbagger that's ruining your own flesh and blood?"

"Momma, first of all, Becky isn't ruining Billy. She's helping him. And second, you know no one will ever take Judith Ann's place with me. I've thought a lot about how she'd see this and I believe she'd be happy about it. Becky is good and decent. Judith Ann would like her."

"Well, I don't like her and I don't like you sniffing around her."

"I know that but I hope you'll respect that this is something for me to decide. Besides, you don't really know her. She's a fine woman."

"I know all I want to know," Gran said. She picked up the bowl and began stirring again. "What're you gon' tell the kids?"

"I'm gon' tell them Miss Reeves and I have become friends and we enjoy each other's company, just the way they like spending time with their friends. And I'm gon' tell Billy that if anyone teases him about his teacher being friends with his daddy, he just has to ignore it."

"You ain't being fair to the boy, Sam. He shouldn't have to go through no razzing just so you can keep company with some woman that's got you all flustered."

"I don't think he'll be bothered much," Sam said, returning the dinette chair to its place.

"When're you gon' tell them?"

"At breakfast, and I'd appreciate it if you wouldn't say anything bad about Becky."

"It doesn't seem to be affecting business at all," Warren Sanders, a wholesaler for Fones Brothers Hardware, said, referring to what he called "the ruckus" in Little Rock. "In fact, there was a piece about it in the El Dorado paper this morning. Maybe you saw it."

A polished man with slicked-back hair and an easy manner, Sanders drove from Little Rock to Union County twice a month, stayed in a motel in El Dorado, and made the rounds of hardware and general stores throughout the area. He and Sam were standing at the cash register table with two huge leather-bound catalogs and an order pad open in front of them.

Until Sanders arrived, Sam had not been able to get his mind off his early morning conversations about Becky. He had expected Billy to worry about being teased, but the boy did not seem overly concerned. He said being picked on about his teacher could not be half as bad as the teasing he got about Crazy Dan. Mary Jane was another matter, though. She asked if Becky would be her and Billy's new mother. When Sam asked how she came up with an idea like that, Mary Jane said, "From Mrs. MacDonald." Sam tried to explain that Becky was only a new friend, and Mary Jane said she understood, but Sam was not so sure. Sanders was a welcome distraction.

"No, I haven't read the paper, yet," Sam said to the dapper salesman. "Last I heard, Faubus was looking to close Central High School, but I don't see how he can."

"Me neither," Sanders said, "but there's talk he's gon' call a special session of the legislature, try to abolish the entire public-school system, and somehow give the money to private schools that aren't integrated. I don't think he's got enough support for it, but who knows. Somebody said more than seven hundred kids are staying home from Central."

"Speaking of seven," Sam said, changing the subject, "add some number seven flat-head wood screws to my order. I need one box of one-inch and two boxes of two-inch."

"Okay. Let me see if we forgot anything else." Sanders licked his right thumb and middle finger and flipped rapid-fire through the catalogs, calling out products as he went, but Sam was not listening. He was thinking about the first time he saw Becky and last night's supper with her.

By the time Ollie Mae arrived at the Tate home Tuesday morning, gray clouds had rolled in from the southwest and brought misting rain. Gran had already put her quilting refreshments on the dinette table, and Mary Jane was sitting underneath it, playing with a shoe box full of paper dolls.

"Morning, Miss Mary Jane," Ollie Mae said, taking off her raincoat and rolling it up. "Are you gon' be keeping me company this morning while your grandmomma's quilting? I saw her sitting out there on the front porch waiting for her friends."

"Gran said I had to stay in here with you so I won't hear something I ought not to. What do you think they're gon' be saying, Ollie Mae?"

"Lordy, child, I don't know, but whatever it is, you best do like your grandmomma says. If you want me to, I'll help you cut some more paper dolls out of that old Sears Roebuck catalog." Ollie Mae hated fibbing, but she reckoned the quilters would be talking about integration again, and she was not about to mention that to Mary Jane.

When Gran's pals pulled into the driveway, she watched silently as they climbed out of Almalee's car onto the wet gravel. Despite carrying her quilting bag in one hand and trying to hold a newspaper over her head with the other, Emma Lou managed to nudge the passenger door shut with her elbow. Almalee struggled out of the driver's side while trying to open an umbrella.

"What's the matter, Ida Belle?" Emma Lou asked, as she clamored up the steps and dropped the damp newspaper next to the door mat. "You look all down in the mouth this morning. You feeling all right? We missed you at church Sunday."

"I was a mite too wore out to go," Gran said. Then she shouted, "Almalee, why don't you just put that fool umbrella back in the car and come on in. It ain't raining that hard!"

"I declare, Ida Belle, I bought this umbrella on sale up at Gene's last week just to go with this dress, and this is the first time I've got to use it. You might at least tell me they look good together."

"They look good. You satisfied?"

"Would you just listen to yourself!" Almalee said, mounting the steps. "You sound like an old sitting hen that's been run off her nest."

"Y'all quit your squawking," Emma Lou said, opening the door.

The three filed inside toward their regular spots. Gran had turned on the overhead light and a table lamp earlier to beat back the gray day.

"Are you worried about why somebody shot out the street-lights in front of your house, like maybe they was trying to get at Sam for some reason?" Emma Lou asked, as they settled into their usual places.

"No, he said it wasn't nothing but some darn fool with beans for brains and nothing better to do with his time."

"Well, I sure hope that's the case," Emma Lou said.

"I know what's the matter with her," Almalee said to Emma Lou, as if Gran were not there. "It's what I told you on the way over. I heard about it up at the Taylor sisters' shop yesterday. She's mad because Sam went out with that Reeves woman. Ain't that right, Ida Belle? I don't blame you, though, hon. I'd be mad, too, if it was me. And, come to think of it, I am mad. A pretty girl like Opal right here in town all this time, and when Sam finally decides he wants a woman, he picks some stranger. Why, I hear he was fawning all over her up at that school board meeting last week. I'd have told you about it Sunday if you'd been at church."

"You think I don't know he spoke up for her?" Gran snapped. "He told me."

"Him and ole Doc Perkins both," Almalee said.

Gran ignored Almalee and reached into her basket for her Monkey Wrench pieces.

"Well, Ida Belle," Emma Lou said, setting to work on her Double Irish Chain, "I know you don't like Becky Reeves, but I think it's good for Sam to be taking up with somebody. From what little I've seen of her, she sure seems nice, and you've got to admit she's mighty pretty. I think you ought to be happy for Sam."

"But she's an integrationist," Gran said, almost desperate for Emma Lou to see things her way, "and she's teaching Billy trash. Sam just can't see it."

"You don't know that for sure," Emma Lou said, "and maybe it don't make any difference anyway. Whatever's gon' happen about mixing with coloreds is gon' happen no matter what she thinks about it, or what Sam thinks, or you either. Seems to me the most important thing about Miss Reeves is whether Sam's happy seeing her."

Even Almalee kept quiet as she and Gran thought about what Emma Lou had said.

"Well, what if he ends up wanting to marry her?" Gran asked after a while. "She ain't our kind of people and she won't ever be."

Emma Lou stopped sewing and looked up at her friend.

"Ida Belle, personally, I don't think them getting married would be such a bad thing, but you're getting your cart way ahead of your horse."

Gran continued stitching. "No, I ain't. My cart's got kids in it and somebody's got to be thinking about what's best for them."

"Ida Belle," Emma Lou said, "I love you, but are you sure you know what's best for them? We're not gon' be sitting here quilting forever, you know. Those kids still have a lot of growing to do, and they could use a momma. And Sam's got needs too. It'd be good for all of them if he was to find somebody, but he's gon' have to decide for himself who that is."

Late Wednesday morning, Upshaw looked at his coffee mug and tried to remember how many times he had refilled it. His desk was piled with newspapers from other towns and cities, and he looked like he had slept in his clothes. He got up and started to the coffee pot then remembered he had turned off the hot plate earlier.

"Do you have this week's feature ready yet?" Pearl asked.

"Mrs. Goodbar, you worry too much," he said. "Have I ever missed a deadline?"

"No, but you've come close, and I don't like having to work late when that happens."

Upshaw did not answer because he knew Pearl's concerns were well founded. He did not have his lead story ready. Things remained tense in Little Rock, but not much new had happened, and he was having trouble coming up with an angle. He picked up the latest El Dorado paper again. According to one story there, Eisenhower had said he would withdraw the federal troops if Faubus promised to maintain order around Central High and not oppose integration. Faubus refused to make a firm promise, so the president said the troops would stay put.

Upshaw studied the reports a while longer then reached for his notebook and flipped through its pages. In a moment, a huge grin spread over his face.

"I've got it now," he said. "We're gon' have two main stories. We'll need at least half the front page for them. I'm gon' write about bad government on two levels. I'm gon' expose Eisenhower for lying and the Unionville, Arkansas, town council for being incompetent."

While Upshaw was struggling, Becky Reeves, pleased with the colorful posters and charts decorating the bulletin board on the back wall of her classroom, was starting something new.

"Boys and girls," she said, after completing her daily reports, "you've worked hard on social studies these past few weeks, and you can be very proud of what you've accomplished. I know I am." She leaned against the edge of her desk and pushed up the sleeves on her sweater. "We're going to continue that work, but this morning and some others over the next couple of weeks, we're going to do something different during the first part of class. You will still work in groups, but we're going to study about two groups of grownups—two teams, actually—that are starting something very special today. We're going to look at some ways they measure what they do. Who knows what teams I'm talking about?"

Billy raised his hand along with Glen Ray Plunkett then Linda Perkins put hers up too.

"Linda, what teams are they?"

"The New York Yankees and Milwaukee Braves, Miss Reeves. They're playing in the World Series."

"That's right, Linda. Baseball is a game that involves a lot of math, and during the World Series, we're going to focus our math lessons on the numbers, calculations, and statistics of baseball. We're going to look at individual and team batting, pitching, and fielding percentages, and we're going to look at attendance and ticket and concession prices and see if we can figure out how much money the teams' owners take in on the games."

Over the next forty-five minutes, Becky taught a lesson on how to figure winning percentages for teams and pitchers and calculate the hurlers' earned run averages.

⁓

Some parents who had been complaining about Becky were still mad about losing the school board vote to get rid of her. Others had simply grown tired of hearing about her. Nearly all heard more on Wednesday night, however. As the most popular sporting event in America, the World Series was all over the evening news. Reporters told in dramatic fashion how neither Milwaukee's Warren Spahn nor New York's Whitey Ford allowed a run through the first four innings and the Yankees went on to win 3 to 1. With the newscasters' prompting, a lot of Unionville seventh graders were eager to tell about yet another unusual day in class.

In the Ames household, the subject came up over supper.

"You already know long division and percentages," Howard said, as he put a pork chop on his daughter's plate. "I don't know why you're so pleased. So she's doing math first again, so what? You just said it's only for a couple of weeks. And besides, you don't even like baseball. It's a boring game."

"Yeah," Barbara's mother said, making a face. "It's just a bunch of men standing around scratching their privates and spitting. Yuck!"

"I don't care about the game, Daddy," Barbara said, ignoring her food. "But the math problems are interesting. Did you know that Mickey Mantle and Hank Aaron had the same homerun percentages this year? It's fun to compare things that way. Miss Reeves calls it 'statistical analysis,' and she says we can use it to study a lot of other things, like weather patterns and ups and downs in the stock market."

"Howard," Barbara's mother said between bites of baked potato, "you're gon' have to try harder to get something done about that woman. Little girls don't have any business studying about baseball and the stock market."

"Well, now," Howard said, looking at his daughter but speaking to his wife, "it's not gon' hurt Barbara to learn about the stock market. Maybe Miss Reeves is finally coming to her senses."

At the Plunkett home, Glen Ray couldn't wait to tell Bobby Jack what the class had learned.

"Hey, Pops!" the boy called as soon as his daddy got home. "I know who's gon' win the World Series."

"How do you know that?" Bobby Jack asked, as he took a beer from the Frigidaire.

"We studied it at school today."

"I don't believe it," Bobby Jack said. He squeezed his wife's behind and plopped down in a dinette chair.

"It's true. Listen. The Yankees' top four starting pitchers all have earned-run averages lower than the Braves' top four pitchers. That means the Yankees' top four pitchers are better even though they didn't win as many games this year."

"Who told you that?"

"Nobody. Me and my study group figured it out."

Bobby Jack took a long draw on his can of Miller High Life. "Listen, boy. I don't know what that woman is up to now but she don't know nothing about baseball. I don't know how they get them earned-run averages, but I know the pitcher that's got the lowest one ain't necessarily gon' win. There's more to it than that."

"That's what Miss Reeves said too."

"Really?" Bobby Jack said. "She must've been guessing then."

Sam started the baseball conversation at his house. Only, he didn't know it would involve school.

"Billy," Sam asked, as he passed around the mashed potatoes at supper, "did you hear the Yankees won the first game today?"

"Yes, sir. And guess what? We studied about the series in class."

"How'd you do that, son?" Sam asked, despite wishing he hadn't started down this path.

"Well," Billy said, taking out a huge spoonful of potatoes, "Miss Reeves let us study baseball numbers and stuff for our math lesson. We learned how to do earned run averages, home run percentages, and a whole bunch of good stuff."

"See," Gran said, forgetting she had agreed not to criticize Becky. "I told you she wasn't no good teacher. The idea! Wasting them kids' time like that."

Sam let his mother's comment pass. "How do you figure an earned-run average, Billy?" he asked, as he put peas on Mary Jane's plate. When Billy explained, Sam said, "Hey, that's right. It's a good way to bone up on your long division, too, isn't it?"

"Yes, sir. Miss Reeves sure is a good teacher and I'm sure glad she's your friend. I didn't say nothing to her about that, though."

"I'm glad too," Sam said, letting his son's grammar slide while picturing Becky on Friday night.

CHAPTER 37

"Daddy, Daddy, wake up!" Billy pleaded, as he shook Sam's shoulder with both hands. "The fire siren's going off."

"All right, all right," Sam said, swinging his feet over the side of the bed and reaching for a lamp. "What time is it?"

"It's one-thirty. Can I go this time, Daddy?"

Sam scrambled to his closet for pants and a shirt. "No, son. You have school tomorrow. Is Mary Jane up too?"

"Yes, sir. She's already putting on her clothes."

"Well, tell her to go back to bed," Sam said, pulling on shoes, "and stay with her till she goes back to sleep."

When Sam got outside, he did not see any sign of a fire, but before he cleared the driveway, he heard the old LaFrance truck roaring in his direction. When he got to the highway, he saw a line of pickups and cars coming from uptown then turning east. He fell in behind them and wondered if someone had burned another cross at Mt. Zion. Then he saw a faint glow well beyond it. The train of vehicles continued past the church and South Arkansas Oak Flooring until the mostly dirt road became too narrow to handle them. After pulling over like the other volunteers, he hurried with them on foot toward Sadie Rose Washington's juke joint.

There were not many fire hydrants in the quarters and volunteer firemen had strung out hose for three blocks. When Sam broke into the open at Sadie Rose's place, he saw men and older boys—black and white—carrying tables, chairs, and boxes of foodstuff out of the rambling, weather-beaten frame building and piling them in the unpaved parking lot alongside a juke box and an upright piano. Flames were shooting from a small storage building a short distance away with a chain and padlock on its door. Most blacks and a handful of white men, including Emmett Ledbetter, knew it held bootleg liquor. Odell Grimes and another man had a hose turned on it but it looked like a lost cause. Norm Patterson from Ark-La-Tex Oil and Fred Vestal from the furniture store were wetting down the roof and walls of the main structure, which served as a grocery store and bar-bershop as well as a pool hall and nightclub. Lester Grimes was tending the pumper and trying to look like he had everything under control.

Sam helped carry things out of the larger building until the smaller one collapsed, ending the threat to its neighbor. When that happened, Sadie Rose, a large, dark woman to whom most everyone gave a wide berth, started directing the haulers to tote things back inside. Even in bare feet and a faded red bathrobe, she was a commanding figure. Whites were not exactly afraid of her. They just did not know quite how far they could push her before she turned on them, and she was so big no one wanted to tussle with her.

As soon as the firemen put out the remaining embers, they began cleaning their equipment and preparing to leave. In the middle of all the scurrying around, council president Neal O'Brien found Sam and pulled him aside.

"It's another cross burning," Neal said. "When we first got here, we could see the outline of it in the flames. It looked like somebody wrapped it in rags and leaned it against the shed. Probably tied the rags on with hay wire, same as last time. We'll find out when everything cools off."

"Damn! The streetlights last week and now this."

"Yeah, and this isn't as simple as the last one," Neal said. "We've got real property damage this time and it's pretty deep in the quarters. I'm gon' talk to the mayor and Jesse Culpepper about getting the sheriff down here."

"Where's Crow Hicks? I haven't seen him around anywhere."

"He didn't ride the truck but he's here some place. He was talking to Preston Upshaw a little while ago."

"What about Jim Ed Davis?"

"Yeah, he was standing around looking when I got here."

"I see Leon Jackson over there," Sam said. "I'm gon' find out if he knows anything."

Leon, who had a special affection for Sadie Rose's joint because of the crap games that went on there, had just grabbed two more straight chairs when Sam walked up.

"Hey, Leon, this was a pretty close call for Sadie Rose, huh?"

"Yes, sir, it sure was." Leon put the chairs down and mopped his forehead.

"I guess you know somebody started it by burning a cross."

"Yes, sir. Sadie Rose told me. She saw it."

"Did she see who did it?"

"No, sir. Her dog woke her up, but by the time she got to a window, all she saw was the cross on fire. It was leaning against the shed and it was burning too. She lives right over there," Leon said, pointing to a white house across the road. "She came running out with her shotgun but there wasn't anybody around."

"She has a shotgun?"

"Yes, sir. Because of all the cash she keeps on hand."

"Do you think she'd have shot whoever it was if she'd seen him?"

"It wouldn't have surprised me none. Folks are kind of edgy now." Leon wiped his forehead again. "What do you make of this, Mr. Sam? I figured the first one had something to do with Little Rock but I don't know about this one."

"I don't know either. Maybe someone has it in for Sadie Rose. Say, I don't see B. J. Long and Charlie Foster anywhere. Don't they live right up that road there?"

"They're over at Reverend Moseley's. Some of us have been taking turns staying with him. We're afraid somebody might try to hurt him and we don't aim to let that happen."

As Sam drove home a little while later, he could not stop thinking about Sadie Rose running around in the quarters with a shotgun and what Leon said about looking out for Reverend Moseley. He also thought about the streetlights being shot out and the shotguns and rifles in his store window. There were guns in plain sight in pickup trucks all over town, and apparently a lot of black folks had them too, just not out in the open. And now he was carrying a pistol under his seat. He wondered how many others were doing the same thing.

⁓

Preston Upshaw had most of his next issue in hand before the cross burning, but despite being up much of Wednesday night, he decided to go to Emmett's for breakfast Thursday morning and see what the regulars were saying. He had been over a couple of times since his talk at the Citizens' Council meeting, and both times folks had slapped him on the back and offered to buy him coffee. As soon as he walked in, folks started asking him what he thought about the second cross burning.

"It's another one of them patriotic jobs, ain't it?" Jim Ed Davis asked. He was wearing his hunting clothes and sitting in a booth with Crow Hicks and Odell Grimes, his fellow Little Rock posse members. "We got us some damn good men in Unionville, don't we?"

Upshaw grabbed a counter stool.

"Yeah," Crow said, nudging Odell. "We ain't gon' let that mess they got up in Little Rock get started down here."

"You got any idea who done that last night, Mr. Upshaw?" Jim Ed asked. He looked at Crow and winked. "Somebody's making old Crow here look bad at his night watching. He's gon' start worrying about his job, ain't you Crow?"

Crow grinned back. "What makes you think I ain't been helping with them things, you old coot? I tell you, it sure does make a man proud."

"Now, boys," Upshaw said, reaching for the coffee Emmett set in front of him, "if I knew who did it, do y'all think I'd tell for free? I'd make y'all read it in the newspaper."

"Uh huh," Jim Ed said, nodding his head and poking Crow on the shoulder. "You don't know. Don't nobody know. It's just like back when the Klan was around."

"Hey, Emmett," Upshaw called. "Bring me a stack of pancakes and some sausage patties. These boys are making me hungry."

When Upshaw got back to the newspaper office, Pearl Goodbar was waiting.

"I suppose you're gon' rewrite everything after last night, aren't you?" she asked. News of the event had already traveled all over town.

"Nope. Don't need to. I'm just gon' add onto it. I'll be done in a little bit."

A short time later, Upshaw laid copy for two lead stories on

Pearl's desk. She reached for them to start copyediting. Under the headline, "President Lies," Upshaw had written:

> The president of the United States has lied to the American people. He said he would withdraw federal troops from Little Rock if Governor Faubus would give in to the whims of the oppressive federal judiciary and stop opposing the integration of Central High School. As disagreeable as those things must have been to the governor, he pledged to do both. Then the president changed his mind. Such an act can only be described as despicable. Mr. Faubus is a great man. It is too bad we cannot say the same thing about the occupant of the White House.

"Mr. Upshaw," Pearl said, when she finished. "Are you sure you want to run this? This is pretty strong language."

"Yes, Mrs. Goodbar. I am. It's good journalism. Get on with it."

The second story bore the headline, "Arkansas-Side Mayor and Council Act Irresponsibly." Here, Upshaw had written:

> Cross burning is an act of free speech, and in these trying times, with the menace of integration bearing down on our community, a person who has the courage to stand up for what is right should be admired as a shining light for democracy. Unfortunately, whoever burned a cross at the business establishment of one of our Negro residents this week also burned down a nearby building. But that property loss was likely accidental and certainly secondary to an act committed for the public good. By contrast, shooting out our streetlights last week was

deliberate and reprehensible and did significant financial damage to our community. More importantly, it would not have occurred if the mayor and members of the Unionville, Arkansas, town council had done their duty. Public safety in this community is a joke, and Mayor Alan Poindexter and the council members—Messrs. Art Nelson, Neal O'Brien, Lawrence Perkins, Sam Tate, Fred Vestal, and Dave Westbrook—all know it. Yet they have failed to provide the people who elected them with a police car and a marshal who knows how to operate it. It is way past time for those gentlemen to retire Marshal Claude Satterfield. He should be thanked for his years of service to the community and given a rocking chair under the whittlers' tree.

"Well," Pearl said, after she finished reading, "when did you decide you wanted to go broke? Don't you know this article is gon' cost you advertising and subscriptions? Mr. Claude is a legend in Unionville. I don't know about where you come from, but folks here aren't used to seeing their leading citizens ridiculed in print like this."

"Mrs. Goodbar, I'm just doing what any good journalist would do, and frankly, I think folks are gon' eat this up."

On Thursday afternoon in New York, the Yankees beat the Braves 4 to 2 in the second game of the World Series, and while millions across the country tuned into the game, seventy-five white students stormed out of Central High School and hung a black man in effigy in the parking lot. For a while, it looked as if there would be another riot, but federalized National Guardsmen, who now had primary responsibility for protecting the black students, restored order. However, the soldiers could not stop some white students from continuing the daily pattern of pushing, shoving, and taunting the nine black ones.

In Unionville, meanwhile, people were still buzzing about the second cross burning. As before, though, no one had come up with any clues about who did it. Neal O'Brien walked over to the Otasco store in midmorning and found Sam on the loading dock installing seat covers on Brother Byrd's six-year-old Chevy. The front and rear benches were lying on cardboard spread over the rough planks.

"Sam, I just saw the mayor. He said the sheriff had a state police investigator down at Sadie Rose's yesterday afternoon and they found the wire from the cross. It was clothes hangers."

"How do they know that?" Sam asked, as he used a hog ring to fasten a fold of nylon to the bottom of a car seat. Made to clamp around the edges of hogs' noses and keep them from rooting out of their pens, the rings had a ton of practical uses.

"By the curls in the ends of the wire. Looks like whoever did it just pulled a bunch of hangers apart and used them like haywire."

"That's strange," Sam said, clamping another fold. "Most people who've got two-by-fours lying around have haywire too. Either that or hog ring pliers like these. I sell a bunch of them."

"Yeah, me too," Neal said, sitting down on Byrd's rear car seat. "Anyway, Jesse Culpepper's wondering if maybe Leon Jackson burned this one. That and the fact that it was so far back in the quarters. Maybe he had something against Sadie Rose, and

275

the first cross gave him a convenient way to cover up. Maybe he meant to burn down that shed."

"That's just plain stupid!" Sam snapped. "Jesse's grabbing at straws. Everybody has coat hangers. Besides, I don't believe Leon would do a thing like that. And even if he did, he wouldn't call attention to himself that way. He's smarter than that. You don't really think he did it, do you?"

"No, I guess not, but Jesse's gon' ask him about it."

Sam shook his head and turned the seat over to check for wrinkles. "I bet whoever did it just picked up the first thing he came across that'd do the job. Do Jesse and the sheriff have any other bright ideas? I mean besides putting extra cruisers down here again?"

"No, and they know that's not gon' stop it from happening again if whoever did it is bound and determined."

"Well, we have to do something," Sam said. "Except for the coloreds, I expect most people probably don't care how many crosses get burned. I don't imagine they'd have cared much if Sadie Rose's joint had burned down either. But this happened too close to the streetlights getting shot out. That doesn't look so much like a prank anymore." Sam started to mention the note he found stuck in his door but thought better of it. He did not want to risk word getting out and starting more trouble or scaring his family.

"Yeah," Neal said, "I think we better talk some more about getting a police car."

Sam lifted the seat he had been working on and placed it in the Chevy. "You want me to go ahead and see Horace Bowman about the money, or do you want to have another council meeting first?"

"Why don't you go ahead?"

"You don't believe the others will think we're rushing to get rid of Mr. Claude?"

"No, I think they all know it's time," Neal said. "They just hate to face up to it."

CHAPTER 38

Sam closed the store early on Friday, and when he drove past the high school about half past five, the Bobcat football bus was pulling out of the parking lot for the short run to Norphlet, north of El Dorado. The team's winning ways had led to calls for a fan bus, and students were fastening "Beat Norphlet" banners to it and the band bus. Musicians were loading their instruments, and parents were lining up their cars and tying black-and-yellow streamers to their radio antennas.

When Sam got home, Billy and Mary Jane greeted him in the driveway.

"I fed Old Ned and did all the other stuff just like you asked me to, Daddy," Billy said, as Sam climbed out of his pickup.

"Thank you, Billy. I appreciate it."

"Daddy, can I go with you?" Mary Jane asked, jumping into his arms.

"I'm sorry, sweetheart, but we've already talked about this. It's a grownup supper. I thought we were gon' read some more before time for me to go. Where're your books?"

"Oh, boy! I'll get them."

Mary Jane went flying into the house and Billy walked along with his daddy. Sam put his arm around the boy's shoulders. "How was school today?"

"It was good. We learned how to do slugging percentages. Hey, can we watch part of the World Series after dinner

278

tomorrow? Bob Turley's pitching and it's gon' be a good game."

"You bet, son."

⌒

"I didn't think it'd be possible to get Billy any more fired up about school but you certainly have," Sam said. He and Becky were headed south on US 167 toward Ruston, seat of Lincoln Parish. "How'd you happen to get so interested in baseball? Was it from your daddy?"

"Mostly," Becky said. "He never played, but he always liked the tradition of it, and I guess that's what I like most about it too. I like the way big things in the history of baseball seem to go along with big things in the history of the country. Walter Johnson, Ty Cobb, and Honus Wagner all played during World War I. During the Depression, the Yankees had Ruth and Gehrig and the Cardinals had Dizzy Dean and the Gas House Gang. Then right before World War II, Joe DiMaggio hit in fifty-six straight games and Ted Williams batted over four hundred, and around the time of the Korean War, the Yankees won five straight World Series."

"I can't believe you know all that stuff."

"Why is that? You think baseball's just for men?"

"Well, no," Sam said. "I just never met a woman who knew so much about it." He looked over at her. She wore a V-neck blouse and a swing skirt she had spread out on the seat to keep down wrinkles. Her breasts drew his eyes and she noticed.

"Hadn't you better watch where you're going, mister?" she said with a girlish giggle.

Becky's teasing sent Sam's blood rushing. He shifted in his seat. "Yes, ma'am," he said, "but I have to tell you that a beautiful woman like you is distracting."

"Why, thank you, sir," she said.

For the next forty-five minutes, as they drove through small towns and along stretches of highway built up through bayous, Sam and Becky continued to talk about sports and school.

"How did you start teaching different from everyone else?" he asked.

"It's a combination of things. I believe learning ought to be fun. Kids get bored doing the same things all the time, so I look for different ways to get them thinking. I learned that from my mom and dad when I was sick for so long. They kept coming up with new ways to keep me studying at home."

A little after dusk, Sam pulled into the crowded parking lot of the Chuck Wagon Steak House on Ruston's east side, near Louisiana Tech. The board-and-batten building looked rustic on the outside, but inside, it had polished dark paneling, booths and chairs covered in red vinyl, and lots of mirrors. A hostess wearing cowboy boots, a low-cut peasant blouse, and a red skirt that stopped well above her knees showed them to a booth next to a huge basket of artificial ferns.

"Your waitress will be with you in a minute," she said, smiling through enough lipstick to cover a barn door.

"Sam," Becky said, when they were alone, "I'm sure the food's going to be good here because you said Tucker recommended it, but this is the first restaurant I've been to that had a personality conflict."

"How's that?"

"I don't think this place can decide whether it wants to be a wild West chuck wagon or a house of ill repute," she said, laughing.

Over thick steaks served with baked potatoes, sour dough bread, and iced tea, Sam and Becky talked about the unusual things that had happened in Unionville since she came.

"Do you have any regrets about moving here?" he asked.

The question reminded Becky of the photographs in the shirt box but she pushed the thoughts away as always. She understood her connection to the people in the pictures, but she did not feel it, and she did not intend to let it affect her. "Well," she said, "I deplore the cross burnings, and I think anyone who does something like that is filled with hate. I doubt most white people in Unionville are like that. I expect most of them are against integration, but Missouri is like that too. The thing that bothers me most is the *Unionville Times*. I've never seen a newspaper so blatantly biased. I don't like the editor's claiming that cross burning is freedom of speech either. I haven't met the man, but I think he's more than just meanspirited."

"Yeah, I think you're right about that."

"Let's talk about something else," Becky said. She took a sip of iced tea.

"Okay, what would you like to talk about?" Sam asked. He watched as she sat her glass back on the table and used both hands to pat her lips dry with her napkin.

"Would you mind telling me about your wife, what she was like? She must have been a wonderful woman."

"What makes you say that?"

"You do, and Billy too. He's such a terrific kid."

Sam was surprised that Becky asked about Judith Ann but he did not mind. He told how he and Judith Ann met, how they came to live with his mother, things she liked and disliked, how she died, how much Mary Jane looked like her, and how Gran was helping him raise the little girl and her brother. Becky took it all in, and both the telling and the listening drew them closer.

Later in the parking lot, when Sam held the passenger door

open for Becky, she slid midway over in the seat. When he got behind the wheel, she patted his knee, and as he drove home, they held hands like teenagers and listened to Fats Domino sing "Blueberry Hill" and Pat Boone croon "Love Letters in the Sand."

It was nearly midnight when they got back to Becky's apartment, and, as before, they said goodbye inside, out of the glare of Hazel's porch light. This time, though, their goodnight kisses lasted longer.

"You know the effect you're having on me, don't you?" Sam asked, holding her close as they stood in her living room.

"Yes, I feel you," Becky answered, smiling and pressing tighter against him. She ran her fingers through his thick black hair. "I feel the same way. Why don't you come over Sunday evening and I'll make supper for us?"

"Are you sure?"

"Very," she said, and kissed him again.

CHAPTER 39

Sam and Billy barely beat Miss Ruthelle to work Saturday, and they had just finished sweeping when Lester Grimes came in carrying the *Unionville Times* and grinning ear to ear.

"Hey, Sam," he called. "You're a celebrity! You got your name in the paper."

"Let me see that," Sam said. He dumped a roll of quarters into the cash drawer, pushed it shut, and tossed the coin wrapper into a trash can.

"It's right there on the front page," Lester said, handing over the paper, "under the headline about the town council."

"What is it, Daddy? What's it say?" Billy asked. He leaned his broom against a display counter, and he and Miss Ruthelle strained to see around Sam. As he scanned the story, his face turned red.

"Why, that sorry son of a bitch!" he said after a moment. "Who the hell does he think he is, attacking Mr. Claude like that?"

"Aw, come on, Sam," Lester said, trying to cross his arms above his big belly. "You have to see the humor in it. That part about putting Mr. Claude in a rocking chair is funnier than a nudist in a briar patch. You just don't like what he said about you."

"Lester Grimes! I've told you about that kind of talk!" Miss Ruthelle scolded. "And shame on you, too, Sam Tate!" She grabbed the paper so she could finish reading the story.

"What's he talking about, Daddy? What's it say?" Billy asked again.

"Son, it just says Mr. Claude shouldn't be marshal anymore and the council ought to fire him."

"Gee, Daddy, I bet that's gon' make Mr. Claude feel bad, isn't it?"

"Yeah, and it makes me feel bad too," Sam said.

Miss Ruthelle handed the paper back to Lester. "What're y'all gon' do, Sam?"

"Whatever we do, it won't be because of anything Preston Upshaw wrote."

Neal O'Brien and Fred Vestal were also discussing the story at City Hardware. They saw Lester go into the Otasco store, and when he left, they walked over. By that time, Billy was taking out trash and Miss Ruthelle was into her paperwork.

"Did you see Upshaw's story?" Neal asked Sam.

"Yeah, I saw it."

"I told Fred about the conversation we had yesterday," Neal said. "I'd sure hate for Upshaw to think he's forcing us into something, but I think you better talk to Bowman as soon as you can."

"I don't care what Upshaw thinks," Sam said. "I'm gon' stop advertising in that rag of his too."

"Yeah, so are we," Fred said.

"I think we need to move fast," Neal said. "While you're talking to Bowman, I'll talk to the other council members."

"What're you gon' say to Mr. Claude if he asks you about the story?" Sam asked.

"I don't know," Neal said. "I can't think of any good way to handle it."

"Maybe we ought to ask him what he thinks about it," Fred said.

"Good idea," Sam said.

Later, after Billy got the Tates' copy of the *Unionville Times* from the post office with the mail, Sam looked to see if Upshaw had run any letters about Becky's teaching. There was only one, a nasty piece in which Bobby Jack Plunkett tried to compare her to Daisy Bates but only showed why he flunked English so many times.

On most Saturdays, Sam went to the bank sometime in mid-morning to deposit checks and get change for the cash register. After Miss Ruthelle made out a deposit slip and a list of change they needed, Sam put everything in a zippered bank pouch and headed across the street. When he opened the front door to Farmer's State Bank, Jim Ed Davis rushed out, bumping into him.

"Hey! What's your hurry?" Sam asked.

"Why the hell don't you watch where you're going?" Jim Ed barked without stopping.

"Crazy peckerwood," Sam muttered to himself.

Once inside, he headed straight to the back and, seeing no receptionist around, knocked on the bank president's partly open door.

"Yeah, what is it now?" Bowman bellowed. Then he looked up and saw Sam. "Oh, it's you. Come on in. How's business?"

"It's fine but I'm not here about the store."

Bowman reached into his humidor for a cigar, bit off the end, and spit it into a wastebasket.

"What do you want?" the banker asked, lighting up.

Sam took that as an invitation to sit down in the only other chair in the room. Straight and armless, it was positioned directly in front of Bowman's desk and had legs so short that anyone using it had to look up at the banker.

"I'm here unofficially as a member of the town council," Sam said. "Did you see today's *Unionville Times?*"

"Nope, I don't read it," Bowman said between puffs. "I advertise in it just so folks can't say I'm not supporting the community but I don't care what else is in it. What about it?"

"Upshaw's after the council to get rid of Mr. Claude and buy a police car, and between you and me, it just so happens we've already been talking about it, only Mr. Claude doesn't know it. We figure if we'd had a police car and a marshal who could drive it, we might not have had these two cross burnings and the streetlights shot out. We're worried that something else might happen and somebody might get hurt. That'd be even worse for business. Problem is, the town doesn't have the money to buy a car."

Bowman glared at Sam then took a long draw on the cigar and blew a smoke ring.

"And you want me to lend it to you. Is that it?"

"Well, not exactly."

"You sure as hell don't think I'm gon' give it to you, do you?"

"Well, sir, we hoped, seeing as how you're a community-minded citizen, like you said, you might consider it."

"Goddamn it!" Bowman shouted, yanking his cigar out of his mouth. "Everybody wants something for nothing. That's all I've heard this morning. Everybody thinks I'm running some kind of goddamn charity here. This here ain't no Community Chest, it's a bank, and I'm sick and tired of every goddamn son of a bitch and his brother coming in here and thinking I'm giving money away like it grows on goddamn trees. People think just because I've got money, I ought to give them some. Well, I ain't gon' do it."

Surprised by Bowman's outburst, Sam could not think of a good response, and the two men sat staring at each other.

"You've got a lot of nerve, you know," Bowman said after a few moments, "coming in here like this, as much money as you owe me on that store of yours. All right. I tell you what I'll do, but only because I think you're right about Mr. Claude. I'll donate half the money and lend the town the rest of it if at least three council members will sign a promissory note to pay it off if the town can't."

Sam said he would take Bowman's offer to the council and see if they could make it work. "I'm sure they'll be much obliged to you, in any case," he said.

"What do y'all plan to tell Mr. Claude?"

"I don't know yet. The truth, I reckon. Times are changing and the town needs more protection."

Bowman picked up a stack of papers, signaling the end of the meeting, and Sam got up and walked out to a teller's window.

As soon as he finished his banking, he went next door to City Hardware. Older and not as well lighted as the Otasco store, it had long rows of tall, over-stuffed shelves. Along each side wall, a well-worn wooden ladder stood on rollers and was connected to a ceiling rail so clerks could reach things way up top. Neal O'Brien was in the back helping a customer find parts for a refrigerator motor, so Sam lifted the lid on the Coca-Cola box up front, dipped his hand into the ice-cold water, and helped himself to a bottle of Dr Pepper. After Neal rang up his sale, Sam flipped him a dime and filled him in on the conversation with Bowman.

"I figure we'd need to come up with about twelve to fifteen hundred dollars," Sam said. "You think we can squeeze the rest of it out of the budget somewhere?"

"Yeah, I think so, and we can see if the Ford place will sell us a car at cost. That'd save quite a bit." Neal fished a Grapette out of the drink box. "I tell you what. I'll talk to everybody as soon as I can get to them, and if it looks like most of them are for it, I'll get us together for a special meeting to make it official. Even if we had a car tomorrow, it'd still take a while to get it all rigged up. Are you willing to sign the note?"

"Yeah, I guess so, if you will," Sam said, taking the last swig of Dr Pepper.

"Yeah, I will too, and I'll get somebody else. Probably Fred."

Sam dropped his empty bottle into a wooden Coca-Cola crate sitting on a wire rack. "You got any ideas about who we can get to take Mr. Claude's place?" he asked.

"I thought we might recruit Jesse Culpepper away from the sheriff's office."

"You think he'd give up his chance for a county pension?"

"I think he might," Neal said. "He'd pretty much be his own boss for a change."

"Well, I guess if he'll do it, we'll be trading age and experience for youth and ability to drive, won't we?"

"I reckon so."

"Feels right and wrong at the same time, doesn't it?"

When Sam and Billy turned on the television after dinner to watch the start of game three of the World Series, KTVE was running a news update about how, overnight, the Soviet Union had launched a basketball-size satellite traveling at the mind-boggling speed of eighteen thousand miles per hour. The 184-pound artificial moon was passing over the United States seven times every twenty-four hours and beeping coded radio signals back to earth. It had captured the attention of scientists everywhere and startled pundits and politicians already worried about growing Soviet military power.

Sam, who had not read a newspaper since the day before, reached over to the coffee table for the *El Dorado Daily News*. A small front-page headline stated, "Soviet Russia Launches Earth Satellite; Beats US."The brief story said it was the start of a new era in science.

"Momma," Sam called to Gran in the kitchen, where she was helping Ollie Mae clear the table. "Come see this. The Russians have put a satellite up in space."

Gran came to the doorway and stared at the TV while wiping her hands on her apron.

"Aw, Sam," she said after a couple of minutes. "That's some kind of trick. Nobody can do something like that."

"Is that right, Daddy?" Billy asked. "Is it just made up?"

"No, son, I reckon it really happened, all right." Sam did not like disagreeing with his mother in front of the boy but did not see how to avoid it. "There wouldn't be any reason for our scientists to say it happened if it didn't."

"Pshaw!" Gran said. "I don't believe a word of it." She turned back to the kitchen.

"Why'd she say that, Daddy?" Billy asked.

"It's a little hard to explain, son. You remember when we were talking up at the store a while back about the Giants moving to California, and maybe the Dodgers, too, and how that's gon' change Major League baseball, and none of us much like it?"

"Yes, sir."

"Well, this is a little like that but much bigger. Gran has seen a lot of change over the years, and she's seeing a whole lot more right now, and sometimes when things are changing really fast, it can be scary. She's aggravated about integration and she doesn't much like me being friends with Miss Reeves. This satellite is just one more thing that's different. She'd rather everything stay the way it is."

"Is the satellite more important than what's happening with integration?"

"I don't know, Billy. They're both important but in different ways."

"Look, Daddy. They're switching to the ball game."

Sam and Billy watched until Mickey Mantle belted a homer in the top of the fourth to put the Yankees up by six runs. As they drove back to the Otasco store, Sam wished he had not mentioned the Russian satellite to Gran.

"Man, they could sure use Ronnie Metcalf tonight," Houston Holloway said shortly before halftime of the Razorbacks' game against the Horned Frogs of Texas Christian University. He leaned forward on the mezzanine steps and brushed a speck of dust off one of his cowboy boots. Even though the Hogs were winning, the game was not holding the attention of the Saturday night loafers. Arkansas managed to get a 14 to 7 lead early, but after that, the teams banged away at each other without effect.

"Say, Sam," Doyle Scoggins said, changing the subject. "You think Upshaw's right about Mr. Claude? You think the town needs a younger marshal and a police car?"

"I don't think Upshaw cares what Unionville needs. He's just trying to sell newspapers," Sam said, not taking his eyes off the radio sitting next to him on the wrapping table. He did not want to start any rumors about Mr. Claude before the town council acted. Tucker noticed his friend's attempt to dodge the question.

"Anybody got any ideas about who's burning these crosses?" the undertaker asked, trying to steer the conversation away from Mr. Claude.

"No," Holloway said, "but whoever burned down that shed must have had it in for Sadie Rose."

"You think there was more than one of them that done it?" Scoggins asked.

"I don't know," Holloway said. "I reckon one man could manage it all right, but it'd be easier if there were at least two of them. Did you see it?"

"No, I wasn't there," Scoggins said. "I didn't see the first one either. I don't like going out in the middle of the night. That's why I quit the fire department. Anyway, if you had to guess, who'd you say?"

"Oh, somebody like Boomer Jenkins or old Jim Ed Davis, I reckon," Holloway said. "Maybe even Crow Hicks. From what I hear, they all seem to be getting a kick out of it."

"It might be any number of folks," Doc Perkins said. He was sitting in Sam's office chair as usual.

"You think they'll burn any more, Doc?" Holloway asked.

"It wouldn't surprise me," Doc said. "I think whoever's doing it is looking for some kind of reaction. I don't know what exactly and they may not either."

"What do you think will happen if there's another one?" Scoggins asked.

"Hard to say," Doc said. "I just hope things don't escalate, like they have in some places."

"Sam, maybe y'all ought to think about getting that police car," Holloway said.

"Speaking of newfangled gadgets, what about that Russian satellite?" Doc asked, shifting the talk like Tucker had earlier.

"I sure hate them red bastards beat us to it," Scoggins said. "I bet they're gon' use it to spy on us somehow. The paper said that beeping might be some kind of secret code."

Before anyone replied, a long Razorback pass play pulled the loafers back into the game, and a little while later, most of them went home thinking more about the Hogs' 21 to 7 win than about burning crosses and beeping satellites.

CHAPTER 40

Walter Byrd had trouble deciding what to preach about on Sunday morning. He did not like using the pulpit for matters other than saving souls and did not want to preach about burning crosses again, but he also did not like seeing people mistreated, no matter the reason. After he had hammered his congregation hard following the first cross burning, attendance had fallen off, but he did not regret saying what he thought the situation required. Since then, Sam had told him about talking to Leon, and while Byrd regretted his deacons had put one of their brethren in such an awkward position, he was pleased to learn that his prediction about blacks preferring their own churches was right. Finally, as he mulled things over and prayed for guidance, he fixed on a message.

When Sam got to the sanctuary, he was disappointed to see Hazel Brantley sitting alone again. She grinned and winked when he passed her on the way to his usual seat with the children. He nodded and wondered if he had blushed. There was no denying he felt like a kid again, though.

He daydreamed through the opening part of the service, hardly noticing the music and announcements. Even a beautiful choir special failed to stir him. The silence that followed the hymn grabbed his attention, however, and he focused on the preacher.

Byrd was standing stone still in front of the podium holding an open Bible in the palm of one hand. His other was extended, open, above his head, and he was looking heavenward, seemingly unaware of the worshipers sitting before him.

Seconds ticked away before the trim preacher looked down and said quietly, "Friends, listen to these words from Proverbs, chapter four, verses fourteen to eighteen, advice from a father to his son and God's words to you. 'Enter not into the path of the wicked, and go not in the way of men. Avoid it, pass not by it, turn from it, and pass away.... For they eat the bread of wickedness and drink the wine of violence.'"

When he finished, he gazed upon his listeners, then remounted the podium, placed his open Bible on the pulpit, and stretched his arms out to the congregation, palms up.

"Did you hear that?" he shouted.

"Amen!" Hollis Cook yelled, coming awake over in the corner.

"Have you paid attention to the words of the Lord?" Byrd asked, still roaring. "You can't drink the 'wine of violence' and live for Jesus at the same time! You can't go watch the wicked work of crosses burning on week nights, talk about it with all your friends and neighbors till Sunday morning, and then come in here and join in Christian fellowship and think that everything's all right in the world!

"'Well, preacher,' you say, 'I didn't burn any crosses. I'm not responsible for what somebody else did.' Well, I say you are! I say you are, because you're not standing up against it. From what I hear, some of y'all are even happy about it. You're so scared of integration, you're willing to see laws violated to stop it—men's laws and God's laws. And you're afraid some of our Negro citizens might want to come to your church someday. I happen to know they don't, but that doesn't matter. What matters is you need to stand up for what's right. You have a Christian duty to oppose cross burnings and those who do them."

Byrd closed the service with "Take the Name of Jesus with You" and watched as even more people left through the back door this time. He knew there would more empty seats next week but he felt he had preached what God wanted said.

Hosea Moseley fretted over his sermon too. People had been asking him, "What're we gon' do? Where's this gon' stop?" All he knew to do was preach about the power of God and tell folks to have faith.

After rousing renditions of "Blessed Assurance" and "Amazing Grace," Moseley rose from his chair on the podium, buttoned his black suit coat, and walked slowly to the pulpit.

"The Lord is my Shepherd," he read from the twenty-third Psalm. "I shall not want."

"Amen! Praise Jesus!" some of the assembled shouted.

By the time Moseley quoted the fourth verse—"Yea, though I will walk through the valley of the shadow of death, I will fear no evil: for thou art with me. Thy rod and thy staff they comfort me"—most of the worshipers were on their feet, and the organist was punctuating each phrase with staccato chords.

"Hallelujah! Praise Jesus!" they called, as they spilled out into the aisles and jumped up and down in unison to the organist's notes.

After carrying the uplifting spirit of the Psalms through the entire service, Moseley sent his congregation home with hope that there would be no more cross burnings, and courage to face them if there were.

Out at the Mercy Baptist Mission, Elmer Spurlock did not give his preparation a second thought. He rolled out a foot-stomping celebration. Clad again in his new white suit and red tie, he told his flock, "My only regret is that the good Lord didn't bless me to see the cross burning with my own eyes. All of y'all who were at prayer meeting Wednesday remember I was sick that night. I tell you, though, I felt the Lord's spirit when I heard about it, and I knew right then what scripture we needed to hear today.

"Y'all just listen to what the Good Book says in Paul's letters to the Corinthians, first book, chapter fifteen," he said, placing his Bible on the pulpit and jabbing his finger at the selected passage. "Here, right here. 'Thanks be to God, which giveth us victory through our Lord Jesus Christ. Therefore, my beloved brethren, be ye stedfast, unmovable, always abounding in the work of the Lord, forasmuch as ye know that your labour is not in vain in the Lord.' God is on our side in this fight and he's gon' give us victory."

Spurlock railed on until he pushed his listeners to the limits of their attention, and when he finally let them go, he soaked up their praises.

After the service at First Baptist, Gran sulked all the way home. She was already aggravated about Sam's plans to have supper with Becky and had only gone to church because of Billy and Mary Jane. Brother Byrd had added insult to injury.

Billy spent the entire ride home reading *Sport* magazine, and Mary Jane spent it drawing on the church bulletin with her daddy's mechanical pencil.

Sam's thoughts bounced from Brother Byrd's sermon to Gran's pouting, and from how he planned to spend the afternoon with the kids to how he hoped to spend the evening with Becky. He was amazed at how quickly they had grown comfortable with each other and how natural and right their being together seemed.

At home, Billy and Mary Jane flew into their normal after-church routines of changing clothes and playing until dinner-time. Sam changed, too, then helped Gran finish fixing the meal she had started before church. They worked without speaking, each aware of the tension between them and each unable to see a way through it.

In a little while, Sam called Billy and Mary Jane to set the table, and during dinner Billy innocently forced the conversation in a direction the adults did not want.

"Daddy," Billy asked between bites of fried chicken, "Brother Byrd said we ought to stop the cross burnings but he didn't say how. What can we do? We don't know who's burning them."

Sam put down his iced tea and glanced at Gran. She took a bite of the green beans she had mashed on her plate and kept her head down.

"Billy, he knows the church members can't really stop them. He just meant we ought to recognize that they're wrong and not be happy they happened."

"I know you're not happy they happened, Daddy. Gran, are you?"

"Now, Billy," Sam started.

"It's all right," Gran cut in. She put her fork on her plate and sat back in her chair. "Billy, when I was your age, we had cross burnings pretty regular, and we never had no race trouble, least-ways not like they've got up in Little Rock now. But you got to listen to your Daddy and do like he tells you. He's the one that's responsible for raising you."

Sam did not know whether to feel gratitude or relief. Gran had not given an inch on her views, but she had conceded to his authority as the children's father. "That's enough about cross burnings," he said. "I expect the Yankees and Braves are already going at it on TV. Let's hurry and help Gran finish up in the kitchen so we can watch the rest of the game. Mary Jane, are you gon' watch it with us?"

"Yes, Daddy, if you'll read to me when it's over."

"You bet, sweetheart."

By the time Sam and Billy helped Gran clear the table and wash the dishes, the ball game was in the fourth inning, with the Braves leading 4 to 1. New York tied the game in the ninth and went ahead by one in the tenth. Then Eddie Matthews homered to give Milwaukee a 7 to 5 victory and knot the series at two wins apiece.

"Wow, that was some game, wasn't it, Daddy?" Billy said.

"Boy, was it ever. I'm beginning to think you're gon' be right about the Braves winning the series. Okay, Mary Jane, where're those books?"

The little girl already had them in her hands. She leaped into her daddy's lap and he gave her a bear hug.

Eight hours later, Sam had his arms around Becky. They were standing in her living room reluctantly saying goodnight.

"I can hardly believe this evening happened," he said, as he moved the tips of his fingers gently over the side of her face. "I haven't felt this way in a long time and I wish I didn't have to leave."

"I wish you didn't either," she said, brushing his hair into place with her fingers. "I feel like I'm floating on a cloud."

He moved his hand behind her neck, kissed her again, and smelled the Chantilly perfume he had driven to El Dorado for yesterday and watched her apply to out-of-the-ordinary places earlier in the evening. She returned his kiss then slid her hands across his chest and stepped back. They both glanced around the room, looking to see if Sam had forgotten anything. He had insisted on helping her clean up their mess and do the supper dishes before leaving.

"Wait right there," she said, and padded barefoot in her rumpled blouse and skirt through the kitchen into the bedroom. Sam stared at her as she went, completely unconscious of her limp. He saw only an attractive, sexy woman who was smart, easy to talk to, and fun to be with. "You'd better not forget this," she said, when she returned a few seconds later with his new red-and-blue striped tie.

"I don't know why I wore it," he said. "I guess I was nervous and wanted to impress you."

"Oh, I'm impressed all right," she said, smiling. "I'm very impressed."

"So am I," he said, looking into her eyes. "So am I." He took her into his arms again. "You don't think Hazel heard, do you?"

"I doubt it," she said. "Right now, I don't care."

CHAPTER 41

Before spending Sunday evening with Sam, Becky planned another curriculum change for her class. With her landlady's help, she rounded up several copies of the front page from the *El Dorado Daily News* with its lead story, "Baby Moon Spins On."

On Monday morning, after completing her reports Becky came around her desk, pushed back a stack of books, and hefted herself onto the front. The students, already in their study groups, watched as she fluffed out her full skirt. She often leaned against the desk and sometimes even perched on a corner with one foot on the floor, but she had never sat on it. She looked out at the class and smiled.

"Boys and girls," she asked, "what is the most important thing that happened in the world since you left school Friday?" Her evening with Sam flashed into her mind, but she shifted her weight and forced herself to focus on her students.

The students looked around at each other for a moment then several hands shot up. One boy guessed it was the Braves beating the Yankees on Sunday and another thought it was the Bobcats winning Friday night. Barbara Ames said it was the Russian satellite going into orbit.

"That's right, Barbara," Becky said. "In time, it's going to have a big effect on how we live—in ways we can't even imagine right now—and I want all of us to remember it. So this morning

we're going to do our math lesson first just like we've been doing these past few days, but we're going to base our problems on
the satellite. We're going to work on circumference, speed, and
distance." She said they would come back to baseball later. Then
with the students still in groups, she handed out the newspaper
stories and asked the students to use math facts in them to make
up problems to give other groups to solve.

Even though Becky had departed from school tradition
again, there was not much talk about her in student homes that
evening. Most of the new stuff she had come up with in the last
week or ten days did not have anything to do with integration,
the children all seemed to like her, and more parents were getting used to her. When Bobby Jack Plunkett heard the students
were making up math problems, he grumbled again that Becky
was finagling to get them to do her work, but Howard Ames was
delighted. He even sat with Barbara and worked up some additional problems for extra credit.

The next morning, when Ollie Mae Greene got to work,
she found a basket of greens on the Tates' back porch, tea cakes
scattered across the kitchen table, and no sign of Mary Jane or
her grandmother. Ollie Mae put her purse and paper bag on the
kitchen counter, stepped into the living room, and called out.
Getting no answer, she went into the hallway and saw the door
to Gran's sitting room closed.

"Mrs. Tate, you in there?" Ollie Mae asked, knocking lightly.

"Ollie Mae? Is that you? What time is it?"

"It's a little after eight-thirty," Ollie Mae said, taking the
question as an invitation to open the door and step inside. Gran
was getting out of her rocking chair, a batch of quilt squares in

one hand and her blue apron in the other. Her oak basket sat on the floor. "I'm sorry I'm running a little late this morning, Mrs. Tate," Ollie Mae said. "I was at my daughter-in-law's house all night. I got two sick grandbabies. Is anything the matter?"

"No, dadgum it! I was just sitting here thinking and I forgot the time. I done piddled around and got everything all out of kilter. I need you to get things ready this morning and look after Mary Jane. She's in her room."

Not long afterward, Emma Lou MacDonald knocked on the front door.

"Ida Belle, you home?"

When there was no answer, Emma Lou said, "Gosh almighty, Almalee, I wonder if she's sick or something. Ida Belle! You in there?"

"Yeah, I'm here," Gran said, reaching the screen door and opening it with one hand while trying to button the top of her dress with the other. She squinched her eyes in the bright sunlight. "Why didn't y'all just come on in?"

"What's wrong?" Emma Lou asked, shuffling sideways through the door. "You look plum tuckered out."

"Yeah," Almalee said. "You sure you're all right?"

"Yeah, yeah, I'm okay. Hurry on up. You're letting flies in."

The friends filed into Gran's sitting room, took their seats, and started getting out their quilting things.

"I bet I know what's eating you," Almalee said. She had on another new dress from Gene's, but instead of trying to get her friends to notice it, she took straight to meddling and gossiping.

"Now, Almalee, don't you start in on Brother Byrd's preaching," Emma Lou said, when she thought her friend was about to bring up Sunday's church service. "We're not gon' talk about cross burnings today. Ida Belle, hon, how're you coming with your sampler? You finished any more squares?"

"Yeah, let me show you," she said, pulling them out of her basket.

Almalee hunched her bird-like shoulders, leaned toward Emma Lou, and said low enough that she thought Gran would not hear, "That ain't what I meant. I wasn't talking about the preaching. It's what I was telling you about on the way over. You know, what I heard from Hazel Brantley's neighbor."

"Almalee Jolly!" Gran said, "You know I know Sam's seeing that Reeves woman and you know I don't like it. There ain't nothing I can do about it, though, and I don't want to talk about it."

"Well," Almalee said, "I just thought you ought to know what folks are saying. After all, Sam's been over to her place an awful lot lately."

"I done told you. I don't want to hear it."

"What they're saying is that Sam's got the hots for her."

"Look, Almalee!" Gran burst out. "That ain't none of your business and I'm tired of hearing about it. I'm tired of Yankee schoolteachers. I'm tired of old Byrd preaching about coloreds. And I'm tired of hearing about that blasted Russian thingamajig on television. Dadblame it! I just want to quilt and if you don't want to do nothing but run your mouth, you can just go on home!"

"Well, I never!" Almalee said. "You got no call talking to me that way, Ida Belle. I'm just looking out for you."

"I can look out for my ownself!"

⌒

"Can you make a council meeting before supper?" Neal O'Brien asked Sam Wednesday morning outside the post office.

"I can get everybody but Dave Westbrook, and I talked to him on the phone last night. He'll go along with whatever we decide."

"Yeah, I can make it," Sam said. "I take it you've talked to the folks at the Ford place too. Are they gon' help?"

"Some. Since the new models are about to come out, we can get a 'Fifty-seven Fairlane at three hundred dollars off dealer's cost, and they'll get the siren, lights, and radio and install them for nothing. I figure we're only gon' have to lay out about twelve hundred dollars up front, not counting the loan."

"Has the mayor signed off on it?"

"Yeah, but he's worried about Mr. Claude or Preston Upshaw finding out before we're ready. I'm going over to the town hall now and put a meeting notice inside the door just to be legal. I doubt Mr. Claude will see it, and I can't imagine Upshaw stopping in there for no good reason."

That afternoon at the Otasco store, Sam tuned one of the Philco TV sets into the sixth game of the World Series, and customers and loafers stopped in to catch an inning here and there. Sam watched when he could. Milwaukee had won game five, the series was back in New York, and the score was tied in the bottom of the seventh when Mr. Claude dropped by. Sam watched him talking and laughing with the other men and dreaded where the town council was headed. After the Yankees got another run and made it stand up for the win, the onlookers began drifting out.

"See you later, Sam," Mr. Claude said.

"All right," Sam said, feeling badly about what that might be like.

After closing time, Sam crossed the street to City Hardware and walked with Neal O'Brien and Fred Vestal to the town hall. Alan Poindexter was waiting behind his mayor's desk, and Art

Nelson and Lawrence Perkins were sitting in folding chairs in front of it.

The new arrivals pulled up chairs too, and Neal wasted no time getting started. "We all know why we're here. The meeting is called to order and the floor's open for motions."

"I move we commit up to three thousand dollars of town funds toward the purchase of a police car and all necessary equipment to go with it," Fred said, "with half to be borrowed from Farmer's State Bank and paid off over time, and that we ask Mr. Claude to resign as marshal, effective as soon as we can hire somebody to take his place."

"I second," Art said, "but I got a couple of questions. How long is it gon' take to get the car and who's gon' tell Mr. Claude?"

"It's gon' be at least two weeks," Neal said, "maybe four, before the car's ready to use."

"I sure wish we could get it sooner." Art said. "A lot can happen in a month."

"All the more reason to hurry up and get it ordered," Lawrence said.

"Okay, but who's gon' tell Mr. Claude?" Art asked again.

"I reckon that's my job," Alan said. "But I sure don't look forward to it."

"I'll go with you," Neal volunteered. "You shouldn't have to do it by yourself."

"Me too," Sam said. "I like that old man and I really hate we have to do this."

"Okay, any more questions before we vote?" Neal asked.

"Yeah," Art said. "Who're we gon' get to take his place?"

"Let's vote first and then talk about that," Neal said. "All in favor of the motion, raise your hand."

All did, and then, having decided to fire the town's only

marshal of the last four decades, they talked for a while about potential replacements and could not come up with a better idea than trying to persuade Jesse Culpepper to give up his deputy sheriff's job. If he would not do it, then maybe they could get Norm Patterson. He was a dependable volunteer fireman and made no bones about hating to commute to work at the Ark-La-Tex Oil refinery. He had no experience in law enforcement, but he was smart, strong, and knew how to drive.

"When're you gon' tell Mr. Claude?" Art asked again, trying to nail down all the details.

"Evening boys, y'all come in," Mr. Claude said, holding his front door open wide. Without his black coat and hat, he looked even smaller than usual to the mayor and council members, who had come straight from their meeting. "What's going on? We haven't had any more trouble, have we?" He ushered his guests through a small foyer and into his spotless living room. It had not changed much in forty years, except for the Philco TV purchased at the Otasco store and new upholstery on the sofa and chairs. "Y'all want some coffee? Irene and me just finished supper and she's got a fresh pot on."

The visitors all declined, and when they were seated, Alan tried to pull himself forward in the padded armchair he had chosen. Everyone could see he was nervous.

"We haven't had anything else happen, Mr. Claude, but we're sure worried that we might, and the boys and me feel like we've got to do more to try to prevent it. Times are changing, you know, especially with integration and all, and, well, we just feel we've got to beef up protection for the town."

"Y'all have come to tell me that you want a younger marshal, ain't you?" Mr. Claude said from the straight chair he'd pulled up.

"Yes, sir, I hate to say so, but I'm afraid that's about the size of it," Alan said, glancing at Neal and Sam.

"Mr. Claude," Sam started.

"It's all right, Sam," Mr. Claude said. "I've been knowing this time was coming and I've been thinking about retiring. Irene's been at me about it for years."

None of the visitors said anything, so Mr. Claude kept talking.

"I've enjoyed this job and I'm proud to have had it this long, but I don't need it anymore, and I know we've got to make some changes in the way we do things. The only thing I hate about it is that jackass Upshaw likely believing he caused it. I've been think-ing about talking to Jesse Culpepper and seeing if he'd take over when I quit, assuming y'all would hire him, of course. I suppose y'all intend to buy a police car. He wouldn't do it without that."

"We've thought about Jesse too," Neal said. "You reckon he'd do it?"

"I don't know but I'll be glad to talk to him if you want me to."

"We appreciate that, Mr. Claude," Sam said, "but we'd rather talk to him first, then let him come see you if he has any ques-tions. Meanwhile, we'd be much obliged if you'd stay on till we get somebody lined up and get a car ready, but we're gon' pay your salary through the rest of the year anyway."

"Sure, I'll be happy to stay till everything's all set. I got a couple of ideas about these cross burnings, and I'd like to keep on checking them out for a while."

"Can you tell us what they are?" Alan asked.

"No, I'm not ready, yet."

CHAPTER 42

"Morning, Pearl, Upshaw," Sam said, closing the front door to the newspaper building and heading toward the editor's desk midway back in the big workroom. Mr. Claude had written a letter of resignation, effective on a date to be determined by the council, and Sam had volunteered to tell Upshaw before he heard about it elsewhere. The councilmen knew as well as Mr. Claude that Upshaw would claim responsibility for it, but Sam could at least tell him the idea did not come from him.

"Mr. Tate, I'm surprised to see you," Upshaw said from behind his cluttered desk. "Have you reconsidered canceling your ads?"

"No," Sam said, towering over the editor, "I was out doing errands and I thought I'd stop by and settle my bill. I think I'm all paid up but I don't want to owe you anything." Sam had not been in the building in years, but except for the Linotype machine and the hastily patched wall and pile of debris where workmen had brought the monster in, things did not look much different from the days when old man Trammell owned the paper.

"Mrs. Goodbar, how much does Mr. Tate owe us?"

"Just a minute," she said. "I've got it right here. It's twenty dollars."

Sam handed Pearl two tens and waited for a receipt. "By the way, Upshaw," he said, "you'll be interested to know Mr. Claude is resigning as town marshal."

A smile of satisfaction spread over Upshaw's lumpy face. "It's about time you people came to your senses," he sneered. "I'm glad to see our community leaders have taken my advice."

"Don't break your arm patting yourself on your back," Sam said. "It was in the works long before you thought of it."

"I doubt my readers will believe that," Upshaw said. He rolled a new sheet of paper into his typewriter.

"If I were you, I wouldn't bet on it." Sam took his receipt, started for the door, then turned back briefly. "Most folks around here have known Mr. Claude all their lives," he said. "You're nothing to them. You keep running him down, all you're gon' do is hurt yourself."

"Just you wait. You'll see," Upshaw shouted through the closing door. He looked toward Pearl but she was on her way to the rest room, hiding a broad grin.

Until this moment, Upshaw had not had the mix he wanted for this week's issue. He had no interest in the Russian Sputnik, and all he had from Little Rock was Mothers' League claims that soldiers, black ones he guessed, were following girls into rest rooms at Central High School. He banged out twelve words on his typewriter: "Integration Threatens Southern Womanhood" and "Arkansas-Side Council Succumbs to Pressure; Fires Marshal."

"Mrs. Goodbar," he called, when she returned to her desk. "Here're this week's headlines. I want them equal size, top of the fold."

Upshaw found it hard not to rush over to Emmett's as soon as the café opened on Saturday morning but he waited, trying to give folks enough time to see his paper. He knew they would be talking Bobcat football. The El Dorado paper said the Metcalf boy had been held under a hundred yards the night before in a tough 13 to 6 home win over the Bernice Bears, from just down the highway in Louisiana. Still, Upshaw felt confident the stories he had written this week would spark talk. When he walked into the café about half past eight, he was pleased to see the man with the wooden leg and several others not often there on Saturdays. They were holding forth at the counter, while the football crowd occupied the booths.

"Hey there, Mr. Upshaw," Jim Ed Davis called from a stool near the back. He was wearing his hunting clothes again. "You're just the man we want to see. We saw your story about coloreds wanting our women."

Upshaw took a stool near his customary spot at one end of the counter. "Yeah," he said, "It's a well-known fact that what the Negroes really want is to get in our bedrooms. That's exactly what integrating the schools will lead to."

"By god, we ain't gon' stand for that," Boomer Jenkins said, banging a fist on the counter. "I don't know about everybody else, but I'm about ready to do some head knocking." Upshaw could tell that the big man knew the password for Emmett's juiced-up coffee and had been using it.

"Yeah, me too," Crow Hicks said. He hitched up his gun belt. "I'm thinking it's about time for another cross burning. Emmett, give me another cup of that there high-test coffee."

"Say, Mr. Upshaw," one of the football crowd spoke up, "If you're so interested in what's best for Unionville, why are you picking on Mr. Claude and the councilmen? They're good people. You ought not be running them down the way you did."

"I'm just standing up for law and order," Upshaw said. "I'm

afraid the marshal and people like Mr. O'Brien and Mr. Tate don't understand what's needed."

"Hey, now," Boomer said in a threatening tone. He slid off his stool and took a couple of unsteady steps toward Upshaw. "I don't know exactly what it was you just said, but don't you be bad-mouthing Mr. Claude and Sam Tate. They're friends of mine."

Upshaw started to say he was just doing his job as a newspaper man then thought better of it. He settled for being glad that this week, at least, the café bunch had read his paper.

"I'm sure it was hard, but I think y'all did the right thing about Mr. Claude," Doc Perkins said Saturday night, after the Otasco loafers had finished talking about how Milwaukee had won the seventh and deciding game of the World Series. "That old man's getting on up in years. I'm worried about him just sitting around, though. He's gon' need something to keep him busy. Maybe if his wife would let him out of the house at night, you could get rid of Crow Hicks. Mr. Claude could walk up and down Main Street a couple of times and otherwise hang around the town hall and nap. It'd make the town look more respectable, and we wouldn't have to worry about Mr. Claude shooting anybody."

"You've got that right," Doyle Scoggins said from his nail keg. "Crow's as liable to shoot a white man as a colored one."

"That's not a bad idea, Doc," Tucker said. "What do you think, Sam? Reckon Mr. Claude would do that?"

"I don't know. We could ask him. I'll talk to Neal about it when the time comes. Right now, Mr. Claude's still marshal."

"Well, Sam, when're you gon' find time to do that?" Houston

Holloway asked from the mezzanine steps. "From what I hear, you're pretty busy keeping company with Billy's teacher."

"Yeah," Scoggins said, digging in a shirt pocket for his Lucky Strikes. "I hear Hazel Brantley's neighbors ain't been getting any sleep because they're too busy watching to see when you're coming and going over there."

Sam's face turned red and he wondered how far his friends intended to take their teasing. He knew Billy was hanging on every word.

"Well, I'll tell y'all," Doc said, "I think Becky Reeves is a fine woman and ole Sam here's a lucky man to get to spend time with her." He looked at Sam and winked.

"If y'all don't quit picking on Sam, we're gon' miss the kick-off," Tucker said. "Arkansas needs to get off to a fast start to-night." He got up from his catalog-padded nail keg and turned up the volume on the radio.

The Razorbacks had not won in their last sixteen tries against the Baylor Bears on their home field in Waco, Texas. Once the game got underway, both teams played tough, but when Arkansas took the lead on a quarterback sneak in the fourth quarter, their chances of winning looked good. During a long injury timeout, Tucker said the pileups from the hard play reminded him of the worst injury he ever had in football.

"What was it?" Scoggins asked.

"Incisoritis," Tucker said.

"What the devil is that?" Doc asked. "You get hit in the mouth or something?"

"Well, not exactly. We were playing Strong, and they had a bunch of really big ole boys, and we were right down on their goal line. I took a hand-off and dove hard as I could right into the line and they just plain knocked the crap out of me. When I came to, I was on the bottom, arms and legs twisted every which way, with the biggest, nastiest rear end you ever saw right in my face. I yelled, 'If you don't move your stinking ass right now, I'm gon' bite a plug out of it.' It didn't move and I bit down hard as I could. Man, it hurt! I couldn't sit down for a week. Had to eat standing up."

The Razorbacks held on to win the game but the Otasco loafers did not hear the finish. Every time one of them looked at Tucker, he grimaced as if in pain, leaned to one side, and rubbed his behind, and everyone burst out howling again.

Sam could hardly wait to share the story with Becky. She had a plain folks' sense of humor and a laugh he found sweet and sexy and loved to hear.

CHAPTER 43

"Sam," Becky said, when she finally stopped laughing, "I don't think I'll ever be able to watch football again without seeing that picture in my mind. Do you know how lucky you are to have Doc and Tucker as friends? When I listen to you talk about them, I'm envious. I've never had friends as close and dear as they seem."

It was Sunday night, and she and Sam were sitting on her living room sofa waiting for the meatloaf to reheat for a supper they had not eaten when it was ready the first time. She shifted her shoulders and Sam pulled her closer. Her bathrobe slipped off one knee and he slid his free hand over her leg.

"Yeah, I've known them a long time. They're good people. Every time I've been with you, Tucker and Gloria have been willing to help out if Momma or the kids needed them."

"You know," she said, "we're either going to have to stop seeing each other or start letting people see us together. I was right about Hazel not talking, but apparently, the fact that she's not is only piquing everyone's interest. Maybe you and I ought to get out around town some."

"Where would you like to go first, and when?"

"How about the Liberty Theater? I haven't seen a movie in a long time."

"It's a deal," Sam said, smiling broadly. He lifted his hand to her face and slowly turned her lips to his.

The next morning, a headline in the Monday, October 14, *El Dorado Daily News* proclaimed, "Prayers and Grid Win Soothe LR."

In coordinated weekend services that both Faubus and Eisenhower endorsed, more than six thousand worshipers had filled more than eighty churches in and around Little Rock and prayed for divine guidance to end racial trouble. According to the Associated Press, the praying, together with the Razorback win over Baylor and prospects of another trip to the Cotton Bowl, had eased the bitter mood in the capital.

Tuesday brought news that Eisenhower planned to reduce the number of paratroopers and federalized National Guard soldiers in Little Rock to around two thousand. "That doesn't change a thing," Faubus responded on Wednesday. "We're still occupied."

"The Governor's right," Elmer Spurlock told Preston Upshaw as they sat talking in the newspaper office. Pearl Goodbar had gone on an errand, and Spurlock, in his splattered painter's garb, spoke freely. "I tell you. We're living in a police state, and I'm so mad I could just about knock the next nigger I see upside the head. I swear I just don't know why God ain't answering our prayers to keep them where they belong. I'm afraid any day now we gon' have them over at our high school. That's why I jumped at the chance to get Martin Smitherman to speak to the Citizens' Council tomorrow, even if it ain't our regular meeting night and there ain't been much time to get the word out."

"I've got the flyers ready for you, but I think your best hope of getting a crowd is gon' be that notice in the El Dorado paper this morning, with Smitherman's picture and all. Anyway, if you just keep on doing what you're doing, I think we'll start to see things happening our way."

"Neal O'Brien's on the phone for you!" Miss Ruthelle shouted to Sam late in the afternoon.

She sounds like Momma's old rooster when she hollers like that, Sam thought. He was out back on the loading dock installing a car battery.

"Hey, Neal, what do you need?" Sam asked, when he got to the phone.

"Can you come over? I've got some news and I don't have anyone to watch the store right now."

"Yeah, sure. Gimme a couple of minutes."

Neal was sitting on his cold drink box when Sam arrived. "What is it?" he asked.

"Couple of things. I just talked to Jesse."

"Is he gon' take the job?" Sam asked.

"He said he'd think about it. I told him what we could pay, and he said that was okay but he'd need medical insurance and a retirement fund. I said I'd take it up with the council on Monday. He also said he talked to Leon Jackson about those coat hangers on the cross over at Sadie Rose's and didn't like his explanation."

"Why not? What did Leon say?"

"Jesse thought he was a little smart mouthed. "He said, 'Why are you asking me? There're coat hangers in every closet in Unionville.'"

"So? He's right."

"Yeah, and I think that's what's really bothering Jesse. He still doesn't have any real suspects."

"Ladies and Gentlemen! Let me have your attention, please!" Spurlock shouted at the nearly one hundred people gathered in the Mercy Baptist Mission. Most were applauding wildly and many were whistling. Jim Ed Davis, Boomer Jenkins, Bobby Jack Plunkett, and the Grimes brothers were all down front again, making more racket than anyone. School board members Herbert Kramer and Travis Swilley sat a few rows back, along with Doyle Scoggins and two Louisiana-side council members. Upshaw had positioned himself quietly off to one side, arms folded and chin in the air, striking a pose next to a young reporter from the *El Dorado Daily News.* The lad sat wide-eyed with pad and pencil in hand, ready to record every word the famous man from Little Rock said.

"Quiet, please!" Spurlock called from in front of the big Confederate flag he had trotted out again. Although mid-October had brought cooler temperatures, he was starting to sweat. He kept his jacket on, though, because he had managed to come up with a Confederate flag tie like Leland Farley from down at Summerfield wore, and this was a proud moment for him. Deciding that it would be useless to attempt a long introduction, Spurlock merely said as soon as he thought he could be heard, "I'm pleased to present Mr. Martin Smitherman."

Most in the audience got to their feet and cheered again as the outspoken segregationist, a tall, graying man dressed in a conservative business suit, approached the pulpit. Few knew he earned so little money practicing law that he also worked occasionally as a long-haul truck driver to make ends meet. When people took their seats, Smitherman thanked everyone for their warm reception and said he was pleased to have the opportunity to speak to them on "Segregation Problems Now Facing Us."

Though he had no office-holding credentials or pulpit experience, Smitherman held the crowd spellbound. He blasted what he called the Gestapo tactics of federal troops and argued the need to keep Central High School lily-white. After an hour, he ended with, "Let there be no doubt, Little Rock is the pivotal battleground. If we win in Little Rock, integration is dead. If we lose in Little Rock, the Republic of the United States is gone forever."

Sam, Doc, and Tucker did not attend the meeting. They had seen and heard enough at the first one. While Smitherman held forth, Sam and Becky went to the Liberty Theater to see *A Face in the Crowd*, starring Andy Griffith and Patricia Neal. Few in Unionville, including Sam and Becky, knew director Elia Kazan had made *A Face in the Crowd* to put down hucksters and rabble-rousers like Smitherman. Most who saw the movie felt sorry for Griffith's Lonesome Rhodes character. After rescuing the seemingly down-and-out drifter from a drunk tank in a small town, Patricia Neal's character helped him become a windy pitchman and back-room politician, slept with him, and then used his own big mouth and mean spirit to destroy him.

"That was a powerful story," Becky said, as she and Sam left the theater.

"Yeah, it was," he agreed. Aware that some folks had been staring at them off and on all evening, he glanced around to make sure no one else was within earshot. "Lonesome Rhodes reminded me a lot of a couple of people I know around here."

"I assume one of them is our newspaper editor. Who's the other one?"

"Brother Spurlock, the preacher that heads up the Citizens' Council. You wouldn't like him either," Sam said, then chuckled.

"What's so funny?" Becky asked, squeezing his hand.

"Oh, I was just imagining Upshaw getting his comeuppance someday like Lonesome Rhodes."

When the fire siren went off a little before three in the morning, Sam was dreaming that Lonesome Rhodes was at the front door yelling about Hadacol, the real-life, alcohol-laced miracle elixir that some former Louisiana politician was huckstering all over the South. As Lonesome's hollering got louder, Sam woke up, recognized the real noise, and started pulling on his clothes. Everyone else in the house woke up, too, and, as always, the children clamored to go along. As usual, he sent them back to bed.

Like the last two times the siren had sounded in the dead of night, Sam could not see any sign of a fire. When he got to the highway, he looked toward town and saw the flashing red lights of the pumper coming toward him. He waited until the fire truck passed then pulled into the line of vehicles following it. A quarter mile up the highway, it turned right and headed east into the quarters, toward the black school.

When Sam arrived at the fire, he could see flames reflected in the sash windows of the huge wooden building and a cross burning on the playground out front. It was wedged into a wooden seesaw frame, which was also burning, and flames were moving along the three seesaws. The fire was a fair distance from the building but the wind was blowing hard in that direction. Worried that floating embers would catch up tall pines next to the school and then the building itself, folks were rushing in and out removing desks, chairs, and stacks of books. As Sam joined them, he heard Odell Grimes say, "This one will sure enough send a message."

The volunteers put out the blaze but the seesaws were burned beyond repair. As the firemen cleaned and stored their equipment, folks toted furniture and books back into the school while several black women looked on, sobbing openly. Even to many whites on the scene, this cross seemed more menacing than the first two because it came closer to children.

As Sam worked, he kept looking around, trying to see who was there. Jim Ed Davis and Crow Hicks stood off to one side, pointing to the smoldering cross and the black spectators and snickering. Preston Upshaw was running around interviewing folks like the last two times. And Leon Jackson, who earlier had helped empty the building, stood at the edge of the playground quietly watching everyone.

While all this was going on, Jesse Culpepper pulled up in his deputy sheriff's car with Mr. Claude inside. Neal O'Brien talked to them for a moment, then they started going through the crowd asking if anyone had seen anything suspicious before the alarm.

"You know, Sam," Neal said, when they met up after everything was back inside the school building, "threatening people's kids is a surefire way to set folks off, it don't matter who they are. I'm afraid if we don't find out who's doing this soon, we're liable to wake up some night and find half the town on fire or folks shooting at each other."

"Yeah, I expect you're right. Mr. Claude said the other evening he had some ideas. Maybe after tonight he can flesh them out a little more. Did you get a look at the cross? Were there coat hangers on it again?"

"I don't know. I'll make sure Jesse and Mr. Claude check it before we leave."

Sam started to walk away then turned back. "Neal, did you notice how worn out all that furniture and those books were?"

"No," Neal said absently, as he looked around for the two officers.

"Whole building's like that."

"Yeah, I reckon it is. Hey, there's Jesse," Neal said, hurrying away. "I'll see you tomorrow."

"I understand Doc has the standby duty tonight," Gloria said, when she and Tucker picked up Sam and Becky at her apartment a little after five on Friday evening.

"Yeah," Sam said, trying to find room for his legs as he and Becky settled into the back seat of Tucker's new blue-and-white Oldsmobile, bought, he said, for relief from driving hearses and his black utility truck. "Doc thought the chance of his being out on a call if Momma and the kids needed him was pretty slim. In any case, his wife always knows where he is."

"He's a nice man," Gloria said.

"It was nice of you and Tucker to invite us to go to the game with you," Becky said, as she glanced around at the vehicle's sporty interior.

"Oh, it's our pleasure. We're glad to have company."

"Hey, Sam," Tucker said, "I was busy with a funeral all day. Is there anything new on the cross burning? Does Jesse or anyone have any leads?"

"Aw, come on, hon," Gloria said. "That's all folks wanted to talk about at the mill today. I'm sick of hearing about it, and I don't imagine Becky wants to talk about it either."

"No," Sam said. "As far as I know, there's nothing new. I heard a lot of talk about Smitherman's speech at the Citizens' Council meeting, though. I'm wondering if that had anything to do with what happened or if someone already had this one planned."

"Yeah," Tucker said, "I hear he's a real spellbinder."

"Then he must be like the character Sam and I saw in the movie last night," Becky said, trying to move them off the cross burning. This one, at a school, bothered her more than the first two, plus she knew she would spend a lot of the weekend planning how to deal with it in class. Tonight, she just wanted to be with Sam and other adults and finally see the Bobcats and Ronnie Metcalf play football.

"Oh?" Gloria said. "Tell us about it."

Becky shifted her and Sam's coats, scooted up against him, and began telling about Lonesome Rhodes. The story entertained them much of the way up US 167 past El Dorado to Hampton, where Sam and Becky attracted considerable attention from Unionville fans and Ronnie led the Bobcats to a 35 to 14 win.

"Smitherman Man of the Hour Here," proclaimed a headline in the *Unionville Times*. "Burning Cross Serves Warning," another declared.

"Yes, ma'am," Lester Grimes said, poking a fleshy finger at the newspaper he laid on the Otasco office counter Saturday morning, "we've had ourselves quite a week. You should've heard Mr. Smitherman. He sure can get a fellow fired up. Upshaw's got most of it right here. You ought to read it."

Sam was in the warehouse dealing with a shipment of roofing paper and shingles, and the talkative barber was stuck with Miss Ruthelle.

"I've already seen it," she said, "and I've heard all I want about Martin Smitherman and that cross." She was sitting at her desk, and when she saw Lester was looking at the headline again, she reached in an open drawer for a jellybean and popped it into her mouth.

"You know," he said, when he looked up, "I wouldn't be surprised if we had us some more cross burnings."

Across the street, Reverend Moseley was paying Leon Jackson a visit.

"I hear a lot of parents kept their children home yesterday," Moseley said. He was standing where he could watch the open door. "Folks are scared."

"Yes, sir, my wife told me last night," Leon said.

"I'm gon' preach again about keeping faith," Moseley continued, glancing at the door, "but I'm not so much worried about folks being scared as I am about somebody getting liquored up on some of Mrs. Washington's new bootleg whiskey and doing something stupid."

"Yes, sir, I've heard a couple of folks popping off some, but Reverend, you've got to expect that. And you know most of us have better sense than to drink and then go where white folks can see us."

Moseley said he knew that but wondered if Leon would talk to the men who frequented Sadie Rose's place. "I sure would hate to see somebody do something to make matters worse," the minister said.

"I'll talk to them. Don't you worry."

"There's something else too," Moseley said, moving closer, as if doing so would make Leon more likely to agree. "I was wondering if you could talk to some of the Arkansas-side council members. You work right here next to three of them. I know you can't ask them if they're really trying to catch whoever's burning these crosses, but you can tell them how we're feeling."

"Well, I can't say for sure, but I believe they're doing about all they can. Anyway, I've been thinking on some things, and I'm just about ready to try them out on Sam Tate. But don't you be telling anybody."

CHAPTER 44

Before the sun went down Saturday afternoon, Darrell Royal brought his University of Texas Longhorns into Fayetteville, put eight men on his defensive line, and shut out the Razorbacks 17 to 0. The loss knocked the Hogs out of the Associated Press top ten, clouded their dreams of the Cotton Bowl, and threw folks all over the state into a foul mood that carried over to Sunday morning.

For most of those attending First Baptist Church in Unionville, it did not help that Brother Byrd preached about the cross burnings again. Even worse, he did it with uncharacteristic calm. Rather than fuming and frothing like he often did, he acted like he was teaching children in Sunday school.

"Listen to what the Bible says in Leviticus, chapter nineteen, verses seventeen and eighteen," he said at one point. "'Thou shalt not hate thy brother in thine heart. Thou shalt not avenge, nor bear any grudge against the children of thy people, but thou shalt love thy neighbor as thyself.' People, I tell you, whatever you think about integration, you have to know cross burning is wrong, and burning a cross at a school, a place for children, is diabolical. As Jesus said in his Sermon on the Mount, 'Verily I say unto you, inasmuch as ye have done it unto the least of these my brethren, ye have done it unto me.'"

Becky had not heard Byrd's first two sermons about cross burnings, but she had seen him in full flower earlier and recognized the change in approach immediately. Having come with Hazel Brantley, she was sitting in front of Sam, Billy, and Mary Jane, the same as before. She and Sam had talked about attending together and decided not to. They both knew that when people their age started going to church together, folks began assuming things about their future intentions.

She was going to the Tates for dinner afterward, however, and the prospect distracted her throughout the service. She sat fingering the buttons on her suit and thinking how Sam made her laugh and how she felt when he put his arms around her. She knew she loved him, but his being the father of one of her students still bothered her some. Then there was his mother to consider. Sam had told Becky enough so that she knew she was not exactly going into friendly territory.

Sunday dinner plans weighed on Sam's mind too. He asked Becky to come only after wrestling long and hard with the idea. Although he had known her only a couple of months, he knew he loved her. He also knew his mother despised her, but he wanted to be with Becky even more than he had been, and he did not want to keep hearing Gran complain about it. He hoped if they spent some time together, Gran might soften up at least a little.

Gran was also thinking about dinner during church. When Sam first mentioned having Becky over, Gran told him flat out he had better not count on her having anything to do with it. Later, after remembering some things Emma Lou MacDonald said, she decided to go along with it. She dreaded it, though. Fixing the meal was easy. Ollie Mae helped her do a lot of it on Saturday. Sitting through it would be something else. She hated the notion so much she did not tell Emma Lou and Almalee about it, even though they were sitting with her in their usual pew.

"You feeling bad again, Ida Belle?" Emma Lou asked after preaching was over.

"No, it ain't nothing," Gran said.

According to plan, Sam drove his family home after church, and Becky, driving her Plymouth, stopped by her apartment. When she arrived at the Tate home, she was carrying a hatbox covered with a piece of bright red cloth accented with tiny yellow flowers. Holding it in place was a long yellow plaid piece tied loosely into a large bow. Sam, Billy, and Mary Jane met her at the front door. Then, still wearing their Sunday clothes and uncertain about what to do next, they all crowded into the kitchen, where Gran was now frying chicken.

"Momma, Miss Reeves is here," Sam said. "Becky, this is my mother. Y'all have seen each other at church."

"It's a pleasure to meet you, Mrs. Tate," Becky said. "I've been looking forward to it."

"Becky's brought us something, Momma," Sam said. "You want to see what it is?"

Gran did not move or say anything for a moment or two, and Sam thought she was about to tell them all to go somewhere and let her finish getting dinner ready. But as she looked up from the chicken legs and thighs sizzling in her iron skillet, she glimpsed the cloth.

"That's pretty material," she said. "Where'd you get it?" The words came out automatically, before she thought about them. It was what every quilter asked on seeing a new piece of fabric she liked.

"I bought it in a little store in my home town," Becky said. "I used part of it for a Sun Bonnet Sue appliqué and these pieces are for you. Sam and Mary Jane both told me you like to quilt."

"Well," Gran said, remembering how she regarded Becky and turning back to the stove, "you'd best move it before some of this here grease pops out on it."

"There's a lemon pie in the box," Becky said. "Where would you like it?"

"You can set it over there somewhere," Gran said without looking up, "but you didn't have to bring nothing. Ollie Mae made us an apple pie yesterday."

Becky felt Gran's coolness and the tension in the room. "Well," she said, "my mother taught me always to bring something when I'm a guest, so it was my pleasure. I have to tell you, though, apple pie is one of my favorites."

Gran reached for some more floured chicken pieces and dropped them into the skillet. The hissing sound they made when they hit the hot grease was her only reply. Sam took Becky's box and put it on the counter top. Then, with the table already set and the vegetables ready, he took her onto the back porch to see the rest of the Tate homeplace.

When they all sat down to eat a few minutes later, Sam said the shortest blessing he thought he could get away with and started passing food around. Everyone loaded their plates and for a long while no one said anything.

Then Mary Jane said, "I helped make the chicken."

"Aw, come on," Billy said. "Gran fried the chicken."

"I did, too, help. I did it yesterday. After Ollie Mae wrung its head off, I chased it all around while it was flopping, and after she scalded it, I helped her pick the feathers off."

"Mary Jane!" Sam said. "Do you think that's appropriate for the dinner table?"

"What's wrong with it, Daddy? I didn't say anything about getting the blood on my clothes."

Becky almost laughed out loud but caught herself. Sam could not think of what to say, and Gran went on eating as if nothing had happened.

No one said anything more for another minute or two, then Billy broke the silence. "Miss Reeves," he asked between bites of chicken leg, "can you tell me about Busch Stadium? We haven't talked about it yet at school."

"Why yes, Billy. I'd love to. I've had some really good times there with my father. What would you like to know?"

"Well, I was wondering what it's like to see a real Major League game. I'd give anything to see Stan Musial bat in real life."

Becky put her fork on her plate and used her napkin. "I expect you know that until a few years ago the stadium was called Sportsman's Park. A lot of famous Cardinals have played there, like Rogers Hornsby, Dizzy Dean, Pepper Martin. The Browns used to play there, too, before they moved to Baltimore, and Babe Ruth, Lou Gehrig, and Jimmie Foxx all played there against them. But you want to know what it's like being there, don't you?"

"Yes, ma'am."

"Well, just walking up outside to buy tickets is exciting. There're lots of cars and buses letting fans off. Street vendors are all over the place selling programs and souvenirs. And you get goose bumps thinking about all the things you're going to see inside. Then you walk in and there's that big stretch of green grass right in the middle of the city. It's like magic. You feel like you're in some other world that's peaceful and serene, and somehow you hold onto that feeling even when thirty thousand people are yelling and screaming.

"There are wonderful smells too. I remember the popcorn especially. They used to sell it in cardboard cones you could use as megaphones to cheer with when you finished eating. They were white with two big cardinals on the sides. And the hot dogs, oh, they were good. I can still close my eyes and smell the mustard."

Billy was listening so hard he was ignoring his dinner. Sam was tempted to interrupt and tell him to eat, but Becky's voice and what she was telling were music to father and son alike.

"Did you ever see Stan Musial hit a home run?" Billy asked.

"Yes, as a matter of fact, my father and I saw that double-header three years ago when he hit five home runs in one day."

"Wow!" Billy said. "I've read about those two games. Did you ever see the Browns play?"

"Yes. Several times."

"That's enough questions, Billy," Gran said, interrupting.

Once more, there was only the sound of knives and forks against plates. Then Mary Jane asked, "Miss Reeves, are you gon' be our new momma?" The split second of quiet that followed seemed much longer, as blood rushed to the faces of the adults.

"Mary Jane!" Gran and Sam cried at the same time.

The exclamations startled the little girl. The corners of her mouth turned down, her shoulders slumped, and she stared at her plate.

"Sweetheart, I'm just your daddy's friend," Becky said.

No one knew what to say next.

"Mary Jane," Sam said finally, "Miss Reeves is right. Like I told you before, she and I are friends." To change the subject he said, "Momma, why don't you tell Becky about the quilt you're making."

"It ain't nothing but a sampler, Sam. I'm sure she knows all about them." Before he could protest, Gran filled her mouth with a huge spoonful of mashed potatoes.

"I would love to hear about it, Mrs. Tate," Becky said. "My mother and aunt have made lots of quilts and I never get tired of looking at them."

"Momma," Sam said, "after dinner, why don't you show Becky the blocks you're working on."

"Yeah," Billy said, "and you can tell us some stories too."

"Please Gran," Mary Jane pleaded, smiling now. Then to Becky, "Our grandmother tells good stories."

"Telling stories is a wonderful talent, Mrs. Tate," Becky said, failing to notice the worried expression that came over Sam's face. "I'm sure I would enjoy them as much as the children."

Gran did not reply, and as they all continued eating, Sam tried making conversation around the weather, gardening, and anything else he could think of other than school and politics. Gran kept quiet, and while that was in part a blessing, it was also a clear indication that Becky was not gaining any ground with her. For dessert, Becky ate a piece of Ollie Mae's apple pie and bragged on it, and Sam ate a piece of Becky's lemon pie and bragged on it. When everyone finished, Becky insisted on helping with the dishes. Gran tolerated her but did not speak as they worked.

Sam and the children pitched in, too, and afterward, he ushered everyone into the living room. Before anyone sat down, Mary Jane asked if she could go get Gran's quilting basket. Unable to disappoint her granddaughter, Gran said, "Yes," with obvious reluctance, and Sam hoped she would not get wound up about Yankees and Negroes.

When Mary Jane returned, Gran started laying out her blocks and telling about them. For a while, things seemed to go well. She named the patterns and told where the cloth came from, and Becky complimented the color schemes and stitches. When Gran brought out her Wild Geese Flying and Monkey Wrench blocks, Becky grew excited.

"Why, Mrs. Tate, those are really famous patterns. Before the Civil War, slaves would put out Monkey Wrench quilts to signal when it was time to run away, and abolitionists used Wild Geese Flying patterns to show what direction to go on the Underground Railroad."

Without even looking up, Gran started putting all her blocks back into her basket. "I don't know nothing about no runaway slaves and no abolitionists," she said, "but them blocks has got my daddy's and my husband's clothes in them, and didn't neither one of them ever have nothing to do with no runaway coloreds."

"Oh, Mrs. Tate," Becky said, "I didn't mean to imply anything about your father or your husband." She looked to Sam for help but Gran responded before he could get any words out.

"I know you can't help it," she said, "but the problem with you Yankees is you think you know everything about the South and you don't know nothing." With that, she picked up her basket and started out of the room.

"Momma," Sam called after her.

"I'm tired," Gran said. "I'm gon' take a nap."

CHAPTER 45

Monday brought heavy thunderstorms to Unionville, and that evening as the Arkansas-side council members waited for the mayor to arrive so they could hold their monthly meeting, lightning flashed across the town hall windows and thunder rumbled far off somewhere.

"Hey, Mr. Tate!" Art Nelson said, when he noticed Sam staring blankly. "You going to sleep on us over there?"

"No," Sam lied, "I'm just thinking about our finances." In truth, he had been thinking all day about how badly dinner with Becky went. As soon as the meeting ended, he intended either to go knock on her door or go to the Otasco store, where he could have some privacy, and call her to apologize again. So far, he had been unable to decide which would be better.

Before Art could reply, the mayor arrived, and Neal O'Brien called the meeting to order. He said Jesse Culpepper had accepted the marshal's job on condition that they provide benefits, call him chief of police, and let him fire Crow Hicks as soon as he could find a new night man. Sam mentioned Doc's idea of offering that job to Mr. Claude, and the other members agreed to suggest it to Jesse when he took over. First, though, he had to give the county sheriff two weeks' notice.

"Just a minute," Becky called in response to the knocking. She raked the photographs she had been looking at into the shirt box and slipped it under the sofa. Then she straightened her bathrobe and started for the door, but it sprang open before she got there.

"When I heard you call out, I just used my pass key," Hazel Brantley said, closing the door behind her. "I guess I should have waited," she added, when she saw Becky's face. "You been crying, hon? What's the matter?"

"No, Hazel," Becky fibbed, "I just have a runny nose. I think I'm coming down with something."

"Why didn't you tell me earlier? I got all kinds of medicine over at my place. We ought to be able to find something that'll fix you up."

"No, that's okay. I'll take some aspirin before I go to sleep. First, I have a lot more work to do for class tomorrow." Becky gestured toward papers lying on the writing desk.

"All right, hon, but you holler if you need anything. And soon as you're up to it, I want to hear all about dinner over at the Tates."

As Hazel started for the door, Becky's phone rang, and the landlady paused.

"Excuse me a minute, Hazel," Becky said, going to the desk to answer. She said hello then after a moment said, "Yes, Sam, I'm fine, but I can't talk now. Hazel's here with me." After a pause she said, "No, tomorrow night I'll have a huge batch of papers to grade." In another moment or two, she ended the conversation with, "Well, I guess Wednesday will be all right. I'll see you sometime after supper. Good night."

"Are you sure everything's all right, hon?" Hazel asked. "I know it ain't none of my business but that didn't sound just right to me."

"Oh, Hazel, you read too much into things. Like I told you, I'm just not feeling very well."

Becky put her arm around her landlady and walked her to the door. Hazel shivered as she crossed the porch to her own apartment and the damp night air was not the only reason why.

Inside, Becky went back to her sofa, took a tissue from a nearby carton, and reached for the box of photographs.

On Tuesday morning, Ollie Mae Green did not ask how Gran's dinner had gone on Sunday. Emma Lou MacDonald and Almalee Jolly did, however. Even though Gran had said nothing about the Tate's dinner plans at church on Sunday, Becky's green Plymouth sitting in the driveway had signaled gossipers all over town, and the quilters came loaded with questions, each hoping for different answers.

"Gosh almighty, Ida Belle!" Emma Lou said, as soon as she got through the front door. "How come you didn't tell us Becky Reeves was coming for dinner?"

"Yeah, Ida Belle, how come?" Almalee asked. She was right on Emma Lou's heels. Both wore blue dresses, one flowered and one striped, and Gran used them to fend off the question.

"Y'all trying to look like twins today?" she asked, as they all filed into her sitting room.

"Come on, out with it," Emma Lou said, as she sat down and started unloading her stuff. "I want to know what happened. I bet you found out she's a sweet girl, didn't you?" When she looked up and saw Gran's pained expression, she said, "Uh oh, don't tell me it went bad."

"I ain't gon' talk about that woman," Gran said, taking her chair. "I ain't got nothing on my mind but quilting. I only got two more blocks to make then I'm gon' be ready to put my sampler together." She reached for her basket but could not hold back her anger. "She said runaway slaves and abolitionists used blocks like mine. Of all the nerve! These patterns have been in my family a hundred years. I told y'all she didn't know nothing about the South."

"I bet she was just awful, wasn't she, Ida Belle?" Almalee said. This was just the sort of thing she had hoped to hear. "It's like I been saying all along. What Sam needs is a nice southern girl with good breeding."

"Oh, hon, I sure am sorry," Emma Lou said to Gran.

"You heard Ida Belle," Almalee said. "That woman's dumb and mean. There ain't no need to be sorry about it."

"Aw, Almalee," Emma Lou said, "why don't you just keep quiet?"

"Lordy! If you're gon' get all huffy about it, I'll do just that." For a long while, the friends sat quilting in silence broken only by deep breathing, loud sighs, and scissor snips.

"Where's Mary Jane?" Almalee asked after a while. "I brought her a new doll dress."

"She's in her room," Gran said. "She's coming down with something. I pinned a Vicks rag to her nightgown and let her stay in bed."

"Aw, that poor baby," Almalee said. "I'm gon' go cheer her up." She fished her gift out of her bag and left the room.

"Ida Belle," Emma Lou said, glancing up after a minute, worry deepening the wrinkles on her round face, "did you throw a fit in front of Miss Reeves Sunday?"

"I told you I don't want to talk about that."

"You did, didn't you? Did you insult her?"

"No," Gran said, keeping her eyes on her stitches. "I just came in here and left her alone."

"Aw, Ida Belle, that was rude." Emma Lou leaned back, took a deep breath, and just looked at Gran.

"It wasn't near as rude as her talking about my quilt patterns like that," Gran said. "I tell you, I don't want nothing to do with her and I done told Sam that too. You ought to seen them young'uns hanging all over her. They're too little to know she ain't no good influence."

"Ida Belle, I think you're making a big mistake. Can't you see Sam's in love with her? When has he ever brought a woman over here for dinner before? And you just said the children like her. You better do some more thinking about this, hon. Besides, she may be right about those quilt patterns. Your family didn't invent them, you know. They're everywhere."

"You done now?"

"Yeah, I'm done."

"Good."

"Sam, I'm very fond of you," Becky said, taking his hands in hers as they sat on her sofa Wednesday night. "The times we've had together these past several weeks have been among the most enjoyable of my life."

Sam's throat leaped into his mouth. This did not sound like it was leading to anything good. He had come to make things right in some way or other, but now dread washed away all the words he had rehearsed. Becky was wearing the same white blouse and blue skirt she had on when he first saw her, and he wanted to take her into his arms and stop whatever was coming next. Somehow, though, he knew he should not. He wished he had insisted on coming over Monday night after the council meeting. After she told him not to, he convinced himself that maybe waiting was better. It gave him more time to figure out the right thing to say and a chance to put on his dress slacks and a good shirt and look his best. Now none of that seemed to matter. He squeezed Becky's hands and struggled to clear his head and concentrate on what she was saying.

"But I don't believe things can work between us," Becky said, "and I don't think we should see each other anymore."

"I don't understand," Sam said, "especially if you've been having a good time. Please don't let Momma come between us. I'm sorry about Sunday and I won't ever put you in a position like that again. We can work around her some way. I don't know how right now but I'm sure we can. Besides, while I don't like saying it, she's old and she's not gon' be here much longer." He knew that sounded awful but he was desperate.

"Sam, wait," Becky said. She started to put her fingers on his lips but stopped. "There's something you don't know about me, and I haven't slept for three nights trying to decide whether to tell you. I'm going to, though, because I love you, because I believe you love me, because I don't believe you'll agree with me any other way, and because I believe if you know this, you'll be hurt less. You may even hate me. I wanted to believe it didn't matter but now I know it does."

She paused and slid her hand gently along his arm.

"Okay, go ahead and tell me," he said, putting his hand on hers, "but nothing you say is gon' change the way I feel about you."

She looked in his eyes, pulled her hand away, and struggled to get her breath.

"Sam, my Great-grandmother Charlene was one-half Negro, and by the way most people define race, I'm a Negro too. Even the Census Bureau says so."

Nothing Becky could have said would have surprised Sam more. Blood drained from his face, his mind whirled, and fear swept over him. He sat thunderstruck, struggling to breathe, unable to speak or move. Part of him wanted to reach out, pull Becky close, feel her warmth, make love to her, and tell her it did not matter. And part of him fought to grasp the full weight of what she had said. He wanted to say it had nothing to do with how they felt about each other and did not change anything about their being together, but like her, he knew it did. Maybe, he thought, he had not heard her right, or maybe her facts were wrong.

"Becky," he finally blurted, "are you sure?" It was a stupid and thoughtless response and he knew it as soon as he said it. It had just come out, like some sort of reflex. He knew he loved her and he knew he wanted to be with her. He knew he should have said that was all that mattered and he wished desperately that he had. While he tried to think of some way to erase what he had asked and replace it with what he felt, a litany of out-side obstacles that were bound to stand between them filled his mind, all in an instant. If people found out—and they would—his mother, his friends, his customers, his church, the school, the whole town, and even his children would be caught up in an inescapable whirlwind. Images of other people's scorn and hate flashed before him, slipping in and out of focus and competing with images of the beautiful woman he loved. Time seemed to stand still as he thought about the two of them trying to make a life in the face of it all. The room spun and he could not stop it. He sat frozen.

"Yes, I'm sure," Becky said. She reached over to the coffee ta-ble, took the lid off the shirt box, and laid out two photographs. "These are pictures of my grandmother and my great-grand-mother. I never knew either of them, but my mother told me about them when I finished high school."

Sam looked at the pictures, then at Becky, and back at the pictures. Tears filled his eyes and words failed him.

Becky knew it was dangerous to tell her secret to anyone, even Sam, but that mattered less to her than her love for him. She hated hurting him, but she knew she had to tell him, and she had thought long and hard about what to say. She saw the disbelief in his face and watched him search for resemblance in the photographs and wrestle with both the suddenness of her revelation and the complexity of the entire situation, and although nothing in his reaction surprised her, it hurt to see him hesitate and wonder. She longed for him to reach out and take hold of her but she was glad he did not. She knew she had made the right choice for both of them. They could not be together, not here, not now, not ever.

CHAPTER 46

"Mr. Sam," Leon Jackson called out. "Miss Ruthelle said you were out here and I should come on back." Sam was sitting on the loading dock, his back against the brick wall of the store and his arms resting on drawn-up knees. He was holding a smoldering Chesterfield. "I never saw you smoking before, Mr. Sam. Is anything wrong?"

"No, I'm just thinking through some stuff." He took a final draw on the cigarette, flipped the butt away, and blew the smoke through his nose. "What can I do for you?"

"Well, sir," Leon started.

"Sit down and take a load off, why don't you?"

It was an unexpected invitation, spoken in the same tone and manner Sam might have used with Tucker or Doc. Leon did not want to sit on the rough boards and maybe tear his pants, so he squatted on his toes, in a catcher's crouch. Wrinkled pants were no problem for a man with a pressing machine.

"You remember, Mr. Sam, a while back you said if I ever found out anything about the streetlights getting shot out, I should come talk to you?"

"Yeah, I remember. Did you find out something?"

"No, sir, not yet. This might not even have anything to do with the streetlights, but then again, it might. I've been thinking about the cross burnings and I have an idea about them. I don't want to stir up any more trouble, but I figure I can trust you, and you'll know what to do if what I'm thinking makes sense."

Sam stood up and brushed off his khakis. Leon rose with him.

"You're right," Sam said. "You can. Let's go out to the warehouse. We won't get interrupted out there."

They walked the hundred or so feet in silence. Sam unlocked the front door, slid it open partway, and led the way through racks of galvanized pipe and stacks of Sheetrock and plywood to a little-used side entrance. There he removed the iron security bar from a smaller sliding door, pushed it open, let in sunlight and fresh air, and stepped back.

"We can talk here," he said. "What're you thinking?"

Leon looked into Sam's eyes as if taking his measure one more time.

"Go ahead," Sam said. "You can tell me whatever it is. I won't repeat anything you don't want told."

"Okay, and please don't take any offence at any of this either. I've been making up two lists in my head. The first one is which white folks in town seem to hate us black folks the most. The second is which ones stand to get something out of burning crosses."

Sam leaned against a post supporting a rack of wood molding. "Who've you come up with?"

Leon leaned against another post. "First," he said, "I need to tell you how I came to my lists. Part of it's from what white folks say and do to us and part of it's from what we hear them saying when they're talking to each other. You'd be surprised, Mr. Sam. Sometimes it seems like white folks don't think we have ears. They talk just like we weren't around. Other times they talk like they want us to hear them. Anyways, what I have is from what we've heard, plus some watching and lots of thinking on it."

"I understand."

"Okay, first, there're a few white folks that always seem to go out of their way to spite us every chance they get. They're always saying stuff to us and talking about us when they know we can hear them. That's Mr. Jim Ed Davis, Mr. Boomer Jenkins, Mr. Crow Hicks, and Mr. Bobby Jack Plunkett. There're a few more, too, but they're the main ones. We do everything we can to stay out of their way because we don't like to hear that stuff, and besides, we can't ever be sure about what else they might do. Then there're some folks who've been talking about us a lot more than usual lately when they think we can't hear them or we're not listening. That's Mr. Horace Bowman, Mr. Lester Grimes, Mr. Odell Grimes, Brother Elmer Spurlock, and Mr. Preston Upshaw."

"Surely you don't suspect Mr. Bowman."

"No, sir, I don't, but let me go back a minute. The next thing I figured is that whoever did all this had to have a truck of some kind. Everybody I named so far drives one or owns one except Mr. Lester and Mr. Odell, so I took them off."

"So, where'd that leave you and what about Mr. Bowman?"

"Well, then I started asking myself what each one of the others might be getting out of what's happening. And it seemed to me that even though most all of them might get a kick out of trying to scare or hurt us, destroying property with the crosses is a mite risky to be doing just for spite or a good time. I don't know what the law will do when it catches whoever it is, but nobody around here has ever gone this far to get at us before, leastways not that I can remember. I know they might think they have more cause now, what with everything that's going on up in Little Rock and all, but so long as it's not too likely that integration is coming to Unionville any time real soon, I don't believe most of them would risk burning down a school or somebody's business. Of course, Mr. Bowman could be getting Mr. Davis to do it. I've been seeing him around the bank a lot lately, and I happen to know he's been over to Mr. Bowman's house a few times too. That seems pretty strange to me and I don't have any explanation for it."

"How do you know that—about Mr. Bowman's house, I mean? I have to admit I've seen Jim Ed over at the bank more often than usual. I thought he might be trying to get a loan or maybe sell some timber."

Leon shifted his weight away from the post.

"If you don't mind, Mr. Sam, I'd rather not say, but it's the truth. I just hear things. Anyway, I can't see nothing Mr. Bowman could be getting out of all this, because half the black men in Unionville work for him, and burning crosses, or hiring somebody to do it, isn't gon' make them work any harder for him. So that leaves me with two folks that could be getting something besides fun out of what's happening, and that's Brother Spurlock and Mr. Upshaw. Both of them are getting a lot of folks to notice them, and one of them is making money off of it, or trying to anyway."

Sam turned to the door and looked toward First Street. He had an angled view of the back of Emmett's Café and the newspaper office. Leon stood waiting. In a few moments, Sam turned back.

"Leon, I appreciate you telling me this. I've been suspecting just about everybody you named except those two. Between you and me, I don't have much use for either one of them, especially Upshaw, but a person doesn't like to think about a preacher or a newspaper man, even one as low-down as Upshaw, doing something like burning crosses and destroying property, despite all the blowing off they've been doing. But now that you've said it, I think you might have something, especially about Upshaw. I haven't trusted him since I first laid eyes on him. You said you wanted me to help you think what to do about it. You got some ideas about that too?"

"Well, sir, I was wondering if you could talk to Mr. Claude and Deputy Culpepper and figure out some way to watch Brother Spurlock and Mr. Upshaw close enough to maybe catch whichever one of them it is if he tries to burn another one. I've been trying to keep an eye on them a little, even to the point of coming back to the shop after work sometimes, but I can't keep track of them all by myself. Besides, no black man wants to be caught sneaking around in the middle of the night alone."

"Okay, suppose we start with Mr. Claude? He told me he's got some ideas, too, but he hasn't said what they are yet. Maybe he's thinking along the same lines as you."

Leon agreed and Sam went to close the door. He did not see the truck that slowed on First Street with its driver squinting through the windshield in his and Leon's direction.

"So, do you think the cross burnings and the streetlights might be connected some way?" Sam asked over his shoulder.

"That's hard to say but whoever burned the crosses could have shot out the streetlights just to throw everybody off, or like we talked about before, to make it look like our folks were trying to get back for that first cross burning at the church. Just like somebody wrapped that second one in coat hangers so maybe it would look like I did it."

"Yeah, could be. Far as I know, this last one didn't have wire on it. That could mean there's more than one person burning them."

The two men headed back to the front of the warehouse.

"Can I ask you something kind of personal, Leon?" Sam said, as they walked.

"Yes, sir."

"I was noticing y'all's school the other night, how run down it is. I'm wondering how it is that when you put that together with all these cross burnings to stop integration, which I guess would mean better education for Negroes, you aren't just mad as hell? You seem pretty calm about all this."

"Mr. Sam, I don't mean any disrespect, but how do you know I'm not mad as hell, and a lot of other folks too? What do you think would happen to me, or any of us, if we let white folks see that? Some of those fellows you and me have been talking about would be looking for some black heads to beat on. We're not afraid to defend ourselves if we have to. But right now, it looks like things might be starting to change, so there's no sense doing something stupid."

For a moment, both men were silent as they walked along, then Leon spoke again. "Mr. Sam, about that last thing I said..."

"It's all right, Leon, I understand."

CHAPTER 47

On Friday morning, October 25, the *El Dorado Daily News* reported that the nine black students at Central High no longer needed military protection to go to class. The paper said soldiers still took them back and forth from their homes in an army station wagon but did not accompany them otherwise.

Authorities cited this as evidence that tensions were easing but they were not. White students continued to kick the nine in their shins, stomp their toes, trip them in hallways, knock books out of their hands, and call them names. The press did not report it, but word of it spread among blacks throughout the state.

Superintendent Vernon Appleby did not know or care what was happening to the black students at Central High, but today he feared violence between white and black students in Unionville even without integration. Clarence Tubbs, who was principal of Unionville's black school and did know about the student violence at Central, shared Appleby's concern. They sat in the superintendent's office talking about how to prevent trouble during the one school function that brought white and black students physically close to each other every year—the white high school's homecoming parade. It always started at the school, moved east on Newton Chapel Road to the highway, went south through town, looped around several blocks on the Louisiana side, and returned the same way it came. Blacks were not allowed to join in but they could watch along a four-block stretch on the east side of the highway north of the business district, close to the quarters. Whites could watch from all other vantage points and the district bused all students to their respective places.

Appleby and Tubbs were trying to decide whether to go ahead with the parade the same as always. Because of the last cross burning, both worried that someone, black or white, might do something—push, shove, flip a finger, or throw a rock—to start a fight, or worse. Appleby considered barring black students from attending.

"I know folks are all tensed up right now," Tubbs said finally, "but nothing's happened in the daytime, and I don't want to penalize my students. Seeing the parade is the only thing they get to do away from school all year and they look forward to it." He thought, but did not say, even if they cannot be in it.

"Aw, all right. We'll go ahead like we always do. But you tell your teachers I expect them to keep those kids in line."

The bright sun had taken some autumn chill out of the air and it was a nice day for a parade. Every grade of the Unionville white school and all of the organizations—pep squad, Future Farmers of America, Future Homemakers, 4-H Club, Science Club—were decorating pickup trucks or tractor-pulled wagons as floats. Sam had promised the Otasco truck to Becky days earlier, and this morning before school, he had parked it in front of her building, left the keys in it, taken his pistol out of the tool box, and walked to work. Now, it was time to go back and drive it in the parade. He wondered if he would see Becky but had no idea what he would say to her if he did. He knew he had crushed her and she had been clear about her wishes. He replayed their conversation over and over in his mind and the replaying always ended the same—with his bumbling response and two people empty and hurt because of it and because of circumstances neither could control.

Sam skipped dinner and arrived back at the school on foot a little before one o'clock, in plenty of time to pull the pickup into line. He found it where he left it, decorated now in paper flowers and streamers, with a hand-lettered "Tame the Bears" sign taped to each door. A sheet of cardboard cut from a bicycle box, also courtesy of the Otasco store, was fastened to the back of the cab and had a circus tent painted on it. Balloons in assorted colors flew from the top. Inside the bed, two students dressed in homemade bear suits practiced rearing on their hind quarters. Two animal trainers wore cardboard top hats and their fathers' hunting jackets.

Becky was nowhere in sight but Billy was there. She had given him permission to ride along with his daddy.

"Hi, Sam," Lily Poindexter, the other seventh-grade teacher said when she arrived a few moments later. "We're all ready to go. You'll be behind the sixth-grade. That's the 'Skin the Bears' float over there on Mr. O'Brien's truck." Sam glanced over and saw three kids waving huge cardboard knives in front of papier-mâché bearskins tied to the cab. "Remember to stay twenty yards apart."

A few minutes after one, Jesse Culpepper and another Union County deputy, along with one each from Tonti and Claiborne Parishes, began detouring traffic away from the parade route. Mr. Claude walked along the highway in the center of town to make sure onlookers did not run into the street.

At fifteen minutes past the hour, the Bobcat drum major blew her whistle, and the Unionville High School band stepped off playing John Philip Sousa's "The Thunderer." The pep squad fell in behind them, and two horse-drawn buggies, a group of men and boys on horseback, and the floats followed. The largest one brought up the rear, carrying the homecoming queen and her court.

As Sam turned the corner onto the highway, the first thing he noticed was all the black children lined up to watch. He had seen them there for previous parades but he had never looked at them the way he did now. They could not play on a football team or march in a band or ride on the floats. They could only watch the white kids. Sam glanced over at Billy, who was waving to folks along the other side of the road, and he remembered his son's questions about segregation the day they were shelving fuel pumps, not long after the trouble started in Little Rock. Now the same beliefs and attitudes that separated the school children also separated him from Becky. He drove the parade route carefully but remembered little about it afterward.

When the parade ended, adults along the route went home or back to work, bus drivers took students back to school, and teachers and students began taking the floats apart and getting ready for that evening's football game and homecoming dance. Billy and some of his classmates helped Sam remove the decorations from the Otasco truck, then he drove back to town. He never saw Becky and wondered all the while where she was.

When Sam walked into the store, Mr. Claude was sitting on the mezzanine steps talking to Miss Ruthelle. "Hey, Sam," he said, "I just came in to sit for a spell. I saw you and Billy go past. This was another good one, wasn't it?"

"I reckon so," Sam said absently. "I need to talk to you, Mr. Claude. Can you walk out back with me? It's council business."

"Y'all just go on and don't mind me," Miss Ruthelle said, as if her feelings were hurt. She was used to Sam getting out of earshot when he had something private to discuss, but still, she liked to get in a little dig about it. As Mr. Claude and Sam walked to the loading dock, they could hear her taking jelly beans from the ceramic jar she had bought to replace the glass one she dropped.

Sam grabbed a couple of empty nail kegs, carried them onto the dock, and put them where he could keep an eye on the door. Unlike with Leon Jackson, no one would be curious about seeing him sitting back here with the marshal.

"Mr. Claude," Sam said, taking a seat, "the other night over at your house, you said you had some ideas about all the stuff that's been going on. I've got a couple, too, and I'd like to see if we're thinking the same thing."

Mr. Claude sat down, took off his hat, and rolled the brim between his fingers.

"All right, Sam," the little man said after a moment, "but I want this strictly between you and me."

"Understood. Go ahead."

"I think it's either that smart-ass Upshaw or that loudmouth Spurlock. Here's how I figure it. There's a whole lot of good ole boys like Crow Hicks, Jim Ed Davis, Boomer Jenkins, and Bobby Jack Plunkett that are enjoying the hell out of all this. But three of them—Crow, Jim Ed, and Bobby Jack—don't have sense enough to do it without getting caught. They wouldn't know horse shit if they stepped in it. Lester Grimes and that brother of his are getting a kick out of it, too, but they don't have the guts to burn crosses, and besides, they were at the football game the night the streetlights were shot out. So were Bobby Jack and Crow, for that matter. And burning crosses ain't Boomer's way. If he was riled up enough to do something, he'd just beat the crap out of somebody and be done with it. To tell you the truth, he's the one man around here I'd hate to tangle with. He's not scared of anything."

"So, why do you think it's Upshaw or Spurlock?"

"Because they're liking it too much and because both of them are capable of thinking through how to do it without being seen, at least so far. I expect whichever one of them it is doesn't want to take time to dig a hole for the crosses and that's why he's leaning them up against things. He doesn't want to just leave them lying on the ground either, because they're not scary enough like that. Upshaw and Spurlock would think of all that. They might also think about making each one of them a little bit different, too, just to throw people off or make it look like more than one person is doing it. They both ought to be smart enough to know they're breaking the law by destroying private property, but they may not care about that because they're so cocksure they won't get caught. That fits both of them too."

"Mr. Claude, I have to tell you something and ask you the same thing you said about keeping it just between us."

"All right," Mr. Claude said. He put his hat back on. "You know something I don't?"

"I don't know anything for sure, but I'm pretty much where you are on this, and so is somebody else I know. I'd like to see the two of you get together before something else happens."

Sam told how Leon had come to a similar conclusion and what they had discussed about watching Upshaw and Spurlock. Mr. Claude said he had been trying to keep an eye on them, too, but he needed help.

"Leon took a big risk talking about this, Mr. Claude."

"I know. I'll go tell him we've talked and not to worry. We'll see what we can do."

"There you are!" Gloria said, when Billy and Sam slid in beside her and Tucker at the football game a few minutes before kickoff. "We'd about given up on you." She and Tucker had been expecting Sam to bring Becky so they could all go to the homecoming dance, but she stopped short of asking in front of everybody why he had not.

Bearden, from way upstate, was always a tough opponent for the Bobcats, but Unionville had not lost since the opening game. Early in the first quarter, Ronnie Metcalf plunged off left tackle, cut to his right, and scampered thirty yards for a Bobcat touchdown. The 7 to 0 score held up the rest of the half, and at the break most folks stayed in their seats to see the homecoming queen crowned and the band put on its fanciest performance of the season. Then came a mad rush to the concession stand. Billy went off on his own as usual and Sam and Tucker rose by habit and fell in behind everyone else.

"Anything you want to tell me, buddy?" Tucker asked.

"No," Sam said without stopping.

"I thought you'd have a guest tonight," Tucker said, guarding his words just in case someone overheard. "I know she didn't have to work the concession stand any more this season."

"I don't think it's gon' work out. Everything's too complicated."

"Well, you know what that means and I don't, but you make damned sure you don't give up on it too soon."

Tucker's words rang in Sam's ears the rest of the evening, as Unionville pounded out a 27 to 10 win. When the game ended, the Tuckers went to the homecoming dance. The Tates walked home. And after Billy went to bed, Sam went out on the back porch and lit a Chesterfield.

Following a sleepless night, on Saturday morning Sam left Billy with Miss Ruthelle at the Otasco store and drove to the county seat. He said he needed to pick up some things at El Dorado Pipe & Supply but his real destination was Ewing Florists. He could have walked across the street to Bailey's Floral Shop, but he wanted two-dozen red roses delivered, and if the delivery was refused, he did not want everybody in town hearing about it. He had written and sealed a simple note to go with the roses: "Becky, I love you, and you said you love me. Nothing else matters. Please call me."

The folks at the floral shop were agreeable, but they were working two funerals and could not make a delivery until Tuesday, after more fresh flowers came in. Sam did not like waiting that long but he placed his order and left his note and directions to Becky's apartment.

On Saturday afternoon, most people in Arkansas and Mississippi, as well as many elsewhere, turned their attention to Memphis, Tennessee, where the undefeated Ole Miss Rebels were preparing to defend their number six national ranking against the Arkansas Razorbacks on a neutral site. Having fallen out of the top ten after losing to Texas last week, the Hogs looked to get back on track.

With the score tied 6 to 6 at halftime, Tucker finished the body he had been embalming, washed his hands, turned off the radio, and went to the Otasco store. He had been thinking about his friend all day.

"Sam," he said on entering, "you ought to be listening to the

Hogs. They're playing a good game. Let's turn it on." Without waiting for a reply, he went to the Philco and flipped the switch.

"I don't have time, Tucker," Sam said. "I've got customers and Billy and I have to put these wagons together." He motioned toward parts of three Radio Flyers scattered about on a large sheet of cardboard near the stairs.

"You need to take a break," Tucker said. "Miss Ruthelle can wait on folks. Besides, I don't see any customers right now."

Tucker drew up a nail keg and Sam and Billy kept on working. The second half began slowly and things looked bad for Arkansas until midway through the third quarter. Then the Razorbacks scored on a nifty run that proved enough to end Mississippi's unbeaten streak.

"Boy, that was some game, wasn't it, Daddy," Billy said at the end.

"Yeah, son," Sam said matter-of-factly.

Tucker knew his friend had not heard a word of it.

After breaking off with Sam, Becky cried often and struggled to maintain her enthusiasm for teaching. She even questioned the wisdom of staying in Unionville. Over the weekend, however, new stories about intimidation of blacks in Little Rock gave her inspiration for more lessons and helped her regain some of her spark, and on Monday afternoon, she went home thinking once more about how well her students were responding to her methods. Her classroom overflowed with posters, drawings, reports, and other examples of student work, and because the children talked about them with friends, other teachers had begun to take notice and ask her questions about her approach. And Gladys Woodhead seemed to have decided, now that parents had

stopped calling, that ignoring Becky was the easiest route to retirement. After mulling everything over, Becky wanted to finish
what she had started.

Schoolboard president Herbert Kramer had a different idea,
however. He hated that Vernon Appleby and Gladys Woodhead
had not been able to devise any new rules or regulations to trip
Becky up. He was also disappointed that only a couple of people
had criticized her in letters to the *Unionville Times*. Unaccustomed
to losing, he decided to take matters into his own hands and see
if he could dig up other grounds for getting rid of her. He did
not know what he was looking for exactly, but he had money and
determination, and he put both to work.

Believing he would not find the help he needed in Little
Rock because folks up there were so consumed with the crisis at
Central High School, he drove down to Shreveport on Monday
afternoon. In addition to being almost as large a city, it was closer, and he knew it better. Folks back home had no idea that he
liked to visit the strip clubs near Barksdale Air Force Base or that
he had serious poker pals there who gambled real money. It did
not take him long to find what he wanted—a private investigator willing to work for a reasonable sum and travel to look into
Becky's past.

CHAPTER 48

A light rain had been falling for several hours, and there was a nip in the air when Emma Lou MacDonald banged on the Tates' front door Tuesday morning.

"Looks like she's locked us out again," Almalee Jolly said, shaking water off her new umbrella. "I wonder if something's wrong."

"I don't know," Emma Lou said. She knocked again and started taking off her raincoat.

"Morning, Mrs. MacDonald. Morning, Mrs. Jolly," Ollie Mae Greene said, as she opened the door. "I'm sorry. I forgot to unlock it."

"Is everything all right, Ollie Mae?" Emma Lou asked.

"Mrs. Tate ain't feeling too good," Ollie Mae said, holding open the screen door. "I found her sitting in there with all her quilting things again this morning. I tried to get her to lie down but she wouldn't do it. She just said to tell y'all to come on in. Miss Mary Jane's in her own room and I'm fixing y'all's refreshments."

When the quilters walked into Gran's front room, she was sitting in her rocking chair holding some of her sampler blocks. Others lay on the floor among loose scraps. She looked pale and her hair bun was partly unwound, as if she had not put enough bobby pins in it.

"Gosh almighty, Ida Belle," Emma Lou said, frowning with worry, "you don't look like you feel like quilting today. Why don't you just go ahead on to bed like Ollie Mae said? We can catch up on talking and stuff next week."

"No. I don't want to. I want to quilt. I got my sampler blocks about done, and I'm thinking about how I'm gon' line them up. Y'all just sit on down."

"Okay," Emma Lou said, "we're gon' do it just so we can keep an eye on you. But I still think you ought to go lie down." She plopped into her customary straight chair.

"I think Emma Lou's right," Almalee said, taking her seat on the sofa and crossing her legs just so.

"I ain't gon' lie down," Gran said, "so y'all just as well shut up yapping about it." She looked down at her lap and pushed several pieces of fabric under the pile resting there.

"What are those pretty red and yellow scraps?" Emma Lou asked.

"They ain't nothing. I just had them lying around and I ain't gon' use them."

"What scraps?" Almalee asked, starting to work on her Triple Nine Patch.

"Ain't nothing!" Gran snapped. "Y'all just quilt."

Emma Lou let her question go and she and Almalee stitched silently for a while. Gran sat holding her blocks, slowly rubbing her hands over them one by one.

"The homecoming parade sure was pretty this year," Almalee said, finally overcome by her need to gab. "Did y'all see it?"

"Almalee, you know Ida Belle don't ever go to the parade," Emma Lou scolded, intent on keeping Gran quiet. "I saw it, though, and you're right about it being pretty. That queen looked real nice. All the girls did."

"Emma Lou, I been thinking," Gran whispered. Before she could say what about, she slumped sideways over a chair arm.

"Good Lord!" Emma Lou cried, struggling out of her chair. "Ida Belle! What's wrong? Oh Lordy! Almalee, she's passed out! Go call Doc! Ollie Mae, come quick!"

Sam had been making a delivery when Almalee's call came into the Otasco store. When he pulled into his driveway, he had to steer off the gravel and around Doc Perkins's DeSoto and Tucker's spare hearse, with its rear door standing open and the inside getting wet. Fearing the worst, Sam skidded to a stop on the wet grass, leaped out, and raced for the porch steps. Before he got there, Doc came through the front door backwards, bumping the screen aside and pulling Tucker's wheeled stretcher. All Sam could make out at first was a form under a white sheet. Then he saw his mother's uncovered head and Tucker beyond, pushing.

"Looks like she's had a heart attack," Doc said without pausing. "We're taking her to the hospital."

"Is she gon' be all right?"

"I can't tell yet, but we're gon' take good care of her. You can ride along. Emma Lou's gon' look after Mary Jane."

Sam wanted to reach over to Gran and kiss her on the forehead or something but everything was moving too fast. He helped Doc and Tucker get the stretcher down the steps while Almalee tried to hold her umbrella over her friend's face. Once they had the stretcher on the ground, Sam hurried back onto the porch and into the hall, where Emma Lou was kneeling on the floor holding Mary Jane. Tears were running down her cheeks. Sam squatted down and took her face in his hands.

"Don't worry, sweetheart," he said. "Gran's gon' be all right. I'm gon' go with her and Mrs. MacDonald is gon' stay with you. I'll be back in a little while. I love you." He kissed her cheek and ran for the ambulance. As he went, he thought about Billy and whether to have somebody get him out of school but there was no time.

Becky had barely closed her front door when Hazel Brantley rapped on it and pushed through without waiting for a reply. She was carrying a long white box with a huge red ribbon tied around it, and the look on her face matched her gray dress and the gloomy weather outside.

"I'm sorry to barge in, hon, but I've been waiting for you. Somebody brought this from El Dorado a little while ago and I'm afraid I've got some bad news too."

Becky finished getting out of her raincoat and put it on the back of her desk chair.

"What's happened, Hazel?" Becky asked, taking the box. She could guess what was in it and who had sent it. She laid it on the coffee table and motioned her landlady, who clearly need to sit down, to the sofa.

"Ida Belle Tate's had a heart attack," Hazel said. "She's up at St. Joseph's Hospital in El Dorado and she's in bad shape. They say Sam's real upset."

Becky drew a quick breath and sat down next to Hazel.

"What does 'bad shape' mean exactly, and who said that about Sam?"

"Emma Lou MacDonald called and asked me to tell you. She's Ida Belle's best friend and she likes you. She's taking care of Mary Jane and Billy. Emma Lou was planning to tell him about it soon as he got home from school."

Becky leaned back on the sofa. All sorts of things ran through her mind. She expected that in addition to worrying about his mother, Sam was probably wondering, as she was right now, if their seeing each other had helped bring on the attack. And he must be worried about the children too. She wished she could do something for him.

"I don't know if Ida Belle can have visitors," Hazel volunteered, "but if you want me to ride up there with you to see Sam, I'd be glad to drive us."

"Thank you, Hazel. That's sweet but I can't go."

Hazel put her hand on Becky's shoulder.

"You two had a spat, didn't you? I've had a feeling, because I ain't seen Sam over here in a while, and you've been moping around so. You want to talk about it?"

"No."

"I bet this is flowers from Sam. Ain't you gon' open them up and see if there's a note inside or something?"

"Hazel, you've been nice to me, and I don't want to hurt your feelings, but I'd really like to be alone now."

"Okay, hon, I understand, but let me tell you first that Emma Lou's organizing church ladies to help out over there while Ida Belle's in the hospital—and after she comes home, too, assuming she does. I told her to put me on the list and I said I figured you'd want to be on it too."

"Can we talk about that later?" Becky asked, sitting forward and putting her hands on her knees.

"Okay, hon," the landlady said, getting up to leave.

"Hazel, if you hear anything more, will you let me know, please?"

"You know I will, hon."

When Hazel was gone, Becky opened the box, put the flowers in her lap, and read the note. She wished Sam knew how badly she wanted to do as he asked and call him, or better still, go to him, but she could not do either. She laid the paper on the flowers and buried her face in her hands.

⌒

Sam wanted to stay at the hospital but he also wanted to talk to Billy and Mary Jane and make sure they were all right. With the help of oxygen and medicine, Gran was resting, and the doctors said there was nothing more to do but wait. After using a pay phone to call his brother Herman in Texas, Sam rode back to Unionville with Doc shortly before suppertime.

Emma Lou and the children were putting food on the table when Sam arrived home. The church women had already been hard at work and the kitchen counter was filled with casseroles, pies, and cakes.

"Hey, Billy, Mary Jane!" he called. "I'm home and Gran's doing fine."

"Daddy!" Mary Jane cried, running to him. "I knew she would be okay. I said a prayer for her."

"That's good, sweetheart," he said, picking her up. "You can say some more prayers tonight and pretty soon she can come back home." He squeezed Mary Jane and put his arm around Billy's shoulders. Both children smelled of soap. Emma Lou had made them take a good wash for supper.

"Emma Lou, I'm really obliged to you for taking care of them. Are you gon' have something to eat with us?"

"No, thank you, Sam. I need to get home and take care of Purvis. Him and Almalee brought my car over this afternoon, and if I don't get on back pretty soon, he'll be worried."

"Okay, but why don't you fix up some of this food and take it home for y'all. Looks like there's plenty."

While Emma Lou filled two plates and covered them with

wax paper, Sam told her what he knew so far about his mother's condition.

"You don't need to worry about nothing here," Emma Lou said. "I've I got it all arranged. There's gon' be somebody that Mary Jane knows here with her every minute you're gone, or else she's gon' be over at Gloria Tucker's on weekends. And even on days Ollie Mae ain't working, there's gon' be food on the table every noon and night. I reckon y'all can get your own breakfast. Anytime you want to stay all night at the hospital, Mary Jane and Billy can sleep at my house. I got plenty of room."

Sam thanked her and asked her to thank all the other ladies, too, and when she left, he and the children sat down and tried to eat without staring at Gran's empty chair.

"Are you sure Gran's not gon' die, Daddy?" Mary Jane asked through puckered lips.

"Sweetheart, I'm sure God's gon' take good care of your grandmother," Sam said, choosing his words carefully.

"But who's gon' take care of us if she dies?"

"Now, Mary Jane, don't you go worrying about that," he said, wishing he could follow his own advice.

That night on the back porch with his Chesterfield, his heart ached for three women and two children, and he could not discuss his pain with any of them.

The next morning, Sam called Art Nelson and arranged for him to help in the store again, as he had last Christmas season. Then began a daily routine of getting Billy off to school, waiting for Ollie Mae or someone else to come and stay with Mary Jane, running by the store for an hour or so, and then spending the rest of the day in El Dorado. His brother Herman flew in from Midland, took a room at the Flamingo Motel, and stayed at the hospital almost around the clock.

CHAPTER 49

"Evening, Mr. Claude." The voice came out of the night without warning.

"Good lord, Leon! You ought not sneak up on a fellow that way. Where'd you learn to do that?"

"I'm sorry, Mr. Claude. I didn't mean to give you a start. I learned it in the army."

"Well, I'm glad you're tracking Upshaw and Spurlock and not me."

Mr. Claude had gone to see Leon on Monday morning and they had arranged to meet back at the dry-cleaning shop late Tuesday night. There, talking in the dark to avoid notice, they swapped theories and came up with a plan to watch their two suspects. They felt sure that after Crow Hicks made his night watchman's rounds about ten o'clock, he did nothing more except sleep in the town hall, so they decided to meet behind the post office every night at ten-thirty. They figured if they watched the highway from the cover of alleys until an hour or two before sunup, they would have a decent chance of seeing Upshaw, Spurlock, or anyone else who was out and about at an odd hour. To help stay awake, Mr. Claude would nap at home during the day, and Leon would catch a few winks right after work.

"Tell you what," Mr. Claude said, as Leon slid in next to him. "Let's walk over behind the Ford place and come back to the highway at Second Street. I stashed a thermos of coffee over there a little while ago. We can see farther up the highway from there and still watch the newspaper office."

The pint-size lawman, wearing his black suit coat, and the strapping ex-soldier, clad in a dark gabardine jacket, moved off in the darkness and took up their new position on a big residential lot with plenty of cover. The two men drank coffee and watched, mostly in silence. Neither expected to see anything this first night but they hoped all the same. Big trucks passed occasionally, most of them hauling freight from factories up north, but little else stirred. Shift workers in El Dorado's oil industry had returned home hours earlier.

"Hey, Mr. Claude," Leon whispered about one-thirty. "Isn't that Mr. Upshaw's stake-bodied truck coming yonder?"

The marshal squinted, trying to see up the highway. "Sure looks like it. I wonder how we missed him leaving, unless maybe it was before we came out here. If that's the case, he probably hasn't been out burning crosses."

"Looks like there's somebody in there with him," Leon said, when the truck drew closer. "I believe it's Brother Spurlock."

"Well, I'll be damned! Maybe they're in it together. He's heading around back. Let's move."

Mr. Claude grabbed the thermos, and he and Leon hustled across the street and crouched behind some more bushes just in time to see Spurlock and Upshaw climb out of the truck in the alley back of the newspaper office. The two talked for a couple of minutes then shook hands, and the preacher got in his own truck and drove off. Upshaw unlocked his back door and went inside.

"That's strange," Mr. Claude said, standing up.

"Looks like they must have been driving for a while," Leon said, rising and brushing off his clothes. "They were walking like their legs were all stiffened up."

"Yeah, I think you're right. I sure would like to know what they were up to."

Folks stopped by the Otasco store in droves to ask about Ida Belle and send her get-well wishes. They came more for Sam than for Gran but he appreciated them all. He also welcomed moments when he could concentrate on other things. Fellow merchant Neal O'Brien provided such an opportunity Thursday morning.

"Hey, Sam, wait up a minute," he called, as Sam was getting in his truck to go to the hospital. Neal hustled across the street between traffic. "The police car's here. It came in yesterday and the Ford place already has everything installed. Boy, wait till you see her. She's a beauty."

"That's great, Neal. Have you told Jesse?"

"Yeah, I'm hoping he can start next Wednesday. He won't have a uniform by then, but he'll have a badge and a gun—and a car."

The businessmen chatted a few minutes more, and Sam drove away wondering if Mr. Claude and Leon had talked yet. As he passed Hazel Brantley's house, his thoughts turned to Becky again. Despite everything else going on, he had tried calling her three times this week, but she had not answered. He still did not know what to say to her, other than he loved her and wanted to be with her, but he hoped if he could see her and hold her, the right words would come.

While Sam was on his way to El Dorado, Upshaw was hard at work finishing his lead story for the November 1 *Unionville*

Times, and Pearl Goodbar was trying to hurry him up.

"I don't know why you always wait till the last minute to do these things, Mr. Upshaw," she said, tossing her pencil on her desk. "One of these weeks, we're not gon' get the paper out."

"I can't help it that I didn't get back from Little Rock till one-thirty this morning, and I couldn't very well write this before I heard the man speak. Here," he said, making a big show of removing a page from his typewriter, "proof and set it."

Pearl got up from her desk and retrieved the story. The main headline read, "Area Leader Wows Capital Audience." The subhead said, "Leland Farley Says Stop Integration by Denying Negroes the Vote."

"Farley's a genius," Upshaw said, rubbing his shoulder while heading for the coffeepot. "It was worth the drive to hear him, and folks around here, especially those on the Louisiana side, are gon' appreciate our covering a local hero like this."

"He's not exactly local, Mr. Upshaw."

"Maybe not, but he's close enough. He represents lots of Unionville folks and he drew a big crowd at that first Citizens' Council meeting out at Brother Spurlock's church. And he's not just head of the Louisiana Citizens' Councils. He's also head of the Joint Committee on Segregation in the Louisiana legislature. He says if every state had intelligence tests for registering voters, it'd keep coloreds away from the ballot box permanently and kill integration. You should have seen the reception he got up there last night. They loved him and Brother Spurlock is gon' try to get him back again."

CHAPTER 50

After taking his brother Herman to the Union County Airport early Saturday morning and watching him climb into a twin-prop for the long trip back to Midland, Sam headed home. He expected to get there about the same time as Doc Perkins and Tucker, who were bringing Gran. Sam had not wanted her to leave St. Joseph's, because Doc and the hospital physicians could not be sure about how much damage her heart attack had done. She was kicking up such a fuss about staying, however, that they decided she would be at least as well off at home. Doc got ahold of an oxygen tank in case she needed it, Emma Lou MacDonald said she would help look after her, and Ollie Mae helped Sam find somebody for the days she could not work. Desperate, Sam met Doreen Dykes only briefly and hired her strictly on Ollie Mae's recommendation and the knowledge that she was Black Tiger B. J. Long's sister-in-law.

Sam got home just as Doc and Tucker were rolling Gran through the front door. Emma Lou was hovering over her and Ollie Mae was keeping Mary Jane out of the way.

"Y'all take care now. Don't be bumping this thing into the wall and scratching it," Gran said. Her voice was weak but, in her mind, this was her house and she was still the boss.

Tucker and Doc maneuvered the stretcher through her sitting room and into the adjoining bedroom, where one of Gran's quilts covered two feather mattresses and a set of box springs on a brass bedstead.

"You men get out of here now," Gran ordered. "Emma Lou and Ollie Mae can help me out of this contraption. Dadblame you anyway for tying me up like this. I ain't no baby."

Everyone did as she asked, and as soon as Tucker and Doc retrieved the stretcher, Gran called for Billy and Mary Jane.

"Lordy, young'uns," she said, as they came into her bedroom, "y'all sure are a sight for sore eyes. Come here and give your grandmomma a hug."

Doc followed them in, and after watching for a minute, he put a hand on each child's back and squatted beside them.

"Now, Billy and Mary Jane," he said, as much for Gran's benefit as for theirs, "your grandmother is a very sick woman and there are two things she's gon' need you to do to help her. The first one is she's gon' need lots of hugs, but real gentle ones, no squeezing hard. And the second one is she's gon' need lots of rest and sleep. That means you have to play quietly and not be pestering her all the time."

"Is she gon' die?" Mary Jane asked.

"Shhh!" Billy said.

Doc looked at Gran and started to speak but she beat him to it.

"Where in tarnation did you get a notion like that, hon'? I'm gon' be just fine. Don't you be worrying none."

A few minutes later, Sam helped Tucker bring in the oxygen tank, and Doc showed the adults how to use it. Then Emma Lou and Ollie Mae started tidying up, and Sam followed his friends into the yard. Doc started to get into the ambulance then turned back.

"Sam," he said, gripping his friend's shoulder. "I wish I could give you a better idea of what to expect. She may pull through this and get back on her feet again but I can't promise you that. She's old and she's tired. The best thing you can do for her, besides seeing she gets her rest, is just go on about business as usual. Keep her in bed till I say she can get up, but otherwise just keep things normal as you can and try not to upset her. It'll be the best thing for the kids too."

Saturday afternoon, while Emma Lou and Ollie Mae looked after Gran and Mary Jane, Sam took Billy to the store. It was the first time since Monday that Sam could spend more than a couple of hours there, but Miss Ruthelle and Art Nelson had everything under control. Little needed doing and all anyone there wanted was to find out about Gran. Sam tried to follow Doc's advice and not worry but it was hard.

Thankfully, Tucker came in and said, "The Razorbacks are about to play the number one team in the country and kickoff's in five minutes. Let's listen to it."

"Yeah," Art said. "Good idea. What do you say, Sam? It's pretty slow right now."

"Yeah, Daddy," Billy chimed in. "Let's."

Sam didn't need persuading. He moved around the table and turned on the Philco. Paul "Bear" Bryant, who hailed from Fordyce, about sixty miles up highway167, had brought his undefeated Texas A&M Aggies into Fayetteville expecting a tough contest and got it. Unfortunately for the Razorbacks, however, Bryant's All-American halfback John David Crow, from not far away in Springhill, Louisiana, pounded the Hogs on both sides of the ball, and the Aggies won 7 to 6.

"Well, there goes the Cotton Bowl," Tucker said, as Sam

switched off the radio. "They might have made it with one loss but they can't make it with two."

"Maybe they can still go to the Sugar Bowl," Billy said.

"Maybe," Sam said. He doubted it but he did not want to dampen Billy's hopes or his own. Neither of them needed anything more to worry about, not even something as simple as the fate of the Hogs.

When Becky answered Hazel's knock shortly before ten on Sunday morning, the landlady stood on the front porch wearing a blue apron over her pink bathrobe and holding a role of wax paper.

"I thought I'd give you one more chance to say, 'Yes,' before I get ready to go over to the Tates," she said. "I'm taking rolls and a salad and I made a chocolate cake for the kids. You still have time to make a little something too."

"No, Hazel," Becky said, keeping one hand on the door and the other on the frame, blocking her would-be guest. "I appreciate your asking but it's not a good idea."

"Okay, hon," the landlady said, backing away, "but I think you're making a big mistake."

Becky, also still in her bathrobe, closed the door and returned to her kitchen. She picked up the *El Dorado Daily News* from the dinette table and looked at the long headline again, "74 Atlanta Clergymen Set 6 Principles to Govern Race Relations." The ministers, all white, had issued a statement aimed at easing racial tensions across the South. It called upon all people to obey the law, preserve public schools, protect free speech, avoid hatred, work toward equal rights, and pray for guidance. It was not the ministers' recommended principles of moderation that drew Becky's attention, however. It was the preamble to them. She sat down and read it again.

> The use of the word *integration* in connection with our schools and other areas of life has been unfortunate, since to many, that term has become synonymous with amalgamation. We do not believe in the amalgamation of the races, nor do we feel it is favored by right-thinking members of either race.

When Becky decided to tell Sam she was a Negro, she had not been thinking past knowing that they could not be together. She just wanted to protect them both from unbearable pain. Afterward, as she went about teaching every day, she tried not to think about the future. Now, she was beginning to realize she could not put her heritage back in the shirt box with the photographs and just keep it there. And she did not know any longer if she even wanted to.

Becky was not the only Unionville resident moved by the newspaper report about the Atlanta clergymen. Elmer Spurlock was not sure why he woke up early on Sunday morning, but he slopped his hogs and dressed for church before the sun came up. His sermon—a rehash of what Leland Farley had said in Little Rock—was ready and there was no need to review it. Restless, he decided to go to the post office and pick up the El Dorado paper. He read about the Atlanta ministers while sitting in his truck on Main Street and chain smoking half a pack of cigarettes. Then he rushed home to his Bible. He did not need to make any notes. He only needed to mark a few passages. Once he got in the pulpit and started reading scriptures, words to expand on them would come easily.

He had preached plenty about what he thought integration would lead to, but he had not devoted an entire sermon to mixed marriages. As the Mercy Baptist Mission filled with worshipers, he sat silently on the podium, wearing his badly wrinkled white suit despite the season and imagining himself rising to the pulpit and addressing his flock.

When the service began, he led the same rousing songs he used back in August when he preached about how, in his way of thinking, God's curse on Canaan, the son of Ham, doomed black people to everlasting inferiority. "Stand Up for Jesus," "Rise Up, O Men of God," and "Onward Christian Soldiers" all spoke of Christians doing battle for the Lord.

After the singing, Spurlock stood dead still as those gathered before him sat down and returned their hymnals to holders on the backs of the pews. Once everyone was settled, he placed his oversized Bible on the pulpit and flipped it open. Then, in the most dramatic voice he could muster, he said, "Listen to what Moses told the Israelites here in Deuteronomy, chapter seven, when he was reminding them about the Ten Commandants and all the other things they needed to do to live right for God. He warned them against mixing with other races, like the Hittites and the Canaanites and a bunch of others. He said don't make any covenants with them, and he said—I'm quoting now— 'Neither shalt thou make marriages with them; thy daughter shalt not give unto his son, nor his daughter shalt thou take unto thy son.' Then he says if they don't obey, the anger of the Lord will destroy them.

"Folks, he's talking about the sin of race mixing. He's talking about mongrelization. He's talking about what's gon' happen to people who promote it, who do it, and who let it happen. He warned the Israelites about it more than once. You can find just about these same words in First Kings, chapter eleven, verse two, and in Ezra, chapter nine, verse twelve.

"God is talking to us right here today through these scriptures. I tell you, if integration ain't stopped right now, right here in Arkansas, it's gon' spread to the rest of the South, and it's gon' destroy the white race!"

Spurlock did not care that Moses actually was warning the Israelites against people who worshiped idols.

⌒

"Sam," Miss Ruthelle called, laying the receiver on the office counter, "It's Emma Lou MacDonald."

Thinking the worst, Sam dropped the Flying-O tricycle wheel onto the cardboard he had spread out on the floor, scrambled to his feet, and hurried around the stairs to the phone. It was Wednesday morning in the first week of November, and he had spent the last several days trying to catch up on putting together Christmas toys.

"Sam," Emma Lou said, "your momma's okay, but you better come home and see to her. She's giving me and Doreen fits."

"What's the matter?"

"She don't want Doreen touching any of her things," came the tired voice on the other end of the line, "and she wants her sewing basket. I don't think she ought to have it because I don't think she needs to be stirring around that much. She's mad as an old momma possum and I can't do anything with her."

"All right, Emma Lou. I'll be right there."

Sam told Miss Ruthelle he would be back in a little while and headed for his pickup. He knew even before he told his mother about Doreen Dykes that Gran would not like the idea of new help, but he hoped that Emma Lou's being there on Doreen's first day would smooth the way.

When Sam turned into the driveway, Emma Lou was standing on the front porch waiting, and she met him in the yard. Her rolled stockings sagged around her ankles and the underarms of her dress showed circles of sweat.

"I hated to bother you, Sam, but she's been carrying on so, I just didn't know what else to do. She's running me all over the house making sure Doreen's doing this and not doing that, and she's bound and determined to quilt. Maybe you can do something with her."

"Okay," Sam said, relieved his mother had not had another spell with her heart. He gave her friend a hand up the steps. "Let me see about it."

"Momma," Sam said, trying to strike a concerned but pleasant tone when he walked into her bedroom, "what's all the ruckus about?"

She was propped up on three large goose-feather pillows.

"It's about that colored woman messing in my kitchen and Emma Lou telling me I can't have my quilting basket. Dadgum it! I been laying up here for four days doing just like Doc said, and now I got me some sewing I need to do."

Sam had to admit she seemed better. And Doc had said to keep things as normal as possible and not upset her. "I tell you what," Sam said. "You stop fussing about Doreen, and I'll get your quilting basket, but you have to promise to calm down. Emma Lou's running her legs off for you and you have to let her get some rest too."

"I know, Sam. God love her. She's a saint. I promise, but you tell that Doreen not to be changing things around in the house. I can hear her and I can tell she ain't working like Ollie Mae."

"All right, I'll talk to her. You just behave." That was almost too easy Sam thought as he fluffed her pillows. He had expected more arguing. He kissed her on the cheek and went looking for Doreen. He asked her to work as quietly as possible, then he thanked Emma Lou and told her to give Gran what she wanted.

Driving back to town past Hazel's place, Sam's thoughts turned to Becky again. She still was not answering her phone, and he was thinking about stopping by unannounced again some evening after work or after supper, even though he still had not come up with how to say all that he felt.

He kept thinking about how he had hurt her, and while he could not put himself in her place, he imagined this was probably harder for her than for him. He did not care if she were black, white, or green. He loved her. To him she was simply Becky, a wonderful woman with whom he wanted to spend the rest of his life. He wondered what the chances were of anyone ever finding out she was passing. Pretty slim, he guessed, since she had kept it from everybody all her life, but he did not know if she intended to keep on doing so or, if she did, for how long. He was not going to ask, though, because he knew that would only hurt her more. One thing was certain. If her past came out, he and Becky could not be together in Unionville or anywhere near it. People would shun them and make life miserable for Mary Jane and Billy. And they could never get married—at least not in Arkansas or in most other states in the South—without committing a crime. Interracial marriage was against the law.

CHAPTER 51

When Sam got back to town, he parked in the alley next to Lawson's Dry Goods and crossed the street to City Hardware. Art Nelson had been opening the Otasco store every morning so Sam could take care of things at home, and he had been so wrapped up in his own affairs he had not kept up with town business. He found the council president filling nail bins.

"Morning, Sam, how's your momma doing?" Neal O'Brien asked, as he shook the last tenpenny finishing nails from a keg. Happy to have a break, he set the keg upside down on the floor, motioned Sam to sit on it, and lugged over an unopened keg for himself.

"I reckon she's doing better," Sam said. "She's still in bed but she's giving everybody orders. Anyway, I was wondering how things are going with Jesse Culpepper."

"He's not gon' be able to start till Friday. Something personal came up that he wants to take care of first. But he's happy as a pig in slop. He was over at the town hall last night after the votes were counted and said he's rearing to go. By the way, we missed you there."

"Sorry about that," Sam said. "I was so busy I clean forgot about the election. How'd we do?"

"No matter," Neal said. "You won. We all did of course. Same mayor and council for two more years. Anyway, Jesse's all set to start on Friday. Mr. Claude says that's okay with him. He also says he wants to rest up some before he starts the night watch-man's job. We'll have to keep on making do with Crow Hicks."

"Yeah, I reckon so," Sam said. He was pleased that Mr. Claude had not mentioned anything about getting together with Leon Jackson to watch Spurlock and Upshaw.

"But Mr. Trammel always ran bios on the election winners," Pearl said. She was standing in front of Upshaw's desk, clutching story drafts in both hands.

"You know I don't give a fig about what old man Trammel did. The only reason Sam Tate and the rest of that bunch won is because no one ran against them. They're incompetent morons and I'm not gon' waste any more ink on them. I'm not gon' waste it on that second Russian Sputnik either. To hell with the red menace. It's the black menace I'm worried about. Go on and set those Farley and Smitherman speeches like I told you."

"But Mr. Upshaw, you've reported on those before. They're not news anymore."

He stared coldly at Pearl. "Mrs. Goodbar, you still don't get it, do you? I don't mind breaking a few rules and conventions to get what I want."

While Upshaw went on using the *Unionville Times* to blast anyone and everything that hinted at integration, elsewhere the Soviet Union dominated the news. The *El Dorado Daily News* pro-claimed, "Soviet Newspapers Predict Russia to Send Rockets to Planets" and "Reds Claim New Super Fuel."

"What I'd like to know is how the hell those idiots in Washington could've sat on their fat asses and let this happen,"

Doyle Scoggins said at the Otasco store Saturday night. The usual loafers had gathered, and about the only thing keeping them anywhere near a good mood was a mess of Sam's peanuts parching on top of the large gas heater while it gave off a warm glow and soothing hum. Doc Perkins was fighting a cold he had picked up from one of his patients, Tucker had hunted all day without much luck, and Sam was worried about Billy taking care of his grandmother alone all evening. There was not even a Razorback game to listen to. Arkansas had played that afternoon and lost 13 to 7 to the Rice Owls. With three losses, their hopes for a bowl bid had grown dim.

"That satellite's not as much of a threat as everyone thinks," Doc said. He got up and grabbed a handful of peanuts. "We'll have our own satellites pretty soon. I'll tell you, though, if the Russians and us end up bombing the hell out of each other, we're not gon' have to worry about who's got the most do-hickeys in space."

"What do you think about that dog they sent up this time, Doc?" Houston Holloway asked. "You think it's gon' survive?"

"No, I don't think they expect it to. They just want to get some medical readings so maybe they can send a man up sometime soon."

"I think Odell Grimes hit the nail on the head up at Emmett's this morning," Scoggins said, flicking cigarette ashes on the floor. "He said we ought to let the Russians send ole Daisy Bates up there. Said it'd be good riddance since she don't know how to stay in her place down here."

Sam looked on in silence. In the past he had not paid much attention to this type of talk, but now it sounded different to him. He knew people would say things like this about Becky if they learned her secret, and it hurt to think about it.

While the loafers gabbed in Unionville, Lucien Bouchard slipped onto a barstool in Lee Ann's Palais de la Femme, just off Bourbon Street in New Orleans. The beefy detective had logged nearly twenty-five hundred miles by car during the last two weeks, walked dozens more, and poured over enough old newspapers, letters, journals, land deeds, and census records to fill an eighteen-wheeler. He had driven first to St. Louis, then south to the Crescent City, and since then, he had gone back and forth to Baton Rouge half a dozen times. He visited two county courthouses, one parish courthouse, one state archive, and three university libraries and walked up and down half the streets in New Orleans, or so it seemed, and talked to dozens of people. He was bone tired but the effort was paying off. He had only one more source to check.

At home amid the smell of cigar smoke and stale beer, he shucked his rumpled sport coat, ran a chubby hand through his thick black hair, and motioned to the stacked blond tending bar at the end of the counter. He wondered if she took a turn stripping on Lee Ann's beat-up stage, empty at the moment. If so, he might stay longer than he had planned. She winked at the customer she had just served, stuck a five down the front of her spaghetti-strap dress, and glided over, all smiles and boobs, aiming for another big tip.

"Hi, there, sugar. What can I get you?" she asked, leaning forward to give him a view intended to loosen his wallet. He admired what she was showing then laid a twenty on the counter and held it down.

"I'm looking for Skinny Red Hérbert," he said, as a five-piece band launched into a lively jazz number on the other side of the dimly lit room. "He's an old trombone player. Fellow down the street told me he likes to hang out around here."

"What do you want with him?" she asked in an almost motherly tone, as she reached for the twenty. Bouchard kept his hand on it.

"Do you know where he is or not?"

"Maybe. It depends."

"I just want to ask him some questions about some of the old joints, that's all."

He lifted his hand and she grabbed the twenty and pushed it in where the five had disappeared earlier. "Go through that green door over there and all the way down the hall," she said. "He's in the last room on the right. He's a nice old man and he's a little down on his luck. Lee Ann lets him come in from the alley and rest back there."

"Thanks for the information, baby. And thanks for the peep show too," he said, reaching for his jacket.

"You come back with some more of them Andrew Jacksons, sugar, and I'll show you a lot more," she said, winking.

Once in the hallway, Bouchard found the door to Skinny Red's room cracked open and the light-skinned old man sitting in a ragged platform rocker, his head on his chest and his feet on a liquor crate. He was wearing a worn black suit and white shirt with no tie. The detective walked over and gently shook his shoulder.

"Yep, what can I do you for?" Skinny Red asked, springing up as if he were used to being shook awake. Bouchard had expected to see a Negro but Skinny Red did not look or sound like one. Although he was well into his nineties, word had it that he still played now and then over at Preservation Hall, an old art gallery turned jazz room. Bouchard thought all those fellows were black, so maybe Skinny Red was a high mulatto or something. That might explain a lot.

"I hear when you were a kid you lived in one of those old Freedmen's Bureau homes and you knew Louise de Mortié. That right?"

The old man looked closer at his guest. Louise de Mortié was one of several people who had organized homes for black orphans in New Orleans near the end of the Civil War. The houses later came under the authority of the bureau and stood for years.

"How'd you know that? That was a long time ago."

"There're some records scattered around and I found out you looked at some of them."

"That was a long time ago too."

"Yeah, but people who keep that stuff generally remember who uses it, especially since not many folks do. I also hear you used to play in the pleasure houses over in Storyville. Did you?"

"Yeah, that was back before World War I when ladies of the evening were legal down here. Man, I could sure tell you some stories."

"That's exactly what I came for, Skinny Red. Do the names Charlene or Abigail Clémence mean anything to you?"

"Well, let me see now. They do sound sort of familiar like." He took his feet off the liquor crate and rested his hands on his knees. "Yes, sir," he said after a moment. "I recollect both of them."

CHAPTER 52

"She's pale as a ghost, Doc, and having trouble breathing, even with the oxygen," Sam said over the phone on Sunday morning. "You'd better get over here fast."

"I'm leaving right now. Call Tucker."

Sam did as he was told then rushed back to Gran. She looked frail with her long gray hair scattered over her pillow and her wrinkled face scrunched up in pain.

"Doc will be here in a minute," Sam said, "and he'll give you something to make you feel better. I expect he's gon' want to take you back to St. Joseph's, so I'm gon' go call Emma Lou and see if she'll look after Billy and Mary Jane."

Gran opened her eyes wider and shook her head.

"I know you don't want to go," Sam said, "but they can take better care of you there."

He touched her gently on the shoulder and went back to the phone in the hall.

"It's a good thing you called when you did," Emma Lou said, after Sam explained what was happening. "Me and Purvis was fixing to go over to Pine Bluff to see his brother. Now don't you worry, hon, I'll be right there."

Sam barely had time to talk to Billy and Mary Jane before Doc, Tucker, and Emma Lou pulled up within minutes of each other. Doc strode directly into Gran's bedroom. He wore his usual black suit and displayed the same sunny manner he always used to calm folks in trouble.

"Morning, Ida Belle. You been behaving yourself?" he asked, not expecting an answer. He set his medical bag on a chair and took out his stethoscope. "Let me take a look at you." He felt her forehead, checked her pulse, and listened to her heart and lungs. "I tell you what, I'm gon' take you up to the hospital just so they can help me keep an eye on you, and in the meantime, I've got something here that's gon' make you feel better." While reaching in his bag with one hand, he signaled to Tucker and Sam with the other. They had already brought the stretcher into Gran's sitting room and they were watching through the door. A couple of minutes later they wheeled her through the hallway.

All this time, she said nothing, but seeing her friend holding open the front door, she whispered, "Wait. Emma Lou?"

Emma Lou leaned over the stretcher and took Gran's hand.

"I finished my sampler top," Gran whispered. "It's in my basket. Promise me you'll quilt it for Sam."

"Aw, hon." Emma Lou patted her hand then squeezed it. "You'll be back home in no time and you can do it yourself."

"Promise me. You have to."

"Ida Belle, you know I'd do anything for you."

Gran closed her eyes and the men rushed her to the ambulance.

"You look beat, Sam. How's your momma doing?" Miss Ruthelle asked, when he arrived at the Otasco store early Tuesday afternoon. Except for a few hours to clean up and see Billy and Mary Jane the day before, he had been at the hospital since Sunday morning. His clothes looked slept in and he needed a shave.

"There's not much change," he said, taking a seat on the wrapping table. "They've got her all doped up, so I don't think she's in much pain. Doc says it looks like there's a lot of damage this time but we're praying she's gon' pull out of it. My brother flew in a little while ago and he's gon' stay with her tonight. Is everything okay here?"

"Art Nelson came in this morning just like he promised. He's out in the warehouse taking a pipe delivery. Neal O'Brien was in here about an hour ago looking for you. He said he had some council news. Lester Grimes has been around a couple of times and lots of folks have asked after you. That's about it. Why don't you go on home and get some rest? Me and Art have things under control."

"All right," Sam said. "I think I will, right after I see what Neal wants."

Outside, Sam nodded to Otis Henderson, passing through town in one of his pulpwood trucks, and crossed the street to City Hardware. Neal was standing by the Coca-Cola box with Fred Vestal. Both were drinking Grapette sodas. They asked Sam about his mother, and while fishing in his pocket for a dime for a Dr Pepper, he told them the same thing he had told Miss Ruthelle then said, "I hear you were looking for me, Neal."

"Yep," Neal said. "Jesse Culpepper's been on the job less than a week and he's already found out who shot out the streetlights."

"Who did it?"

"A bunch of high school kids from Pineview," Fred said. "They didn't like their football team getting beat by the Bobcats so they did it for spite."

"How'd Jesse find out?"

"He had a suspicion about it," Neal said, "and when he didn't get anywhere with the Webster Parish sheriff's office, he went down there, talked to the high school principal, and asked him if he'd been having trouble with any boys who might have been at the game that night. Turns out he had, and when the principal started questioning them about the streetlights, they just up and confessed. Apparently, they'd been arguing for several days about where to put the blame once they got caught."

"That was a break. What's gon' happen to them?"

Neal said they had been suspended from school and their parents were trying to work something out on the damages.

"Now we just have to find out who's burning the crosses," Sam said. "Does Jesse have anything on that?"

"No," Neal said, "but since we haven't had one in nearly a month, maybe whoever burned them is done with it."

"Let's hope he is," Fred said, dropping his bottle in a crate with other empties.

Sam hoped so too. He was starting to think the crosses scared Becky more than she let on. There was also still the matter of the threatening note in his door. He had returned his new pistol to the tool box in his truck after the homecoming parade, and he planned to keep it there.

A jarring racket of disjointed sounds propelled Sam upright in bed. He identified the fire siren but could not make out the others. He switched on a lamp and looked at the clock. One-thirty in the morning. Darn it, he thought, he could not even get a good night's sleep at home. Then he realized that the mill whistle at Bowman Lumber Company was blowing and the telephone was ringing. He swung onto the floor and ran into the hallway for the phone but Billy beat him to it.

"It's Mrs. MacDonald," he said, handing over the receiver.

"Daddy, what's happening?"

"I don't know, son. Your sister's crying. Go see to her. Hello. Emma Lou? Is that you?" He wondered if she were calling about his mother. Maybe she had taken a turn for the worse. But no, if that were the case, Herman would be calling. "What is it, Emma Lou? What's wrong?"

"Have you looked outside, Sam? It looks like the whole town's on fire. I don't know what it is but I figured you'd need somebody to keep Billy and Mary Jane, so Purvis is getting the car out. We'll be over there in a minute."

"All right. Thanks."

He hung up the phone and rushed onto the front porch in his pajama bottoms. The southeastern sky was lit up like a sunrise. For a moment, he feared the business district was burning, then he realized the blaze was too far away for that. Bowman's lumber mill must be on fire, he thought. That would explain the whistle.

Sam tried to reassure Billy and Mary Jane then hurried into his clothes. Emma Lou and Purvis arrived moments later and Sam dashed to his truck. This was the first time he could remember when one or both of his children had not asked to go with him. They knew this one was different.

The closer Sam got to State Line Road, the more he worried. This looked like way more than Unionville's volunteer fire fighters could handle. He guessed it took a long time for him to wake up, because so many people had already turned out that he could not get within six blocks of the mill. He saw the new blue-and-white police car parked in the middle of an intersection, lights flashing, with Jesse nowhere in sight. After pulling into someone's yard, Sam grabbed his fireman's hat and joined others sprinting toward the fire. The night seemed almost bright as day. Huge flames shot above the houses and trees in front of him.

Sparks flew all over and the smoky smell of burning pine and hardwood hung in the air. Three blocks up, he passed some men dragging hose back to tap another fire hydrant. They seemed to have the job in hand so he ran on. Suddenly the mill whistle stopped—itself a victim of the fire—and Sam could hear the blaze roaring and timber cracking.

When he got to the mill entrance, he saw the fire truck in the service yard, just past the office. The old LaFrance was over-matched by the flames. A hose ran off each side. One snaked past the giant lumber shed nearly to the sawing building, where volunteers and Bowman employees manned the mill's own pumper, so small it was mounted on a hand truck. Both the sawing and planing buildings were engulfed. Sheets of tin on their roofs and sides curled in the heat and fell to the ground, and flames leaped to the lumber shed.

On the other side of the yard, another group of volunteers had the LaFrance's second hose trained on the mountains of dry lumber stacked in the open. Caught up by flying embers, it burned like kindling. Closer by, commissary owner Rufus Keller stood on the front porch of the old building shouting orders to a host of folks, black and white, who were hauling merchandise out and piling it in the gravel parking lot.

Preston Upshaw ran around taking pictures just as he had at the cross burnings, and Lester Grimes and Neal O'Brien stood behind the LaFrance talking to Horace Bowman, who looked out of place in his dress pants and grimy white shirt. Sam ran over to them.

"I don't give a good goddamn about the lumber, you fat turd!" Bowman shouted at Lester. "You turn that hose on my office building and wet it down. I can't afford to lose my files."

"Mr. Bowman," Lester yelled back over the roar of the truck

engine and whine of the water pump, "we've got more than your office to worry about here. The whole neighborhood's liable to go up if we don't get this thing under control."

"Well, you better get me some help. Poindexter and me can't empty that building by ourselves."

Sam looked toward the office and saw the Arkansas-side mayor, Bowman's long-time bookkeeper, come out with a cardboard box of papers and dump them into the trunk of Bowman's Lincoln.

"I'll help you," Sam said, squinting into the glare of the raging fire. "Just give me a second." He turned back to Lester and Neal. "This is bad. We got any help coming?"

"Yeah, Alan started making calls as soon as he heard the mill whistle," Neal said. "The El Dorado department ought to be here in a few minutes. Homer and Farmerville are on the way too. You go on and help Bowman. It'll keep him out of the way. I got to get over there and stop Rufus from blocking the other trucks with all his junk."

Sam climbed the steps to the mill office just as Alan came out with another box of files.

"Does anyone know how it started?" Sam asked, stepping aside.

"Not that I've heard," Alan said, pausing, "but it looks like it started in the sawing building."

"Isn't Crazy Dan's shack back over there somewhere?"

"It's down at that end all right, but it's on the other side of the access road, close to the log sprinkler. Look, this is the last pasteboard box we've got. Just grab up whatever files you can carry and toss them in the back seat. I'll worry about sorting everything later."

As Sam dumped his fifth stack of files into the Lincoln, two

El Dorado fire trucks, warning lights spinning and sirens blaring, rolled into the yard. Meanwhile, the fire grew bigger by the minute.

"Mr. Bowman," Sam shouted through the front door of the office. "You better get yourself and your car out of here now. I got to go help the boys."

Leaving the mill owner and his bookkeeper to fend for themselves, Sam raced over to catch what the El Dorado fire captain had to say. According to letters stenciled on his coat, his name was Archer. Recognizing that the locals were in over their heads, he seized command. No one, including Lester, objected.

"Y'all are wasting your time on that lumber. You ain't gon' save it," Archer shouted. "Y'all got anybody wetting down those houses over there?" he asked, pointing past the crackling stacks and the chainlink fence beyond them.

"No," Neal said. "We've only got this one truck."

"Are any other departments coming?"

"Yeah, at least two more," Neal said.

"Okay, is this building over here some kind of store?" Archer pointed at the commissary. The growing mound of merchandise between it and State Line Road looked like a huge garbage dump.

"Yeah, it's the commissary," Lester said.

"All right, this is what we're gon' do. Hunter," he said to the El Dorado lieutenant who had now joined the group, "back your truck out and take your boys over there and spray those houses." Then to Lester and Neal, "Y'all think the town's water system has enough pressure for that?"

"I believe so," Neal said.

"What about the houses over yonder in the quarters?" Sam asked, motioning past the railroad tracks. "If those sparks from the lumber shed set them off, we'll lose every one of them."

"Y'all got hydrants over there?"

"Yeah," Sam said. "We've got one but it's way down at the far end. If you've got a drafting hose, you can tap into the mill pond. It's just past the sawdust pile and you can get at it from the quarters. You'll have to run a hose across the tracks but I expect the depot man has already stopped any trains. I can show you the way."

"Okay," Archer said. "Let's do it." He turned to Lester, "When those other boys show up, put one of them on the commissary and one on that big shed."

Sam climbed into the first El Dorado engine beside the driver and Archer followed. "I sure hope whoever owns this bastard has plenty of insurance," he said, "because there ain't gon' be nothing left of it."

By dawn, the fire had pretty much burned itself out and most of the spectators, except those who lived nearby, had long since returned to their homes. As the sun cleared the horizon, the fire fighters and mill workers hosed down the remaining hot spots and sifted through the rubble. Remarkably, none of the houses in either the white neighborhood or the black section were damaged. The commissary still stood, but most of Rufus Keller's merchandise, even the stuff carried outside, was soaked. Everything else in the mill compound, except the sprinkled logs and the rail fence along State Line Road, was reduced to ashes and scrap metal. The sickening smell of wet, charred wood was almost overpowering.

"Did anybody see a cross last night?" Neal asked. He and Sam stood in front of the sparse remains of Bowman's office talking with Jesse, Captain Archer, Lester, Alan, and Louisiana-side mayor Eddie Dunn. All of them were wet, dirty, and exhausted.

"Aw, Neal," Lester said, "you don't think whoever's been burning crosses started this, do you?" He took out a red bandana, wiped his face and arms with it, and shoved it back in his pocket.

"If he did, you'll play hell finding any evidence of it now," Archer said, taking off his helmet and running a hand through matted brown hair. "Besides, it started down by the sawing building and I don't see why anybody would burn a cross back there. What would be the point? I do think it might be arson, though."

"Why's that?" Lester asked. "It could just be spontaneous combustion. Happens all the time in these mills. You get all that sawdust under the right conditions and it just catches up."

"Couple things," Archer said. "According to Mr. Metcalf—I believe he's one of the mill foremen—it spread too fast in the beginning for that. And my men found a two-gallon gas can back there in the ditch beside the tracks. There's no good reason for it being there and it was scorched. Looks like somebody might have been trying to carry it off and dropped it. Could've been because they got burned themselves."

"It's worse than that, sir" Lieutenant Hunter said, coming up from farther down in the mill yard and breaking into the circle. "We found a body back over there between the sawing and planing buildings. It's burned real bad. We're probably gon' need forensics to identify it. The poor devil died holding onto some kind of metal wheel. Looks like it might have come from a push cart, or maybe a wheelbarrow."

"Crazy Dan," several men said at the same time.

Archer looked puzzled.

"Fellow named Dan Malone," Alan said. "He lived in a shed back there. Did odd jobs for us."

"Looks like a support beam might have fallen on him,"

Hunter said, "and he couldn't get out from under it."

"My god," Neal said. "That's a terrible way to go. I wonder why he was messing around in the sawing building at night? He always did his roaming in the daytime."

"Maybe he saw somebody or heard something," Archer speculated. "Anyway, if this is arson, then it's also manslaughter."

"I think one of the Tonti Parish boys is still around here somewhere," Jesse said. "I'll let him know so he can get the sheriff up here from Farmerville."

As Jesse moved away, Sam pointed toward the depot. Reverend Moseley, Leon Jackson, and a couple dozen other black men were standing with their heads bowed. They looked as if they were praying.

"What's going on over there?" Archer asked.

"We've lost more than the mill and Crazy Dan," Sam said grimly. "A lot of those men and a whole bunch more don't have a place to go to work today."

"If I know my boss, he'll build it back," Alan said. "I know he's insured, and ever since he read about that new chip mill up at Warren, he's been wanting to put in an operation like that down here."

"Let's hope so, for all our sakes," Neal said.

No one felt any sympathy for Horace Bowman but everyone had a friend or relative who worked at the mill. The fire brushed aside nearly every other concern. Long after the firemen had gathered up their gear and gone home, people got in their cars and drove to the site, both to satisfy their curiosity and to convince themselves it really happened. They talked about it all day—everywhere except at the barbershop and newsstand. For the first time anyone could remember, it was closed on a weekday. Lester and Odell Grimes were too tired to open.

One person in Unionville seemed anything but tired. Upshaw wore a huge smile on his face all morning and typed faster than Pearl had ever seen him.

"Mr. Upshaw, I don't see how you can be so happy about a disaster," she said, when she could not stand it any longer. "I know this is a big story but it's a terrible thing for this town."

"Here," he said, "read this copy." He snatched the sheet of paper from his Underwood, put it with several others, and held them out for her. She got up from her desk and retrieved the pages.

"Fire Destroys Mill; Town Officials Baffled," the headline said. Pearl assumed he would want it set in the largest type possible. She continued reading to herself. "Early Wednesday morning, November 13, fire destroyed the Bowman Lumber Company mill on State Line Road. The blaze left one dead and scores without jobs. Unionville officials are clueless about the cause or how the town can recover from this economic disaster."

"This isn't a report about the fire," she said after a few minutes. "This is another attack on Mayor Poindexter and the town council."

"Yep. This is gon' be one of our best issues. If you don't like the story, wait till you see my editorial," he said. "You'll hate it. From all I heard, it looks like somebody set this fire. This new police chief they hired isn't much better than that old man was, and I'm gon' roast them all. Pun intended."

"But Jesse Culpepper caught the streetlight shooters," Pearl protested.

"What he did was get lucky. Just proof that and set the type."

"I don't see much in here about Dan Malone."

"Old Crazy Dan? He was nothing but a bum. Nobody'll miss him. Set the type."

When Sam got home in midmorning, Emma Lou had already left, and Doreen Dykes was taking care of Mary Jane.

"Your brother called," Doreen said, "and Mrs. MacDonald told him what happened. He said your momma hasn't changed much and you should rest up. Mrs. MacDonald left you this note too." Doreen pulled a folded paper from her apron pocket.

"Sam," Emma Lou had written, "I'll be back before Doreen leaves and I'll stay with the children tonight if you want to spell Herman at the hospital. You get some sleep." Sam was too exhausted to disagree with Herman's and Emma Lou's advice. He cleaned up and, strange as it felt, set his alarm for two in the afternoon.

When Billy got home from school, Sam told both children what he thought they should know about the fire. That done, he ran to the store to pick up some cash and headed for El Dorado. When he passed Hazel's house, she was crossing her front porch and waved. He returned the gesture and wished he were standing where she was, ready to knock on Becky's door knowing she would open it and welcome him inside.

CHAPTER 53

"Where the hell's Tucker?" Boomer Jenkins bellowed when Sam walked into the Otasco store early Thursday afternoon. The gruff outdoorsman's clothes and wooden leg were caked with dried mud and he smelled of swamp water and sweat. Miss Ruthelle had her chair backed up against the office wall and a handkerchief to her nose.

Aw, crap, just what I need, Sam thought. He was in no mood to put up with any bull. Gran had taken a turn for the worse and he was not sure how much longer she could hold on. He had driven back to Unionville only to get Mary Jane and Billy and take them to see their grandmother after school. With a few minutes before classes let out, he had stopped by the store to make sure everything was okay there. He wished now he had called instead.

"What makes you think I know?" Sam said. "I'm not Tucker's keeper. I expect he's at the funeral home."

"Goddamn it! Don't you think I looked there? Where's Mr. Claude? He ain't home neither," Boomer growled. He took off his hat and beat it against his pants. Dirt flew all over the floor and Miss Ruthelle slammed her free hand against her desktop. Boomer ignored her.

"What do you need them for?" Sam asked, aware now that something was wrong. "Maybe you haven't heard, but Mr. Claude's retired. Jesse Culpepper's chief of police now."

"Is that right? Well, where the devil is he? I been over to the town hall too."

Then Sam remembered. "I bet he and Tucker are burying Crazy Dan today. I forgot because my mother's in the hospital. I didn't notice anybody when I passed the cemetery, but they'd have been over in the back, in the pauper's yard. What do you need them for?" Sam asked again.

"What happened to Crazy Dan?"

"Didn't you hear about Bowman's mill burning down the other night? Crazy Dan got trapped in the fire."

"Do they know how it started?" Boomer asked. Sam noticed he did not seem surprised.

"They think maybe it was arson but they aren't sure," Sam said.

"Well, I reckon they're right." Boomer put his hat back on and hitched up his pants. "I came to get Tucker and Mr. Claude because Jim Ed Davis is dead."

Miss Ruthelle got up and came around the stairs, still holding the handkerchief to her nose.

"I found him this morning," Boomer said. "I been camped over on Big Corney running trotlines and frog gigging for near on two weeks, and when I come home, I seen him sitting in his truck about a mile from the house. He was burnt bad. Poor bastard must have been hurting like hell before he gave out and run in the ditch. I figure he was too scared to go see Doc and he thought I could help him because I used to be a corpsman. He must've been sitting there for hours. Anyway, there wasn't anything I could do for him. I called his name, and he came to for a minute or two, but the only thing he said before he croaked was, 'I fixed the son of a bitch.' So, I expect he set the fire."

Sam sat down on the wrapping table. "Why's that?"

"Because he'd been trying to blackmail old Bowman and he wouldn't pay."

"Blackmail?" Sam asked, surprise showing in his voice. "For what? Do you know?"

"Yeah. It ain't nothing. Bowman used to bootleg for Jim Ed's daddy. That's how the old bastard got the money to get started in the land and timber business."

"Well, I'll be damned. That's why I've been seeing Jim Ed over at the bank so much."

"I told him Bowman don't give a rat's ass about what people think. Hell, bootlegging never hurt nobody anyway."

"Did Jim Ed have any proof?"

"Only what his daddy had told him."

"That boy never was the sharpest tack in the box," Miss Ruthelle said.

News about Jim Ed spread like the fire he'd started. Sam walked with Boomer over to City Hardware, left him with Neal O'Brien, and headed home to get Billy and Mary Jane. Boomer repeated his story to Neal, and he called the Tonti Parish sheriff's office then went looking for Jesse. Boomer went to Emmett's to get some of his special coffee and wait for the authorities. Because the café crowd was already talking about the fire, the big outdoorsman saw no reason not to tell what he knew, and soon Lester had wind of it. Meanwhile, Miss Ruthelle called her good friend Nettie Wilkerson, who was Hazel Brantley's chief rival as town gossip, and in no time at all, everyone knew.

Elmer Spurlock's wife told him and he called Upshaw. He hung up without a word and rushed outside to try and spot Jesse's police car somewhere. When he saw Boomer's truck in front the café, he ran over to get a firsthand account. By the time he got back to the newspaper office, Nettie Wilkerson had called Pearl.

"I guess you want to change the layout now," she said.

"No, it's not worth the trouble," Upshaw said. "We'll just run a little box beside the story we've already set."

"Don't you think Jim Ed's the one who burned all those crosses?" she asked from her desk.

"No. He didn't have the brains for it." Upshaw sat down and rolled a sheet of paper into his typewriter.

"How can you be so sure?"

"I'm sure. That's all. Anyway, if he'd burned the crosses, that'd be the end of it, wouldn't it? Why would I want the suspense to be over? I've got them on the run—the new police chief, the council, and the coloreds—all of them, and I aim to keep them there."

Upshaw and Pearl were not the only ones speculating about whether Jim Ed Davis burned the crosses. A little before five o-clock, two Tonti Parish deputies huddled in the Arkansas-side town hall with Jesse Culpepper, Alan Poindexter, and Neal O'Brien. The mill fire and the two deaths were Louisiana matters, but Arkansans had done most of the fire fighting, and there were still some loose ends to tie up. Everyone was tired and nerves were frayed.

"I still think we ought to search Jim Ed's place and see what's out there," Neal said, when the deputies finished asking questions. He had pretty much convinced himself that Jim Ed had set all the fires but he wanted to be sure.

"We'll have to get my old boss down from El Dorado to do that," Jesse said. "These Louisiana boys don't have any jurisdiction out there and neither do we. But I don't know what you think we'd find that would tell us anything. Just about everybody's got stuff for crosses lying around."

"Look," said a red-faced Tonti Parish deputy. "I really don't give a shit about your goddamn cross burnings." He closed his notebook, stuck it his shirt pocket, and buttoned the flap. "Frankly, if I knew who was doing them, I'd probably give him a hand. Far as the mill fire is concerned, with what you just gave us and what we got from them El Dorado boys and that peg-leg fellow, this thing is about wrapped up."

"I'd sure like to believe that," Alan said.

"Well," the deputy said, "y'all can do what you want but we're done here." He motioned to his partner and they left without another word.

The Unionville officials were not done, but they did not know what to do next, except hope that either Jim Ed had burned the crosses or that Jesse in the new police car would keep it from happening again.

Leon Jackson and Mr. Claude were not done either. As soon as Mr. Claude heard about Jim Ed, he stopped by Leon's shop with some dry cleaning. Despite the cool autumn air, the tin shack radiated heat from Leon's cleaning equipment.

"Did you hear the talk that maybe Jim Ed Davis burned the crosses?" Mr. Claude asked straight off. He assumed Leon knew about the ne'er-do-well's death.

Leon laid Mr. Claude's bundle on a table and began sorting it. "Yes, sir, but I don't put much stock in it. Do you?"

"No. What do you say we put in a few more evenings? I got a feeling our boy's not done yet."

"Usual time and place?"

"Yep."

Friday morning found Upshaw more depressed than angry at being scooped yet again. He liked his mill fire stories, but new developments in Little Rock happened too late for him to get them into Saturday's *Unionville Times*. "White Boy Suspended at Central High after Striking Negro," read the headline on the front page of the *El Dorado Daily News*. This was the kind of story Upshaw craved.

"One of these days, I'm gon' have a daily and this kind of crap isn't gon' happen to me," he said, as he sat slumped in his desk chair, the countywide paper in one hand and a cigarette in the other. A spiral of white smoke rose toward the pressed-tin ceiling.

"Mr. Upshaw," Pearl said, "I feel sorry for that boy that got hit, but things are starting to settle down up there, and it looks like they're going to get through the rest of the school year without any more trouble. The Associated Press is just trying to create headlines. I should think that you, of all people, would understand that."

"That's just the problem, Mrs. Goodbar," he said, glaring at her. "There's too little happening. I've got to get things moving, and by god, I know just how I'm gon' do it."

A few blocks north of the newspaper office, Becky's seventh graders were also struggling with current events. Accustomed now to studying what was going on around them, they wanted to talk about the mill fire and the two deaths.

Becky had put them off on Thursday then tried all day and into the night to come up with some connection to the past that would not be upsetting, especially to Billy. From what Hazel had told her, Gran was close to death and Billy realized it.

"We all know the lumber mill burned early Wednesday morning," Becky said to the class after finishing her reports, "and I expect we all know someone who worked there. Until the mill is rebuilt, those people won't be earning a paycheck. And that will affect a lot of other people, too, because the town's economy depends a lot on the mill. There was a situation like that before the Civil War, only it was much, much bigger. The North had an economy that depended on factories just the way we depend on the mill, and the South had an economy that depended on agriculture and slavery. One of those economies was destroyed by the war and one wasn't. In fact, it prospered and grew. This morning, we're going to skip ahead and begin studying the causes of the Civil War."

Several hands went up. "Yes, Glen Ray, what is it?" Becky asked.

"I don't understand, Miss Reeves. "What's all that got to do with them two people getting killed?"

She did not have a good answer and knew it. Meanwhile, she could see Billy was not listening.

CHAPTER 54

On Saturday morning, steady rain and distant rumbles of thunder matched the mood of many Unionville residents. Sam was at his mother's bedside in El Dorado, along with Herman. Emma Lou MacDonald was at the Tate home helping Ollie Mae take care of Mary Jane and Billy. And Reverend Moseley was home trying to find comforting words for his congregation come Sunday.

Even the café crowd was quiet. They did not exactly miss Jim Ed Davis's big mouth, but his crime and his death hit them hard enough to dampen their usual carrying on.

That afternoon the sun came out but brought little cheer, and the Razorbacks, playing their next-to-last game of the season, made things worse for people who were still paying attention to them. At the Texas state fairgrounds in Dallas, Southern Methodist University handed the boys from Fayetteville their third loss in a row.

Although Emma Lou could not tell a quarterback from a shortstop or an SMU Mustang from a Rhode Island Red rooster, she tried to listen to the game with Billy and play dolls with Mary Jane at the same time. Then she busied both children baking cookies until suppertime. As they were setting the table, they heard Sam's truck pull into the driveway. They hurried to the front porch and saw Uncle Herman, a shorter version of his brother, but thinner and wearing glasses, climb out with him.

Sam mounted the steps, kneeled, and put his arms around both children. "Gran has gone to be with Jesus," he said, "but as long as you carry her in your heart, she'll always be with you too."

Early Sunday, Becky sat in her bathrobe and read the lead story in the *Arkansas Gazette*. "Little Rock Echoes throughout the South," proclaimed the headline. An Associated Press reporter wrote that although most federal troops had been withdrawn from the Arkansas capital, southerners seemed more determined than ever to resist the *Brown v. Board of Education* decision. Membership in segregationist organizations was growing everywhere and a new push for a third political party seemed likely. Legislators in several states were proposing measures to make public schools private, and numerous merchants were denying blacks credit, "to keep them in line" the paper said. "So, in many ways," the story concluded, "the shadow of Little Rock lies heavily over the nation."

Hazel Brantley knocked on the door, and, as she often did, barged in without waiting for a response. "Ida Belle Tate died last night, hon. I hear the funeral's gon' be tomorrow morning. Do you want to go with me?"

"I'm sorry to hear it, Hazel," Becky said, lowering the newspaper, "but no, I can't go. I'll be teaching."

"Aw, come on. I'm sure you can get a substitute."

"No, I need to be with my class."

"You just don't want to go, do you?"

"I can't, Hazel. Please don't press it."

"I'm making a casserole to take over. You want to send something?"

"I don't think so."

"All right," the landlady said, as she left, "but if you change your mind, let me know."

Becky sat a long while staring at the door.

Later that morning at Mt. Zion Baptist Church, Reverend Moseley fixed on a theme of trial, tribulation, and faith for his first service since the mill fire. B. J. Long and other deacons got things started by lining out phrases for the congregation to sing "Faith of our Fathers," about remaining true to one's beliefs "in spite of dungeon, fire, and sword." Next there came the old standby, "Amazing Grace," and then a moving choir special about Jesus caring for those whose hearts are touched by grief.

When the song ended, Moseley rose slowly to the pulpit, laid his open Bible on it, grasped the lapels of his black coat, and looked out on his flock like a kindly grandfather.

"You know Jesus cares, don't you?" he asked quietly.

"Yes, Reverend. Praise Jesus," came the responses, in the same solemn tones as the pastor's.

"You know I'm gon' preach about Job today, don't you?"

"Preach, Reverend! Tell about Job!"

"You know God tested Job, just like he's testing us right now, right here in Unionville. He took away everything Job had, just like he has taken away the place where a lot of y'all work. And what did Job say when God did that?"

"Preach, Reverend! Tell what Job said!"

"It's right here in chapter twenty-three, verse ten. Job said he's gon' have faith. He said he's gon' persevere. He said he's gon' defeat trial and tribulation. He said he's gon' beat back adversity. He said he's gon' triumph in the end because he's got faith!"

"Amen! Praise Jesus!"

"God delivered the Israelites out of the wilderness. He delivered Daniel out of the lion's den. And He's gon' deliver us out of this mess we have here in Unionville today. I talked to Mr. Bowman and I got faith he's gon' rebuild that mill and hire a lot of y'all that worked there to help him do it. Y'all got to have faith too."

"We got faith! Praise Jesus!"

Underneath the open-sided cemetery tent, Sam, wearing his navy suit and striped tie, tried to concentrate on Brother Byrd's words, but few stuck. Back at the church a little earlier, the pastor had delivered a short but moving eulogy, the choir had performed a medley of Gran's favorite hymns, and Opal Jolly had sung a beautiful version of "What a Friend We Have in Jesus." Then the Townsend Family Quartet, from nearby Haynesville over in Louisiana, closed the service with a lively version of Gran's favorite country gospel song, "I'll Fly Away." As the Townsends sang it, he imagined her flying away home to glory.

Now, sitting before his mother's casket, Sam stared at the blanket of pink and white carnations and thought about Billy and Mary Jane. They were sitting on either side of him, each holding one of his hands. They would miss Gran the most. Herman sat on the other side of Billy and Emma Lou on the other side of Mary Jane.

As Byrd spoke on, Sam glanced around Oak View Cemetery and felt more gratitude than sorrow. Gratitude for Gran and gratitude for those gathered with him, and for others in the community too. Friends and church members arrived with food and condolences not long after he and Herman got home on

Saturday night, and a steady stream of callers had come at all hours since. Now, near noon on Monday, more than a hundred stood around the gravesite, still showing support and respect. Although the cemetery was oddly situated along the highway next to the high school baseball field, stately oaks and handsome dogwoods dotted the grounds, and Sam knew his mother's remains would rest peacefully here next to his daddy's.

When the ceremony ended, Emma Lou took the children so Sam and Herman could thank the minister and those who came to say goodbye. Fifty yards to the west, beyond the cemetery fence, Becky Reeves climbed down from the top row of the baseball bleachers and walked away unnoticed.

CHAPTER 55

As Sam drove back from El Dorado late Wednesday morning, two days after his mother's funeral, he still could not get Becky out of his mind. He replayed their time together and imagined holding her again. More and more now, once he started thinking about how she felt in his arms and how he might get her back, he had trouble focusing on anything else.

This time, Lester Grimes broke the spell. He came lumbering up the sidewalk as Sam parked in front of the Otasco store and climbed out of his pickup.

"Morning, Sam," Lester said. "It's good to see you." In addition to having not been around much the previous week, Sam had kept the store closed the last two days.

"Morning, Lester," he said, crossing the sidewalk. "Come on in." This seemed as good a time as any to start getting the word out about the new arrangement he had made with Art Nelson.

Sam's brother Herman, whom Sam had just dropped off for his return flight to West Texas, suggested the deal Monday night, Sam approached Art the next day, and he eagerly accepted. In exchange for a modest salary and an office on the Otasco store's mezzanine for his tax work, Art would open the store every morning and be available any other time Sam wanted to be with his children. He could see Billy off to school every day and go home to be with Mary Jane anytime Doreen or Ollie Mae called and said he was needed. Emma Lou remained available too.

"Let me introduce you to our newest downtown business-man," Sam said to Lester when they got inside. Miss Ruthelle looked up from her perch in the office and smiled for a change. She was as pleased as Art. Sam had gone to her house and told her the news on Tuesday afternoon so she would have time to adjust and not feel threatened. He need not have worried, though, because she knew as well as he did that he needed both her and Art now. She also knew that having Art around would reduce the number of times she would have to get up from her desk.

"I'm a little stiff. Let's cross back over behind the post office to your place and go up the alley between the bank and the furniture store," Mr. Claude said. It was a little past two o'clock on Thursday morning and he and Leon were hiding behind cars outside the Ford dealership. They had a good view of Emmett's Café, the newspaper office, and Main Street, but so far, they had not seen anything suspicious.

"Okay," Leon said, rising from behind the flared tail fins of a new Fairlane. "I got a hunch something's gon' shake loose any time now."

"Yeah, me too. That's why I brought my Smith & Wesson," Mr. Claude said, standing up, "but the blame thing's hurting my back." He reached under his black suit coat and brought out a short-barreled .38-caliber revolver he had tucked into the back of his trousers.

"I never knew you carried a gun, Mr. Claude."

"I never did, except once in a blue moon, but I decided it might come in handy."

Moving off quietly, the pair swung by the town hall, peeped in, and saw Crow Hicks sound asleep in his usual spot.

"He's a real crime fighter, isn't he?" Mr. Claude whispered.

"A sure enough Dick Tracy," Leon said with a low chuckle. In the hours they had spent together, Mr. Claude had told Leon the plots of some of the western novels that led him to law enforcement, Leon had told Mr. Claude stories about serving in Italy during the war, and they had grown comfortable with each other.

They passed back of the post office and adjoining stores and went up the alley next to the bank. With Mr. Claude leading the way, they hugged the wall of Vestal's Furniture Store, staying in the shadows as they approached Main Street. Suddenly, Mr. Claude stopped and reached back to halt his companion. The gesture was unnecessary, as Leon heard the noise too. A vehicle was moving somewhere in front of them but the engine sounded distant. Clearly it was not on the highway. Seconds later, at the end of the alley directly across the street, a large shadow came into view then a brief flash of red. Someone driving on the warehouse access road without headlights had braked behind the Otasco store.

"I wonder who the hell that is?" Mr. Claude whispered. "Maybe we've got something else than cross burning here."

"You'd think if whoever it is wanted to burn a cross on Main Street, he'd just drive on up the alley," Leon said quietly.

"Well, if he lights it up behind the stores, we're not gon' get a look at him. He could cause a lot of damage back there, but if we go down the alley he'll see us. Let's just stay put for a bit."

Seconds dragged into minutes.

Eventually, a figure edged out of the darkened alley and into the low glow of the streetlight along the highway. Whoever it was wore dark clothes and a cap of some kind pulled low on his forehead. Sensing Leon ready to pounce, Mr. Claude put his arm out again. The figure walked to the edge of the sidewalk, looked up and down Main Street, then turned toward the front of the Otasco store. Leon and Mr. Claude saw a large object in his hand just before he hurled it toward one of the display windows.

The initial crash and then the crunching of splintered glass made so much noise that the culprit did not hear footsteps behind him as he scrambled through the debris on the sidewalk to get at the display of guns and ammunition. He reached in, grabbed the locked gun rack standing in the center, and started to pull it onto the sidewalk. Just as it came free of the window ledge, Mr. Claude's blackjack smashed against the back of his head, knocked his cap off, and dropped him to the pavement. He fell face down on top of the gun rack and split his chin on one of the bolt action shotguns. Blood ran from both wounds.

Leon bent down and turned the figure over. He was out cold but still breathing.

CHAPTER 56

Across town, at about the same time that Mr. Claude and Leon spotted the vehicle behind the Otasco store, a man driving a pickup cut his headlights, eased off the gas, and rolled to a stop on the dusty road. He had decided that this time he would fix things once and for all. Despite the cool air outside, he had both side windows down, and only the low hum of his truck engine broke the silence. Looking around, he could not see another soul moving anywhere. There were not even any dogs barking.

This was good. This was everything he had hoped for. He could feel his heart pounding. He thought if he got lucky, he might burn up every blooming house on the street. Then the black sons of Canaan would not even look at a white school, much less try to go to one.

He shifted into neutral and pulled up the emergency brake. Then he eased the door open and slid out with the motor still running. Once he started the blaze, he would jump in and drive away before anyone woke up. He believed burning crosses were scarier when no one saw who set them. Still, he did not rush. So what if some mongrel set up a howl? What he had planned now would keep the black bastards too busy to worry about him, and if they did see his truck, they would have a tough time telling it from others in the dark.

He took another look around, went to the back of the truck,

and lifted out the cross. He had made it just large enough to fill up the bed and not stick out, just like always. It did not look like much now, but by the time he finished soaking it and setting it on fire, it would burn good and look ten times bigger. He hefted it onto his shoulder, crossed the ditch, and leaned it against a fence post under a big tree with lots of limbs and dry leaves reaching over the corner of the white frame house.

Then he went back for the gasoline. He wished he had kerosene like before, but he had run out and did not want to attract attention by buying more. The gas he siphoned out of the truck would be fine. Probably burn even faster. He just had to be a little more careful with it. Blasted fumes burned his eyes but he liked the smell. He lifted the rusty jerry can and carried it to the cross without noticing the puddle the container left behind on the truck bed or the wet trail he was making on the road and in the grass. He poured the contents on the burlap-covered cross and returned the can to the truck.

Everything was still quiet. He crossed the ditch again and admired his work. Then he stepped back a few feet, reached into his pants pocket, and took out a new book of matches from the café. He hated the damned things but they made good torches. He opened the cover, tore off one of the sticks, lit the whole pack, and tossed it toward the wet cross.

The sudden swoosh sent him reeling backwards, arms flying up to protect his face. He smelled hair burning and felt like bees were stinging him all over. Then he saw flames racing toward his truck.

CHAPTER 57

"Well, I'll be damned!" Mr. Claude said, when he got a look at the burglar. "I would've never thought he had the balls for something like this."

"I'd have thought he had better sense," Leon said.

"Yeah, that too," Mr. Claude said, as he put away his blackjack and took out his handcuffs. "But why'd he do it? I had him figured maybe for burning the crosses but this don't add up."

"I sure don't know. Maybe he wanted it to look like a black man did it."

"Why would he think people would believe that?"

"Well, everybody knows white folks have guns, lots of them. Y'all—well, not including you, Mr. Claude—even drive around with them hanging in the back of y'all's truck windows so everybody can see them. We've got guns, too, but nobody sees them. So maybe being new around here, he didn't know we had them, and maybe he wanted folks to think we were trying to get some to use on white folks. He could print that in his paper to make more trouble."

"He must have gotten pretty worked up to think that was gon' work, or that nobody'd hear all this racket," Mr. Claude said.

"You don't suppose he thought all those rags he wrapped around that brick would kill the sound, do you?"

"Well, I don't know, but the dumb son of a bitch ain't gon'

414

be throwing anything else, or printing anything else either, for a long time, and he's gon' have one hell of a headache when he wakes up. Goddamn tinhorn! I wish I'd hit him harder."

"I wish you hadn't hit him hard as you did. I'd liked to have taken a poke at him too. Anyways, what are we gon' do with him now?"

"Why don't you crawl through the window there and use Sam's phone to call Jesse Culpepper and Doc Perkins. I don't think this pea brain's gon' bleed to death, but he's sure gon' need some stitches. Better call Sam too. I'll keep an eye on Upshaw, just in case he comes to."

Just as Leon started picking his way through all the broken glass and sporting goods in the window display, an explosion split the night air. He and Mr. Claude turned toward the sound and saw a fireball rising in the eastern sky.

"What the hell was that?" Mr. Claude exclaimed.

Dogs were barking now. Lights were coming on everywhere. People were screaming and hollering all over the place. "Holy shit!" the cross burner shouted. Blinded by the glare, he ran.

"There he goes!" someone yelled. "Get him!"

He managed only a few steps before he smacked into a porch and fell. A sharp pain sliced through his side. He thought for a moment he had landed in broken glass. Then something shattered against a porch post and he realized someone was chunking near about whole bricks at him.

He got to his feet and took off hunched over, running between houses. He could hear someone running and shouting behind him but he did not look back. He crossed a backyard, bolted over a fence, and sank to his ankles in a hog pen. Shotgun blasts roared somewhere off to his left. He pushed through a gate and disappeared into the darkness.

———◯———

"I knew Upshaw was a real scumbag, but Doyle Scoggins— man, that's hard to believe," Sam said. Dawn was breaking and he and Art Nelson were sweeping up the last bits of glass from the busted window display. Neal O'Brien had just come from the jail, where Upshaw and Scoggins were both locked up awaiting transfer to county authorities. "Scoggins has sat back there with me and Tucker and Doc and Billy on Saturday nights more times than I can remember—talking, listening to ball games, telling yarns, and running on. I knew he didn't like Negroes, but I just never would have figured him for something like that. You say Jesse Culpepper found him at home?"

"Yeah," Neal said. "Jesse said when he knocked on the side door, Scoggins said, 'Come on in,' and he was just sitting in a little room there—hair singed near about off, face all blistered, and hog shit all over him. He was smoking a cigarette and muttering about some uncle of his who'd been in the Klan way back in the twenties. He had a double-barreled shotgun in his lap but it wasn't loaded. Jesse said he must not have had it with him in the quarters, because it was clean as a whistle. What we don't know is how he got out from over there without getting shot, because he sure stirred up a hornet's nest. There wasn't much left of his pickup except enough to tell it was his. At least four houses caught on fire, and two of them burned real bad before Lester and the boys put them out. Leon Jackson's was the worst. It's a shame, especially seeing as how he's been helping Mr. Claude all this time. Anyway, we passed the hat, and I think we got enough money to get him started on fixing it up."

"I'll put in as much as I can," Sam said, "and I'll check with the other merchants, too, just in case some of them weren't at the fire. None of this was Leon's fault. Fact is, I expect a lot of it's mine for playing baseball with him. I remember Scoggins asked a lot of questions about it."

"No, Sam. I don't think it was your fault," Neal said. "I think Scoggins picked out Leon just because he looks like he's got a little money. I imagine that just got under Scoggins' skin along with all the integration stuff. He had all kinds of Klan papers and a whole room full of guns, and he said next time instead of trying to scare coloreds or burn them out, he was just gon' shoot a bunch of them. He said that's what his uncle would've done. His wife said she knew he hated them but she didn't know what he'd been up to. She was still in bed asleep when Jesse got there. She hadn't even heard the fire siren. When they told her, Doc had to give her a shot to calm her down."

Sam dumped a dust pan full of glass into an empty nail keg. Three others, filled earlier, sat next to it.

"What about Upshaw? Is he saying anything?"

"He's swelled up like an old toad. Hasn't said a word."

"The pompous asshole. I wish I could have seen Mr. Claude coldcock him."

"You know," Neal said, "even assholes get a trial and he's gon' need money for legal fees. I wonder if we could persuade old Bowman to lend Pearl Goodbar enough money to buy Upshaw out so the town can still have a newspaper."

CHAPTER 58

On the Sunday before Thanksgiving, most people in Unionville had a lot to be grateful for. No one except Elmer Spurlock had really liked Upshaw and most people were glad to see him go. Folks who worried about the cross burnings no longer had to wonder any more when there would be another. And Bowman hired back a lot of his workers to help clean up the mill site. Even Razorback fans were happier than they had been in weeks. The day before in Fayetteville, the Hogs had closed out their season by running up five hundred seventy-five yards of offense and beating the Texas Tech Red Raiders 47 to 26. It was the most points a Tech team had given up in thirty years. Arkansas would not be going to a bowl game but at least the boys from Lubbock said they thought the Razorbacks were the best team in the Southwest Conference.

When worship time rolled around, the Unionville ministers all noted the need to thank God for his blessings, but there the similarity in the services ended. To a relieved and happy Mt. Zion congregation, Reverend Moseley preached a rousing sermon of thanksgiving and celebration based on First Corinthians 15:37, "Thanks be to God, which giveth us victory through our Lord Jesus Christ." He did not know Spurlock had recently misused that same passage trying to stir up hatred.

Brother Byrd surprised his flock, like he had done so often of late. He took his text from Hebrews 5:2 and called, as the

418

scripture said, for "compassion on the ignorant, and on them that are out of the way."

Out at the Mercy Baptist Mission, Brother Spurlock read from Romans 12:1, "I beseech you therefore, brethren, by the mercies of God, that ye present your bodies a living sacrifice, holy, acceptable to God, which is your reasonable service." Twisting meanings like he nearly always did, he ignored the call to goodness in his text and praised Scoggins as a hero and Upshaw as a man of vision. "It's true they got a little crosswise with the law," Spurlock railed, "but these are dangerous times we live in and these men gave of themselves for a cause that's right. Now we have to carry on their fight."

When church was over at First Baptist, Sam and the children followed Emma Lou MacDonald home to have dinner with her and Purvis. Sam did not want to go, but Emma Lou insisted, and he owed her so much he felt he could not refuse. She promised a surprise for everybody, and that got the children's attention just enough to keep them from putting up a fuss. Further, Purvis, who welcomed any excuse to miss church and was known to be the best deer camp cook around, said he would have a feast ready for them as soon as they hit the front door.

The MacDonalds, whose own children were long married, lived in a rambling white frame house just off State Line Road on the west side of town, and the meal proved as good as advertised. Purvis set out venison roasted with onions in a pressure cooker and, to go with it, mashed potatoes, black-eyed peas, and corn bread. For dessert, there was pecan pie and homemade ice cream.

After dinner, Sam insisted that the Tates help clear the table before they all retired to the living room. There Emma Lou pulled out a box of old toys for Mary Jane, and Purvis started showing Billy a staggering collection of pocket knives.

"Sam, come out to my sewing room," Emma Lou said, once the children were busy. "I've got something to show you too."

"Don't get your Sunday clothes dirty," Sam told Billy and Mary Jane, then followed Emma Lou into a sunny corner room with windows on two sides and armoires along the other walls. A sampler quilt, spread out on a wooden frame, filled the center.

"I keep my quilts and scraps in those," she said, when she saw Sam looking at the armoires. "Two of them belonged to my momma and two of them came from Purvis's family. But this quilt is what I wanted you to see. It's your momma's sampler. The last thing she said before y'all took her to the hospital that last time was, 'Promise me you'll quilt it for Sam.' I thought that was a little peculiar, because one time she'd told me she was making it for Mary Jane. Anyhow, I just now got it all laid out with the backing and batting so I can work on it. That's gon' take me a while but I thought you'd like to see it now."

As Sam looked at the quilt, decades of memories flashed before him lickety-split, like he was thumbing through the pages of a Fones Brothers Hardware catalog.

"This was the last top Ida Belle made," Emma Lou said, her voice cracking. "She told me all the pieces are from clothes y'all wore and she chose every one of the patterns special."

"Yeah, I remember when she started it, and she showed me some of the pieces several times."

"Do you know the patterns and can you guess which ones are whose?"

"No," he said at first, but he kept looking. "Well, I know some of them. "That one's a Log Cabin and it has to be for my granddaddy. Those black pieces are from one of his suits. And the one that looks like a little girl has pieces from some of Mary Jane's baby dresses, so it must be for her."

"That's right. It's a Dutch Girl. Do you know this one?" Emma Lou pointed to a square near the center.

"I don't know the name of the pattern, but I see some of my old shirts in it, and I see pieces from some of Judith's Ann's things in the one next to it."

"Yep, you've got two squares in here and there're two for Judith Ann too." Sam smiled. His mother and Judith Ann had quarreled from time to time, usually over how Judith Ann was raising Billy, but Gran had loved her daughter-in-law.

"See that square near the middle there with the red and yellow?" Emma Lou asked, pointing. "That one's a puzzle to me. I've never seen one like it. I reckon it's supposed to be for Ida Belle. She told me she was making a Sunflower for herself, but that pattern usually has just one big flower, and this one's got four little ones. I don't know where the pieces came from either. I saw them that day she had her first heart attack, but I don't remember ever seeing her wear anything made out of material like that."

Sam stared at the square for a moment. Then he rubbed his fingers over the cloth and felt his knees grow weak. "I know where this came from," he said, after taking a deep breath. "You say she handed this top to you all put together just like it is now?"

"Yeah, well, in a manner of speaking. Like I said, she asked me to quilt it, and I found it in her sewing basket with these last pieces just sort of tacked together. I stitched everything up proper. Why? Do you know where they come from?"

"I almost don't believe what I'm seeing. Becky gave Momma that cloth the Sunday she came to dinner. Momma put Becky in the quilt with the rest of us. I guess she knew she was dying and changed her mind about Becky and me. I bet those four flowers are me and Billy and Mary Jane and Becky."

"Well, God bless her heart."

Sam did not say anything more. He was trying to think of what else he could do to get Becky to see him.

CHAPTER 59

"If that son of a bitch Bouchard hadn't spent the last two weeks shacked up with some whore in New Orleans, I'd have had this sooner," Herbert Kramer said, tossing the thick brown envelope on Superintendent Appleby's desk early Monday morning. Instead of the white shirt he wore when presiding over school board meetings, Kramer looked like he just came from tending his livestock. He wore a plaid work shirt, overalls, and a denim jacket. Without waiting to be asked, he took a seat and ordered, "Get that Reeves bitch over here and let's get this over with."

"Why? What's in here?" Vernon Appleby asked, his face growing redder than his paisley tie. He was both irritated and cowed by the big farmer's manner.

"I'll tell you what's in there. It's everything we need to fire her ass. Call Mrs. Woodhead and tell her to send Miss High-and-Mighty over here on the double."

Ignoring the sweat starting to bead on his forehead, Appleby picked up the telephone. Kramer took out a cigar, bit off the end, and spit it in an ashtray he lifted off the desk. He intended to enjoy these next few minutes.

The cigar was half gone and Kramer was a few degrees hotter under the collar by the time Becky arrived at the door to Appleby's cluttered office.

"You sent for me, sir?" she asked Appleby. No summons to see the superintendent in the middle of classes could be routine but she had not expected to see the board president there. He sat with his back to the door but she recognized him anyway.

"No," Kramer said coldly. "I sent for you." He took a long drag on the cigar, tilted his head up, and blew the smoke out slowly. He watched it rise and without turning around said, "Come in and sit down. This'll just take a minute but I want a clear view of the look on your face when I have my say."

Shaken, Becky took the only other chair in the room, tugged at her skirt, and put her hands in her lap. Kramer continued to watch the cigar smoke. Becky looked over at Appleby and saw his usual blank expression give way to a silly smirk. Then Kramer turned toward her and the look in his eyes sent chills down her spine.

"Miss Reeves. Becky!" he said, raising his voice and drawing out her first name, "This time I don't need no goddamn vote. You are a goddamn, deceitful nigger bitch, and as of this moment you are fired from the Unionville School District for lying about your race on your contract. I want your sorry black ass off these premises right this minute!"

Becky sat stunned. She had never been called black before, let alone nigger. Ever since telling Sam about her great-grandmother, she had been thinking plenty about all the meaning those words carried for her, but still, part of her wanted to say, "No, that's not right. You're mistaken, I'm not black." For what seemed an eternity but was only seconds, she thought this cannot be happening. She wondered if she should deny Kramer's assertion, but everything about him told her it would be useless. The type of hate she saw in his eyes was no longer something to read about, or hear about, or observe being aimed at others. This was aimed directly at her, and she realized she had entered a new world.

Sam pushed away the half-eaten plate of chicken-fried steak and sat back in the booth at Hattie's Diner. He never wanted to go through another Thanksgiving like the one he just spent or another week like the one just past. With the town still reeling from the mill fire and caught up in the news about Scoggins and Upshaw, no one said much of anything to him about Becky, even though Herbert Kramer made sure everyone knew what happened. Not even Miss Ruthelle or Lester brought it up. They would eventually, he knew, but he did not care about that. He thought only about Mary Jane, Billy, and Becky, and how she left town without a word to anyone. The Tuckers tried to make him and the children feel at home at their house for the holiday. Gloria cooked a delicious meal. Tucker told Billy one yarn after another. And to entertain Mary Jane, the Tucker kids dragged out toys they had not played with in years. But Billy and his sister moped through the day, and not only because they missed their grandmother and Thanksgiving in their own home. They also missed their daddy. He was unable to give them the attention they needed because what happened to Becky kept distracting him.

The worst part came after dinner when he told Gloria and Tucker he still loved Becky and still wanted to be with her somehow. Looking back, Sam did not know why he thought they would react any differently than they did, but he had known them a long time and hoped they would understand.

"Sam, you're not giving this enough time," Tucker said. They were sitting in the kitchen drinking coffee while the children played elsewhere. "Too many things have been happening and you're still grieving. I know you're lonely, and on the surface,

Becky is a mighty appealing woman. Hell, I'm as open-minded as anybody, but she's a Negro for god's sake. Come to your senses man."

"You need to listen to Tucker," Gloria said, reaching over and putting her hand on Sam's shoulder, "Look, I've never offered this before because I didn't think you'd want it and because I didn't want to butt in, but Tucker's sister has a bunch of attractive friends up around Smackover that I bet you'd like. I'd love to introduce you to them."

"Gloria, I know you mean well," Sam said, "but you don't understand. Neither of you do."

He realized then that he should have known better than to think Tucker and Gloria would react any other way. But they were wrong. They were wrong about Becky and they were wrong about him. He had taken all the time he needed. He knew what he wanted—for himself, for Billy, and for Mary Jane.

When he got them home and in bed, he phoned Art Nelson and asked him to take charge of the Otasco store for a few days. Then he called Emma Lou MacDonald and asked if Billy and Mary Jane could stay with her for a while. He did not tell either of them why.

He did not tell the children much before leaving them with Emma Lou early this morning either, except that he loved them, he had to go on a trip, and he would be back as soon as he could. He asked Billy, however, if he would like to live some place where he could be on a Little League baseball team, wear a uniform, and see the Cardinals play. The boy grinned from ear to ear and his eyes sparkled like Judith Ann's used to.

Sam put a five on the table and left the diner. Having made good time in the Ford Victoria, he was less than fifty miles from St. Louis. He did not know if Missouri had mixed marriage laws

like the ones in Arkansas, but if it did, there were other states
with different laws and other places where Billy could see the
Cardinals from time to time, just like there were other places
where a man could own an Otasco store. Sam felt sure Becky
loved him and once he found her, he did not intend to let her go.

AUTHOR'S NOTE

South of Little Rock is a work of fiction, but it is set within the context of a real crisis of government and civil rights, and throughout the South, people reacted to it as deeply and variedly as the residents of imaginary Unionville. References in the book to historical events, real people, or real places are used fictitiously. Other names, characters, and events are products of the author's imagination, and any resemblance to actual events, places, or persons, living or dead, is entirely coincidental.

What happened in Little Rock and its environs started long before 1957 and lasted long after. For a historical overview, see especially: Karen Anderson, *Race and Resistance at Central High School* (Princeton: Princeton University Press, 2010); John A. Kirk, *Beyond Little Rock: The Origins and Legacies of the Central High Crisis* (Fayetteville: University of Arkansas Press, 2007); and Grif Stockley, *Ruled by Race: Black / White Relations in Arkansas from Slavery to the Present* (Fayetteville: University of Arkansas Press, 2009).

Among many other helpful works are the published recollections of several of the Little Rock nine. See also: Daisy Bates, *The Long Shadow of Little Rock* (New York: David McKay Company, 1962); David R. Goldfield, *Black, White, and Southern: Race Relations and Southern Culture, 1940 to the Present* (Baton Rouge: Louisiana State University Press, 1990); Gene Roberts and Hank Kilbanoff, *The Race Beat: The Press, the Civil Rights Struggle, and the Awakening of a Nation* (New York: Alfred A. Knopf, 2007); Neil R.

McMillen, *The Citizens' Council: Organized Resistance to the Second Reconstruction, 1954-64* (Urbana: University of Illinois Press, 1994); Roy Reed, *Faubus: The Life and Times of an American Prodigal* (Fayetteville: University of Arkansas Press, 1997); Charles F. Robinson, II, *Dangerous Liaisons: Sex and Love in the Segregated South* (Fayetteville: University of Arkansas Press, 2003); and Juan Williams, *Eyes on the Prize: America's Civil Rights Years, 1954-1965* (New York: Penguin Press, 1987).

I am grateful to many for invaluable assistance with *South of Little Rock*. Charles Phillips provided encouragement and editorial help without which this book would never have happened. Carol Sandler of the Strong National Museum of Play and Nancy Arn and Jeana Finley of the Barton Library gave critical research assistance. Friends and colleagues Susan Asbury, Juanita Battle, Richard Battle, Don Daglow, Kathleen Dengler, Scott Eberle, Lisa Feinstein, Charles McElhinney, Jean McElhinney, Allison McGrath, Susan Vogel-Vanderson, and Dawn Williams-Fuller read all or portions of the manuscript in various drafts and provided invaluable feedback. Patricia Hogan assisted with copyediting, and Shane Rhinewald assisted with preparation for promotion and marketing. Amy Collins and Keri-Rae Barnum of New Shelves Books assisted with production of the second edition.

My quilting and novel-loving spouse, Diana Murphy Adams, read and critiqued every draft and supported my efforts all along the way. The quilting conversations in *South of Little Rock* are not based on her and her friends, but the quilting patterns in the book are real. Lastly, I am grateful to our children, Brady, Amy, and Amanda, who not only showed appreciation for the creative process and time required to produce this book, but also demonstrated every day the importance of accepting cultural differences and showing good will toward all—critical values I hope this work conveys. To these four diverse and caring souls whom I am fortunate to have in my life, this book is lovingly dedicated.

See my website at georgerollieadamsbooks.com, and watch for my next novel, *Found in Pieces*.

QUESTIONS FOR DISCUSSION

To what extent did the racial views of various white characters in *South of Little Rock* differ? Which characters exemplified which views?

In what ways did Sam's views about race evolve? What events, conversations, and other factors contributed to those changes?

Why do you believe Becky felt so confident about succeeding in Unionville? Did she succeed? Why or why not?

What do you think about Becky's teaching methods? Are they like or different from methods you remember from when you were in school? In what ways? Why do you think the students liked them?

Did you enjoy history and social studies in school? Why or why not? Do you believe that understanding the past is important for understanding the present? Why or why not?

To what extent has what you learned about history in school affected how you regard the world?

How did individuals with different perspectives interpret or spin information about what was happening in Little Rock to support their own views about it? How usual or unusual do you think that is in American social and political history?

Did Upshaw separate reporting from editorializing? To what extent? How do his journalism practices compare with those of today?

ABOUT THE AUTHOR

GEORGE ROLLIE ADAMS is a native of southern Arkansas and a former teacher with graduate degrees in history and education. He is the author of *General William S. Harney: Prince of Dragoons* (a finalist for the Army Historical Foundation's Distinguished Book Award); coauthor of *Nashville: A Pictorial History*; and coeditor of *Ordinary People and Everyday Life* (a book of essays on social history). Adams has served as a writer, editor, and program director for the American Association for State and Local History and as director of the Louisiana State Museum in New Orleans. He is president and CEO emeritus of the Strong National Museum of Play, where he founded the *American Journal of Play* and led the establishment of the International Center for the History of Electronic Games.

12/19

CPSIA information can be obtained
at www.ICGtesting.com
Printed in the USA
LVHW091523281119
638726LV00009B/1462/P